FLAME IN THE SILVER STORM

FLAME in the SILVER STORM

THE ETERNAL CURSE BOOK TWO

ROCIO CARRANZA

QUEEN OF WANDS BOOKS
since 2024 | Austin, Texas
contact@queenofwandsbooks.com

Library of Congress Control Number: 2025914913
eBook ISBN 979-8-9921892-4-7
Paperback ISBN 979-8-9921892-5-4
Hardcover ISBN 979-8-9921892-6-1
www.rociocarranza.com

Cover Art by Irina Koryakina
Cover Design & Map by Rocio Carranza
Editing by Heather Hudec, Simply Spellbound Edits
Interior Formatting by Mariska Maas, Rubre Art
Interior Illustrations by Irina Koryakina, Natalia Tyczyńska, Nolwenn Lagrenee, Maria Erić, Karolina Wucke, Cheyanne Bueno, Wiktoria (@maniagania), and @_nereart__.

First edition September 2025
Published in the United States
9 8 7 6 5 4 3 2 1

For the loud girls who were told to be lawyers...
we probably didn't do that but look at us now,
reading and writing books like hobbits.

And I love that for us.

P.S. When they ask for silence,
don't you dare give it to them.

CONTENT WARNINGS

FLAME IN THE SILVER STORM IS A DARK FANTASY NOVEL AND BOOK two of The Eternal Curse series. This story contains content that might be troubling to some readers, including, but not limited to, depictions of and references to abuse, attempted sexual assault, blood, death, genocide, gore, manipulation, PTSD, strong use of language, and violence.

Unclaimed Wastes
Gods Protection
Horned Cove
Teros
Dragon Sea
The Clutches
Alcanza Peaks
Mytar
Rubianes Keep
nsmir Realm
Larrea
Bay of Chaos
Azurea Sea

Azurea Sea

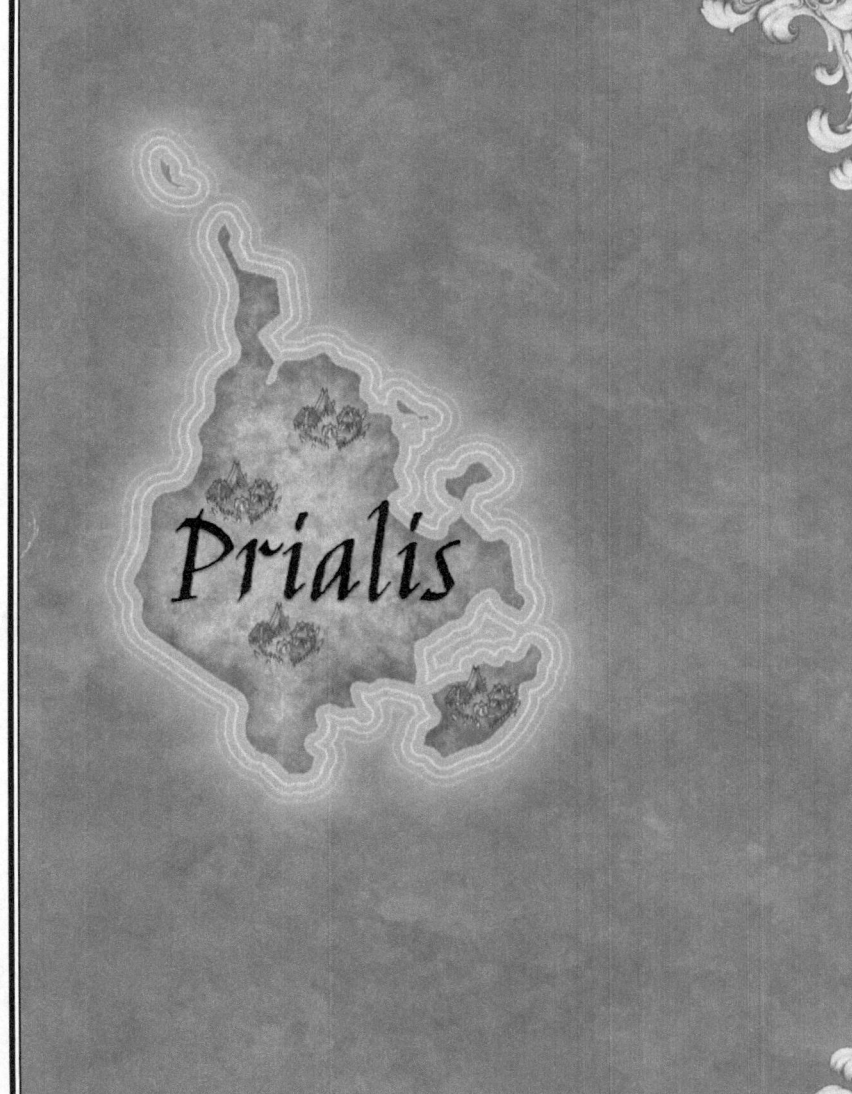

Prialis

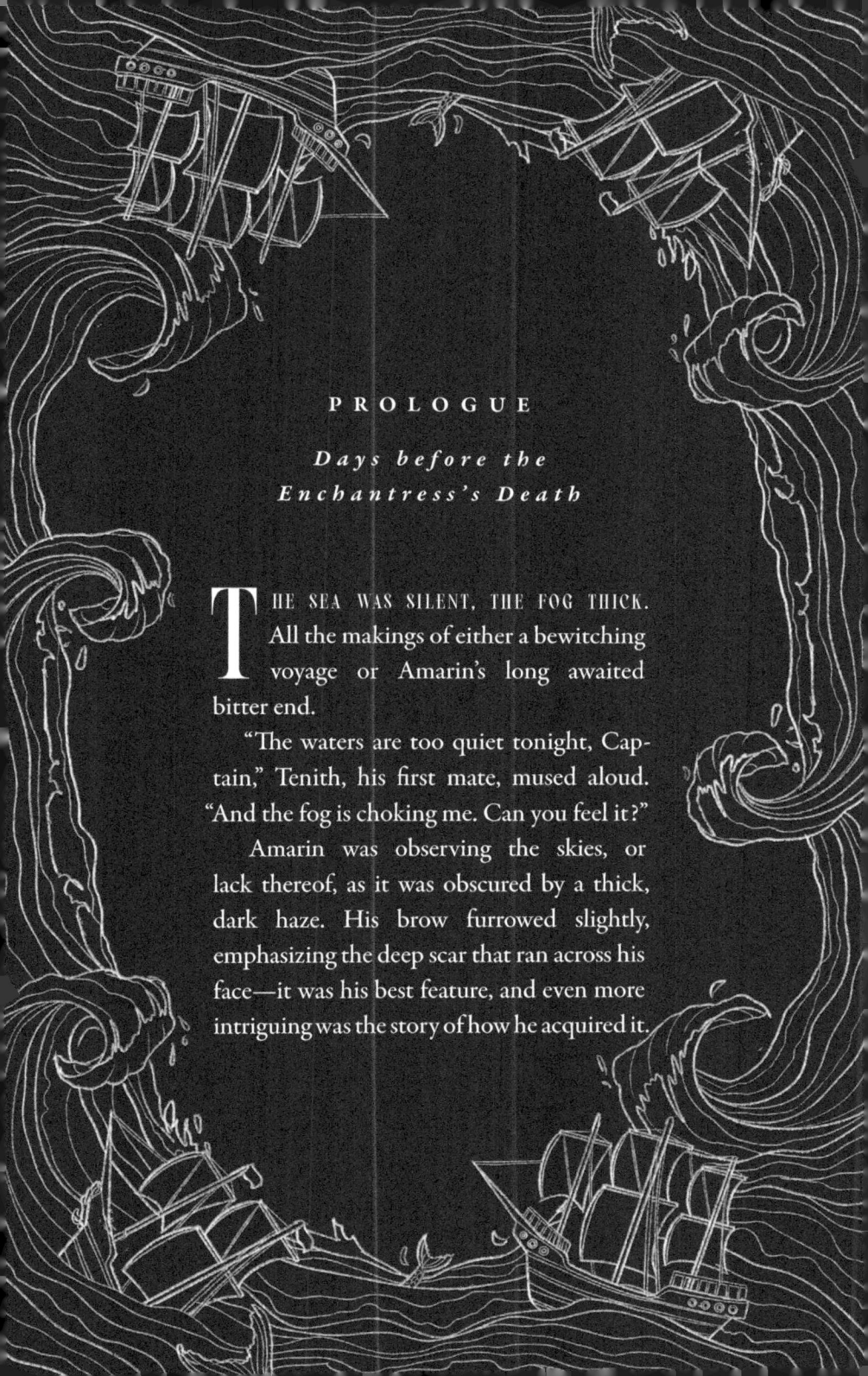

PROLOGUE

Days before the
Enchantress's Death

THE SEA WAS SILENT, THE FOG THICK. All the makings of either a bewitching voyage or Amarin's long awaited bitter end.

"The waters are too quiet tonight, Captain," Tenith, his first mate, mused aloud. "And the fog is choking me. Can you feel it?"

Amarin was observing the skies, or lack thereof, as it was obscured by a thick, dark haze. His brow furrowed slightly, emphasizing the deep scar that ran across his face—it was his best feature, and even more intriguing was the story of how he acquired it.

Tales of single-handedly defeating monsters of the depths, being captured by his enemies, and fighting his way to freedom in nothing but shackles, and other incredulous stories added to the allure of Captain Amarin. The lore and mystery amongst speculation bolstered his reputation over the decade as one of the greatest pirates of Serit. Yet, the truth—that was another thing entirely.

He could feel Tenith studying him.

"Yes"—Amarin breathed deeply, pinching the bridge of his nose—"I have noticed."

"Should I awaken some of the men to stand post in case something were to go awry?"

Tenith, a man of nearly sixty, had been born and raised on a ship for nearly every one of those years, but his superstitious nature tended to prevail in the silence. Silence was not good. Not when they were far offshore.

"What is it you think we should be looking for?" Amarin's voice was calm, but a fierceness held Tenith's gaze.

The *Wretched Sentinel* rocked gently and the only discernible noises around them were the soft creaking boards of the ship as it moved and the occasional snores of some pirates who typically found purchase on the decks for the night. It was as if they were floating on air rather than water, and Amarin looked overboard once more to confirm the waves lapped against the ship. There was a crisp chill that clung to the air surrounded by fog, but no wind could be heard.

"I don't know, Cap'n," Tenith began, "but I feel it in my gut. Something is very wrong."

"So be it, if it calms your nerves," Amarin said with a wave of his hand. "If I hadn't known any better, old man, I'd think you're becoming soft on me now."

Tenith cocked his head and smirked. "If it weren't for me, you'd still be anchored to the bottom of the ocean. Perhaps the sirens would've made pretty necklaces from your bones."

Amarin smiled broadly, clasping his hand on Tenith's shoulder. "And you will never let me forget it, will you?"

"Not for as long as I breathe."

Amarin considered making another quip at Tenith's expense but thought the better of it. The old man had a point, and the night felt too unsettling to idly stand by.

For all his flaws, Tenith had truly been the backbone of his immense success, the reason they were able to keep nearly a dozen ships at their disposal with nearly a hundred men aboard them, all of which were scattered across the seas completing their various tasks for him. Amarin regretted not bringing another ship along with him as Tenith suggested, but time and the need for swiftness did not allow for it. None of his other ships were as fast as his own.

"Wake some of the men, have them keep watch with the rest of the skeleton crew."

Tenith nodded and scurried down the steps of the quarter deck and disappeared through the fog.

Amarin stood rigid, trying to listen to any of the other familiar sounds that he had grown accustomed to over the years, but again, it was unusually quiet. Even the snoring had ceased, but Amarin supposed they were the few that Tenith woke. An unsettling thought crossed his mind then, and try as he might, its bitter truth could not be pushed away. Perhaps their success was turning them into old fools, frightened by anything that may threaten the splendor and riches they had accumulated—the protection it bought.

At some peace, quiet, and a little fog, he and Tenith were like frightened children. He would be a walking disgrace to his younger self.

Amarin began walking down the stairs of the deck, the quiet still unsettling as he made his final step and turned toward his cabin. He closed the door behind him, allowing the darkness of the room to consume him and let out a long, drawn-out breath.

How could he be frightened of a little fog?

He was Captain Amarin, Conqueror of the Serit Seas, a man with warrants from numerous kingdoms—the largest boasting two thousand silver pieces to the person who'd bring him to the Blackthorn realm *alive*.

He shivered a bit at the thought.

"Hello, Amarin."

The captain's eyes shot open, and he turned to the source of the voice, sword drawn and ready for an attack.

It took mere seconds for the candles of the room to come alight and even less to make out the woman before him lounging about his plush blood-red chair, seemingly unfazed by his brutish stance.

"Cassandra?" Amarin lowered his sword slowly, but did not sheath it. "What are you doing aboard my ship?"

Cassandra smiled gently and rose to her feet, her long, plum colored dress clung to her figure, the ends pooled on the floor around her. Her dark curls fell just below her bare, bronzed shoulders, and bounced slightly as she moved toward him. She was no doubt a beautiful woman, but what lurked beneath her flesh was the evil incarnate. Amarin knew this too well; had witnessed it too many times.

"It's been a long while, Amarin. I've missed you."

"Get out."

"Get out?" she scoffed, a playful smile on her lips. "And go where?"

"You can drown for all I care."

"Tsk, tsk, Captain," she drawled, coming closer still, "is that any way to treat your guest?"

Amarin stiffened, frozen on the spot as she came nearly nose to nose with him, her bright silver eyes shining playfully. He found himself unable to speak, the words—his curses, rather—were lodged at his throat, begging for release.

Cassandra placed her hand on his and the sword clattered to the floor. She kicked it away with her foot, and it slid under the door.

"Now, if I let you go, will you promise to be on your best behavior?"

She grinned, nuzzling her nose against his, as she waited patiently for words his body was incapable of speaking aloud. She looked upon his lips for a moment, lingering there as if to place her own on them, before slowly stepping out of his way.

Amarin lunged forward suddenly, all of his movement coming back in a sudden rush, and fell hard. Cassandra watched as he rose cautiously, a wicked gleam in her eyes.

"I won't ask *how* you came about my ship," he growled, "but *why*."

She sighed, stretching her arms above her, "I want what any woman wants, Amarin."

"You are vile, Cassandra," he spat. "You have a black heart that spreads misery."

"My, my, is that really what you think of me? How disappointing." She walked about his cabin, her fingers tinkering with random objects on his shelves. "There was a time you would have praised my kind."

"I was a fool then." He stood slowly, trying to consider his options. He could kill her, there was a knife hidden just under his desk, but her calm demeanor told him she had something up her sleeve and damn him for his curiosity. After over a decade, why did she choose to seek him out now?

He took a hard look at her as she moved, slowly, methodically as if she were a predator assessing the nest of her prey—cold and calculating. She was in no rush, nor was her age; she looked nearly the same as when they had last parted, barely a wrinkle adorned her face. It was as if time had stopped for her until this moment. It unsettled him.

Her eyes skimmed the maps on his desk. "Bound for Givensmir are you?"

"What business is that of yours?"

"More than you know."

"Damn you to five hells."

"Aren't we there already?" She smirked as she continued looking through his papers. Her eyes widened with delight when she found what she was looking for and held up a small scroll.

"Ah, it seems you haven't left the past behind you, Amarin. Were the two thousand pieces not enough to sway you?"

Amarin stalked over and snatched the parchment from her hand. "What do you want?! Damn you, witch, get on with it!"

Cassandra sighed dramatically and lounged back on his chair. "Can we at least have a drink? I'll answer your questions and more . . . cross my little black heart." She made an X over her breast and winked.

Amarin eyed her suspiciously before grabbing a bottle from his cabinet and two glasses.

She patted a seat next to her, and he moved warily to sit, filling their cups.

"Go on," he said, handing her a glass. He had to remind himself to breathe calmly, to loosen his white-knuckled grip.

The witch took a long drink before handing the empty glass back to the captain, batting her eyelashes. She leaned back further in the chair, pulling the slit of her dress high upon her leg and giving Amarin a mischievous smirk. He snatched the glass and placed it on the desk beside him, avoiding her temptations.

"Drink, Captain," she insisted. "You will need it."

He swirled the contents in his glass before drinking, emptying it in one sitting. Before he proceeded to threaten her, she spoke in a serious tone, all former pretenses forgotten.

"The king is sick; he is expected to join his gods very soon. His heir, as you know, is preparing for a swift ascension."

"There are many kings, Cassandra, which one?"

"King Byron of Givensmir."

Amarin nearly dropped his glass, his eyes wide. "How can this be?"

The king was not a young man, but neither was he too old. Last he heard, the king had even participated in a fighting contest for sport weeks prior. Amarin tried to imagine the strong man now weak and feeble on his deathbed—it just wasn't possible.

"Humans are mortal, Amarin; it's how these things work." She raised her hand to silence him before he could respond. "He has taken ill over the past week, an unusual illness that has a far stronger hold than anyone expected. His healers are at a loss."

"If I didn't know better, I'd suspect you had something to do with it."

"Amarin, darling." She sat forward, slowly moving her fingers up his thighs. Her silver eyes danced with the candlelight as her voice lowered suggestively. "Now why would I do that?"

"Because it's what you do." He pushed her hands aside, turning away from her.

"You are not wrong, Captain"—she smiled warmly—"but this was not my doing. It lacks a certain *creativity*."

A question he craved to ask bore itself to the forefront of his mind, torturously demanding to be free upon his lips. He knew what the king's death meant, he knew what the prince's ascension meant. He considered his words carefully before speaking, not wishing to reveal his true concerns.

"How much time does he have?"

"Four days."

A shiver went down his spine, that was barely enough time, even with good winds and luck.

"Why are you telling me this?"

"Because I know why you are sailing there, and powers beyond my control prevent me from letting you for that reason."

His breath caught, fear and apprehension in his eyes meeting her sinful gaze. Amarin's head began to swim, but anger prevailed.

"I cannot—I will not—let her suffer."

"It is not your place to interfere with fate."

"You cannot stop me!" He stood, chest heaving as he glared down at her.

7

She returned his gaze, a cat spying a mouse. He was somehow caught in a trap of her making, but he couldn't figure out what that was. It reminded Amarin of all those years ago; he could still see the hint of chaos in her eyes as she destroyed everything around him, the smell of burnt flesh and ash, his ungodly screams, just before he began sinking down, down, down into the sea. He shook the memory away.

"I will go to Givensmir if I have to swim there myself." The room begin to spin, and he sat upon his chair once more. He had to control himself; this was not a friend with whom he was speaking.

"I sincerely doubt it. However, I have come to offer you a proposition. One that you will either accept"—she hesitated, her eyes darkening, a ghost of a smile on her lips—"or die refusing. The choice is yours."

Amarin tried to speak, but he gasped for air. He clutched his neck, his body convulsing as he fell to the floor. Cassandra grabbed the bottle, poured herself another glass, and winked, sipping the drink calmly once more.

"You only have a few moments before your heart fails you. Before all that you have amassed becomes some other captain's treasure." She bent down to his shaking body.

His face turned pink as he tried to gasp for air that wouldn't come. He clawed at his throat, his eyes bulging and reddening.

"You will go to Givensmir and transport the enchantress's daughters—and *only* her daughters—to the Blackthorn. The queen's adviser, a witch named Malin, will see you on the southward port and provide you a pardon by the realm in exchange for your services." She hesitated, looking at him as if admiring her work.

Amarin's face turned purple, he could feel himself on the brink of death, the blackness closing all around him. The enchantress's face came to mind, memories of their time together filling him as his body began to succumb. Hot tears stung his eyes and the pain, the pain . . .

Cassandra snapped her fingers, and Amarin sucked in a breath, gulping it as if he had never breathed before. The room brightened slowly once more in a dizzying motion.

"I wasn't ready to let you go." She mockingly pouted and drank the last of her glass. "Now, do we have a deal?"

Amarin nodded as he coughed and gasped some more, his body shaking from the aftermath of the poison she no doubt slipped in his bottle while waiting for him. He could feel the lingering effects still weighing heavily on him, and his eyes grew heavy.

"I will kill you," he groaned.

"Perhaps, but not today."

"Don't be so sure."

"Oh, but I am."

"Why me?" His breathing began to steady, but he could only turn on his side, too weak to stand, too weak to sit.

"Because you are the world's greatest pirate on the world's fastest ship. You should be honored."

"Why does the Blackthorn want her daughters?"

"You ask too many questions, Captain."

"You told me you would answer them."

"That I did." She sighed contemplatively. "Her daughters are believed to hold more power than the enchantress herself. Together, Malin is convinced they could rule the mortal kingdoms—*all kingdoms* and restore Isila to her former glory."

"A fucking prophecy?"

"Yes, we witches love our prophecies."

"They are half-witches; rumor has it one has shown no signs of magic."

"True, but I am merely a messenger, and my message has been delivered."

"Does she know?"

To this Cassandra seemed taken aback.

"Does the enchantress know?" Amarin pressed. "Does Lucia know?"

Cassandra turned. "Soon."

"Soon?"

"Yes."

"What the hells does that mean?" He coughed, not expecting his anger to take up so much of his strength.

"She does not yet know that only her daughters will gain passage."

"You know what will happen to her. You know what kind of man the prince is."

"I did not take you for a merciful man when it did not benefit you. You surprise me, Captain."

"But her letter—the scroll. She must not know that she will soon follow the king in death."

"Not yet."

His heart felt heavy in his chest, the thought of seeing Lucia once more ripped away in a single conversation. The spawn of chaos as the messenger made it all the more sour. He shut his eyes tight, and opened them once more, trying to stay awake, trying to not fall into the depths of rest his body begged for.

"I can save her, please," he beseeched. "I will do anything."

The witch leaned closer, pulling his hair back and forcing his eyes upon hers. "There is nothing you could give me that would prevent what must happen. Even if you could, my answer would be the same."

Amarin met her eyes with a mixture of horror, anger, and heartbreak. He was far from a good man; many would argue he was the worst of them—merciless, cold-blooded, and vile to any of his enemies. But Lucia held a power over him that he could never explain, unlike any other witch of her kind. He needed her, desperately.

Cassandra gave him a wicked smile as she stood and procured a note from thin air. She laid it atop his desk. "This has your instructions."

She walked over his body, her dress skirts practically suffocating him in the process, and made her way toward the cabin door.

"This is a very generous offer. It would be a shame if you were to fail." She smirked and turned the knob. "Oh, and it's good to see you again, Amarin, especially under such great circumstances."

She smiled beautifully as if they had been discussing their favorite pastimes and not the imminent death of the woman he loved while forcing him into a contract he wanted no part of.

A deal with a witch.

Amarin relented, closing his eyes and giving into sleep—no longer able to fight his body's desperate need for recovery.

She no sooner shut the door than a knock rapped on it.

"Damn you, leave!" he yelled, his eyes shut tight.

There was silence again, then a slow creaking as the door opened carefully.

"Cap'n?" Tenith whispered carefully. "I only came to give you some good news."

"Tenith?" the captain nearly choked on his words, barely able to lift himself onto his elbows. He realized the room was pitch-black save for the moonlight filtering in from beyond the door.

"Yes," he replied as he struck a match. "The fog has cleared. Everything seems to have returned as it was."

Amarin suspected the reason for this but said nothing.

"I reckon we're becomin' soft ol' men after all," Tenith chuckled, lighting a few candles.

"Perhaps," Amarin murmured, eyeing Cassandra's letter on his desk, "perhaps not."

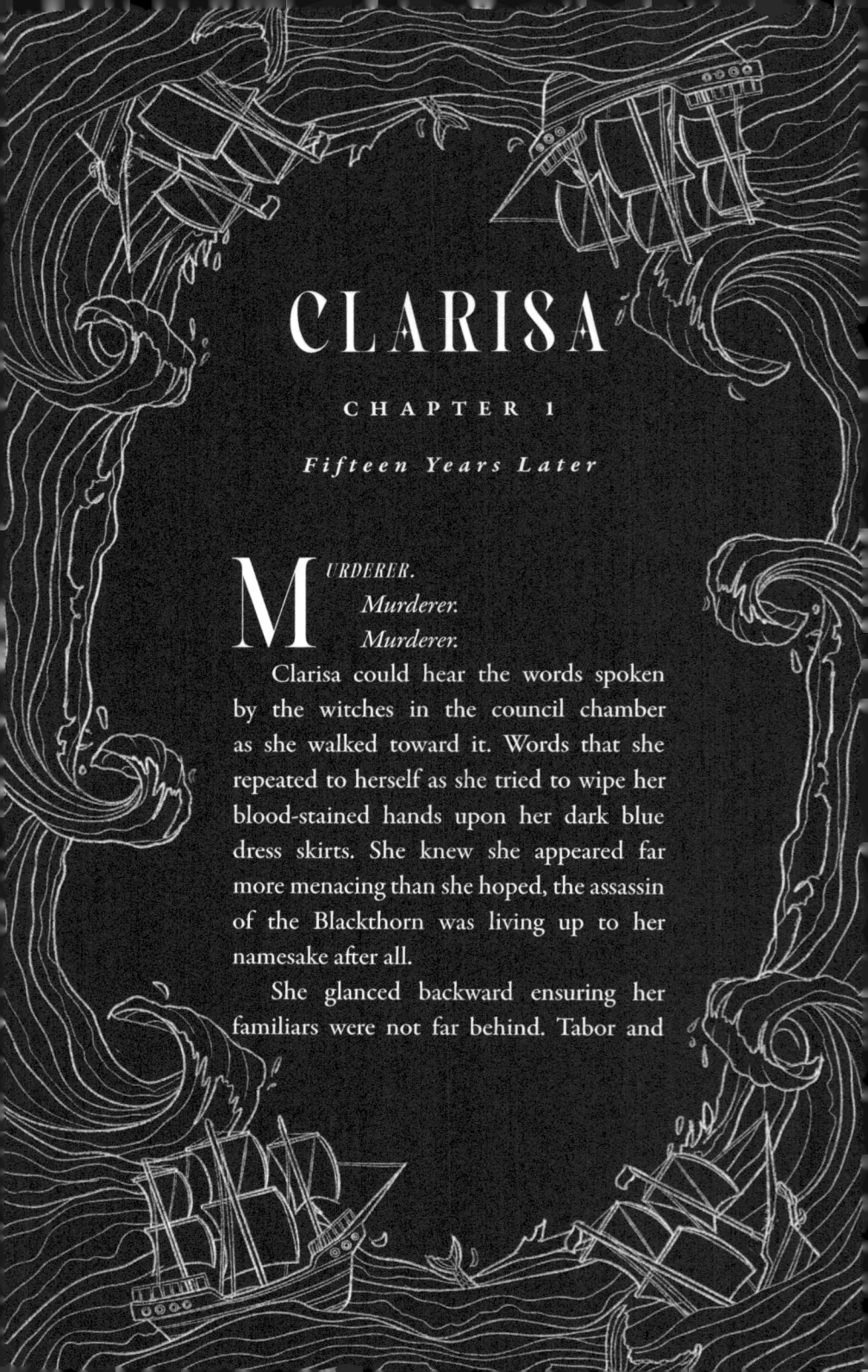

CLARISA

CHAPTER 1

Fifteen Years Later

MURDERER.
Murderer.
Murderer.

Clarisa could hear the words spoken by the witches in the council chamber as she walked toward it. Words that she repeated to herself as she tried to wipe her blood-stained hands upon her dark blue dress skirts. She knew she appeared far more menacing than she hoped, the assassin of the Blackthorn was living up to her namesake after all.

She glanced backward ensuring her familiars were not far behind. Tabor and

Brisa kept their heads low, avoiding the gazes of the witches that lingered in the hall. They, too, appeared disheveled and exhausted; the magic used to assist her the night prior had nearly depleted all their strength.

Navir, who waited patiently outside the council doors, embraced her as she approached.

"They are quite impatient to speak to you."

"So I've heard."

"We haven't had all six heads of the covens here since the last trial for your dear Malin."

Clarisa narrowed her eyes. "What of my cousin and the prince? When can I see them?"

"In due time, I promise," Navir responded. "They are under watch by the queen's guards until negotiations with the mortal king can be made. When they are properly healed and the queen allows, I will take you to see them myself." Clarisa raised a brow, and he continued, "They will not be harmed, I promise."

She breathed a sigh of relief. Since their arrest she had been waiting to see them, to ask them about Eve and the kingdom. In all the darkness of the past night, she was thankful that they were not killed by her.

The voices in the council chamber were louder now, echoing into the hall.

Murderer! Uncontrollable! Dangerous!

Clarisa let out a deep breath. "What do the queen and the covens want from me?"

"To discuss your attack."

"The one against the mortals?"

"No"—his lips thinned—"the one against Giselle."

Clarisa blanched, faltering slightly as she stood. The room was suddenly too hot, the hall too cramped, her vision too blurred. She had forgotten that she had nearly killed the high priestess in the midst of all the chaos of the previous night, much too plagued by the other events. Now, her consequences lay bare before her. It was treason to harm a high priestess.

Navir grabbed hold of her shoulders, righting her. He leveled his gaze with hers. "You need to trust me. If you can remain calm, I can get you out of this. Can you do that?"

Clarisa could hear the heavy footsteps of the Blackthorn guards approaching the door from the other side, ready to open it. She had no time to challenge Navir's words.

"Yes. I can."

The doors were opened and Clarisa, Navir, and her familiars entered the council chamber. Behind a large circular table sat the head of each of the six covens—Petris, Veneno, Arric, Alvyna, Luna, and the Capital. The queen from the capital chair watched Clarisa as she entered. The three other women and two men were far too embroiled in arguments amongst each other to notice her.

Clarisa did not have time to reconcile the destruction she caused, still could not believe the power that surged within her only hours before the guards arrived to escort her to the castle.

The thought of the bodies washing ashore, painting the beach red with death sent a chill down her spine. So many men, so many that had been killed at her hands. How many fathers, brothers, sons? Innocents who were sent unwillingly to do the bidding of the mad mortal king?

She had gone too far—this she knew for certain—used her gifts and failed to control her impulses. Too many lives were taken at once. More than she had ever taken before in a single night. Lives that must be repaid to maintain balance. What would the goddess demand of her for this blatant neglect? Perhaps, this was her destined retribution.

Guilt and fear threatened to seize her, and she shook her head to try and dispel the thoughts.

Calm.

Be calm.

There were pitying glances amongst the few other witches present, concern, but most of all fear as they parted ways to allow her to walk toward the council table. Once more, King Gareth, seated behind the queen, seemed to be dazed and uninterested in the affair, his eyes lazily shifting between the faces in the crowd. He seemed paler now than he had the last time she laid eyes on him. He met her stare for a moment, his formerly emerald-eyed stare now traded for one of misty green hues and clouded grays. Clarisa shifted her gaze, feeling uncomfortable.

Deyes and Giselle stood on either side of Queen Saryn, the latter giving Clarisa a twisted, scornful look. Clarisa expected the witch to be bitter, but didn't expect to have this outcome. It was all too much at once. Her head rested heavy upon her shoulders.

"We are here for you, whatever may come," Tabor whispered from behind her.

Clarisa walked precariously into the chamber and stood before the council table. As the rest of the covens noticed her, the room soon fell silent, save for the sound of rain tapping against the windows.

"Your Majesty," she said, bowing and trying to maintain a neutral tone. She hoped her blood-stained dress was not as horrifying as the other witches made it appear. She sensed how they distanced them-selves from her.

The queen lifted her chin, and the sound of the doors closing echoed throughout the room.

"I take it on good authority, my dear, that you have tried to kill a witch, defied coven orders, slaughtered countless mortals, and have taken responsibility for our prisoners—the Prince of Givensmir and his knight."

Clarisa clenched her jaw, the memory coming back to her in full force—her power, how it took over her, how it ravaged their coast in death, and how she found her cousin Pedro and her old friend Theo miraculously alive in the carnage. Then, more stupidly, how she vouched for Pedro's claims to be the prince before the witches stormed the beach and arrested them. A switch that both confused but concerned her.

Be calm.

Clarisa righted her shoulders square at the queen and leveled her gaze against hers. "Yes. It is true."

"What you are confessing to is treason," Saryn explained.

"If it is a crime to save my fellow witches from the onslaught of mortals that threatened our land so be it," Clarisa snapped. "I had the magic to stop the attack, and I did. Is that not what you have me here for?"

"Bite your tongue," Giselle growled. "You wanted nothing but power and used my suffering as a sacrifice to get it!"

"I would do it again to keep our covens safe."

"Selfish half-breed!"

"Silence!" the queen demanded, glaring at Clarisa and Giselle. "With their attack on our lands, the mortals have declared war. We will need every witch to fight against them, and I will be damned if I allow anarchy to thrive at the expense of innocent witches." She turned her gaze solely to Clarisa. "Your blasphemous attack on our high priestess is indeed treason. And while you have subdued our enemies *for now*, you have become unruly and dangerous to our coven. Your mortal thirst for bloodshed threatens us all."

The air in the room thinned, and Clarisa's eyes widened with disbelief. Nearly every kill in her life was at the command of her queen; every death she caused stained her soul and damned her to a purgatory of guilt. She was nothing like the mortals.

"My Queen, I—"

Saryn raised a hand to silence her. "The punishment for such an act is death."

Clarisa's breath hitched, unable to respond. Surely this could not be her final demand.

Tabor and Brisa stood in front of her, readying themselves for an attack. Deyes, large and menacing, moved toward them.

"No!" There was a plea from the corner of the room and Clarisa turned to see Ana's face ashen with fear as she stepped in front of the small crowd. The guards blocked her path, warning her to move back. Clarisa's eyes met Ana's, and her heart clenched, regretting their tense last parting.

Death?

No, not after everything Clarisa had done for the coven. The lives she had taken to save them all. Tears threatened as she turned back to the queen.

"Your Majesty, might I speak on behalf of Clarisa?" Navir stepped forward.

Saryn eyed him suspiciously but waved Deyes back. "Quickly."

Navir nodded, turning toward the heads of the covens. "It is no secret that we brought Clarisa here in hopes that she will resurrect our goddess. No secret that she was to be used as a weapon to save our kind from the brutality of the mortals. She has succeeded in one of her tasks. We would have faced certain death if not for Clarisa's bravery—"

"He lies!" Giselle snapped.

"Let him speak," the queen warned. Giselle clenched her jaw, her nostrils flaring as she stepped back.

Clarisa watched as each of the coven members looked warily upon Navir as he continued.

"Let me be clear. We are alive because of Clarisa's magic. The mortals severely outnumber us, and we will not survive another invasion without her." He hesitated, letting his words sink in with the council.

"If she means to keep us safe, why did she attack our high priestess?" Rinya, head of the Alvyna coven spoke. Her gray braided hair fell to the small of her back, the wrinkles deepened on her face, her raven eyes narrowed at Clarisa. Ana bore a striking resemblance to her mother.

17

"The high priestess tried to stop Clarisa from saving the coven, wishing to take the credit for herself."

"Blasphemy!" Giselle cried out.

Clarisa found her voice. "It's true. I told you that I was your only chance at survival, and you refused to step aside."

"And how did you know this?" Silas, head of the Petris coven, asked. He was balding with a thick black beard he brushed with his fingers.

"I foresaw it."

"Did Isila visit you?"

"No, it was in a dream."

"Impossible," Rinya breathed.

"Not for her," Navir remarked. "What we saw was not chaos unleashed, but the power to destroy our enemies. We have misunderstood because we have never seen anything like it."

He gestured to Clarisa, announcing proudly, "The Original Witches have finally claimed their descendant."

"It cannot be," Giselle breathed, her face paling.

"But it is," Navir replied. "Clarisa has embraced the ancient power of her ancestors. Why must we wait to summon Isila, when we have the magic of the Original Witches willing to defend our lands at any cost?"

The chamber filled with murmurs and gasps. Deyes warned that those who would not be silenced would be thrown from the room, but the crowd made no attempt to hush themselves.

The queen stood from her chair. "My son, do you mean—"

"Yes, Mother. The prophecy has begun."

"How can this be?"

"Is it true?!"

"Can she still resurrect the goddess?"

Navir ignored their words and turned to Clarisa. He held her hands in his, and even though he was saving her life, her flesh crawled at his touch. He smirked. She was unsure of how to respond. She met Navir's eyes, within them a promise there would be no turning back from.

"Clarisa *is* our Blood of the Blackthorn!" he declared.

The chamber roared to life with shouts and bickering.

Use it, Navir mouthed to her.

Clarisa lifted her hand up before her and channeled her magic. Water whirled above her palm like the storm from the night before. Bits of lightning flashed, and thunder rumbled outside. She silently begged for Isila to have mercy on what she was about to do. For this magic had been within her all her life, hidden from the rest of the witches to blend in. Now released there would be no going back. The queen would never let her leave. The bright paradise she once hoped to be in with Ana would be forever out of reach.

The gloomy daylight turned to darkness, the lightning cracked dangerously close to the windows providing the only semblance of light; the thunder roared, and the storm fought for purchase in the skies.

As the magic made its way through her veins, Clarisa relished in the power, forgetting why she refused it before. The excited *tink, tink, tink* of the oracles in their crystal cage about her neck was music to her ears. Her fingers trembled with the enormity of her strength.

Perhaps paradise could be here too.

The room erupted into a medley of celebration and worship.

And shamefully, all the while, the only thing that came to Clarisa's mind was that if she was this powerful without Isila, imagine how much more she would be when she took her from Eve.

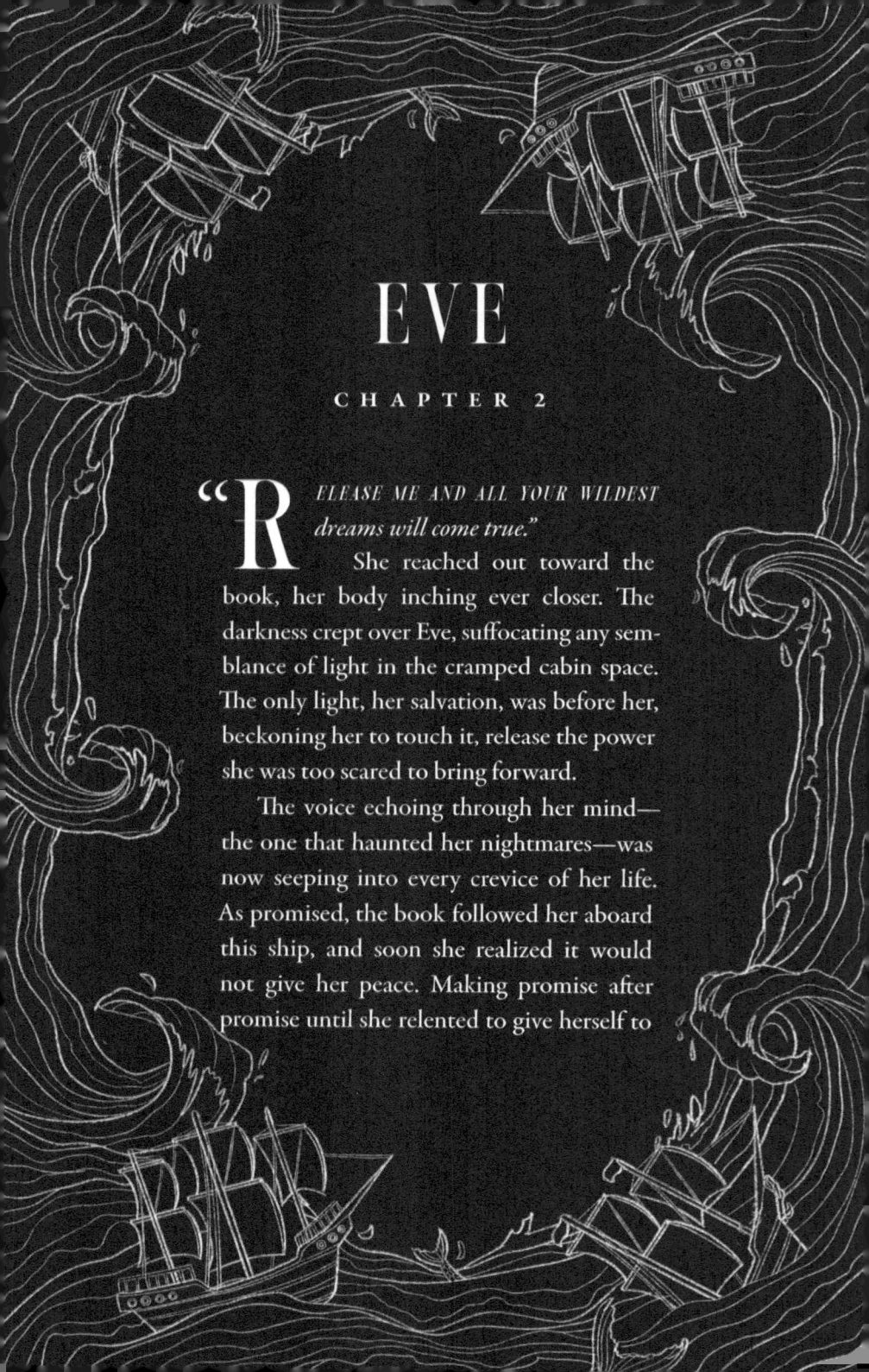

EVE

CHAPTER 2

"RELEASE ME AND ALL YOUR WILDEST *dreams will come true.*"

She reached out toward the book, her body inching ever closer. The darkness crept over Eve, suffocating any semblance of light in the cramped cabin space. The only light, her salvation, was before her, beckoning her to touch it, release the power she was too scared to bring forward.

The voice echoing through her mind—the one that haunted her nightmares—was now seeping into every crevice of her life. As promised, the book followed her aboard this ship, and soon she realized it would not give her peace. Making promise after promise until she relented to give herself to its weathered pages. Each time, she was able to resist . . . barely.

"I am not ready," she managed, no more than a whisper.

"We are ready."

She tried to pull away as fear seized her, pricking her skin. Tears fell down her cheeks, cooling her heating skin. She ground her teeth, struggling against the invisible tie pulling her ever closer.

Branches danced in her vision, clawing their way out of the grimoire in erratic, horrid motions. The book she had willingly given herself to months ago was now consuming her dreams and every waking hour. She closed her eyes, remembering the cut on her finger, her blood drops on the pages, mixing with the blackthorn ink, tying themselves together for eternity. They were bound in life, of this she was certain. But she couldn't bring herself to give it anything more, no matter how it called for her.

The sharp branches began to wrap themselves around her, cutting her flesh, drawing blood, and forcing her toward the Blood of the Blackthorn. She tried to scream, tried to fight, but darkness sapped every bit of her vision and strength.

"Please, no," she whimpered. Her fingertips were too close to the parchment, she could nearly feel it pulsing as if it were a beating heart beneath her hands. It wanted her, *needed her*. It could not unleash its power without her.

The pain, the stinging pain of the sharp, thorny branches, the voices, the darkness. She closed her eyes, all the fight within her nearly gone.

"Help me," she breathed.

"Eve? Eve!"

She slowly opened her heavy eyes and raised her hand to shield her face from the powerful brightness of the sunlight. Her head pounded unrelenting against her skull, and she moaned against the pain. The slow movements of the ship beneath her rocked her back into life, as everything came to.

I am on Captain Amarin's ship. I escaped Givensmir. I am somewhere over the Dallise Sea.

"Eve," a voice repeated, softly. Her familiar's voice.

She shuddered weakly as Dakon grasped her arms between his. She was covered in handprints and scars, dark as the ink that filled the pages of the grimoire. Memories of the branches pulling her to the grimoire resurfaced and she shuddered, rubbing her aching head.

"What is that?" Pazel gasped from behind him, his wild, dark curls nearly covering his eyes. It had been over a moon since they boarded the ship.

"I'm not sure," Dakon responded, focusing on the scars, "but I don't like it."

They were deep black rivers across her skin that worsened with the nightmares.

He lifted his head to Eve. "That was close, Eve. Too close. You need to tell me when the book calls for you, not when it's nearly too late. You promised me. Had Beast not woke me, who knows what could have happened."

Eve pulled her arm back and turned from him, unable to meet his disapproving stare. She sat up on the bed, focusing instead on Beast who lay about a small rug in the far corner of the cramped cabin the four of them shared. His blood-orange eyes watching her curiously, his black fur like a shadow that covered him even in the daylight. He was proving to be worth the struggle it was becoming to keep him a secret while aboard Captain Amarin's ship. So far, none of the crew noticed the gytrash; Eve considered they may not be able to. She hoped this continued, as she did not wish to divulge any more news onto the captain. Harboring a witch—one being pursued by an angry, powerful kingdom—was damning enough for one lifetime, she supposed.

"Thank you, Beast." She sighed. The gytrash cocked its head, and Pazel petted its long fur gently.

"It's happening more often," Pazel mumbled. "Nearly three times this week alone. Ever since that book appeared—"

"Enough about the book," Eve snapped, pulling down her sleeves to cover the marks. With limited options aboard the ship, she had donned spare blouses and trousers from the quartermaster. Thankfully, the sleeves reached over her wrists, hiding the blackthorn's marks.

Until the next time it comes for you. She shook the thought from her head, unwilling to go down that path.

Dakon crossed his arms. "Fine. But you cannot avoid this forever. That *book* is dangerous. We have to figure out what it wants or how to subdue it."

"Perhaps we should tell the Captain—" Pazel began.

"You will do nothing of the sort!" Eve snapped. "Not until we know more."

"Seems impossible since you refuse to speak of it, or anything else for that matter," Dakon challenged.

Eve rolled her eyes, lifting herself off the bed. "Not this again."

"Yes, yes this again." Dakon grabbed her arm once more turning her to face him. "You cannot keep secrets. At least not from me, Eve. I am your familiar, remember? My life depends on your survival, which I cannot guarantee without knowing as much as you do."

"I am not ready." She pulled away, and he released her.

"We are far past that now," he replied, frustration taking over his tone. "I'm sorry, but we cannot delay any further. We are meeting the captain tonight to discuss plans, and we cannot go in there unprepared because you refuse to talk to us—to me."

Eve gritted her teeth. It was not long ago that she had lost nearly everything—her life at court, her friends, Adriana, Pedro, Theo, Callum. *Callum.* Her heart sank. Memories of him fighting bitterly against the knights to his sure death chipped away at her soul. No. She was not ready. Not yet.

"No." She gave Dakon a hard look. "I said no."

Dakon narrowed his eyes. "So you will damn me too?"

Eve gasped. "How dare you."

They glared at each other, the heat of Eve's skin rising with her anger.

"He defies you," a voice inside her whispered.

She looked upon his face, one that she had only become used to these past few weeks. So long ago, yet not long at all.

Who does he think he is?

To command me, to order me?!

"He wants your magic, your power."

The voices were swimming through her head; her jaw tensed, and her hands began to shake as they grew louder within her. And slowly Dakon's glare subsided into concern.

"Eve?"

"You must kill him."

"Eve, your eyes are turning red again." Pazel inched cautiously between Dakon and Eve. He raised his hands slowly. "I think what Dakon meant to say was that we want the same things you do. We are a team. A family."

Eve felt a tug at the bottom of her tunic. Beast nuzzled against her legs, looking up apprehensively. She took a deep breath, feeling his fur beneath her fingertips. She closed her eyes, trying to silence the voices. She could feel her skin become cooler as the seconds passed. She opened her eyes, taking in the men in front of her, they were her familiars, her saviors, her friends. Her life would have been damned if not for them.

"I—I'm sorry," she breathed, shame filling her.

Dakon and Pazel gave each other worried looks.

"I feel as if I am becoming a host for something awful," she explained. "It terrifies me."

It was silent for a moment as the words weighed heavily in the tense air.

Dakon reached for Eve's hand. "We are not your enemies, Eve. We would not have returned to the king's tower that night if we did not mean to save you. Every day of my life will be dedicated to ensuring your safety. I promise."

She blinked as thoughts of Callum filled her once more, and tears pricked at the corners of her eyes. He was the last one to make a promise to her, and he had kept it until his dying breath. The last one who gave his life for her and paid the price; would Dakon have to too? Her lips quivered as she remembered Callum's last words, the look in his eyes as he stood to face the knights alone. "*I meant what I said in the tower.*"

How many times could a heart break before it gives up?

Dakon's green eyes locked in on hers, they were intense, but sincere. His copper hair was longer now than it had been only weeks ago, the scars and bruises he had received from their escape healed quickly, as if they were never there to begin with—a new magic of his that had emerged in recent weeks.

Eve cleared her throat, feeling the burden of everything heavier upon her.

"I understand."

Before Dakon could respond, Eve felt a second hand upon theirs.

Pazel gave her a playful grin. "I love it when our family gets along."

"What are you doing, Pazel?" Dakon sighed.

"I didn't want to feel left out." He shrugged. "I already lack magic; I am at a bit of a disadvantage if you haven't noticed."

Dakon released Eve's hand, rubbing his temples. "You may not be born with magic, but you can see Beast, which is more than many mortals can do. Perhaps there is some magic in you we've yet to discover."

Pazel reached down, giving Beast a hug. "Of course I can see you, boy. Who is the best feral creature out there? You are, you are."

Eve smiled, allowing herself a brief bit of peace watching the gytrash wave his tail and roll on the floor happily.

"Come"—Dakon gestured Eve to the floor—"let us heal your wounds."

Ah, yes. The scars.

Pazel took Dakon's words as his cue, leaving Beast to retrieve a candle and Cerene's book. The small green book could fit in his palm and was full of stories, spells, and scribbles. He opened the correct page, handing the book and candle to Dakon.

Dakon took them silently, focusing on placing the candle as still as he could between him and Eve despite the rocking of the ship.

"Thank you, Pazel. You are the greatest apprentice in Serit," Pazel mocked, bowing before them. "Oh, you're welcome, Dakon. Of course, only making sure I am worth my keep."

Dakon cocked his head. "Thank you."

Pazel grinned and sat on the floor next to them. "If you don't treat me well, I may find another familiar to apprentice with. I hear they are in high demand."

Eve couldn't help but let out a small giggle. She was grateful someone like Pazel could dispel the tension even in these dark moments. Dakon joined her, patting Pazel on the back.

"I am grateful, truly." He turned to face Eve. "Now, let us see your scars again."

Eve's smile quickly faded, and she nodded, lifting her sleeves. The dark marks filled her skin, harsh and eerie, and spindled out like the trees the book had shown her all those months ago. They were the branches of her nightmares that tried to force her toward the grimoire etched into her skin. A chill went down her spine, and she shuddered against the memory.

What lengths would the grimoire go for her to accept its full power?

She squeezed her eyes shut, pushing the thought from her mind. Not now. She couldn't let herself think about that now.

Dakon lifted a hand over the candle, focusing on it as Eve and Pazel watched silently. After a few agonizing moments, it finally lit weakly. Dakon let out a shaky breath.

"You are getting better at this."

Pazel nodded. "My good charms are finally wearing off on him."

Dakon placed his hands on Eve's arms, locking his eyes with hers. "Ready?"

"Yes," she breathed, bracing herself.

Pazel raised the book to Dakon, and he read from the small fine ink on the parchment.

"Isila, hear my plea. Remove her pain and give to me."

He repeated these words again and again until the marks began to slowly disappear from her arms and reappear slowly on Dakon's. She tightened her grip on him, seeing the pain across his face as he continued repeating his words.

Finally, it was done. Her wounds were removed, transferred to Dakon's arms. If only this healing magic would have come sooner, then maybe things could have turned out differently.

Dakon breathed deeply, shakily.

"Thank you," Eve said, holding his hands in her own.

"As I said"—Dakon blew out the candle—"I am not your enemy."

Eve inspected his wounds, guilt creeping in. "I hope they heal more quickly than the last. Perhaps before the end of today."

"Hopefully."

"Come"—she stood, helping him from the floor—"let us get some fresh air."

He took her hands, and they stood rather awkwardly, as if waiting on one another to make the first move out the door. Pazel, much to Eve's relief, strutted past them and opened it.

"I have a few questions," Pazel called out over his shoulder. "Are the five gods our enemies now? Do we have gods? I want to make sure I choose the winning side here."

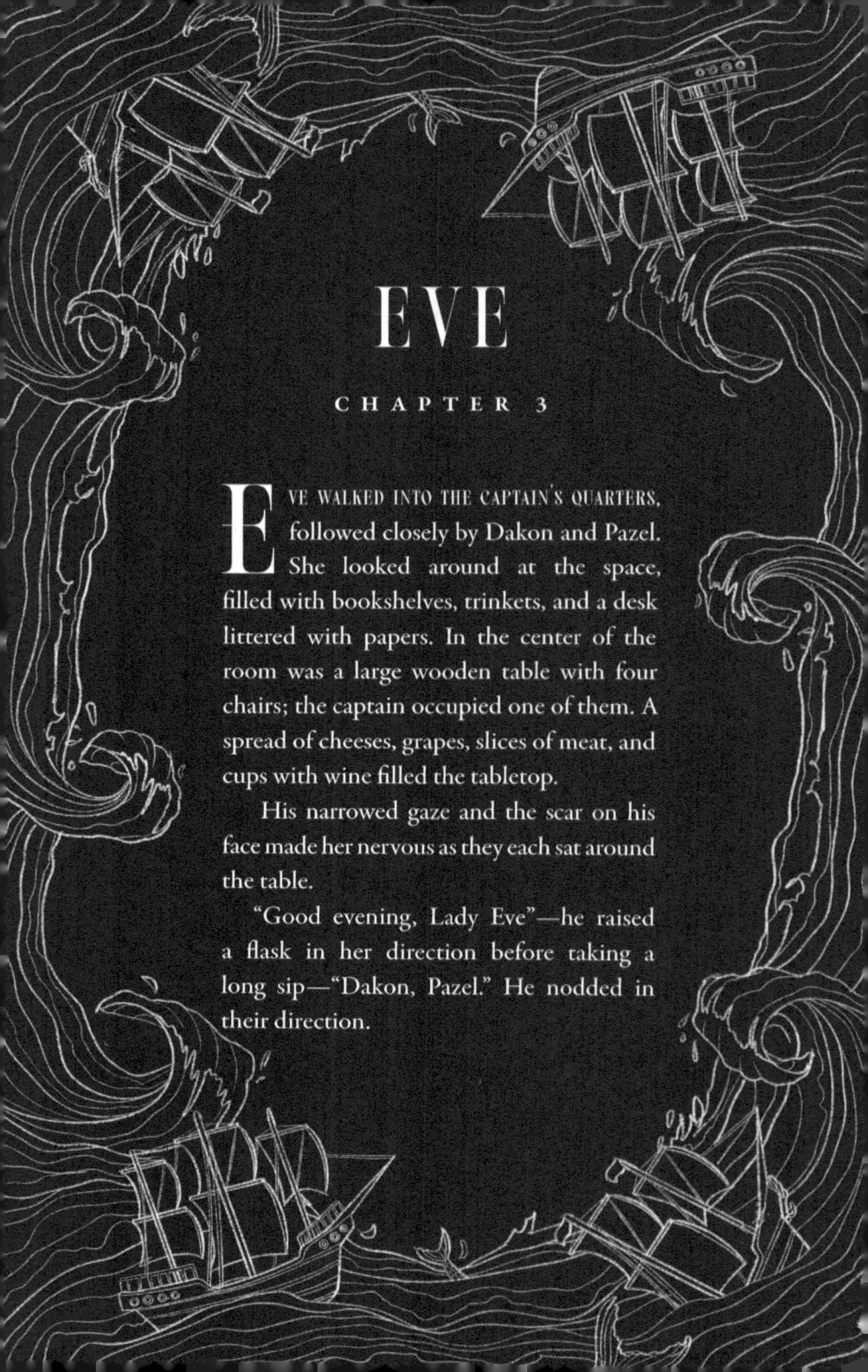

EVE

CHAPTER 3

E VE WALKED INTO THE CAPTAIN'S QUARTERS, followed closely by Dakon and Pazel. She looked around at the space, filled with bookshelves, trinkets, and a desk littered with papers. In the center of the room was a large wooden table with four chairs; the captain occupied one of them. A spread of cheeses, grapes, slices of meat, and cups with wine filled the tabletop.

His narrowed gaze and the scar on his face made her nervous as they each sat around the table.

"Good evening, Lady Eve"—he raised a flask in her direction before taking a long sip—"Dakon, Pazel." He nodded in their direction.

"Good evening, Captain," Eve replied, straightening her posture. "As I've said before you can simply call me Eve."

He ignored her. "How are you enjoying my ship?" He brushed his fingers curiously through his long, red beard.

"Good, thank you. The crew has been respectful of our privacy during this time; we very much appreciate it."

"The idea of a witch aboard spooks them," he grumbled, sipping once more.

Eve nodded, the gossip surrounding her fire spectacle the first day aboard the ship had spread rather quickly. "Understandable. However, my familiars and I—"

"Ahem, apprentice," Pazel coughed.

Eve glared at him, and Dakon elbowed him in the ribs.

"Don't think I've forgotten you retching on my clothes, boy." Amarin sneered in Pazel's direction. "You owe me a new coat and shoes."

Pazel blanched, shifting his gaze. "Once we reach land, I promise to pay you back. I think green with some black trim may bring out your eyes."

"Stow your tongue, or I will cut it out," Dakon gritted through his teeth.

Pazel bit his lip, focusing his attention on the cheeses, throwing one in his mouth.

Eve rubbed her eyes, annoyed. Amarin raised a brow at Pazel before turning his attention to her.

"Speaking of reaching land. I think the time has come to discuss your options. I cannot keep the ship over the sea forever. She has graced us with good weather and tides, but in my experience it does not last long. We must go to land and replenish our supplies."

"Of course."

She watched as the captain righted himself, pulling a scroll from his coat.

"I received a letter earlier this morning, a dove from one of my spies in the Mistral Islands." He handed it to Eve. "You are now worth three thousand coins alive. I must admit, I'm impressed."

Eve unfurled the scroll; a sickening feeling came to her stomach before she quickly closed it and handed it to Dakon instead.

"I'd rather you tell me what else it says." Eve locked eyes on the captain.

He took another drink. "Besides the tempting reward, Givensmir has officially crowned a new king as expected."

Her heart fluttered hopefully. *Eryce? Theo? Did they make it back alive after all? Was Pedro with them?*

Dakon spoke up. "Who?"

"King Marc. It is reported that his elder brothers were killed by an attack on their ships. Only the youngest heir made it back. Lucky bastard."

Eve couldn't breathe. She turned away, her heart cracking as the bitterness of hearing her nightmares confirmed overpowered her.

"Are you well?" Dakon asked.

Eve shook her head.

"What else was reported?" Pazel asked.

Eve could feel the captain's stare on her as he answered. "The Strix—the exiled witches living in Givensmir—have continued growing their following. My informant believes they may be working with the new king as there are a number of them sighted within the castle. Though, witch burnings have increased throughout the kingdom, nearly four since we escaped. He suspects it is from errant witches who refuse to join their cause."

Why is Marc doing this?

She recalled their dance in the ballroom, how he hinted at knowing her affinity for magic. Then, how Adriana confirmed her suspicions. Marc *was* curious, but did that mean he was welcoming it?

"What can we do?" Eve asked.

"Do?" Amarin scoffed. "There is nothing to do. The kingdom will soon be in another war. The best thing for all of us is to venture far from the destruction."

"And leave innocent people to die?"

"They aren't innocent in the king's eyes; they are witches."

Eve stood, the force of it knocking her chair down behind her. "And witches are guilty by existing?"

"He sees you as a threat." The chilling voice within her spoke, whispering softly as if it were right behind her.

Amarin leveled his gaze at her. "I never said that *I* believe that. Only that the king does."

"He defies you."

Eve shook her head, squeezing her eyes shut to block out the noise. She tried to concentrate.

Theo was dead, Callum, Pedro, Eryce.

But what of Adriana?

Would Marc harm her?

She realized Amarin was speaking. "—and in case you have forgotten, your sister killed the princess too. Of course, they don't trust them."

Eve recalled seeing her sister standing in the hall while Felicity lay dead at her feet. She didn't look smug or proud but confused. Maybe there was a reason for all of this. Something that Clarisa could explain if given the chance.

But where could she be?

The Blackthorn?

"I—I want to go to the Blackthorn," she announced suddenly, standing.

Amarin choked on his drink, coughing until he began to breathe normally once more. "Are you mad?!"

"I'm quite serious."

"Eve"—Dakon placed a hand over hers—"we cannot go there without a plan."

"I cannot risk my crew, my ship, *my life* trying to go to the Blackthorn! I might as well offer myself in chains," Amarin continued. "No, absolutely not."

"We can pay you," Eve insisted, her body heating with frustration.

"No amount of money is worth meeting Death."

"Then how will we get there?"

"That isn't my problem."

Eve pounded her fist on the table, her hands shaking with anger. "I can make it your problem."

"Kill him before he kills you."

"Eve," Pazel reached to hold her back, his fingers barely closed around her wrist before he screamed. She ripped her glare from the captain and turned quickly to Pazel. His hand was raised before him, red and blistered.

No, no, no.

"Pazel!"

Dakon ran to him, wrapping Pazel's hand in a wet cloth from the table. Pazel groaned. "It was like touching steel in a stove!"

"I'm sorry!" Eve reached out, but he flinched away from her.

"No, Eve," Dakon raised his hand, "I will take him to our cabin. He needs to be healed."

Eve lowered her hand, nodding. "Of course, I'm sorry, Pazel."

Guilt overcame her as she watched them leave the room. She hadn't realized how angry she had become, hadn't realized her skin had heated so quickly.

She placed a finger in her cup, the wine steamed slightly.

Relax, Eve.

Amarin sighed, rubbing his forehead. "How often does that happen?"

Eve turned to him, her eyes wide and shameful. "More than I'd like to admit."

He nodded, mulling over this. "I used to know a powerful witch, very quick to anger."

"Have you met many witches on your travels?"

Amarin huffed. "Too many to count."

Eve sat, taking a long drink. The wine, even warm, felt good against her lips. She needed to focus her thoughts, figure out how to express what she really needed from Amarin, but the only words that came from her were, "Am I damned?"

"I couldn't tell you." He shrugged, chewing on a roll. "I think that depends on how much you can control it."

"It?"

"The magic."

"This witch you knew, did she control it?"

She watched as a ghost of something crossed his eyes, haunting. "No."

"Oh."

"But she had very different wishes. Wanted for power. Thrived on the pain of others. Is that what you want?"

"I hope not."

"Nor do I. It isn't good for business to mingle with a witch who wants you dead."

Eve bit her lip. "What happened to this witch?"

He shook his head. "I do not know, nor do I wish to. I haven't seen her in fifteen years."

She nodded, letting his words settle on her. A lot seemed to have happened fifteen years ago.

"But you remind me of another . . ."

He shifted to face her, his eyes softening.

Eve waited for him to finish his sentence, but instead the captain grabbed another cup of wine. He drank it on and off until the words that hung in the air disappeared. Moments passed between them in silence.

"Who do I remind you of?"

Amarin faced Eve again, studying her. His brows creased, emphasizing his scar as he stood, walking toward his cabin window facing the open, darkening sky and sea. "We will go to Bastard's Haven."

"Bastard's Haven?" Eve sat straighter, trying to recall the stories of the abandoned island where the heathens of the world congregated.

She was more than a little nervous at the prospect of going so wholly unprepared.

"Yes, you can find someone there who will gladly risk their life to take you where you want to go."

"And if I don't?"

"Trust me. There's always someone with a death wish."

CLARISA

CHAPTER 4

"I FEEL IT IN THE AIR, TIME IS ESCAPING us," Brisa said, her hair changing into a blonde hue, her eyes nearly black, in Clarisa's candlelit room, "and you have yet to tell us why Navir defended you."

"Navir has always defended me—"

"He has never helped anyone he wasn't benefiting from. That includes you." Tabor huffed. "He wants something."

"I know, I know," Clarisa was weak from the magic she used before the coven council earlier, the sheer force of its power settling into her bones. She was barely able to brush her fingers nervously through her hair, then abruptly stopped, noticing it was dampening the strands. She shook her hands of the water, but it continued to pour from her palms like raindrops.

Brisa approached her, gently placing Clarisa's hands in hers. The water began to dry, instead settling on Brisa's new curls, weaving them in wet tendrils. "We were born for you, and we will die for you. But it feels as if our sacrifice is not enough for you to trust us even after all these years. Why must you remain so guarded?"

Brisa released Clarisa.

Clarisa swallowed, unable to meet her eyes. Not every witch had a familiar, but every familiar had a witch. One they were destined to be tethered to for the rest of their lives, even if some would never meet theirs in their lifetimes. Clarisa understood she should be grateful that she had not one, but two; yet she couldn't reconcile the feeling that their connection was slightly fractured from the beginning.

It was a peculiar thing, *familiars*—to put one's trust in another so blindly, and have little reservations about their commitment. To cross a witch was to tempt a brutal death itself. It is how they were first made by the Original Witches, to be wholly, unequivocally, and undeniably dedicated to their witch until they were called to Isila.

Clarisa stepped foot in the Blackthorn fifteen years ago, devastated by the loss of her sister, fearful of the unknown, but with the overwhelming feeling that they awaited her. She had felt it, dreamt about it as a child, but even when they were there in the flesh before her eyes, she couldn't bring herself to accept them, not completely. As if more to love meant more to lose.

"I'm sorry," Clarisa responded, "I have not been fair to you, to either of you."

Tabor rubbed his temples. "None of this is fair to anyone. But we need to know what you and Navir have planned. You tell us to keep the coven at bay so you could channel your magic, you find two strangers—mortals—and vouch for them, and we support you in front of our high priestess, the very one you tried to kill. And Navir's presence throughout it all. . ." He hesitated, his nostrils flaring with built up frustration. "We are in the dark and cannot fight a war we cannot see."

Clarisa released a breath, shaky and unnerving. She instinctively reached for the oracles' crystal about her neck; feeling its smooth texture beneath her fingertips soothed her.

"I don't know what Navir has planned. It happened so fast, and the queen . . . you heard what she said before Navir stepped in. For all my power, all the deaths at my hands at her request, I am no longer valuable on my mother's blood or the prophecy alone. I had no choice but to reveal my true power."

Tabor adjusted the sling of arrows on his back. Brisa fiddled with her fingers. The air thickened in the room with her confession, her most vulnerable fear laid bare for them out loud.

"The reason I have not divulged a plan is because I don't have one," Clarisa admitted. She moved away from them, hands still clutching the crystal as she paced around her chambers.

The silence was nearly too much to bear as she finally settled in front of her window.

Rain, endless and dreary, tapped on the glass. She placed her cold hands on it, feeling the chill beneath her fingertips, she closed her eyes concentrating on the rhythm.

Tap. Tap. Tap.

Her mother would do the same—sitting and looking out to the sea from her window in Givensmir, touching the glass longingly for hours, more so as the end of her life neared. There behind the glass was not a powerful enchantress, but a woman yearning for something on the other side of it.

What did her mother see through the window?

Clarisa opened her eyes and could barely make out the distant forests through the downpour. She allowed herself to wonder how it would feel to be free of the rain. To walk through the grass without the weight of the gods' tears upon her; to go beyond the lands of the

Blackthorn where stories of such places existed. Ana would be with her, creating charms from the precious, delicate petals of blooming flowers and the vines that grew in a garden of their making. They would bring life, not death, to their sanctuary.

"We could leave . . . escape," she heard herself whisper.

Brisa approached, looking out the same window as if studying what made Clarisa come to such a conclusion. "We can't," she said simply.

"Do you think that we ever could? To see the sunlight after the storm?"

Tabor and Brisa exchanged a worried look.

"One day, maybe."

Clarisa nodded, taking a final glance out the window. "I will speak to Navir—"

As if on cue, the door to the chambers opened, startling the group. Navir walked through with a dark, damp cape in his hands. He hung it on the rack and closed the door carefully.

"I heard my name?" He smirked.

Tabor stepped forward. "What do you want from us?"

"I don't negotiate with the help." Navir waved his hand non-committally as he approached Clarisa.

"Don't speak to him that way." Clarisa stood.

Navir folded his arms, unbothered. "We need to talk . . . privately."

She narrowed her gaze, ready to deny his request.

"We will give you a moment," Brisa said, pulling Tabor's arm toward the door. They left quickly, closing it behind them.

Clarisa glared at Navir, "I want the truth, now."

"My dear, Clarisa, when have I ever lied to you?"

She blinked a few times, sure she heard him incorrectly. "You told the queen that I was on the precipice of fulfilling the prophecy. Might I remind you the grimoire has never appeared for me and without it I cannot bring back Isila. Everything you told the coven was a lie."

The candlelight around her flickered; the furniture shook. She was sure she could hear the rats scurrying within the walls, fleeing from certain chaos.

Navir raised his hands between them. "I can explain, but let us remain calm, shall we?"

Clarisa desired to release her anger and frustration on the man before her, but instead she steadied her breathing until the room was still once more. She met Navir's eyes, in the blue hues, there seemed to be an urgency and sliver of amusement.

"What I said before the coven, is not a lie. For one, your bloodline is the reason you have magic."

Clarisa grimaced, and he continued.

"The Strix have risen in Givensmir and are rumored to be working with the new king. A second attack is no longer a possibility, it's a guarantee. They have already attacked you in your sleep; it is only a matter of time before they send far better assassins to your chambers. I fear as it stands now, we are not a formidable match against their alliance. We are an island full of witches, but—"

"Magic is not immortal."

"Precisely."

Clarisa considered this. They had magic in spades, practiced witchcraft for healing, manifesting, and channeling with their world, but it was rare to have magic like she did. And while she was able to destroy a single fleet of ships, she was sure she couldn't destroy an entire army of both mortals and witches. Not alone.

"You are still capable of resurrecting Isila," Navir continued. "You can bring the mortal realms to heel."

"It's not possible." *Not with Eve alive*, she wanted to say but kept the thought to herself.

"Yes, it is. Your mother was originally believed to be the one destined to recover the grimoire, to bring back our fallen goddess and restore our rightful place in this world."

She had been told the story countless times over the years by mentors, tutors, high clergy of the craft, and even by her mother. How her mother was an orphan found and prophesied by visions to Queen Saryn and the high priestess Giselle to resurrect their fallen goddess. The blood of the sole heir of the Original Witches ran through her, and now it was in Clarisa.

And someone else—if they really did possess magic . . .

"'Of mortal blood and wicked nature,'" Navir continued, quoting the prophecy. "You have the mortality your mother lacked. The final piece that was missing is in you. Damn the book, you have what you need, you just need to take it. Quit holding yourself back." He took a few steps toward her, closing the distance.

Clarisa instinctively took a step back. "I can't," she breathed.

"You can."

"No, you don't understand," her pulse began to quicken, her lips quivering. "It's a curse I can't control. Every assassination, every time I take a life and see it drain from the eyes of my victims, it grows within me." Her eyes began to water, and the nightmare she was sure would never leave came to mind. Malin, the innocent princess, the dead littering the beach, the waves bringing in body after body, names before and since that she couldn't recall. "This power has made me relish in what I was doing, as if I enjoyed it. All that death . . ." She closed her eyes, tears trickling down her cheeks. "I'm a murderer, a *monster*."

Navir cupped a hand on her cheek, "I did not see a monster on the shore when you embraced your true self." He lifted Clarisa's face, his eyes staring into her with a fierce intensity, "I saw our *salvation*."

The last words were barely a whisper but said with vigor. His lips were too close, his body touching hers. She shook from his grasp, taking a few steps back to put space between them once more. She did not like his touch on her skin, the way it made her tremble, the way his aura gave her dread. She wiped the remaining tears from her face. "What do you want from me?"

"I want for magic to reign again in my lifetime." He scowled. "I want to save the Blackthorn and the innocent witches who are at the mercy of a tyrant."

"I didn't realize you were such a martyr." Her words were venom.

"Without me, my dear," he replied, a ghost of a smile on his lips, "you would not be here making such cutting remarks about my character."

"So, you want me dead too?"

"I am the only one who doesn't."

He approached Clarisa once more, lifting his hand to her necklace. "I knew this looked familiar."

She instinctively placed a hand over the luring crystal, snatching it from him.

Damn me for not hiding it beneath my collar.

"You thought you were clever in Raven's Holdfast, that I wouldn't recognize it," he mused. "It's a wretched blessing you hold in your hands. But I suspect you know this already."

She didn't respond. Ever since she first summoned the oracles, she found herself unable to part from them, gazing at the crystal at odd hours of the day and night. Transfixed by what lurked within.

"You can't have it."

"I don't want it." He placed a tender hand on hers, gently loosening the crystal from her grip. He inspected it as she released shaky breaths, watching as he held it in his fingers. The crystal went dark and smoky, the faintest tapping against it from the oracles themselves had become a comfort and a source of fear for Clarisa.

"I want you to summon them again."

Goosebumps rose on her flesh. "The last time I did, they told me I would have to do terrible things. Things I will not be able to recover from."

"But you've thought of it."

Clarisa's eyes widened. "No, I—"

"Damn what everyone around you says. In here, between us, Clarisa, you can be your truest self without shame. Power has a way of controlling us, but we can control it too."

41

"You don't know that."

"These oracles can see what we ourselves are too scared to admit. Whatever it is they want from you, will be worth the price, I assure you."

"No, no it's not."

"Yes, it is."

"No!"

"Yes!"

"I will not kill my sister!" she shouted, releasing her frustration into the room. The furniture rattled and toppled over, the trinkets and glass upon them fell to the floor shattering into tiny, indiscernible pieces. The candles burned out, shrouding the two of them in a darkness only impeded by the foggy night sky filtering through the windows.

Navir hesitated for a moment, taking in her sudden outburst. He raised a hand, and the candles flickered back on. His eyes locked on Clarisa's. "She is not the child you left behind all those years ago."

"You can't make me." Hot tears fell down Clarisa's face, her rage and frustration building up once more. Her hands shook, her lips trembled, and even with this visceral reaction, there was a horrible, terrible thought that whispered deep within her.

But I could.

"Clarisa"—his eyes softened—"your sister was responsible for King Eryck's death."

"He murdered our mother!"

"She killed him in cold blood," he continued calmly. "She set fire to the castle, killing dozens of people, trapping them inside. *Innocent* people, horrible deaths . . ."

"No, she wouldn't—"

"Her magic is taking over her. And soon she will want her revenge."

"No." She tried to move back, but Navir moved closer.

"You are the one who killed her friend, ripped her from a life of vanity. She blames you."

"That's not true," she shoved him away, moving for the door. To get Ana, to escape and find Eve and explain everything. They could get away if they left now, they could put some distance between themselves and the Blackthorn before they found out. They could . . .

Navir grabbed her arm, turning her to face him. "It's true and if you don't believe me, ask your oracles. Do it. Do it now."

His words sent chills down her spine, tears fell down her cheeks. She tried pulling against his grip.

"This land will not survive her wrath," Navir said. "She will destroy everything good in this world. She may even try to get even."

At this, Clarisa stopped fighting. Her heart stopped beating, the rain seemed to stop falling. Everything was still and unsettling.

Would Eve kill Ana?

Clarisa killed the princess and watched as Eve was arrested shortly after, and she did nothing to save her. What ties they had before, Clarisa's inability to act certainly severed them.

"I can talk to her—"

Navir shook his head slowly, "I fear we are far past that now."

She bit her lip. "What can I do?"

"The only choice we have is to raise powerful allies." He lifted the crystal delicately from her neck once more, admiring it. "Ask them about the Unclaimed Wastes. It's time we claim what is rightfully ours . . . together."

THEO

CHAPTER 5

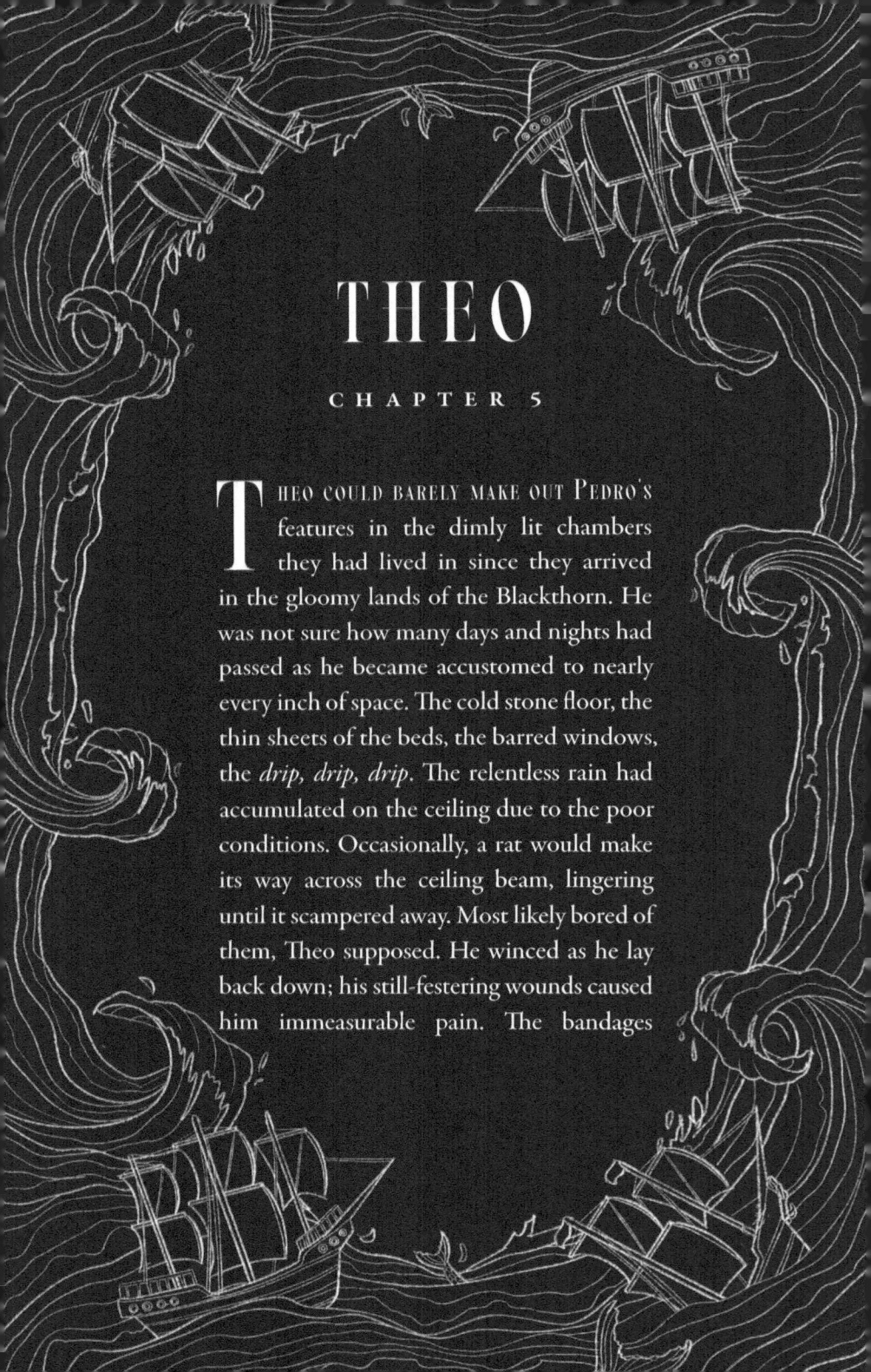

Theo could barely make out Pedro's features in the dimly lit chambers they had lived in since they arrived in the gloomy lands of the Blackthorn. He was not sure how many days and nights had passed as he became accustomed to nearly every inch of space. The cold stone floor, the thin sheets of the beds, the barred windows, the *drip, drip, drip*. The relentless rain had accumulated on the ceiling due to the poor conditions. Occasionally, a rat would make its way across the ceiling beam, lingering until it scampered away. Most likely bored of them, Theo supposed. He winced as he lay back down; his still-festering wounds caused him immeasurable pain. The bandages wrapped around his torso where Marc's sword pierced him now tinged a murky amber. He hoped the witch healers would return soon to give him their tinctures so he could sleep the pain away. Theo still coughed blood, though it lessened as the days passed.

Pedro gazed out at the midnight rain, tapping gently against the window. Theo could sense his frustration; it emanated off him as if there was something he wished to say but couldn't. Pedro had stood at that window for hours and hours, nearly every day since their arrival, and Theo wondered what went through his mind—was he searching for a means of escape? The guards interrupted them only to provide food, but otherwise did not answer any of their questions or requests to speak with Clarisa. Theo hated how powerless he felt, and for the first time he truly understood the precarious danger his mortality afforded him.

"How much longer do you think they will keep us here before they kill us?" Theo asked, fear prickling down his spine as his thoughts spiraled once more.

Pedro shook his head, jaw tightening as he kept his gaze toward the window. "I'm not sure. They wouldn't continue healing us if they were planning to kill us. It would be a waste."

"I wouldn't put anything past them."

"Surely Clarisa has put in a good word for us."

"Clarisa," Theo scoffed, coughing into his sleeve. "The one who watched us get taken away by our mortal enemies."

"They are not mortal, and if it wasn't for her we would be dead."

"This seems like a nasty trick, waiting for us to be healthy and whole before they set us apart for torture."

Pedro ripped his gaze from the window, glaring at Theo. "Thinking that way only makes this situation worse. We are alive by the skin of our teeth, and instead of thanking the gods, you are here spitting in their faces."

"Our gods abandoned us on the sea."

"*Us.* You are not alone, Theo, lest you forget you have a friend here."

"As you wish, *My Prince.*"

Pedro stomped over to Theo, kneeling by his cot with daggers in his eyes. "Must I explain again why that was necessary?"

"As a prince or a knight, you and I are not long for this world of theirs. Switching birth rights does not change that."

"In case you have forgotten, enemies typically hold their high-value prisoners hostage and send back someone of lesser worth as the messenger. I made sure to give you the best chance of survival. We are still in danger, and while they may spare a rich knight, they will not so easily release a prince of their enemy."

Theo clenched his jaw; he could taste the blood on his tongue. "Even if they released me, how would I get anywhere like this?" He gestured to his wounds. "I can barely stand for a short time. Riding horses is out of the question."

Pedro inspected the bloody bandage. "It is better than it was when we first arrived, I promise you. These witches seem to have far better healing than we do back home. You will get better."

Theo looked up at the dark ceiling; it seemed to go on forever into a void. *Witches.* The beings he had been taught to fear most of his life after the enchantress were now the ones healing him. It was both unsettling and unreal.

"I didn't believe Eve when she told me."

Pedro furrowed his brow. "Told you what?"

"Our last night in the capital, I visited Eve, and she told me Clarisa was the one who murdered Felicity. I ignored her, thinking that she was trying to use any excuse to be free. Perhaps, I didn't want to believe it." Theo shook his head. "A coveted half-witch presumed dead for years comes back to her home and kills an innocent woman and for what?"

"Eve said Clarisa killed your wife?"

"Yes."

"Did she say why?"

"No."

"You're a shit listener."

Theo grimaced from the truth of it. "I was as wary as anyone would be. I had nearly convinced myself that witches were no more than folklore anymore until that night."

"Did something else happen?"

"Eve, she"—he swallowed remembering, and brought his hands together in front of him. He could still feel the scars of the blisters that had now faded in his palm—"she became like fire in my arms, her skin burned mine, but there she was . . . standing before me as if she was unbothered. As if she were not becoming ash in front of me."

Pedro took a deep, shaky breath. "So the rumors were true."

"Of her being a witch, yes."

"How did she hide it all those years? The king had brought her to his chambers after her mother's death, the healers conducted tests. How did she do it?"

"I don't know."

"And Clarisa being a murderer? Why would she save our lives after being so capable of something like this?"

Theo shook his head. "That's what I have been asking myself. All these deaths and secrets. They make no sense. We are missing something."

Pedro opened his mouth as if to respond, but the door opened and the candles in the room came alight. A man he had never seen before with crow-black hair and blue eyes and dressed in dark clothing walked in.

Theo shifted on his elbows, groaning against the pain. Pedro stood between them.

"Who are you?"

The man removed his gloves, placing them inside his pocket before responding. "My name is Navir, Prince and heir of the Blackthorn. I presume you are Prince Theo?"

Navir reached a hand out to Pedro, and Theo watched as he took it. Navir turned his gaze to Theo. "Ah, and here is the brave knight. Pedro, is it? Of Rubianes?"

Theo nodded, unable to think of anything to say.

"Why are you here?" Pedro asked, his shoulders back and his stance tall against Navir's.

"Sit, would you?" Navir gestured to the other side of Theo's cot, where a table with two chairs appeared.

Theo was stunned, and his heart pounded against his chest as the two men moved to take their seats.

"I hope you are finding these accommodations far better than the dungeons?" Navir smirked.

Pedro narrowed his eyes. "Yes, though we thought we would have spoken to you much sooner, since we've been held hostage."

"Hostage? You are our guests under confinement. Perspective, I find, tells a better story."

"You are spinning words that mean the same thing," Theo said. "We are not allowed to leave and therefore we are under your imprisonment."

Navir turned to Theo, his blue eyes meeting his hazel ones. "You are quite clever for a knight."

"I was raised by some of the best tutors in our kingdom," Theo replied.

"Ah, yes. A rich boy who wished to become a hero. Tell me, do you feel so heroic here?"

Theo swallowed.

"What is it your queen wants?" Pedro asked.

"My mother wants for your kingdom to leave us in peace. To stop the murder of innocent witches, and to forfeit ties to the Unclaimed Wastes."

"The Unclaimed Wastes?" Pedro nearly laughed. "The name says it all, it is unclaimed and a waste."

"Then it will be simple enough for your brother to let us in?"

"My brother?"

"Yes, my spies tell me King Marc ascended the throne shortly after his return to your capital."

Theo's heart raced in his chest, the horror of the words settling on him in a disarray of mangled pieces. Marc truly achieved what he wanted—ultimate control, ascending a throne not meant for him, and now with unchecked power at his fingertips.

Pedro and Theo shared a look. From the corner of his eye, Theo noticed a slight smile on Navir's face.

"I did not think this would be surprising to hear, Prince. After all, your elder brother must have died during the attack, though we have yet to find his body in the wreckage."

"What about my father?" Pedro asked.

"He was killed by his cousin, of course." He pointed to Theo, smirking. "At least, that is the rumor abounding these days."

The room began to spin.

Eve? How is that possible?

"And Lady Eve, what became of her?" Pedro asked, trying to quell his shock.

"My little doves tell me she has escaped."

Where did she go?

It took all of Theo's willpower to remain silent as Pedro spoke.

Pedro's nostrils flared. "I see."

"I imagine when you return and take your rightful place as king, we will achieve an understanding. Some wasteful land and our kingdom in peace in exchange for your lives. That is, if your brother agrees."

"We will need to write to him to negotiate. If you don't kill us first."

"Why would I want to do that?"

"For the same reason our men were killed by your witches on our ships. For the same reason you killed my brother."

Navir smirked, amusement crossing his face. "My dear, Theo. None of our witches were aboard your ships and neither was I. The witches you met were of the Strix."

"The what?" Theo asked, confused.

"The Strix. A faction of our kingdom we banished nearly a century ago for their *interesting* ways of practicing the craft. It seems the men aboard your ships were the target of these witches for some reason or another. Though, admittedly, the destruction of the ships and the remaining deaths were our doing. Your dear cousin, Clarisa, can take the credit for that."

Theo shifted too suddenly from the shock, wincing and coughing against the pain.

Watching Theo, Navir clapped his hands, and a guard came in with cups and a pitcher, placing them on the table before leaving quickly. Navir poured the drink into the cups, handing one to each of them.

"Sorry, gentlemen, only water this time. Need us all to have clear minds."

They raised their glasses, and Navir clinked his against theirs. Theo and Pedro each raised a brow but said nothing as they took a sip. Theo did not realize how feral his thirst had become. He couldn't remember the last time the guards offered him something to drink.

"When can we see Clarisa? Or send a letter to my brother?" Pedro asked.

"All in due time, I assure you. Preparations are still underway as our queen discusses her plans for you with her trusted advisers."

"Why did she send you and not one of them?"

Navir smiled but ignored his question. "Secrets are never far from my ears, gentlemen. I would advise you to think over your intentions for when I return."

"We came here because your kingdom ordered the murder of an innocent princess," Pedro snapped.

"Your wife."

"Wha—"

"Your wife," he repeated, "not just any innocent princess."

Pedro stilled.

Navir stood, walking toward the door. "Enjoy your health, dear prince. I suspect your knight will want you to share in his pain soon enough."

The candles burned out as Navir left the room, drowning Theo and Pedro in darkness once more.

Later that evening, Pedro coughed himself to sleep.

And all the while, Theo wished that wherever Eve was she was safe and free from harm.

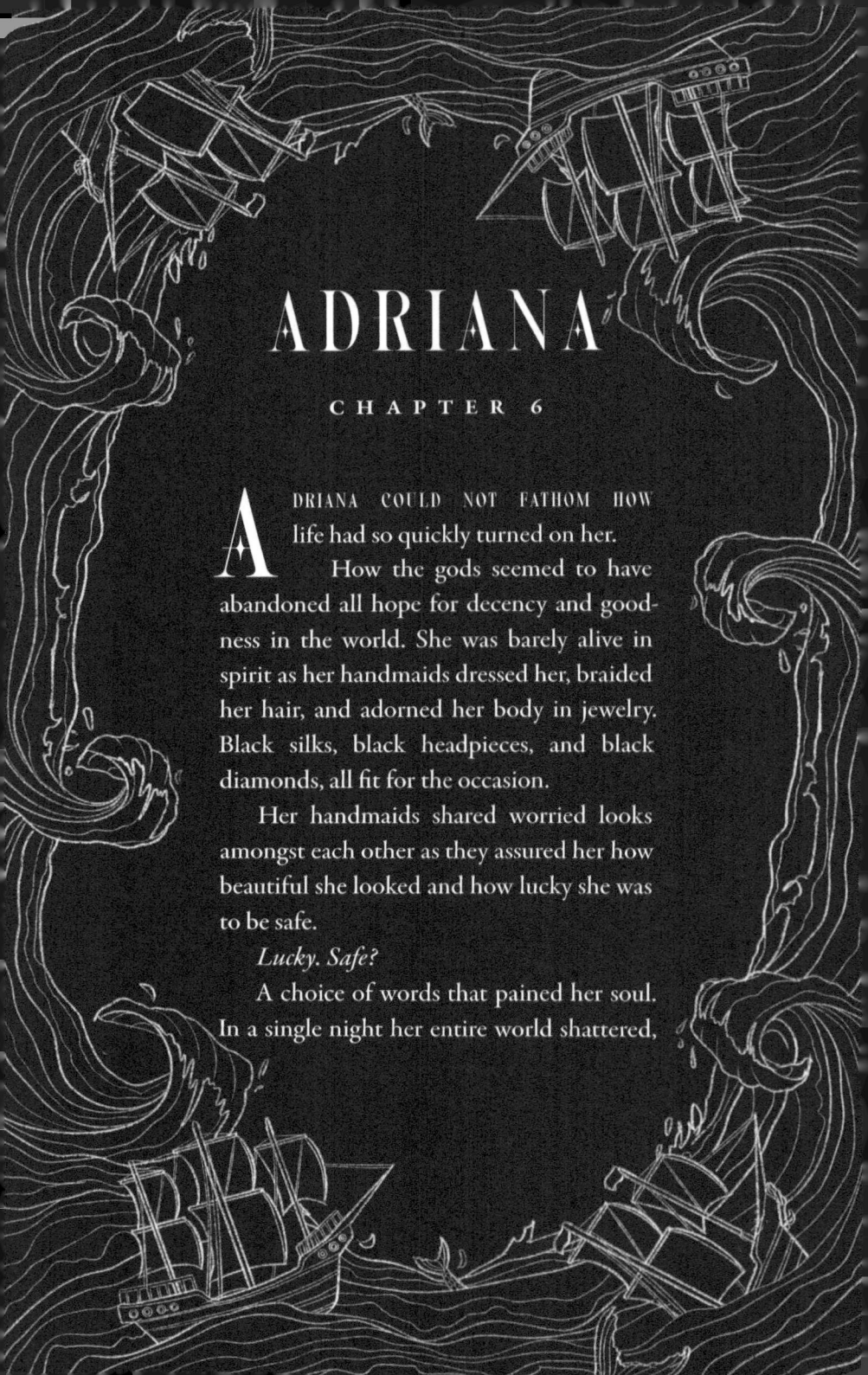

ADRIANA

CHAPTER 6

ADRIANA COULD NOT FATHOM HOW
life had so quickly turned on her.
How the gods seemed to have
abandoned all hope for decency and goodness in the world. She was barely alive in
spirit as her handmaids dressed her, braided
her hair, and adorned her body in jewelry.
Black silks, black headpieces, and black
diamonds, all fit for the occasion.

Her handmaids shared worried looks
amongst each other as they assured her how
beautiful she looked and how lucky she was
to be safe.

Lucky. Safe?

A choice of words that pained her soul.
In a single night her entire world shattered,

taking with it her father, brothers, Eve, Callum, and Dakon.

Dakon.

His name filled her with a mix of confusion, sadness, and betrayal. Tears pricked her eyes, and she squeezed them shut.

"Leave me, now."

The handmaids bowed and made their swift retreat, closing the door quietly behind them.

Adriana sobbed into her hands, recalling the fire from her father's tower not so long ago. A night fettered in panicked chaos, she was awakened by her guards and handmaids. They barely made it past the carnage, all of them quickly escaping to her mother's private castle a short distance east of her home.

There they stayed for days, praying to the gods for safety and for her father's soul to Death. Hours upon excruciating hours they were cared for by servants with little information on what had occurred the night they all fled, save for rumors that occasionally made their way from the guards.

Gossip of Eve attacking her father, and Callum assisting her escape with servants ran rampant. Her brothers had not been heard from, and the start of a promising war against the witches was delayed by lack of news on the status of the ships.

According to her court, the fault solely lay with Eve. She was a witch with a vendetta to curse the royal line by any means necessary. Callum was but a pawn under her spell, forbidden to be mentioned on pain of punishment. Everything they did or said could be subject to punishment now . . .

In those early days after the fire, fresh with her memory of Dakon kissing her that same night, Adriana wondered if perhaps she had been used.

Was he one of the servants that ran away with Eve?

Did he come in that night hoping to distract her?

Was he responsible for Eve's escape, or worse, her father's death?

She bit the inside of her cheek as the emotions warred within her, mulling over every detail trying to understand. There had to be a reason Eve killed her father, something that she was missing in the stories that abounded.

When Marc eventually returned from the failed invasion, Adriana was questioned by him and Lord Wesley, but she knew little. She considered telling them about the secret passage behind her wall, the one Dakon came from that night, but she couldn't bring herself to.

Adriana touched her lips, remembering Dakon's embrace and the softness of his lips, a kiss that she had dreamed about ever since. Those green eyes, verdant and welcoming, as they looked upon her sweetly. Perhaps that final look was what kept her quiet, silently hoping that he would one day return through the wall and whisk her away from her wretched life.

A knock at the door gripped her from her thoughts.

"Lady Jayne, Your Highness." Her guard opened the door letting in Jayne from court, who bowed happily as she entered the princess's chambers.

It was apparent that the ladder climbing and scheming did not stall for even the murder of monarchs. The days following Marc's coronation were riddled with men and women at court feral for a taste at elevating their standing and remaining in her family's good graces. Jayne was one of the many noblewomen who vied for her brother's attention, despite him being swiftly married to Eryce's widow, Gabrielle. As recompense, he gave Jayne the now vacant position of lady-in-waiting to Adriana despite her protests.

A bitterness filled Adriana at the thought of her brother. It was quite unfathomable how he had so quickly situated himself in Eryce's life without remorse.

"Your Highness, you are a vision," Jayne gushed, approaching the princess. Her cheerful disposition calmed as she closed the distance. "While I very much look forward to our blossoming friendship, I wish to impart my deepest condolences. I understand you are grieving, as am I and the rest of the kingdom. If there is anything you should need, I am at your service."

Adriana gently squeezed Jayne's hands and withdrew them slowly from her grasp, not wishing to divulge anything to someone chosen by her brother for reasons she had yet to reveal.

THE TEMPLE OF THE FIVE WAS CROWDED BEFORE ADRIANA AND THE rest of the court arrived in their carriages. She peeked at the hundreds of city folk lining the streets as she passed. Her throat began to close, her heart thundered in her chest, and her hands felt clammy as she grabbed her handkerchief from her dress pocket to clench onto something, anything. She longed for the days when she had not given crowds a second thought.

The carriage she shared with Jayne pulled to a stop at the front of the temple, and a guard opened it; Timothy's eyes met hers, a bruise visible beneath his right eye. She wondered if it had anything to do with the fire.

"Your Highness," he nodded.

"Timothy?" she breathed. She had not seen him since the night Dakon had snuck into her chambers. She bit her lip, feeling awkward.

"Ser Timothy, I am glad it is you escorting us. I feel much safer already!" Jayne exclaimed, placing her hand before him.

"I am glad to be of service, thank you for your generous compliment." He grasped it, helping her down the steps of the carriage.

"Princess," he reached his hand out, and she grasped it firmly.

"Thank you."

She gazed upon the temple as she had done nearly all her life. It was made of a remarkable white stone shaped into a dome that reached into the sky. Large statues dedicated to each of the five were carved all around the temple embedded into the structure itself. The entrance boasted a massive archway leading down an outdoors walkway toward the large twin doors with intricate outlines of grapevines and the five grapes carved on top. Golden details outlined the temple leading up to the top where a pointed sun shined upon the city, reflecting the light of the gods upon them.

Timothy walked alongside them as the rest of the guards kept the crowd at bay. She tried to keep her eyes fixed on the doors, not wishing to rile up any of the people. As she walked, she had an overwhelming sensation that one of the city folk would leap for her skirts and pull her under. She fiddled with her handkerchief to quell her nerves.

They entered the threshold of the temple, and Adriana's lips trembled. The outline of her father's body rested underneath a thin white sheet at the altar below. Elder Borgias and his religious apprentices were preparing the ceremony as the rest of the court waited patiently in their pews. Gabrielle sat alone at the front, waiting for Marc to join her. She appeared beautiful as ever, in a black gown and veil, but her eyes were fixed on nothing, staring blankly and cold.

Adriana moved to speak to her, but the bells in the temple chimed, and she instead rushed to the pew across from her. There Adriana's mother, Queen Alondra, sat rigid and disapproving.

"You are late, my daughter."

"The streets were crowded."

"Always an excuse with you." Her mother clicked her tongue.

Adriana ignored her, not wishing to start an argument amongst such a keen audience. "Where is Marc?"

"The king, you mean."

She rolled her eyes. "Yes, the king."

"The king's guard is escorting him from his solar. Unlike you, he has much business to attend to. We are bound to his schedule, not the other way around."

"Mother," Adriana began, "it has been difficult—"

"Do not speak to *me* of difficulties," she hissed. "Now pray in silence that the gods may forgive your insolence and for your father's soul to Death."

Adriana clenched her jaw and faced the front. There were many words she wanted to release that sat like venom on her tongue, but instead, amongst such a large crowd, she decided to forgo any response. She settled her eyes instead on the silk sheets covering her father.

They were never close, rarely spoke, but she was conflicted about his demise. The gods and elders always spoke of loving your mother and father, to pay them heed and follow their lead. And she believed that some part of her did. Maybe, she even pitied how he died.

But a larger part felt that the gods had finally enacted their karmic retribution upon him. Too many deaths at his hands and now, hopefully, war would end. Surely after his bitter defeat, even Marc must know that war with the witches is futile. Givensmir had plenty of land and a massive kingdom, there was nothing more to conquer.

"All rise for the King Marc of Givensmir and the Four Seas, Defender of Mortality and the Faith of the Five!"

She stood along with the rest of the temple and averted her eyes in the direction of the voice by the entrance. Her brother, surrounded by his king's guard, walked down the aisle toward where Gabrielle sat. Everybody bowed as he moved past them, like a wave around a ship. Marc walked with a steady confidence, his head held high, and a slight smirk upon his face despite the occasion. He was dressed in the finest black-and-gold fabrics, a sword affixed to his hip. Adriana could not keep her eyes off her brother, as uneasiness ran through her. This was not a man in mourning, but in triumph.

He slowed as he approached her pew, and the three women bowed as he reached out for their mother's hand.

"Mother, you can be assured that Father will not die in vain. With the blessing of the gods, I will scour the ends of our world to bring justice. This I promise you in sight of the gods in their holy temple."

He kissed her hand, and Adriana watched as their mother let silent tears fall, a look of pride upon her face.

"By the will of the gods, my king, my son, you bring me light in this darkness."

Marc released her hand gently, and for the briefest moment, narrowed his eyes at Adriana. Just as quickly, he softened them.

"Sister, my condolences," he remarked curtly.

"Thank you, my king." She willed a tear to fall down her cheek. "We are touched by your benevolence."

"Lady Jayne"—he moved to kiss her hand, lingering his touch for a moment longer than necessary—"thank you for accompanying my sister. There is no one better suited."

Jayne blushed, the redness of her cheeks nearly filling her pale face. "Of course, Your Majesty. It is an honor."

Marc lifted his lips in a smile that did not reach his eyes as he lowered and raised his gaze over Jayne's body. Adriana pursed her lips, wishing this spectacle would end.

Finally, he left, taking his seat next to his wife as Elder Borgias began his sermon.

Adriana tried to remain still and composed throughout the funeral but found herself fiddling with the handkerchief on her lap. Her skin prickled and her fingers shook as she tried to focus on her prayers. Her nerves had seeped into her thoughts as she recalled everything she had been told about Marc, her father, and Eve until this point.

She snuck a glance at Marc, whose hazel eyes were locked on their father's corpse. It disturbed her how much he looked like their father, smug and bold beneath a golden crown he didn't deserve. And no matter how she tried to avoid him at court, his threat followed her around when she was alone in her thoughts. The blackmail that still loomed in the back of her mind, the one she knew was due to be paid for her failure to procure proof of Eve's magic all those weeks ago.

"*Wars are expensive.*"

It was a promise to sell her to the highest bidder.

And with nothing in his way, her future was at his mercy now.

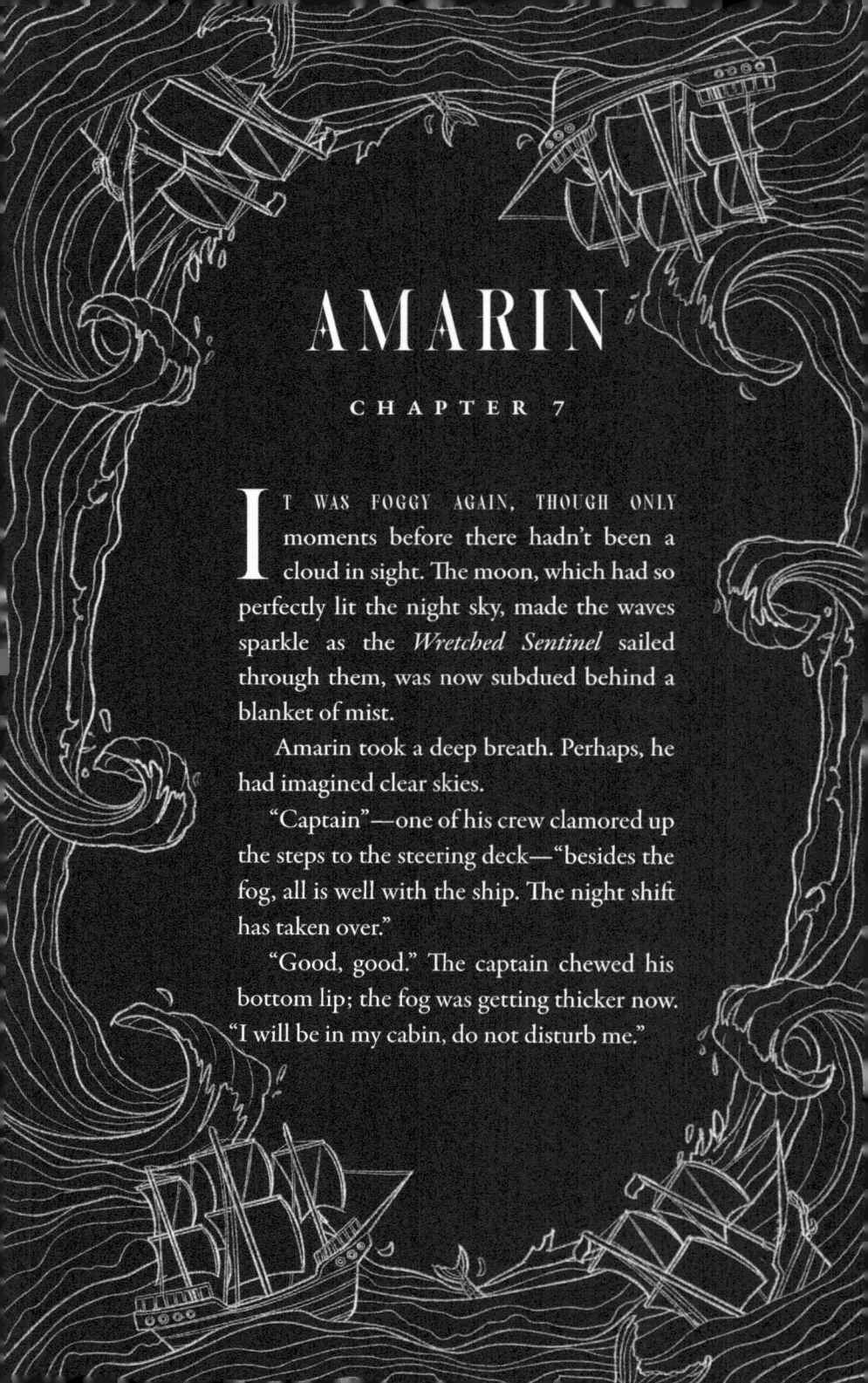

AMARIN

CHAPTER 7

I T WAS FOGGY AGAIN, THOUGH ONLY moments before there hadn't been a cloud in sight. The moon, which had so perfectly lit the night sky, made the waves sparkle as the *Wretched Sentinel* sailed through them, was now subdued behind a blanket of mist.

Amarin took a deep breath. Perhaps, he had imagined clear skies.

"Captain"—one of his crew clamored up the steps to the steering deck—"besides the fog, all is well with the ship. The night shift has taken over."

"Good, good." The captain chewed his bottom lip; the fog was getting thicker now. "I will be in my cabin, do not disturb me."

"Yes, Cap'n."

Amarin pushed past him down the steps, quickly grabbing a lit lantern before shoving open his door. His cabin was empty.

He took a few steps inside, placing the lantern on his desk as he rummaged with the cabinets, fishing out candles and matches. He lit them quickly, knowing his time was limited. He glanced up toward the window that lined his back wall; there was only black-gray fog.

Panic began to set in, as he recalled the last time they faced each other. Fifteen years ago and a failed quest that resulted in him avoiding the Blackthorn since. His fingers fumbled with the last match as it refused to light. It was becoming damp in his fingers, and soon it felt as if water had drenched it.

She was here.

He whirled around and came face-to-face with her.

Cassandra.

"Hello, Amarin, I've missed you," she purred, lifting a finger to his lips before he could speak. "I won't be long, I promise."

She wore a long, jade-colored dress with its signature large slit. Her silver eyes danced and shined in the flickering candlelight. Cassandra's long, black hair fell below her breasts, accentuating her curves. If she were not his nightmares come to life, Amarin would have surely thought her a beautiful woman.

"W-what are you doing here?"

"Oh, you wound me." Cassandra pouted. "I was hoping to feel more welcomed by you." She traced her finger down to his chest, lingering there. "Did you miss me too?"

Amarin swallowed, trying to get a hold of himself. "You only miss torturing me senseless. Tell me what you are here for and be done with it."

She smiled brightly, wrinkling her nose at him before turning toward his desk. "Would you like a drink?"

"No."

"Ah, so you do remember." She winked, taking a seat on his desk, leaning back ever slightly to emphasize her breasts. "I was hoping we could amuse ourselves, make up for lost time."

Amarin shook his head, keeping a safe distance from her. "Every time you see me, I lose a bit of my fucking soul. Why would I want to spend any time with you?"

Cassandra threw back her head and laughed. "Oh, my apologies. I meant amusing for me."

Amarin stood there, arms crossed, unwilling to rise to the bait nor give her any satisfaction of banter.

She sighed. "I hear you are headed for Bastard's Haven. Dropping off some precious cargo, are we?"

"What business of that is yours?"

"Everything that happens in the seas is my business. Or have you forgotten our agreement?" She cocked a brow at him.

He let out a shaky breath. *And so the sea witch needed a favor.* "No," he breathed.

"Good." She smiled. "Now, I see you have a witch on board. Well, half of one."

Eve.

He straightened. "She travels with two familiars. I'm taking them to Bastard's Haven. There she can determine her own path."

Cassandra walked toward him, eyes meeting his in a silver daze. "This one looks familiar, does she not?" She walked around him, her fingertips tracing his shoulders and back. Her voice dripped with sweet, poisonous words. "A beauty to be envied. Rich, warm eyes that remind you of the sparrows that flew over your home and a sweet smile that makes you feel quite *enchanted* even after all these years."

Amarin swallowed. "I don't know what you're talking about."

"Oh, you do, my pirate." She continued walking around him, whispering in his ear, "Heartbreak is often stronger than any memory. I wonder how it feels to look upon her face every day and be reminded of what could have been."

"She is not her mother."

"Of course not." She came back in front of him, placing her hands on the sides of his face, her cool touch like ice in the winter, unwelcome and unwanted. "But she reminds you of her. That is why you want to be rid of her."

Amarin shrugged out of her touch, "I cannot take her where she wants to go."

"And where is that?"

"You know damn well."

She cocked her head and laughed once more. "Oh, this is delicious. A half-witch with little control of her witchcraft wishes to face her powerful sister in a magical war of the ages. Is that right?"

Amarin nodded, trying to maintain some semblance of control.

"I want you to take her there." Her eyes sparkled.

A panic went up his spine. "Why me?"

"We have been over this before, Captain—fastest ship, best captain on the seas, it can only be you."

"No," he said before he could stop himself.

"What was that?" She raised a brow, amused.

"I—I can't. They will kill me."

"Oh, Amarin. You forget one daughter, break your promise to a powerful witch kingdom, and suddenly you think the world is out for you." She sighed dramatically. "Of course, that one daughter was the answer to taking over the mortal kingdoms and resurrecting our fallen goddess, but who really remembers, hmm?"

"I barely escaped with my fucking life the last time. I lost half my crew and Tenith who I had spent nearly my entire life pirating with. This will not go as planned and because you're practically powerless on land, you'll not be able to stop what they'll do to me!"

"Powerless?" She let out a short laugh. "*Powerless?!*"

Quickly, her soft voice was deep and terrifying. Light began to emanate from within her, she rose inches off the floor, her hair wild as she scowled at him. Parchment flew across the room, the glass of his lantern broke, his desk shook, and the cabin descended into madness. The waves whipped at the cabin window and nearly cracked the glass.

"No! No, Cassandra, that is not what I meant!" Amarin fell to his knees, shielding his eyes from the torrent of flying objects around them. A few books hit his body, and a knife slashed his face. "You are the most powerful!" He closed his eyes, shielding himself on the floor unable to stop her.

Then it was silent.

He lifted his arm from his eyes trepidatiously; the cabin was untouched, the cut on his face gone. Cassandra continued sitting on the desk, her legs crossed. She focused on her nails as she spoke, "I am but a powerful, beautiful woman, Captain. And you are"—she eyed him up and down—"a man. Lest we not forget our place."

Amarin nodded, moving to stand before her. "I apologize."

Her bright, silver eyes shined, and she reached her hand out. Amarin felt a sinking feeling in his stomach but grasped it. She pulled him close, too close. Her lips lingered next to his ear, "Bastard's Haven is but a stop for you. Take Eve to the Blackthorn. Fail me and I will sink you and every ship and every crewmate in your charge into the sea. Please me"—she led his hands beneath her dress—"and we can continue our little arrangement."

Amarin's heart thundered in his chest. She was poison. "Yes."

"Yes, what?"

"Yes"—he squeezed his eyes shut, hating the words leaving his lips—"m-my witch."

She smiled bewitchingly. "There now, was that so hard?"

Before he could answer, she wrapped her legs around his waist and pulled him even closer.

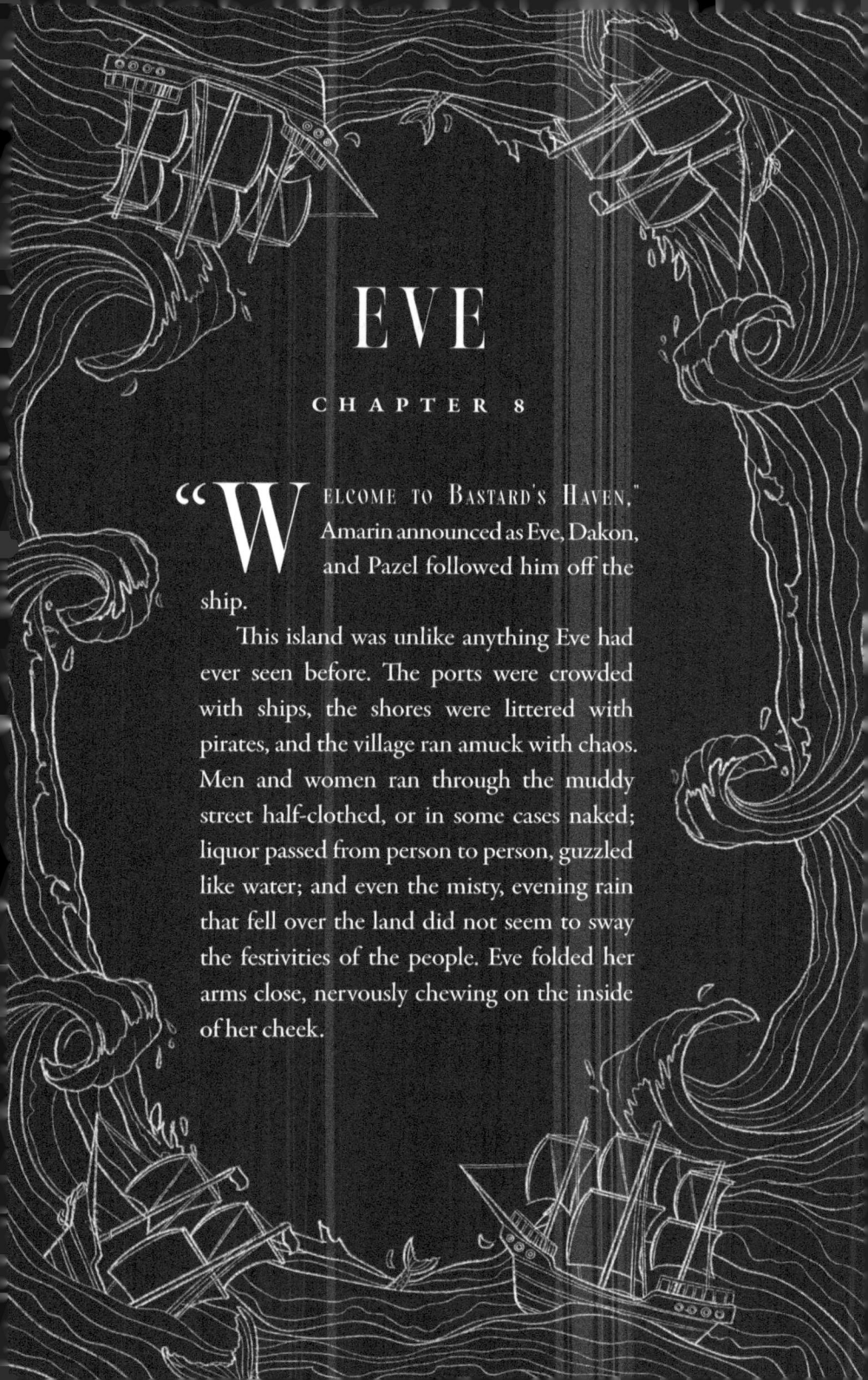

EVE

CHAPTER 8

"**W**ELCOME TO BASTARD'S HAVEN," Amarin announced as Eve, Dakon, and Pazel followed him off the ship.

This island was unlike anything Eve had ever seen before. The ports were crowded with ships, the shores were littered with pirates, and the village ran amuck with chaos. Men and women ran through the muddy street half-clothed, or in some cases naked; liquor passed from person to person, guzzled like water; and even the misty, evening rain that fell over the land did not seem to sway the festivities of the people. Eve folded her arms close, nervously chewing on the inside of her cheek.

"How long do you think we'll be here?" Pazel asked, eyes wide as he took in their surroundings.

"As long as it takes to get everything in order," Amarin grumbled. He gestured to the village before them. There were a few buildings that seemed to barely hang on to their structures, as if a brisk wind would certainly knock them over. Merchants packed up their carts as the dusk settled over them, dwellers lurked in the darkened alleys, commiserating with one another. The rest of the villagers flitted about, as if the night sky signaled the start of a celebration Eve could not understand. "Keep yourselves busy," Amarin continued, "I have work to do."

He took a few steps before turning back to face them, pointing at a dilapidated structure full of people, a short distance down the path. "The tavern is that way."

Without waiting to hear their response, Amarin left, disappearing into the crowd.

Eve faced her companions, unsure of what to make of their situation. Her tunic now was too loose, her braided hair too long, and she shoved it in her collar for good measure. She was vulnerable here.

"I've never left Givensmir before," Dakon admitted, as they continued taking in the feverish strength of the village. "I didn't think it would be so . . . lively."

Eve nodded. In the castle, it was considered beneath the nobles to even speak of Bastard's Haven. It was a place for exiled, low-life people on the fringes of society. It wasn't far from the truth. She grimaced, realizing that included her now too.

Pazel took a step forward, facing them. "Come now, let's not judge before we get to know the good people—"

A woman screamed angrily nearby just as a man with chickens under his arms barreled through them, Eve jumped back in time to avoid making contact. The woman followed close behind, throwing shoes and stones at the man's back. They took off behind a cluster of tents.

Eve huffed, cocking a brow at Pazel. "You were saying?"

His face split into a playful smirk, placing a hand over each of their shoulders and bringing them in close. "Let's get a drink." He gestured to the tavern. "The gods know we need one."

"I never thought I'd rather be on a ship than off," Eve muttered, holding her mug close as she sat in the corner of the brothel. Dakon had ordered them three ales, and Eve sipped the bitter drink as they spoke. Though she had to admit it was better than the rations aboard Amarin's ship.

"We could head back, but something tells me Pazel would have a problem." Dakon gestured to the other end of the tavern where Pazel sang off-key amongst a crowd of fascinated, drunk women.

Eve grinned, taking a sip of her drink, grateful she had something to do with her hands besides fiddling them. Her braid tickled her back, but she was determined to keep it there, adjusting her posture occasionally for some relief. There were mostly men in this establishment, and she wished to remain as inconspicuous as possible.

"I wish I was like him." She sighed, staring into the frothy mixture in her mug. "To be able to find bliss in the chaos."

Dakon glanced at Pazel then her. "He is quite the happy companion."

She watched as he took a swig of his drink, the way his long curls now brushed his brow and the way his stubble was forming into a beard. His green eyes reminded her of the lily pads in the pond of the castle gardens, making her feel homesick and melancholy. "When were you the happiest?"

A bittersweet expression crossed his face, a ghost of a smile that was obscured by the knit of his brow and the darkening of his eyes. "When I would ride among the silver birches this past summer and anytime I could hear Cerene tell her stories."

Before she could pry, he quickly added, "You? Was it when you were engaged?"

He eyed her apprehensively, but Eve tore her gaze from his. She ignored his question and instead drank the rest of her ale, lifting up her now-empty cup until she caught sight of the barmaid. "Let us speak of anything else."

"Eve"—Dakon placed a gentle hand on hers—"we are friends. We can only build our trust by being open with one another."

She bit her lip and removed her hand as the barmaid brought over her drink.

"I'm not ready to speak about Callum."

"What about Theo?"

"What about him?"

"His death must have affected you." He kept his gaze firm on hers, "I don't want you to feel as if you cannot speak to me about what troubles you."

"Then we'd be here all night," she snapped, harsher than intended.

Dakon raised a brow. "If we must."

Eve sighed. "I'm sorry, I hate losing sleep."

"I know."

She knit her brow, unable to think of a reply. He gave her a gentle look as he continued. "We can start small, Eve. Learn about each other. Not as what we've become, but who we are."

Eve took a sip, her words sluggish. "I'm not nearly as interesting as you might think."

"I find that hard to believe. Tell me, what is your favorite food?"

"Lemon cake."

"Cerene made those." Dakon smiled, the memory warm in his eyes, it was infectious, and she returned his grin.

"You were very close?"

"She was the only mother figure I had."

"I'm certain she was lovely," she mustered, then hesitated for a moment. "I'm sorry about your loss."

Dakon tensed slightly. "Sometimes, I can still hear her voice. I wish you would have seen her storytelling; it was magical, she could captivate anyone." His eyes glinted against the candlelight, and Eve could nearly feel the joy the memory brought him.

"It sounds wonderful."

Dakon sipped his ale. "What do you remember about your mother?"

"Not nearly as much as I wish I did. It was as if she was a ghost in my life until one day she was gone for good."

"At least you found out the truth—about her death."

Eve considered this. "I still feel as if I'm missing something, and I have so many questions left unanswered. How did my mother know to bind my magic? Did my father know? Did Clarisa know? Who did my mother correspond with to take Clarisa away? Who took her away?" She mulled over this before meeting Dakon's eyes once more. "Did Cerene ever tell you anything else, as my mother's familiar I imagine she must have known something?"

Dakon shook his head. "I only know what you know now." He pushed away his empty mug, taking a deep breath before continuing. "Have you ever considered that the grimoire could tell you? It appears to you, and you are tied to it, as you've said before. Perhaps, we can make it work to our advantage."

Eve blinked a few times, uncertain she heard him correctly. "Have you so easily forgotten the scars it leaves me, the nightmares?"

"No, believe me, I haven't."

"I am nothing but a means for it to release something. Until I know what that is, I am not willing to risk my life finding out."

"I know, but we can't continue to do nothing. It'll only get worse. I feel it."

"He disrespects you . . ." the unwelcome voice echoed in her mind.

"It's evil." She narrowed her gaze, but Dakon seemed blurred in her vision.

"Do you know that? Or are you just scared of what truths it could show you next?"

"Of course I'm scared," she snapped, and the sound of boiling liquid filled her ears. It was irritating. "All my life I was told witches were the reason for our mortal failings, that my mother was this monstrous and deadly enchantress. I considered myself blessed to be nothing like her, only to find out that it was a lie. All of it was a lie. This grimoire is death, bound in parchment, and gives me nothing but memories of a past I cannot change."

"Eve, I wouldn't suggest it, but we are running out of options. I am nowhere near where I should be in my abilities—"

"He wants your power. He will take it from you . . ."

"Oh, so this is about you getting more magic?" she slurred, standing awkwardly before him. She could hear the bubbles of the drink popping.

"No, it's about a grimoire that's haunting us, clamoring for your attention, and your repeated attempts to ignore it or tell me anything about it have only made things worse. Without it, you would have never known the truth of your mother, you would have gone to the grave believing that she was some murderer keen for power."

"The reasons she was killed doesn't matter as much as she lied to me about who I am, tore my sister from me with no explanation, and left me at the mercy of a court hells-bent on my demise at the end. It is because of her that I am in this mess!"

"Kill him before he kills you."

Pop. Pop. Pop.

The tavern was warm, too warm. Sweat coated her skin; her braid itched her back.

Dakon approached her, they were both nearly nose to nose now. "You can be angry; you can even hate her. But you can't blame her for the rest of your life, if you aren't willing to find out the rest of the story—"

"Kill him!"

"Here's the story: a noble girl of unfortunate blood gets torn apart by mother's actions and is left with a power-hungry familiar that can barely light a candle!"

Eve didn't realize she had been shouting until her voice echoed in the once loud tavern. She looked up, seeing everyone frozen in place. Pazel was mid-drink still surrounded by the women, the barmaid held four mugs expertly in her hands, a fight was about to begin in another corner, a man was eyeing his opponent's cards as they gambled. The bubbles popped louder now, and she looked down at her drink. It was boiling, the bubbles simmering over the top of the mug and spilling on the table in a steamy mess. It drenched the candle next to it, putting out what little flame had been there before.

Dakon noticed, too, turning around and taking in the scene.

"So, every time you're upset you hurt people, control them"—he gestured to the still room—"but it's I who has the bad intentions?"

"I didn't mean to."

"No." Dakon stood, waving his hand methodically across the room. Eve startled as the people resumed their movements once more. "But it's easy when you have someone to fix it, isn't it?"

He blew on the candle, and it resumed its flame once more.

She watched as Dakon placed a few coppers on the table and left, not bothering to turn back.

Eve ran out into the street; it was late, and relatively silent outside except for the random men drunk and asleep along the path. She removed her braid from her tunic and let the raindrops fall onto her hot face, watching as the steam rose off her skin and into the damp air. It was a welcoming feeling, cooling her skin as she tried to forget about everything. She was a drunken, stupid fool.

She closed her eyes, wishing she could remain under the drizzle forever—to let the rain wash away her worries, her burdens, and the filth of this place.

"Do you need help, or do you just like to get wet?"

She quickly turned to the source, placing her braid awkwardly behind her as if that would save her from notice. A man, tall and broad shouldered, with tattoos lining his arms and chest leaned against the wall of the tavern, a sly smile on his face. She did not realize anyone was watching her and now wished she had been more mindful of where she stood.

She chose not to respond, moving quickly out of the rain to go back inside.

Eve was nearly past him, when he moved out to stop her. The strength beneath his muscled arm was firm against her waist.

"Excuse me," she huffed, brushing him aside.

"It's strange," he mused aloud, "I've never seen smoke come off someone's body in the rain. And you are still quite warm despite the chill."

Eve stilled. "You are either mad or drunk. Either way, leave me be. I have no interest in speaking to you."

"Of course." He raised his hands in mock defeat and winked.

Winked?!

She made for the door, ready to put separation between them.

"This doesn't seem like the place for someone like you," he called after her.

She turned back to face him. "What business is that of yours?"

"None at all. I am simply curious as to why a lady chooses to spend her time in taverns or does your trick in the rain explain it?"

He smirked, and Eve despised how inviting and striking his smile was. She focused on his eyes instead, and much to her detriment they reminded her of the amber-brown orchids that bloomed in early spring. He stared back at her with a wicked gleam.

"I am no lady," she seethed, trying to sound convincing.

He laughed, revealing a few dimples. He might have been attractive if not for his arrogance and nerve. "And I suppose I'm not a pirate. Tell me, how does a lady end up in this part of Serit?"

Eve bit her lip, a slight panic setting in. She did not want to be known as a lady in this place, nor draw any unwanted attention. Without a second thought she pushed him against the railing, grabbing his collar with both hands. He seemed amused as she gritted through her teeth, "You have a lot of questions for a man I don't know. And because you don't know me either, let me tell you a little secret, I am a lot more dangerous than you think. Do *not* underestimate me. Do *not* question me. And do *not* follow me."

She released him forcefully, patting down her clothing and straightening her posture. The man only grinned, his eyes coming alight with a silver hue as they stared back at her. It took considerable effort to rip her gaze from him, but she did so, moving quickly past him and walking up the steps to the tavern once more.

Hopefully one of the crewmates would accompany her back to the ship.

"Wait!" he called. "What is your name, *Lady*?"

She ground her teeth, not bothering to turn around. "Get fucked."

"Is that an invitation?"

She turned around to him incredulously, mouth open but words failing her.

This would never have happened at court!

He smiled mischievously, his dark eyes sweeping over her as he folded his hands across his chest and leaned once more against the railing. A slight drizzle fell upon him, making his dark tendrils glisten in the moonlight.

She turned back to the tavern and pushed open the door, making sure it closed between them. She waited a few moments making certain he didn't follow her.

He didn't.

Thoughts of him leaning against the railing, so at ease and arrogant,

73

came to mind. She hoped he wouldn't spread gossip that she was a lady on the run. She bit her lip, walking through the crowd and back to her table trying and failing not to think about the stranger in the rain.

Whoever he was, she was already certain of one thing.

She hated that man.

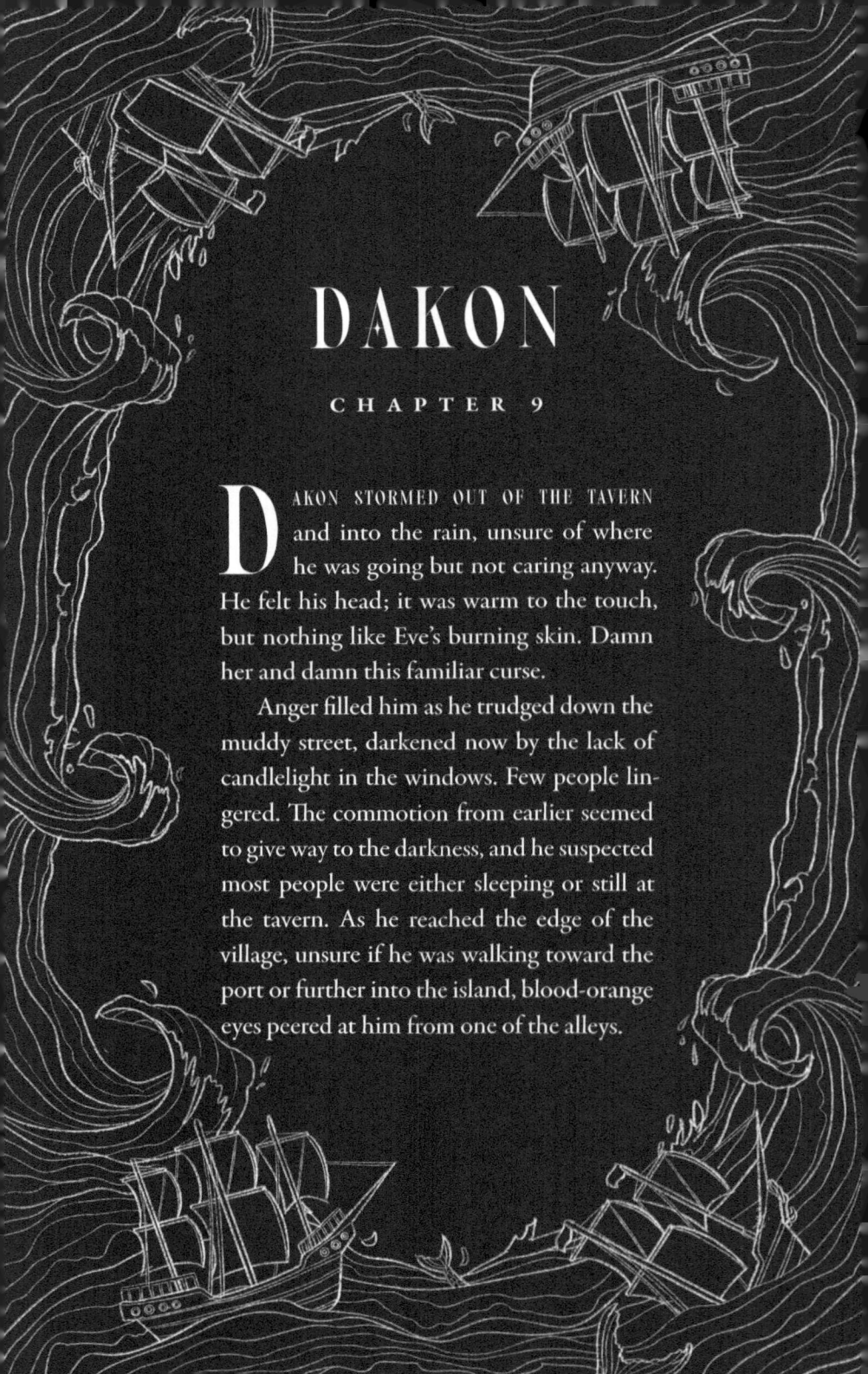

DAKON

CHAPTER 9

DAKON STORMED OUT OF THE TAVERN and into the rain, unsure of where he was going but not caring anyway. He felt his head; it was warm to the touch, but nothing like Eve's burning skin. Damn her and damn this familiar curse.

Anger filled him as he trudged down the muddy street, darkened now by the lack of candlelight in the windows. Few people lingered. The commotion from earlier seemed to give way to the darkness, and he suspected most people were either sleeping or still at the tavern. As he reached the edge of the village, unsure if he was walking toward the port or further into the island, blood-orange eyes peered at him from one of the alleys.

He thought of the last time he was out late—when he fought Amarin in the bar, met Beast on the street, and discovered the Strix for the first time, a lifetime ago—when he was simply a mortal in love with a princess and not a familiar on the run with a witch.

He reached Beast, embracing him and running his fingers through his thick, dark fur. The gytrash was large and nearly invisible in the night. Dakon rested his forehead against Beast's, squeezing his eyes and letting his frustrations melt away.

"I can always count on you to show me the way."

The gytrash looked up at him, and Dakon could have sworn it smiled.

As the darkness loomed through the path, he felt his hips for his trusted daggers. Still in place, safely on his belt. After all they had been through, he would never be without them at his side even with Beast next to him.

He considered his companion, the large wolf-like animal that walked alongside him. Besides Cerene's tales, he knew little to nothing about the creatures created by the first witches, how they appeared, and why only few could see them. Without access to the castle libraries and high doubt that one existed on this island, he could only hope that he would learn from experience or meet someone who knew of them. He wondered briefly if there was some-one on Bastard's Haven that could.

Dakon followed Beast over a small hill, down a beaten path, and finally he could see the port a short distance away. He flexed his fingers beneath him, the fur no longer present. He looked down; Beast was no longer there.

Of course.

Dakon walked to the edge where the brush of the forest and sand of the beach met. The pirates from earlier seemed to have disappeared, most likely sleeping in the brothels or on their ships to avoid the gloomy rain.

He sat under a large palm tree, looking out to the sea as he pulled out a worn parchment folded in fourths from his pocket. It was weathered and damp, but otherwise still intact by some mercy of the gods. He kissed it once, squeezing his eyes shut as he brought it to his lips.

When he opened them once more, he unfolded the parchment carefully and read for perhaps the thousandth time, Adriana's last note to him—or rather, her secret admirer.

Dearest Admirer,

I have been told and nearly convinced that secrecy is what you desire. For months I have bargained, promised, and pleaded with Dakon to give me your name or even a hint as to who you may be, but to no avail. You have surely found a loyal friend in him, of that I am certain. And in truth, so have I. While you have chosen to stay in the shadows, another has come to claim what you seek. One who gives me their affection through trust, friendship, and lack of secrecy.

It is not your fault, entirely. For if not for you, I would not have been willing to open my heart and mind to him. And for that, I thank you.

But in the spirit of honesty, I must confess that I no longer wish to admire in secret. But to love unconditionally in truth. And for that reason, I will now end all correspondence with you.

No ill will, and with much love in my heart,

Your dear friend,
Adriana

A smile involuntarily came over him; her wit and attitude were prevalent throughout the letter. Never mincing words, never one to waste time.

His heart ached to speak with her once more, to be under the soft candlelight, safe and warm in her embrace. Adriana was out there in that castle, under the rule of her tyrant brother, and instead of saving her, he was here on a beach, a lifetime away, powerless and miserable.

He raised his head and looked out onto the sea before him. It was a cloudy night, the moon barely visible in the sky as rain fell like teardrops into the water. The waves lapped back and forth over the sandy shore as the ships in the distance followed suit, rocking gently along the port. This was his new life. Under clouded skies with bitter memories, resentment brewed within Dakon.

Could I have convinced Adriana to come with me that night?

Would she have abandoned her life of luxury for a life on the run with a man of no wealth or status?

He mulled over that last thought, knowing the likely answer but unwilling to say it out loud. He shoved the note back into his pocket, feeling sour.

He stood, brushing off the damp sand from his clothing, when he saw it. Just a short distance from him, a woman in a dark dress walked along the water. Her hair trailed down her waist and clung to her body in a mess of tangles. Her eyes wandered aimlessly, and she appeared to be speaking—no, singing. Though he could not make out the words.

Dakon's skin prickled. A peculiar sensation filled him, as if he were a child again running away from the stable boys in the castle gardens. Goosebumps formed, and his shallow breathing grew stilted as he trembled. He kept his eyes locked on the figure, taking slow, deliberate steps back into the forest. Bending down behind the brush, he peeked through the leaves to avoid meeting her gaze.

She continued forward slowly, her movements gentle as she danced along to her voice. The rain picked up, the waves grew louder, and still she sang. Her skin was pale and nearly translucent in the night, a crown of seaweed rested on her blonde head, and her feet were bare as she moved between land and sea.

He glanced through the foliage, unable and unwilling to rip his gaze from her captivating voice. The song became clearer, echoing in his head as she grew closer.

"The goddess calls for her share,
Enchanting though it is to me,
All their souls are mine to bear,
We send the witches back to sea."

As the words settled upon him, he felt the urge to move toward it, filling him with a powerful desire to speak to her, despite every bit of his body begging him to turn the other away. He lifted himself up from his knees before familiar soft fur tickled his fingers.

Beast whined quietly, tugging at his trousers and pulling him back further into the brush.

Dakon peeked once more at the water. But the woman was gone.

You're tired, Dakon. Get some rest before you imagine singing sea serpents too.

Beast tugged once more, and Dakon relented.

No sooner had he stood, than he heard the singing once more.

"All their souls are mine to bear,
We send the witches back to sea."

It was too close, but he couldn't see the woman or from where the voice had come. He pulled out his daggers following Beast quickly through the brush and back to the other side of the port.

"We send the witches back to sea."

He could see Amarin's ship in the distance, and he picked up his pace wanting to be out of the rain and in the safety of the cabin.

"Back to sea."

The gytrash began to run alongside him as the song grew louder and louder.

"Back to sea."

He could no longer hear his thoughts as he climbed aboard where his surroundings were foggy and eerie. Not a soul, not even the night crew lingered about the main deck. But the voice carried through as he ran to his cabin door.

"*Back to* me."

He slammed the door shut behind him, the singing was overwhelming, overpowering every thought. His hands trembled as he realized his daggers were in a death grip. He had no intention of letting them go.

He was not sure how long he stayed in that position, but soon he heard a loud noise on the other side of the door, muffled sounds and raucous voices. He moved back a few steps, readying himself for what may come.

The door swung open, and his heart nearly gave out.

Pazel stumbled into the cabin, nearly falling over himself. On either side of him, two of Amarin's crewmen, Giovani and Alonso, lifted him up and placed him gently on the floor.

Dakon nearly collapsed himself, leaning against the wall as he placed the daggers back in his belt.

"This one is quite the entertainer." Giovani chuckled, tapping Pazel's leg with the outside of his shoe.

"Sure is," Alonso agreed. "Was singing for the whole tavern. Two more drinks and I think he would have started dancing on the tables."

The two men howled with laughter, surely drunk themselves.

Dakon looked down at Pazel, who groaned and hiccuped as he lay on his back. His eyes were closed, but a lopsided grin was plastered on his face.

"Thank you for bringing him back; I'm sure he would have made more of a fool of himself had he stayed." Dakon sighed, trying his best to smile.

"Our pleasure, we needed a good laugh," Giovani grinned as he and Alonso retreated.

"Tell him that we expect him to come out tomorrow night," Alonso called over his shoulder, closing the door behind him.

The two men roared with laughter on the other side of the door. Finally, it faded away until it was silent once more in the cabin. He looked over Pazel, whose tunic was ripped at the chest, but otherwise he was unharmed.

He knelt beside him, tapping his cheek. "You alive?"

Pazel slowly opened his eyes, full of effortless humor and a hint of mischief. "More than ever."

"I heard you had quite the night."

"You wouldn't believe it, Dakon, the women were feral for me." He gestured to his ripped tunic, a wide smile splitting his face. "I think I like it here."

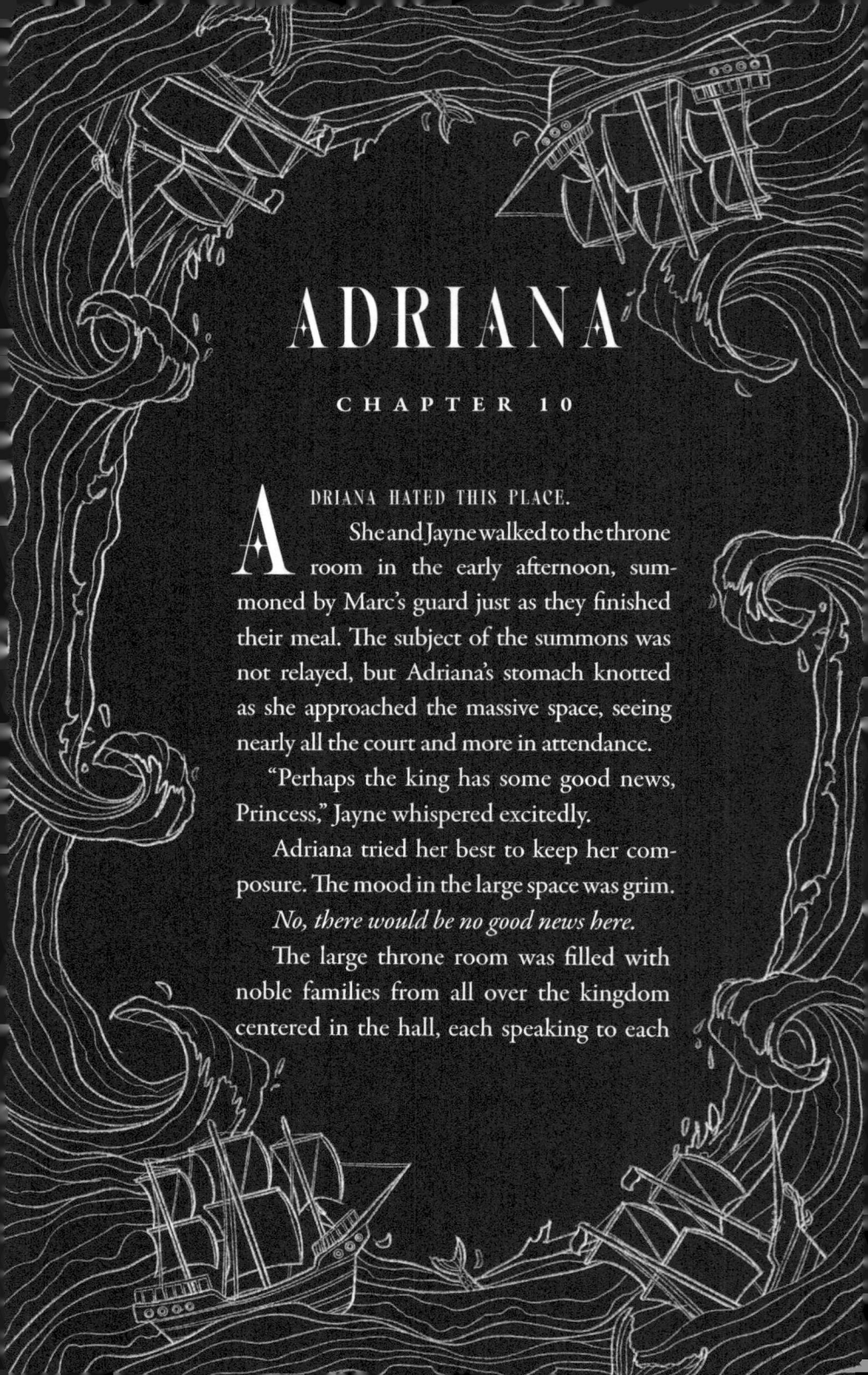

ADRIANA

CHAPTER 10

ADRIANA HATED THIS PLACE.

She and Jayne walked to the throne room in the early afternoon, summoned by Marc's guard just as they finished their meal. The subject of the summons was not relayed, but Adriana's stomach knotted as she approached the massive space, seeing nearly all the court and more in attendance.

"Perhaps the king has some good news, Princess," Jayne whispered excitedly.

Adriana tried her best to keep her composure. The mood in the large space was grim.

No, there would be no good news here.

The large throne room was filled with noble families from all over the kingdom centered in the hall, each speaking to each other in confused, hushed voices. Guards crowded around their space—stoic in their armor and helmets, dressed as if they were prepared for battle. The members of the royal court were positioned along one of the balconies, watching down below; the nobles looked like prey in shark-infested waters.

Adriana approached her mother. "What is happening?"

Her mother rolled her eyes. "Silence, dear. Our king has summoned us to listen, not speak."

"Then where is *our king*?" She studied the group. "There are at least one or two members of each house here, including the minor ones."

Though she noticed Lady Tyrina, Callum's aunt and Lady of Teros was not in attendance. She hoped that Marc had not sought to punish her.

"Hush, now!" her mother scolded, looking around to see if anyone was watching them. "You are no longer a child, but a woman grown. The questions end now. Do as you are told, listen to orders, and follow them."

Her mother's steely gaze met hers, and Adriana felt a lump in her throat. Whatever it was, whatever reason Marc summoned everyone, it had their mother on edge.

She bit her tongue, grabbing Jayne by the arm and moving her further toward the railing where she had a better view of the throne.

"All rise for His Majesty, King Marc!" Ser Elliot announced, tapping his staff on the marble floor.

"Oh! Here is your handsome brother!" Jayne whispered excitedly, gripping Adriana's arm fiercely as the doors of the throne room opened.

Her mother glared at them, giving Jayne a peculiar look that silenced the girl immediately.

Marc, clad in dark royal garb brooded from the side door of the throne room. He was escorted by at least four of his king's guard flanked on his sides and Lord Wesley who followed closely behind them. Marc moved leisurely up the steps to his seat and turned to take in the massive room. All including Adriana bowed, and she watched as he smirked, sitting tall and proud on the chair. The room was silent, waiting.

Wesley approached Marc and they whispered to one another, much to the uneasy tension of the room around them. Adriana's heart pounded in her chest, her breath shallow as she tried to make out their words.

Wesley soon smiled at Marc, then stood tall, addressing the room. "Our benevolent king, sole heir and noble survivor of the Blackthorn attack on our seas, demands that each noble here swear fealty to the new orders presented today without question or resistance."

The room grew cold. This was a first for the royal line. Adriana felt an icy grip on her heart.

Wesley continued. "Witches have entered our borders, encroaching upon our lands and poisoning our people with thoughts of resistance and anarchy. We have been encumbered by civil war, disobedience, and death of our free society under the rule of our noble and just kings. It is hereby ordered that each house conduct a thorough review of their provinces, enact a preservation council dedicated to removing witches that are certainly hidden in our society and cleanse our lands of witchcraft and evil. These councils, under the authority of myself, will include four noblemen searching for women who possess the following traits."

Women?

Adriana had a lump in her throat. Surely, she had heard him wrong. Witches could be anyone . . .

Lord Wesley procured a scroll from his coat and unfurled it. "Civil disobedience, intent to harm others, unfamiliar healing practices, speaking out of turn, immodest dress, unnatural abilities, praising the fallen goddess, and other such abominable acts against the will of the gods."

He furled the scroll again.

This was unthinkable.

A man below spoke up. "My lord, this list—it is quite impossible to understand. Is every woman who speaks out of turn a witch and not possibly a headstrong daughter or a tired mother after her naughty children? This order certainly undermines the consequences it will have against innocent people. Furthermore, witches can be men, too, can they not?"

Marc stood. "Are you saying you are a witch?"

The man looked bewildered. "Of course not, Your Majesty. I am simply questioning the reason for such an order. Can you not see that innocent lives are at risk?"

"Do you believe witches to be innocent?" Marc began to make his way down the steps, slowly, methodically.

"N-no."

"Have you met a witch before?"

"Not that I am aware, Your Majesty."

"I have." Marc stood at the bottom of the steps and announced loudly to the crowd, "They look like us, speak like us, and can even act like us."

His voice echoed, though he did not yell, and Adriana began to tremble.

"But they are *not* us. They thirst for blood, for sacrifices to feed their power and their wicked goddess. And it only took one hiding in our court to nearly destroy a royal bloodline. The reason my father, the late King Eryck, was murdered in a horrific fire, the reason my brothers were slain and taken from us too soon was because of a witch. We will not let it happen again."

Guards closed in on the man, and before he could respond, they were upon him, cuffing him and taking him out a side door.

"Lord Marcelo," her brother called out.

Adriana grew cold as she watched Eve's father make his way through the crowd to Marc. He bowed and kissed Marc's rings.

Marc lifted him back up, embracing him in a hug before addressing the crowd once more.

"Even half-witches, no matter how rare, are dangerous. If Lord Marcelo could so bravely save the realm from his wife and daughter, then you can look upon your family and make the sacrifice for the good of the kingdom. We will not be taken hostage by evil!"

Lord Marcelo stood awkwardly, shoulders slightly slumped, but he nodded along with the king. The sight of it made Adriana ill.

How could a father betray his child?

"My people, it will be under this rule that we are kept safe from the vicious creatures that would seek to harm us and our children. Should you not have any secrets to hide, you will be safe from any risk of persecution. Questioning my orders is not up for debate. We are in the midst of a war brought upon us by the greedy and soul-sucking witches of the Blackthorn. I will not allow my kingdom to fall to heretics and beasts!"

The room clapped slowly, uncertainly, before the guards turned their weapons on the nobles. Very quickly, the crowd erupted into unfettered cheers for the king.

Adriana looked to her mother, who held tears of pride in her eyes and clapped along with the crowd. To her right, Jayne kept her gaze locked on Marc, grinning with unadulterated admiration. The faces of everyone around her seemed fixated on triumph and not the loss of humanity that was at their fingertips. This was not a war the Blackthorn started, but her father.

Lord Marcelo looked hollow but clapped along with the crowd. It terrified Adriana how easily these people had been swayed. And something told her it would only be a matter of time before the losses grew.

Marc moved back to his seat, allowing Lord Wesley to list off other orders of business regarding taxation and the need for increased logistics to temper the growing population in the capital. Adriana was set to leave before Lord Wesley made a final announcement.

"And finally, I would like to formally announce the engagement of Princess Adriana to Lord Joseph II of Mytar. Many blessings to their union by the will of the gods!"

"By the will of the gods!" the crowd thundered.

Adriana was stunned in silence. She met her mother's eyes—cool and assessing, as if to say, "*look happy, now.*" Adriana smiled, trying her best to appear pleased, when all she wanted to do was run away. Thoughts of Dakon entered her mind, and a silent heartbreak began to fill her.

She finally settled her gaze on Marc, who stood clapping, a sinister grin on his face.

"My goodness, can you keep a secret princess!" Jayne remarked, "Many blessings to you! Oh, look, how she is crying. It is truly a happy day indeed!"

Adriana had not realized the tears that came from within her. Any hope she had of escape gone with them.

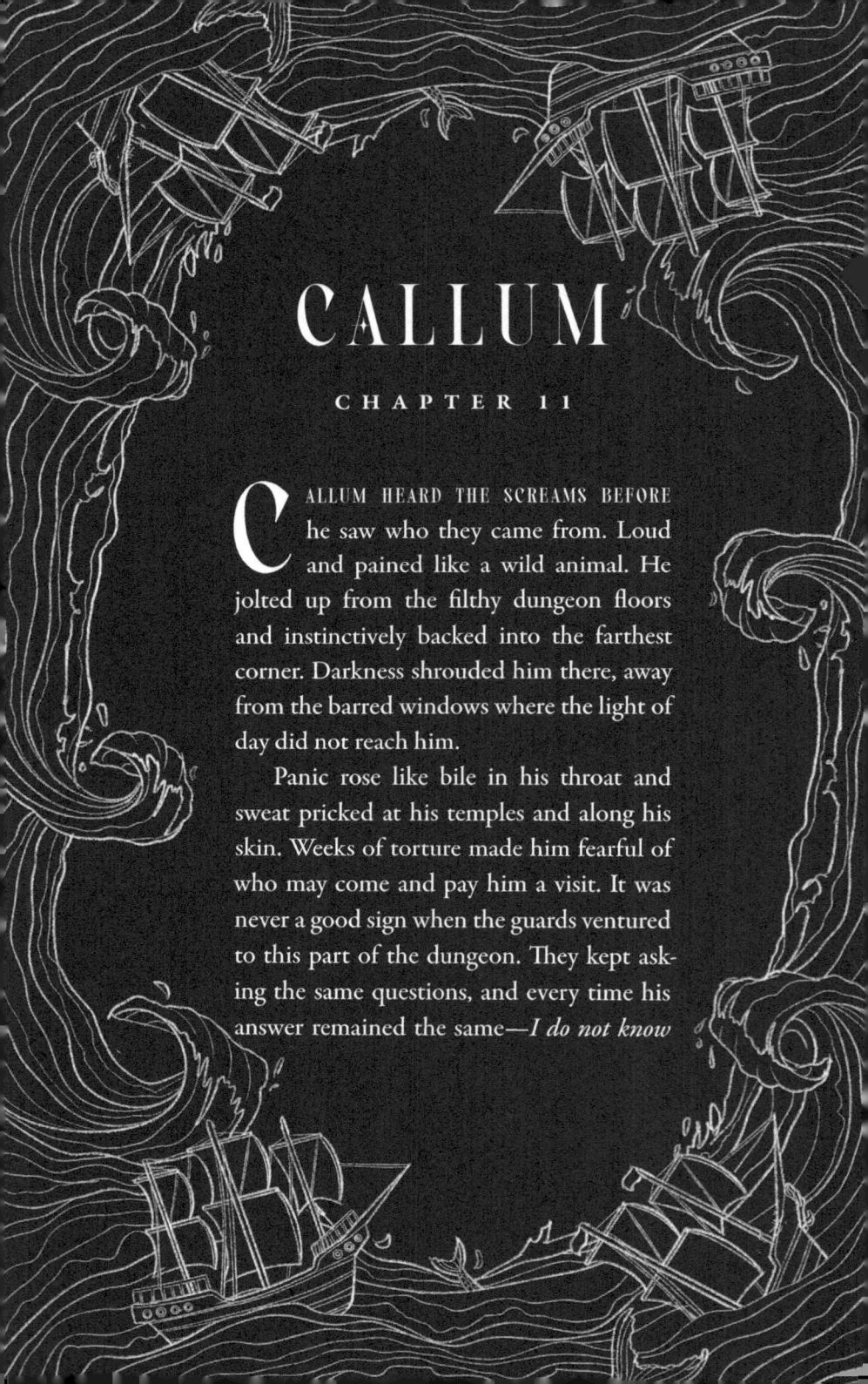

CALLUM

CHAPTER 11

CALLUM HEARD THE SCREAMS BEFORE
he saw who they came from. Loud
and pained like a wild animal. He
jolted up from the filthy dungeon floors
and instinctively backed into the farthest
corner. Darkness shrouded him there, away
from the barred windows where the light of
day did not reach him.

Panic rose like bile in his throat and
sweat pricked at his temples and along his
skin. Weeks of torture made him fearful of
who may come and pay him a visit. It was
never a good sign when the guards ventured
to this part of the dungeon. They kept asking the same questions, and every time his
answer remained the same—*I do not know*

where Eve is. I do not know where she went.

It was the truth.

But it damned him all the same.

He looked around; the few cells in this part of the dungeon were empty where he was. Callum figured very soon after his imprisonment that it was to keep him alone and prone to madness from solitude. He did not know if it was working, or if he had already been mad for choosing the path he did. Helping Eve, staying behind so she could escape, losing Eryce.

Eryce . . .

His heart thundered in his chest as the screams echoed again throughout the dungeon, breaking his thoughts. They were growing close. Callum clutched himself with both hands, hugging his body as if that would make the voices fade and the nightmares that had become his life disappear.

"Go away," he whispered. "Please go away."

Tears pooled at the corners of his eyes as he began to tremble. He was not ashamed to admit he was afraid, petrified of what he didn't know lay ahead for him.

A small voice filled his head. *Perhaps death, hopefully death.*

Callum did not have time to consider this as the screams grew, and he squeezed his eyes shut, placing his hands over his ears. He prayed to the gods to make it stop. To make it all stop. To have mercy on him. He could not breathe, could not move, he was nothing but a body against a wall.

For a fleeting second, he wondered if it was his own screams echoing throughout the halls. But his mouth was dry and parched, his lips chapped, and his voice fickle and weak within him from the little sustenance they gave him

He willed his eyes open, unable to hinder the curiosity and fear of what lay ahead for him.

Three guards were dragging a man toward the end of the dungeon hall—to the cell across from Callum.

He took in a quick breath, pushing himself further into the stone wall behind him as if somehow it would hide him from their view.

"Open that cell there, move it!" one of the guards ordered. He was a large, bald man Callum recognized as Ulric. A smaller guard, with dusty blond hair and beady eyes, rushed with a set of keys and unlocked the cell door across the narrow hall from Callum, swinging it wide open.

The prisoner fought and screamed against the guards and their tight grips, using all his strength to try and free himself from the large men that held onto him. A futile attempt, Callum noted, as Ulric was one of the largest men he ever laid eyes on, and one of the strongest. Callum flinched as memories of his torture surfaced; he lifted a hand to his blackened eye remembering Ulric's brute strength.

Without a weapon, no one stood a chance against him.

The guards thrust their prisoner inside, and he landed on the floor with a sickening thud. He was slick with blood across his tunic and a cut on his chin. He had honey brown hair and eyes, and his attire was made of fine, silver cloth, but torn from the skirmish that led him here. Callum did not recognize the man.

"You have no right to do this to me!" the prisoner shouted from the floor, looking pained but confident of his words. "When my father hears of this—"

"Your father is not the king, you pompous prick," Ulric sneered at him.

The beady-eyed guard locked the cell quickly, moving back as if the man would bite his hand off in the process.

"Do you know who I am?!" The prisoner rushed to the doors, shaking it violently enough that Callum truly thought it may break under his strength. It didn't.

The guards began to snicker amongst each other. "It don't matter, you fuck. New king, new rule. I wager you won't be around before the next moon."

The prisoner grew silent, and Callum watched as fear crept into his once steely gaze. Any retort lost upon his lips as the guard's words settled upon him.

"That's what I thought," Ulric grunted, sounding pleased with himself. He turned toward Callum, a wicked gleam in his eyes. "I'll be seeing you *real* soon. Don't miss me too much."

He winked, and Callum nearly vomited, his legs buckling beneath him as he cowered into a feeble ball in his corner.

Ulric laughed along with the other guards and moments later they retreated, leaving back from where they came.

Callum stayed in the corner, eyes shut tight as he hugged himself.

He tried to think of good memories, something, anything to bring him out of the hole his soul was being sucked into, but each time Eryce filled his mind grief seized his heart once more. He choked out a few sobs, heartbroken for the man he loved and would never see again.

He was not sure how much time passed, but when he opened his eyes once more, the prisoner was leaning against the bars of his own cell, staring at him impatiently.

"You cannot cry forever." He sighed, running his fingers through his hair. "It will only make the pain last longer. I doubt it works on their wicked hearts."

Callum swallowed, unable to think of a reply. It had been a long while since he had spoken to another so casually.

"My name is Emilio"—the man pushed a hand through the slats, it lingered in the space between their cells as he waited for Callum to shake it—"Second heir to Pleasant Peak, sworn to Larrea."

Callum did not move, unsure of himself, unsure of this man. He knew of Pleasant Peak but had never met any of the lords of that house. They assisted Givensmir in defeating Larrea in the war. He shook his head, the war that only ended months ago now seemed like a lifetime away. He focused on the man before him, distracting himself from his memories. Emilio appeared slightly taller than him as he stood against the bars, with tanned skin and a chiseled jaw that was now slightly darker as the bruises began to form.

Callum could only watch him, speechless and wary, as Emilio slowly pulled his hand back through. His eyes assessed Callum, narrowing slightly before a smirk tugged at the corner of his mouth.

"And you must be Lord Callum. I can't imagine they would leave anyone else in solitary confinement at this precarious time."

Callum opened his mouth to speak, but words were unable to reach his lips. Instead, he nodded slightly, keeping his eyes on Emilio who grinned, revealing a lovely smile, and shook his head.

"And here I was thinking you had become a ghost."

He folded his arms across his chest and cocked his head.

"Tell me, is it true you like to play with fire or was it your witch?"

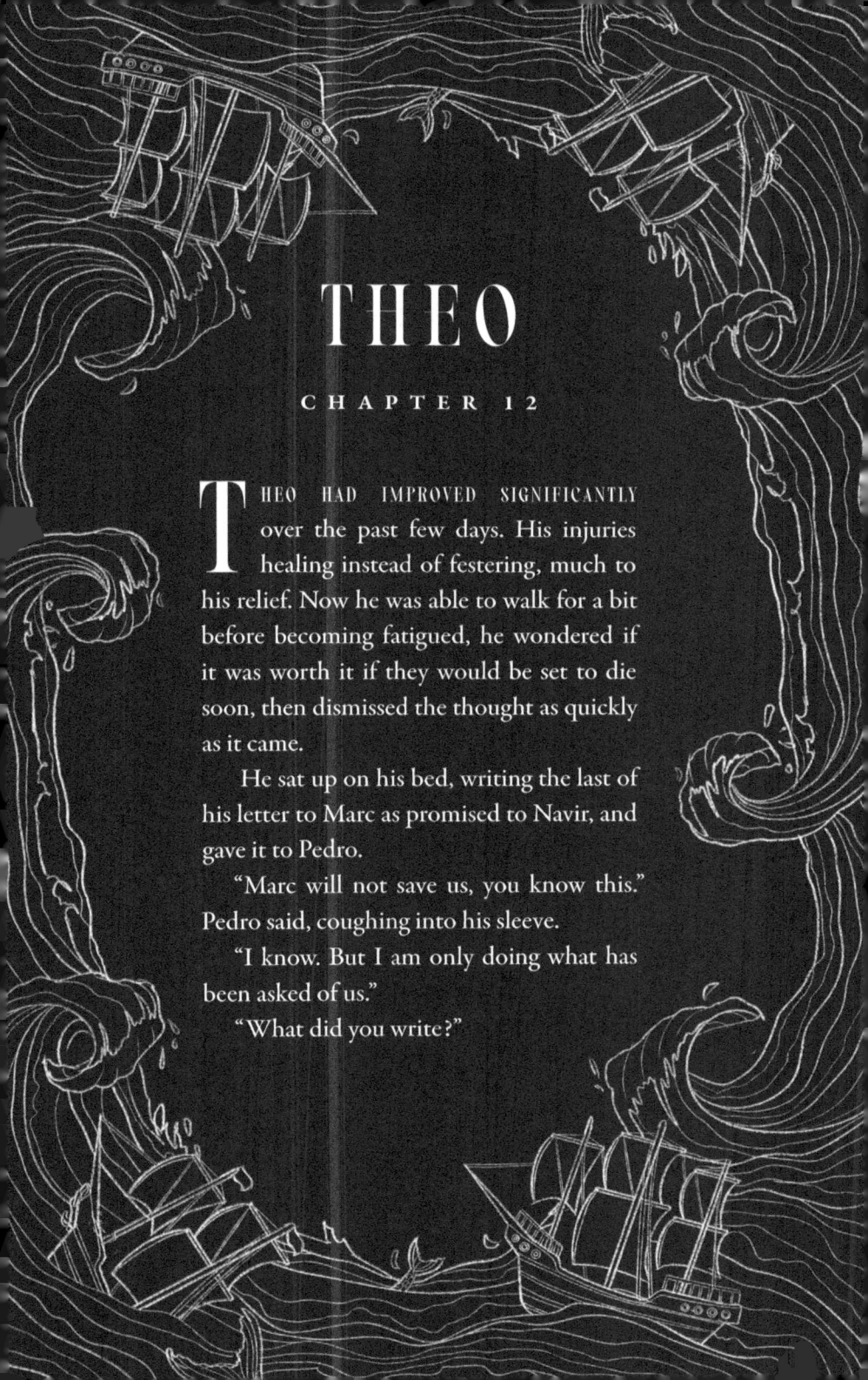

THEO

CHAPTER 12

THEO HAD IMPROVED SIGNIFICANTLY over the past few days. His injuries healing instead of festering, much to his relief. Now he was able to walk for a bit before becoming fatigued, he wondered if it was worth it if they would be set to die soon, then dismissed the thought as quickly as it came.

He sat up on his bed, writing the last of his letter to Marc as promised to Navir, and gave it to Pedro.

"Marc will not save us, you know this." Pedro said, coughing into his sleeve.

"I know. But I am only doing what has been asked of us."

"What did you write?"

"That I will not contest his reign, for him to give up the Unclaimed Wastes, to bring no more harm to magicfolk . . ."

"And?"

"For him to accept us back home."

"If only it were that simple, he'd sooner pass the crown to a dog." Pedro placed the letter in his pocket, coughing once more. "It is much too cold in here, and it rains far too often."

Theo looked toward the window, beyond it was a gloomy, foggy day obscuring most of the scenery. A slight drizzle clung to the glass. "Best we get used to it, I suppose."

"I never imagined I would be here, much less die here. I figured it would be in Givensmir in some battle your father would force us into."

"Isn't this?"

"Well, it doesn't hold quite the same honor as a death by sword fight."

Theo took a deep breath and let it out, seeing a bit of it before him in the chilly, dank room. It was cramped in here, barely big enough for the two of them to pace, though the barred window at least allowed for some light. Surely, the queen did not intend to keep them both alive, he couldn't imagine this kingdom taking much longer to execute them either.

"Why do you think Clarisa hasn't come to see us?"

"Maybe she can't?" Pedro mumbled, unconvincingly.

"Or maybe she has changed her mind?"

Pedro turned to face him. "No, that can't be it."

"We know that she's capable of killing innocents. Why not us?"

"Because she can't." He clenched his jaw. "At least, I can't allow myself to believe it, because then, the last bit of hope we have to leave would be gone."

A squeaking of a rat on the wooden beams above them startled Theo, making him lose his train of thought. The rat scurried across the beam, and settled at the end, staring in his direction. It unsettled him.

The door to their room opened, and much to his surprise, Clarisa walked through. The guard closed it behind her. Her short, wavy hair barely touched her shoulders. Her eyes, a dark, warm brown, hardened as she looked upon them.

"Where have you been?" Pedro said, trying and failing to stifle his cough behind his handkerchief.

"Busy."

"Is meeting mortals beneath you now?" Theo asked.

"As I said, I have been busy. The queen—"

Theo shifted his weight, sitting up straighter, relief washing over him.

Pedro looked stunned and hopeful. "Is she coming?"

Clarisa raised a brow. "She is not able to come at this time, Prince."

Prince?

"Clarisa, I'm the prince, remember? It's me, Theo," Theo said, pointing at himself.

Clarisa gave him a curious look but smiled. "Of course."

"What sort of trick is this?" Pedro asked.

"There is no trick, I assure you."

"Then what of our fates?" Theo pressed, "What will become of us?"

"I haven't been told."

"Well, glad to see you could make time to visit your flesh and blood," Theo scoffed, lifting his chin to Pedro.

Clarisa narrowed her eyes. "The same flesh and blood that would have killed me like my mother."

"I had no hand in that!" Pedro shouted.

"You might not have"—she turned to Theo—"but your father did."

Theo swallowed. "I am not my father. I have loved Eve since we were children. I considered you a sister."

She pursed her lips. "Speaking of, what do you know of Eve?"

Theo and Pedro shared a look.

"You do realize we are being held prisoner?" Pedro huffed.

"I do."

"Did the queen send you to question us?" Pedro asked, hurt in his eyes.

She crossed her arms, refusing to answer him.

"What about Eve do you want to know?" Theo asked.

Clarisa turned to him. "It is rumored that she killed the old king. That she may have magic after all. In truth, we believed she was dead this whole time. Her being alive and with magic . . . changes things."

"We left before Eve had escaped. We have no knowledge of where she is now."

"But did she ever say anything? Do anything of particular notice?"

Theo recalled how she burned his hands with nothing but the touch of her skin. How ashes fell from her fingertips, her confession to him.

"No," he responded, trying to meet her eyes with similar conviction. "Until you killed my wife, we did not suspect anything."

"Hmm," she sighed, unimpressed.

"Why did you do it?"

The rat squeaked, and Clarisa peered up at it. She tensed, barely discernibly, before she responded. "We have our reasons."

"So, now my cousin is just some ruthless assassin?" Pedro stepped toward her.

"I do what I must, as we all do."

"We don't kill innocent people," Pedro said.

"And what of the witches, what of all the wars your kingdom has waged on itself? Was every person on the other end of your blade a villain?"

Theo watched as Pedro bit his tongue, unwilling to give her the answer she wanted him to.

She took a step toward Pedro. "I used to wonder why so many mortal men would willingly kill each other. Was it for land? Protection? Riches? Or for something else entirely?"

Clarisa raised her empty palms between them, and Pedro

swallowed nervously. She closed the distance, nearly face-to-face with Pedro. "I don't trust any of you mortals." She flexed her fingers, and an hourglass appeared in her hands.

"What is this?" Pedro managed.

Clarisa ignored him. "Power. The reason you all would destroy each other and everything else around you. And bloodlust is the only way your kind gets a taste of it. You thrive in fear of those you conquer, relish in delicacies as the poorest among you can barely scrape by. You kill because you want to. Because you *love* to. Because without death counts like notches in your bedposts, you would have to face the bitter, harsh truth that your time is running out and you have nothing to show for it."

She handed Pedro the hourglass, and he held it limply in his hands. Theo was too stunned to speak.

Clarisa took a few steps back and knocked twice on the door.

As the guard opened it, Pedro seemed to have found his voice. "And do you have power? Are you as free as you'd like us to think?"

Clarisa stalled for a moment, and Theo was convinced she would turn with more parting insults. But she didn't, instead leaving the room and not bothering to look back. The door closed and locked once more, echoing loudly in their space.

The two remained in silence for a long while, ruminating over every word she spoke.

Theo had always considered himself a war hero, saving the kingdom from the injustices of bitter rivalries and warring factions set upon causing discourse in the realm.

But was that true? Was every battle I faced one solely of heroism?

Pedro placed the hourglass on the bed, and Theo took it into his hands. It was the size of his forearm, and only a single grain of sand fell to the bottom.

"This is odd," he mused.

"What are we counting down toward?"

"I'm not sure, but it's not good."

The rat squeaked again, and Theo caught sight of it for a last time before it retreated into a crack in the wall. Pedro began to cough, barely grabbing his handkerchief in time before blood fell from his lips, staining the white fabric red.

CLARISA

CHAPTER 13

CLARISA WAS STARTLED AWAKE, ROUGH hands shaking her violently.

Her eyes sprung open, fully expecting to meet those of her intruder.

The Strix? Did they send another assassin?

Instead, there was nothing but the dim twilight from her window. She rose quickly, sweat pricking at her temples, her heart thundering against her chest. From the corner of her eye, she saw the ends of someone's tendrils as they ran through her open door and into the dark hall beyond. Without restraint, Clarisa gave chase, rushing into the hall barefoot and vulnerable.

As her body passed the threshold of her chamber, Clarisa could feel herself suspended between realms. She was in a cold, foggy purgatory that transcended the limitations of her world. Like a dream that pulled at her spirit, beckoning it to follow. She recognized this feeling, the same as when she had the visions of the ships not so long ago.

But what she beheld before her eyes was something entirely different. Her breath left her lungs with reckless abandon, her eyes widened as she took in her new surroundings.

She was in Givensmir's castle.

Clarisa whirled around, seeing her chambers behind her open door. Ana slept peacefully in her bed, her dark hair sprawled out over the pillow, an owl flew past her window, a dim candlelight flickered on her nightstand.

What is happening?

She shakily lifted her hand, reaching back through the doorway. Her fingers touched the space between, abruptly stopped by the feeling of cold glass.

A veil.

Panic rose within her, but she tried to hold onto hope as she pushed more forcefully against it, praying to Isila that it was only her imagination.

But it did not budge.

She tapped on it, pounded her fists against it, screaming at Ana to wake up and save her. Any bit of restraint buried along with her good sense. Until, suddenly, she could no longer see her chambers, the veil was now a mirror and within it was Clarisa's disheveled, horrified face.

She took a step back, stunned.

The sound of laughter pierced the air. A child's laughter.

Slowly Clarisa turned, barely catching sight of a burgundy dress skirt as its wearer ran down another hall.

"Wait! Who are you!" Clarisa called out, but there was only laughter once more.

Lips trembling, legs feeling as if they were in quicksand, Clarisa forced herself forward. Following the laughter, hoping against hope that they could bring her back home.

She took note of how bleak and lifeless the castle felt, much unlike how she remembered it from her childhood. The warm colored stones of the walls traded for graying fragmentations of what once held the mighty structures. A growing fog began to permeate the space, and she held out her hands to guide her.

Clarisa turned the corner where she saw the dress and found herself facing what appeared to be the maiden's keep. She recalled this part of the castle where she and Eve used to sleep in a shared room. A safe place where they traded innocent secrets, played together, and laughed late into the night. Memories she had tucked so far within, now threatened to overwhelm her.

In the foggy keep, down the long stretch of hall, was a single lit room barely visible at the far end. It was their old chambers. She hesitated, unsure of what lingered there, until she heard a familiar voice followed by more childlike laughter.

"Play with me, Clarisa. I've been waiting for you."

"Eve? Is that you?"

Clarisa took a few steps forward, the laughter growing. It wasn't terrifying, but welcoming. A sound she didn't realize she missed that tore down the fortified walls within her soul. Because something about how Eve laughed pulled at Clarisa like an ethereal tether that urged her to continue forward into the shadows that loomed ahead.

She approached her old chambers and peeked from the open door. Within it, all was as she remembered. The brightness of the day bathed the room in sunlight, their vanities positioned next to each other against the wall, their comforters bright and colorful in soft blue hues, paintings of their favorite fairy tales adorned their walls in shows of elegance and childlike wonder.

And in the center was a young Eve, laying on her stomach upon the floor, laughing as she beheld something in front of her.

Clarisa moved to close the distance, but the veil appeared once more, stopping her.

Before Clarisa could think to push against it, Eve turn to face her. She was small and fragile, her long hair poured over her shoulders, her legs crossed before her, and cradled in her hands was a grimoire, an owl beneath three stars etched onto the cover. Clarisa's heart sank, and the small hairs on the back of her neck rose.

This was the Blood of the Blackthorn. It had to be.

"Eve! Eve, don't! Let me in!"

Clarisa pounded against the glass, crying and shouting, helpless and powerless as she watched Eve open the book.

Then slowly, disturbingly, Eve raised her head to Clarisa.

But it wasn't quite her anymore.

Her eyes were a vermilion shade, her expression sordid and depraved as she lifted her lips in a wicked smile. Tears fell from Clarisa's eyes, the terror of seeing what her sweet sister had become, what the book turned her into.

Eve opened her mouth as if to speak, but instead the sounds of laughter took over. Claiming the space, loud and treacherous. The veil cracked like glass, distorting Eve into many tiny reflections.

Laughing and baiting and torturing Clarisa with what she had become.

CLARISA GASPED AS SHE LURCHED FORWARD IN HER BED.

It was morning, at least, the daylight dim and filled with gray clouds and drizzle.

Eve.

Clarisa thought about the girl she had just seen, no longer the sister she remembered but something far more sinister. Perhaps Navir was right, Eve was no longer who she used to be.

Ana mumbled unintelligibly next to her, rolling over but not yet waking. It had been days since she last saw Ana, and they had barely spoken. Their conversations were nothing more intimate than remarks on the weather and meals. Though it was tense between them, Clarisa was still comforted by her presence.

Clarisa pulled herself from the covers and looked at the hag stone that rested on her nightstand.

"What good are you if you can't hinder my nightmares?" she whispered to it.

She grasped it in her hands; the oracles had imparted her and her familiars with one the last time she spoke to them. The stone was light and smooth in her grip.

Hag stones were meant to ward off nightmares, to offer some protection to the one who wielded them, and to reveal the disguises of magic folk. But thus far, it had not worked to keep her sinister dreams at bay. She wondered if perhaps this was some deception by the oracles, a way to guarantee she would conjure them once more for answers.

Clarisa pulled the crystal from her neck and inspected it as she had nearly every day since she received it. The dark smoke tapped gently against the glass as if to beckon her. The urge to let them out was nearly overpowering now. And an unsettling thought arose, *had Navir not asked me to seek their wisdom, how long could I have gone without doing so?*

"Is something troubling you?"

Clarisa turned to face Ana, placing the crystal instinctively back in her nightgown.

"No," Clarisa responded, placing a gentle kiss on her lips, "not anymore."

Ana smiled groggily, running her fingers through Clarisa's hair, brushing back the loose tendrils that stubbornly fell forward. "You would tell me, though, wouldn't you?"

Clarisa nodded but couldn't quite speak the words aloud. Ever since their last argument, the night of the Strix's attack, things between them had been . . . cracked.

She shook away the vision of Eve in her dream.

Ana gently rubbed her back, and guilt rose within Clarisa. She didn't deserve how good Ana was to her.

"I never told you how sorry I was that night. It wasn't fair to accuse you of anything," Clarisa managed, finding it difficult to meet her gaze.

Ana sat up on the bed, tenderly pulling Clarisa to face her. "I'm sorry for ever making you doubt me."

Brown eyes, dark and mysterious, met Clarisa's. Even after all these years, there was something about Ana that equally consumed her and kept her astray. As if secrets made their way inside and were kept locked behind those beautiful eyes, never to be revealed.

Would it always be this way?

"I trust you, Ana. More than even myself."

A tense silence lingered between them. Ana's brow knit slightly, her lips parted, a battle so clearly raging within her. Disappointment, concern, worry all flashing across her eyes.

Finally Ana whispered, barely discernible, as if she were regretting the words as they fell from her lips. "You shouldn't trust anyone."

Before Clarisa could respond, Ana pulled her in close. She kissed her deeply, almost desperately. Her hands wrapped around Clarisa's waist and in her hair. It had been so long since they last were together like this, so long since Clarisa had allowed herself to rid her mind of uncertainty and truly embrace Ana.

She let herself go. Falling into Ana's caress, the softness of her lips. She needed to forget about the burdens upon her shoulders—she needed her paradise.

"I've missed you," Clarisa breathed between kisses, helping Ana remove her nightgown. "Do you have to leave again?"

"Yes, I don't have much time." Ana groaned back, returning the favor and tugging Clarisa's dress over her head. She gently pushed her back down on the bed, trailing kisses from Clarisa's neck to her collarbone.

Clarisa closed her eyes, relishing in the feeling of her warm skin and the tickling sensation Ana's lips gave her. "What does Navir have you doing that's so important? Can't you stay with me instead?"

Ana ignored her, moving down her waist now and spreading her legs further apart.

Clarisa arched her back instinctively, meeting Ana's eyes once more. They were intense and captivating, pulling her into the pleasure she had so longed for. Eyes that captivated her senses, blurring all her thoughts until there was only desire.

And Clarisa forgot what she had asked.

She supposed it didn't matter anyway.

DAKON

CHAPTER 14

"TELL ME AGAIN WHAT YOU SAW?" PAZEL asked Dakon as they rifled through Cerene's book in the cabin.

Beast nuzzled in Dakon's lap, and he ran his fingers through his thick fur in return. "I told you, there was a woman on the shore. She was alone, singing. And then she disappeared." He clenched his jaw, the memory of the woman sending a chill down his spine. "Her voice, though, it followed me all the way here."

Pazel handed the book to Dakon, meeting his eyes. "Could it not have been just any woman out for a walk? What is it about her that troubles you?"

"No." Dakon furrowed his brow as he

thumbed a page with various sketches of herbs. Nothing of particular help. In truth, he wasn't sure what he was looking for. "There was something about her words, the way she sang. I felt nervous, but . . . it was as if I wanted to go with her, and I nearly did before Beast pulled me away."

"You weren't drunk?"

"Yes, I mean, no. I—" Dakon sighed, trying to distract himself. Perhaps he was drunk, perhaps that would explain why he pushed Eve so far that night. Perhaps it was all nothing but his nerves. "It's not important."

Dakon flipped another page in the small book depicting ways to use animal bones in witchcraft; various skulls and body parts were drawn meticulously on the next several pages with explanations of their importance and uses, though, nothing that caught his attention.

"I don't understand why Cerene gave me this. So few pages, and yet the only thing of value was learning how to heal Eve. Most of it is her stories." Dakon let out a frustrated breath.

He could practically hear Eve's words from the tavern echoing within him; she didn't consider him worthy. It didn't matter that she looked sorry, she had spoken her truth, and her words could no longer be taken back.

He had hoped Cerene's book would help him, somehow. Teach him something so he didn't feel so useless next to Eve's growing power.

There was a moment of silence, before Pazel moved closer, inspecting the book from behind Dakon's shoulder.

"Have you tried asking it?"

"What?"

"The book." He pointed. "Have you tried asking for what you need?"

"What are you talking about?"

"Well, Cerene's stories were like magic. You are magic, Eve is magic. We have a haunted book that follows us like a scorned lover. Why not this too?"

Dakon closed the book, inspecting it.

Maybe Cerene's stories have the answers . . .

"You're brilliant."

"I know," Pazel said smugly, petting Beast, "it's part of my charm." He handed Dakon a candle.

Dakon smiled, placing it next to the book on the floor. "You're getting too good at this apprentice thing."

"Aren't I?"

Dakon placed his palm over the candle, and this time it only took a second to light, the flame tickling his hand.

Patience and practice, Dakon repeated this to himself. It made him feel better somehow, as if the more he thought it, the more likely it was to be true.

He looked down at the book once more. "What would I even ask?"

"Pretend it's Cerene and ask her anything. As if she were still here to help."

Dakon focused on the book in front of him. It was dark forest green and faded, the pages yellowed, and the spine torn at the edges. There were no symbols, pictures, or titles on either cover. It was simply Cerene's personal booklet, the last of her, and he would cherish it forever. He clenched his jaw as he tried to focus on the good memories of her—telling her stories, caring for him like a mother would, loving him like the son she never had. Anything but her final moments, forged and defeated in fire.

He cleared his throat. "Cerene, thank you for giving me this book. I hope I am taking care of it like you wish." The book was unmoved, but Dakon continued, "I must admit, I'm lost. I am trying to be a good familiar, but I don't know what I'm doing. I am trying my best to learn, but it's hard without a good teacher; you would have been a good teacher."

Dakon stared at the book, willing something into occurring by mere wishing itself. "I would like to start at the beginning, if that's at all possible. What do I need to know?"

The book opened slowly, and even Beast raised his head to look. The pages within flipped until it neared the end, where it lay open in complete stillness. There, the words were written in elegant script:

Magic Transference and the Original Witches

Dakon breathed the words aloud.

"Who are the 'Original Witches'?" Pazel asked, eyes wide.

"Do you not remember Cerene's tales?"

Pazel shook his head. "Not this one. Ask me about the silver storms or even the sea nymphs, and I could recite it nearly as well as she could, but this . . ."

Dakon sighed, taking in the pages before him, beneath the script was a single drawing of an owl beneath three stars, and he had the odd sensation that he had seen it before. His finger traced the outline on the parchment as he spoke. "The Original Witches were the first created by Isila in a trick against the gods."

He could remember the first time he heard Cerene tell the tale. He was a boy, sitting in her lap as she entertained the servant children with the story. Dakon could nearly see her smile if he closed his eyes, her hands waving to and fro as she theatrically recounted the lore.

He continued. "'Gods are only powerful so long as they are believed in,' Cerene would say."

"And she used their souls to create the witches?"

Dakon nodded. "Yes, but the witches became too powerful and ruled over the mortals instead. The Original Witches used their own magic to make other witches, creatures, familiars . . ." It was a disturbing feeling, knowing himself to be destined by and for witches to do their bidding. Forever fated to be a servant in or out of the castle, a line of work he could never truly free himself from.

Dakon tried to ignore this realization as he finished his thoughts.

"And Isila became 'the goddess who fell from the skies,' her soul damned, but not before she placed it into a grimoire." He hesitated, the truth finally settling on him. "The one that Eve avoids."

Of course, how had I not realized it before?

And why has Eve not told me?

Pazel gave him a wondrous look. "You remind me of Cerene, when you tell stories that way."

Dakon lifted his lips, the compliment too great, but one he would accept with pride.

"What happened to the Original Witches?"

"The gods destroyed them, making sure they would never again be able to usurp their reign. Binding the other, less powerful witches, seemed the better option, I suppose."

Pazel nodded. "Why does Cerene want us to learn about 'magic transference'?"

"I'm not sure." He lifted his fingers from the book, concentrating on it. "Can you tell us?"

They both watched as the small sketch disappeared from the parchment and words in Cerene's handwriting began to emerge on the pages.

"That's incredible," Pazel breathed, eyes wide.

Dakon's breath caught; he couldn't think or speak until the final words were written in thin, black ink.

"Well"—Pazel elbowed Dakon back to focus—"read it to me."

Dakon shrugged him off gently, and taking in the words before him, began to read aloud.

The blackthorn fire died down, and the three mortals came to life bearing magic. Known as the Original Witches, with powers unlike any had seen before, marked the Age of Witchcraft.

Isila forged a grimoire from her soul, Blood of the Blackthorn, written from the ink of the tree, containing the darkest of her spells and incantations. The goddess gave it to her witches, ordering them across the Dallise Sea, where their tumultuous natures sent the mortals running to the gods for their protection. Using the Blood of the Blackthorn, the witches created more of their kind and released creatures of malice throughout the land, giving up pieces of their magic with each creation. With Isila, the witches gained control of the kingdoms, wreaking havoc and thriving in chaos.

Fearful and repentant, the mortals returned to worshiping the five gods whose strength soon eclipsed the goddess.

Angered by her trickery, the gods banished Isila from their sanctuary in the skies and stripped the witches of most of their powers. Cursing them and their magic to the Blackthorn trees on the island. The gods attempted to destroy the grimoire. The source of Isila's immortal power, and the reason she had not yet been completely defeated.

But it could not be found.

Unbeknownst to the gods, the Original Witches sacrificed and transferred all their magic to their only heir, a daughter hidden in the Blackthorn. From whose bloodline the grimoire would be found once more to resurrect the goddess when one of mortal heart and wicked nature united.

The gods soon burned the Original Witches, now mere mortals, who refused to reveal the location of the grimoire despite their torture, in a fire that lit the night sky.

Their daughter was never found, lost among the centuries.

And thus ended the Age of Witchcraft.

Dakon finished, the last words leaving his lips in a breathless whisper. It sounded much like something Cerene would say: a warning to impart a lesson with.

"Witches can lose their magic?" Pazel said, surprise lacing his tone.

"That's what I gathered," Dakon replied, re-reading the story.

"And when they lose it they are mortal?"

Dakon nodded, unsure of how to feel about this. "Eve is the heir, clearly. The Original Witches gave up their magic to an ancestor of hers so that Isila could have a chance to return."

Pazel grew quiet for a moment, before speaking once more. "What happens if Eve doesn't want to help her?"

"She may not have a choice."

Silence filled the cabin, an ominous weight on their shoulders.

"You should tell her."

Dakon bit his cheek, recalling their argument the night prior. "It may be better coming from you."

"We're a family, remember?" Pazel placed a hand on his shoulder. "And I'm not a messenger."

Dakon put out the candle, shoving it in Pazel's direction. Then he stood, grabbed his daggers from his satchel, and fastened them to his belt. "Fine but let us get a bit of fresh air first."

Dakon, with his daggers, and Pazel, with his sword, practiced their fighting on the beach which was once again littered by pirates now that the sun had taken over the skies. Every so often, Dakon would sweep Pazel onto the sand, and despite raining colorful expletives, Pazel would right himself and try once more. He improved greatly in such a short time, that Dakon could not help but praise him often.

Various pirates formed a circle around them, watching with jeers or admiration. As the day wore on, sweat glistening on their foreheads under a relentless sun, different crewmates would challenge Dakon to a fight. And each time, win or lose, the burdens of Dakon's life fell away as he focused instead on the opponent in front of him.

Because, truthfully, Dakon was practicing more than his swordsmanship. With each swing of his opponent's blade, Dakon was learning how to better control the time around him—slowing it down and resuming normality as he fought. All were oblivious to Dakon's magic.

The bright sun began to falter behind the clouds and with it emerged an orange-pink sky beyond the sea. His muscles ached and his palms blistered from holding his daggers in such a fierce grip for so long.

Dakon began to sheath his blades, ready to eat with Pazel, when someone called out to him.

"Oy, mind if I take a swing at you? I haven't had a proper fight yet."

Dakon took in the lanky pirate before him, sweat-stained white blouse and dark trousers, and in his right hand was a blunted blade, no doubt borrowed from some quartermaster of his. This pirate was young, no older than fifteen, and his eyes were wide with hope.

"I think he's had enough for today," Pazel responded, clasping a hand on Dakon's shoulder. "Perhaps tomorrow."

The young pirate lowered his head. "I may not be here tomorrow."

Dakon took pity as he eyed the boy. "Have you fought anyone before?"

"Just some of my crew"—he gestured to a group of pirates far off from where they stood—"but never with a trained fighter."

Dakon grinned. "Then I shall be honored. What's your name?"

"Tomas."

"Dakon."

"Are you sure?" Pazel asked, removing his hand from Dakon's shoulder.

Dakon nodded. "It shouldn't be long." He unsheathed his daggers once more, settling them into his palms, their weight in his blistered hands familiar and welcome. He rolled his shoulders back and stretched out the tension in his neck. Then, he twirled them in his hands, making a show of it for fun, and much to his delight, Tomas looked at him with sincere admiration.

"Let's begin."

Tomas immediately charged at Dakon, swinging his sword not nearly close enough to be of any damage to anyone but himself. Though full of strength, the boy was utterly exposed. Dakon shifted his weight, avoiding the attack and knocking the blade from Tomas' hands with a simple elbow to the wrist.

Tomas fell forward onto the sand, his cheeks reddening as he fumbled for his sword.

"Don't give away yourself too soon," Dakon said, giving Tomas time to resettle before closing the distance, his blades ready for another uncoordinated blow.

Tomas swung his sword from above his head, and Dakon deflected the attempt, clashing the sword down and away with one of his daggers, using the other to show Tomas how open his body was.

"Try to avoid leaving yourself so vulnerable." Dakon took a few steps back. "I hear a knife to the heart is painful."

Tomas huffed, raising his sword once more. "I was just getting warmed up."

The boy rushed, though with more control, and the two settled into a dance of swords and daggers. The clashing of their weapons was music to Dakon's ears, as they twisted, spun, and fought in the cooling sand. He briefly recalled his time as a sparring partner in the castle. To fight with the nobles as their equal, even if for a few moments, and to watch as the greatest swordsmen in the kingdom sparred before his very eyes. Now, he was on his own, teaching others an art that he held dear. A skill that no amount of servitude would take from him.

He was so consumed by these thoughts, he did not realize time had once again slowed. His movements were far quicker than Tomas', too quick. His dagger was mid-strike as Tomas had again left himself exposed. And before Dakon could stop himself, he drew blood, slicing deep into Tomas' ribs.

Tomas' screams pierced the afternoon, and time resumed. At Dakon's feet was a boy, who only wished to train as he once did, now bleeding profusely on the sand.

Memories of his fight with Timothy quickly clouded his mind, how shocked Dakon had been to nearly kill him. He initially stabbed him intending to defend himself but with enough rage to rival ten lifetimes.

Dakon dropped his bloodied dagger as Pazel rushed to the boy. "Shit, Dakon! What happened?!"

Pirates, having heard the commotion, began to run from a distance.

Tomas continued screaming, holding his side and crying out from the pain.

"Heal him! Quickly, before they come."

But the blood was too great, and Tomas' screams were beginning to fade. His face paling as blood began to pour from his lips.

Dakon fell to his knees, trying and failing to chant the words he knew now by heart, to hold out hope that the witch goddess would take pity on him and save this boy.

No sooner had he failed with the spell a second time, then a man rushed toward them. He pushed past Pazel, inspecting Tomas, "I'm a healer. Quickly, shield me, and I can save him!"

Dakon met the man's eyes, dark and serious, with a silver speck glinting then disappearing.

"Be quick!" the man repeated, shoving Dakon and placing his hands above the now too-quiet boy's wound. Dakon and Pazel stood behind him, covering him from the approaching crowd.

"What's wrong?" one of the pirates demanded, his face etched in distress. "Where is my son!"

Dakon couldn't find the words to explain, couldn't imagine the pain of the man before him knowing that he was the cause of the young boy's demise.

Dakon opened his mouth to speak, but the words that came out were not of his own.

"He has a cut from sparring, I imagine it'll be better with some rest after a moon."

Dakon turned, seeing the healer bent over a now-coherent Tomas. Blood filled his blouse and lips, but the wound now was only a large cut compared to the fatal gash Dakon inflicted moments before.

Tomas' father shoved Dakon out of the way, bending to his son and scolding him as the rest of the pirates lost interest, walking back to their tents.

Pazel grabbed Dakon by the arm. "What happened?"

Dakon wasn't sure, unable to rip his eyes away from what could have been his first known kill. And to a boy who wanted nothing more but to learn.

The healer continued speaking to the father and son, and Dakon could no longer watch. Grief and shame filled him. Perhaps Eve was right, he was not nearly as skilled as he thought he was becoming . . .

He ripped his arm from Pazel, grabbed his daggers, and ran back to the ship. Not bothering to see if anyone followed.

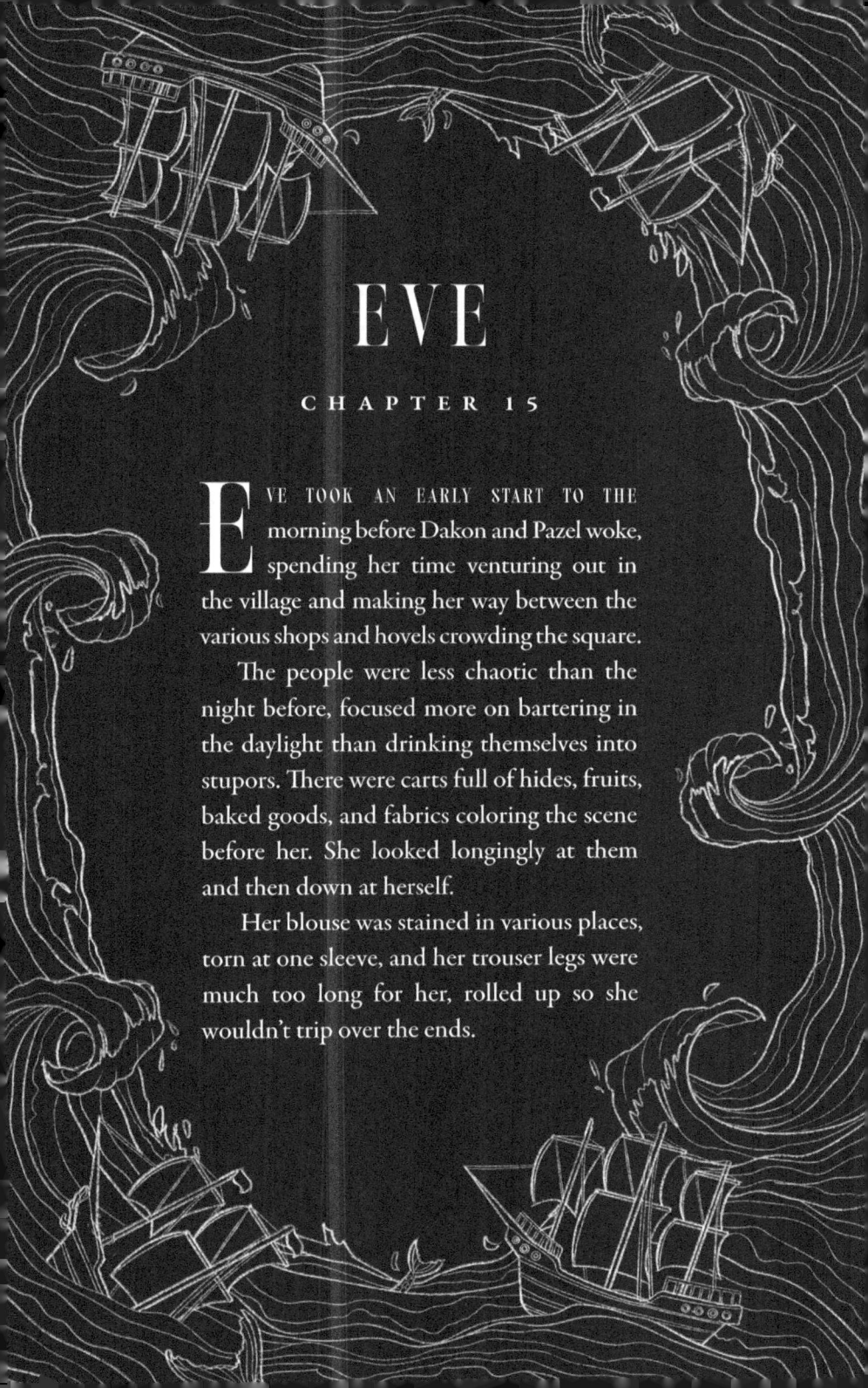

EVE

CHAPTER 15

EVE TOOK AN EARLY START TO THE morning before Dakon and Pazel woke, spending her time venturing out in the village and making her way between the various shops and hovels crowding the square.

The people were less chaotic than the night before, focused more on bartering in the daylight than drinking themselves into stupors. There were carts full of hides, fruits, baked goods, and fabrics coloring the scene before her. She looked longingly at them and then down at herself.

Her blouse was stained in various places, torn at one sleeve, and her trouser legs were much too long for her, rolled up so she wouldn't trip over the ends.

She missed being a lady at court, having finery and dresses embroidered by the finest tailors of the kingdom, going to balls and dances. She walked toward one of the more colorful stalls, the fabrics surrounding nearly every inch of it. Eve's eyes widened as she took in the deep purples, joyful pinks, and gorgeous greens. She held a teal silk between her fingers, missing how it had once felt on her skin. It was nothing like the kingdom's, but somehow the connection was still there. She imagined how she would sew the fabric, pairing it with gold lace and white trim. It would make an excellent gown.

"Are you going to pay for that? If not, get your filthy hands off it!"

Eve startled, releasing the fabric as a burly man with a white beard called out from behind the stall, his eyes narrowing suspiciously on her.

She looked down at her fingers, noticing truly for the first time how callused and unrefined her hands were. Ash stained them a tinge of gray. In only weeks they had become unrecognizable.

"No, I'm sorry," she muttered.

I am a lady of one of the richest houses in Givensmir, I could afford thousands of these if I wanted to!

At least, that is what she wished she could yell. Instead, she found herself running out of the square and past the village itself. Her boots pounded on the beaten path leading up a small hill, clouded by thoughts of her life before it had turned to ruin. Of admiring her jewels in the daylight from her balcony, her engagement to Callum, being the heir to Rubianes Keep, it all seemed not so troublesome now. All her woes were child's play before the grimoire surfaced.

The damn book.

She reflected on her discussions with Dakon since their escape; Cerene was her mother's familiar helping to bind Eve from her magic until her twenty-fourth birthday. Leaving her alone without the crucial knowledge she instead so willingly gave to her murderous sister. Clarisa surely put their mother's teachings to good use, killing innocent people and framing her kin instead.

Eve scoffed aloud at the sarcasm that laced her inner voice. She couldn't understand, with all of Clarisa's power, why she never sought Eve out, never let her know that she was alive. Did their childhood together mean nothing?

Eve's skin heated again. She was not meant to be a fugitive on the run with pirates, she was supposed to be with Callum in Teros where they would have shared in heartbreak about her lost childhood loves.

She slowed to a walk as the sun beat down onto every inch of the island not obscured by the greenery. Sweat pricked at her skin uncomfortably beneath her clothes. Eve braided her hair quickly, doing anything to give herself relief. She was a considerable distance from the main village and near the peak of one of the hills that overlooked the port.

Eve settled beneath one of the large palm trees and watched the sea sparkle in the distance, the pirate ships rising and falling with the gentle waves. It would have been breathtaking if not for her foul mood.

It had been a long while since she was truly alone, having shared a cabin with Dakon and Pazel aboard a crowded pirate ship for so long, and part of her felt as if she could think, truly think, away from the mayhem below her.

There were three things of which Eve was certain: She was a prophesied witch with a grimoire that wanted something from her, she wanted to confront her sister and see if there would be any chance at peace, and lastly she needed to control her magic.

The last thought gave her more concern than the others. She was reckless, she knew, and now voices had emerged, whispering deadly thoughts at her most vulnerable, emotional peaks.

Eve recalled her argument with Dakon and the venomous words that slipped off her tongue too easily. What she really meant, what she neglected to say, was that she felt inferior. While he was able to correct her mistakes, heal her from the wounds of her nightmares, and risk his life for hers, she was utterly useless.

Eve closed her eyes and listened to the island—heard the buzzing of insects, the call of the seagulls, the scampering of animals through brush nearby. The wind rustled softly through the trees and cooled her face under the shade. She concentrated on her breathing and her surroundings, connecting with the nature beneath her—the gentle, tickling grass, the pebbles lining the worn path, the soft dirt still drying from last night's rain—hoping that something primeval would guide her.

She brought her hands together before her, eyes still closed, imagining a small flame within them. A fire burning nothing but air in her palms. She concentrated on it, envisioning it would stop mid-dance, as would the day around her.

A silence encroached upon Eve, heightening her senses.

She opened her eyes and her heart nearly stopped.

The flame was a reddish orange in her palms, the space around her frozen in time. The waves in the distance unmoving, as were the ships along the port. She looked up seeing a seagull mid-flight so close, its wings spread out balancing itself on the gusts of wind that no longer moved.

It was incredible. Tears sprang from her eyes as hope began to bloom inside her. Maybe, just maybe, she could control it.

She nearly forgot that all sound had ceased, until she heard a faint rustling from behind. Eve turned quickly, feeling time resume once more and the seagull flew out of reach, much to her disappointment.

"Why, hello there, *Lady*."

Eve came face-to-face with the stranger from the tavern. She quickly shook her hands and the flame went out, leaving only bits of ash on her fingers.

"W-what are you doing here?"

"Smoke from your skin and now birds stop before you? You are a walking curiosity."

A shiver ran down her spine, she was caught. She nearly forgot to breathe, her mind searching for any excuse to explain away what he might have seen. But as the moment stretched into an unwelcome silence, his suspicious gaze narrowed further.

"I don't know what you are talking about," she managed.

"Of course, you don't." He folded his arms across his chest but moved no closer.

"I told you to leave me be."

"I never promised to obey." He smirked.

She rolled her eyes. "Why are you following me?"

"I happen to be staying at an inn up the way." He pointed to a cottage on the ridge. "I was walking to the port when I saw you. You are not exactly hidden from the path."

Feeling foolish, but unwilling to admit it, she turned away. "I am not in the mood to entertain such conversations."

Eve took a few steps.

"Wait, can I have your name?"

"No," she said, continuing walking down the hill, but hearing him close behind.

"He will hurt you." The voices, they were back. Eve breathed shakily as she tried to focus on her steps, anything to distract herself.

"Ah, so you prefer 'Lady'?"

She refused to look at him, counting her steps. *Six. Seven. Eight.*

"So, I am expected to keep your secrets, but am not given the courtesy of your name?"

"He defies you."

She turned, exasperation molding into pure aggravation. "There are no secrets. I will not give you my name. And if I ever see you again, I swear by all the gods that exist on this damn island I will make you regret ever speaking to me."

"Kill him."

"Quite the temper," he mused. Then his tone grew serious, his eyes narrowed. "It matches your eyes."

"He will hurt you."

Eve blinked quickly, knowing the red within them gave her away. She turned, feeling foolish for thinking a bit of practice would change her fate.

"Do it now."

"What are you?" he breathed from behind her.

"Kill him."

And before she could take off running, he placed his hand on hers, gently stopping her. At his touch, skin to skin, a strange vision came over her.

THE MAN RAN QUICKLY THROUGH STREETS IN AN UNKNOWN VILLAGE, moving as fast as he could toward the sea in the distance. He pivoted between alleys and the shadows of the buildings, trying to fade into the darkness.

Someone was giving chase, and they were not far behind. Of this he was certain. The man's heart raced in his chest, goosebumps lined his flesh. He wouldn't let them capture him, not again. Never again.

He caught his breath behind a building and could see the water beneath the starlight in the distance; it was so close. He just had to touch the water. He would be safe if he could only touch the water.

He willed his legs to move, despite their protest, despite how weak his body felt. It had been hours on the run, an eternity on foot. He raced toward the edge of the village where a stone wall separated the land and shore and climbed quickly over it. The sand beneath his boots gave him a sense of comfort, but he didn't dare to slow his pace.

As he was about to reach the water, a figure in a dark blue, hooded robe grabbed him from behind. He screamed against them, fighting and flailing. More emerged from beyond the wall, rushing to help subdue him.

He tried in vain to touch the water; *he only had to touch the water.* He called out for someone, but the words were muffled by the overwhelming force. He didn't want to do it, he didn't want to hurt anyone, but he could no longer keep his oath.

He couldn't go back. He couldn't.

He unsheathed a single knife from his belt, turning and planting it in the neck of the hooded figure. He watched as the man lowered in his arms and fell with a sickening thud on the sand.

There were shouts and weapons thrown in his direction. He couldn't mourn the man he killed, not yet. He rushed and touched the water, where it welcomed him in its embrace.

He was safe, for now.

"DAMMIT!" HE RELEASED HER, CURSING AT THE BURN MARKS ON HIS hand. Blisters bubbled on his palm where he touched Eve.

She gasped for air, feeling as if she had nearly drowned herself. Her body was scalding; ash fell from her fingertips. The last time she had a vision like this was with King Eryck, the memory making her tremble. This power was still new, still petrifying. She backed up a few steps, trying to regain her strength.

This man was running from something. Something she could not quite understand, and that terrified her.

Though pained, he looked at her with a mix of confusion and fear. Much to her relief he did not attempt to close the space between them, instead holding his wounded hand in his other.

"Who are you?" she demanded, steadying her breath as she leaned against a tree for support.

Before he could respond, a group of people began to make their way up the path where they stood, speaking loudly in jovial voices.

Eve did not wait for him to respond, instead leaving the strange man and his unfortunate past behind.

She hoped she would never see him again.

CALLUM

CHAPTER 16

"**I**T MAY TAKE A LIFETIME TO EXPRESS how much I love you. And even then, I will gladly spend our afterlife telling you again and again."

Eryce reached out and caressed Callum's cheek, delicately gazing upon him. His hazel eyes soft, gentle, and loving in the warm candlelight. His light brown hair was tousled, and the curls fell gracefully over his forehead. The sound of Eryce's voice as he hummed a familiar folk tune, just moments prior to his admission, was pure bliss to his ears. Eryce was not just a prince, but a work of art come to life in front of Callum's very eyes.

The night was peaceful and cool, inviting a brisk autumn breeze throughout Eryce's chambers. The crickets sang softly, and the night herons flew gracefully across the balcony. The drapes of the archway danced gently with the wind, and the sea waves lapping against the shore were distant but comforting.

With Eryce, the chaos of the world stopped, and peace was real.

Callum returned his gaze, smiling against his touch. His heart fluttered with the intensity of their connection; one he was convinced rivaled the greatest love stories heard in his childhood. Perhaps, one day, their story would be told and revered throughout the kingdom. The thought was fleeting, and he shook it away before the truth set in to damper it.

"You stopped humming to tell me you love me?"

"Wouldn't you?" Eryce laughed.

Callum returned his smile. "You have my heart, Eryce."

"I hope I can deserve it."

"Without question," he promised.

Eryce sighed, holding Callum's hands between his. "I wish we could be here forever."

"You wouldn't get bored of me?"

"Never."

"Well, thank the gods the war is over. Now we can spend even more time together and test your words for the truth of them."

Eryce laughed, but the humor did not reach his eyes. "Yes, I hope so."

Callum furrowed his brows. "Your father is sickly, and your turn to reign is shortly upon us. There is no need to worry about leaving anymore. You will be expected to stay behind as heir considering your father's health."

Eryce nodded, unconvincingly.

"Eryce, listen to me. They cannot separate us. Not anymore."

"My father is not dead yet, Callum. The Gold Council still has considerable influence—"

"We are doing nothing wrong."

"Of course not. But they do not see like we do. What we are doing, what we have done, can put us, you, in grave danger."

"I would die for you, Eryce, you know this."

"Don't say what you don't mean."

"I do mean it, though."

Eryce grimaced, appearing conflicting with what to say next.

"I am tired of death. Of causing it, witnessing it. Do you think I want to be responsible for yours?"

"I love you," Callum brushed his fingers against Eryce's cheek. "You cannot make me change my mind. As long as I breathe, you are my life."

"Stop it." Eryce pulled his hands away. "Please. Let me think."

Callum's heart sank as he tried to think of ways to salvage the evening.

How had it turned so wrong, so quickly?

The silence stretched before Eryce finally spoke. "Perhaps we haven't been as careful as we thought."

"Of course we have. No one has seen us; I am sure of it."

"I don't know. Some nights I feel as if we are being watched."

"Watched? Do you hear yourself?" Callum let out a nervous chuckle.

"I am serious."

"As am I. We are safe in your chambers, I assure you."

Eryce looked toward the far wall of his room.

"They have eyes everywhere. We have just not found them yet . . ." His voice was distant, detached. Eryce rose from the bed, moving away from him.

"Wait!" Callum pulled him back into his embrace, but something was wrong. Eryce did not feel warm anymore, but cool to the touch. Callum looked down at his hands, now stained a dark, deep crimson. He screamed, letting go, revealing a large wound in the center of Eryce's chest.

"What happened?! Eryce, speak to me!"

Eryce turned, unblinking, walking away once more.

Callum reached out, desperate to bring him back. But it was too late, he was moving further away, out of his grasp and out of his life.

"Eryce, wait!"

But Eryce was no longer in his sight, disappearing into the shadows that crept into the room. Goosebumps pricked at Callum's flesh, and a sharp pain throbbed on his side, forcing him to the ground. He shouted in agony, holding himself as everything turned black.

"Eryce!"

In the bitter silence that followed, Callum spiraled between pain and darkness. A single thought kept repeating itself in his heart.

Can the dead hear the living?

CALLUM WOKE IN PAIN, HIS BODY ACHING AFTER THE BRUTALITY HE faced from another round of torture the night prior. Slowly, he came back from his dream and into the nightmare of his reality. He groaned, clutching his ribs in a futile attempt to sway the discomfort. He made note of all his new injuries—*bruised ribs, cut on shoulder, bruises on face, broken finger* . . . It took all his effort not to break down as he lay in the cell. A dank, wet smell filled his nostrils, and he gagged as he clutched his body on the floor.

A mouse scampered away, squeaking as it went into a crevice in the stone wall down the corridor. Callum almost envied the feral creature, wishing that he could escape just as easily.

"Finally, I've been bored waiting for you to wake up."

Callum turned to the cell across from him, his golden eyes reaching the honey, humorous ones of Emilio. He did not respond, focusing his efforts instead on raising himself into a sitting position. It was more excruciating than he expected, but he rested his back along the wall for support. He breathed heavily, trying to endure the throbbing in his side.

"Although, I must admit your sleep talking was quite . . . entertaining," Emilio added, tilting his head.

Callum glared at him silently.

Emilio lifted his hands defensively before him, smiling. "No need to worry. Your secret is safe with me."

Callum was unsure of how to respond, wishing he were alone in the dungeon once more.

"It has been days since I arrived," Emilio continued, rolling up his sleeves, "and you have not even spoken a word to me. Did they cut out your tongue?"

Callum raised his head, leveling his gaze with this stranger. He hated to admit it, but he was curious about the nobleman before him. He assessed Emilio—honey brown hair that nearly matched his eyes, a slight stubble adorned his face, and he appeared strong and healthy despite the small cuts and bruises visible. It was apparent this man was one many ladies of the court would swoon over. He was sure Emilio was already promised to one back in Larrea.

Callum wondered many things in those few moments about the man in the cell across the narrow hall . . . but curiosity did not bring back Eryce, nor would it lead him to freedom.

Callum chewed on his lip and painfully faced his body away from Emilio.

Without Eryce or Eve, bonds did not seem to matter anymore. When your body was broken along with your heart and spirit, where else could one go but to sleep? Dreams were the ideal escape.

He lay once more on the floor, letting the tears silently fall onto the dirty, cold, stone floor begging the gods to bring slumber. To have mercy and pity him.

Instead, Emilio's voice, now a whisper he could barely make out, said, "They will not kill you, Lord Callum, you are too important to Teros. From what I heard before my arrest, your lords are fighting against your imprisonment as we speak."

Callum squeezed his eyes shut, not wishing to discuss any matters of the real world.

Escape. Dream. Sleep.

Moments passed, then hours, and before he knew it he could hear Eryce's song once more. A tune he could no longer recall the words to, but one that had settled itself on his heart. As long as the sound continued in his soul, Eryce had never truly left.

And he escaped into a deep sleep, letting his dreams consume him in a semblance of peace.

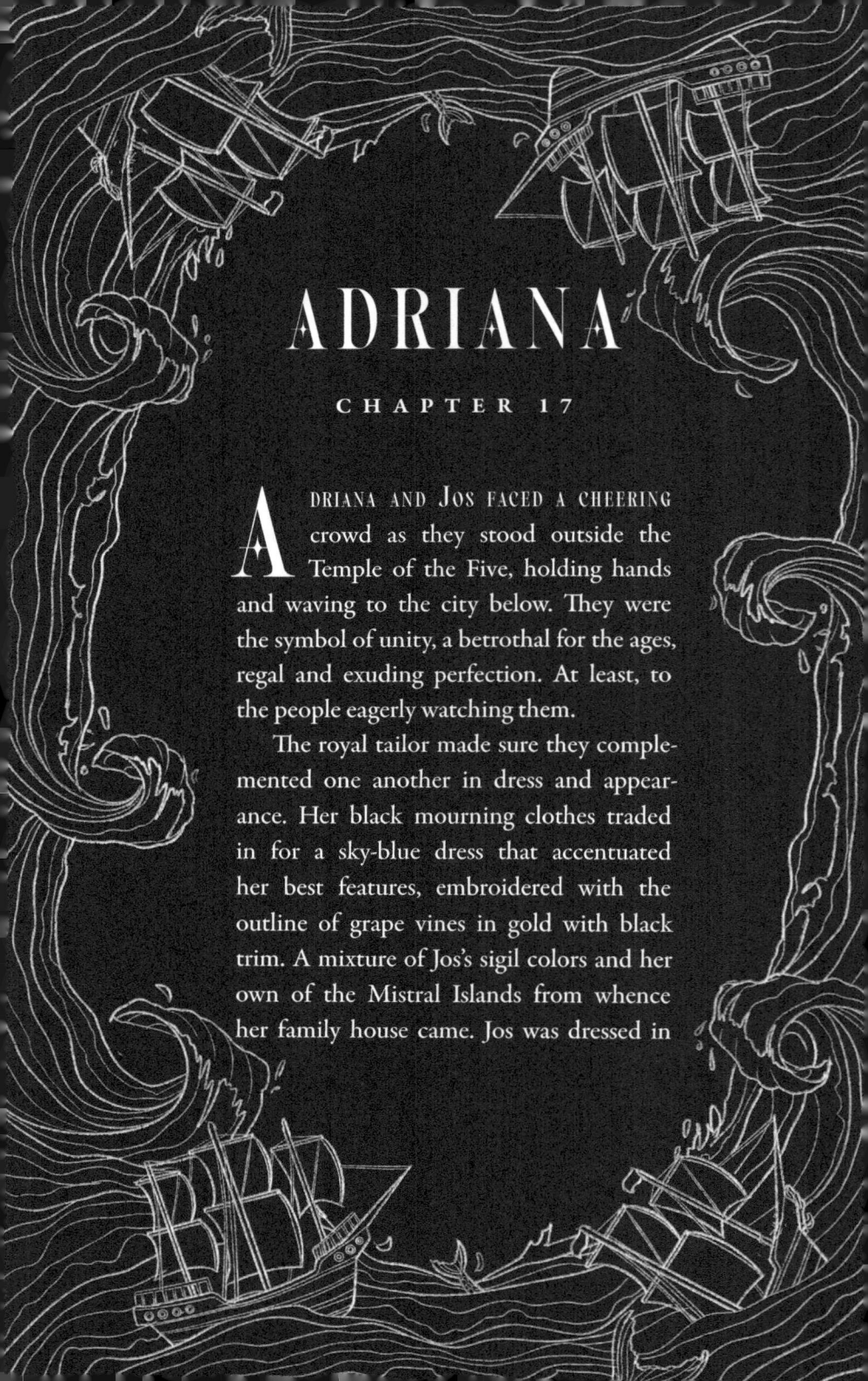

ADRIANA

CHAPTER 17

ADRIANA AND JOS FACED A CHEERING crowd as they stood outside the Temple of the Five, holding hands and waving to the city below. They were the symbol of unity, a betrothal for the ages, regal and exuding perfection. At least, to the people eagerly watching them.

The royal tailor made sure they complemented one another in dress and appearance. Her black mourning clothes traded in for a sky-blue dress that accentuated her best features, embroidered with the outline of grape vines in gold with black trim. A mixture of Jos's sigil colors and her own of the Mistral Islands from whence her family house came. Jos was dressed in his nobleman's garb and coat of the same shades. Her mother had bragged that the brisk blues of Mytar represented the never-ending view from the mountaintops within the skies from which their castles rested. Adriana couldn't care less about skies; she could only look upon them as her brother willed it.

She peeked at Jos from beneath her lashes—his green eyes were alight with joy, mirroring his broad smile as he waved to the crowd—much to their excitement and fervor.

He is good at this.

"We thank the five for their many blessings on this betrothal," Borgias announced from the podium next to them. "Our princess of grace and piety, and our strong and valorous future prince of the mountain. By the will of the gods, may they have a long and happy marriage!"

"By the will of the gods!"

More applause, more cheers of support.

All to distract, she thought, all to keep the people blind to the deaths around them. The winter wind brushed through her hair, and a tense chill ran down her spine.

How soon everyone forgot about the fallen—Callum, her brothers, her father, the numerous women the council declared witches in recent weeks—all because a pair of beautiful faces greeted them from the top of the temple steps.

A group of small birds flew past them, above the crowd and toward the sea. Adriana wished she could leave, to send a dove out to wherever Dakon was now and beg for him to come back and take her away. She bit her lip to fight back the tears that threatened.

Jos lowered their hands, a grin on his face as he turned to her and kissed her knuckles. For the briefest, nearly indiscernible, moment, he raised a brow curiously looking at a lone tear that escaped down her cheek. She reminded herself to smile and blush, making a show of her affection.

Exactly what *they* wanted to see.

The spectacle seemed to last for eternity, until the elder finished his speech and Jos led her, hand-in-hand, back into the temple.

The doors closed behind them, separating the couple from the crowd outside, and Adriana pulled her hand from his grip. Jos furrowed his brow, giving her a pointed look.

She glared, unsure of what to make of him. From Theo's wedding until today, they had not so much as spoken a few words to one another.

Who was this lord of the mountain?

An excited cry rang out in the temple. "Oh, you were wonderful, Princess!" Jayne rushed to her. "Absolutely breathtaking."

"Thank you."

"And *you*"—Jayne's eyes met Jos's—"many blessings to your new betrothal. The princess has finally met such a handsome match."

Adriana rolled her eyes, not bothering to conceal it.

Jos cocked his brow. "And you are?"

Adriana sighed. "This is my lady-in-waiting, Lady Jayne. Daughter of Ser Elliot, commander of the peace."

"Yes, apologies, my lord." Jayne bowed quickly.

"No apology needed," he replied, disinterested. He faced Adriana, "I shall see you at court."

"Of course," she said, refusing to look his way.

Without another word, he straightened his coat and walked away.

She could feel the tension on her face and made a deliberate effort to appear relaxed.

"Shall we go, as well?" Jayne asked, placing her arm in Adriana's.

"Yes," she murmured, watching as Jos met his father at the other end of the temple. Lord Joseph seemed frailer than she last remembered, as if he had aged considerably since Theo's wedding. His hair had grayed; his eyes were wrinkled and dark beneath his lids. His face was in a perpetual state of gloom, much unlike the elated man she had met at the wedding.

Loss, she assumed, had taken his youth and happiness, leaving behind a father that was nothing but skin and bones and heartache.

What did loss take from me?

She continued watching as father and son embraced one another and left. She couldn't remember the last time her father, or even her mother, held her with such affection. Not at her father's funeral, not even when she was in her mother's castle waiting on bated breath for news of her brothers.

Adriana swallowed a lump that had formed in her throat and instead of giving in to her sorrow, she focused on the anger of the injustice of it. Quickening her steps to the carriage, she allowed her anger to fester and build as they rode home.

Until finally, she could not contain it any longer.

"You ambushed me," Adriana snapped as the guards closed the door behind her.

She watched as her mother sat in front of her vanity, barely registering her daughter's presence.

"Hmm?"

"You heard me, Mother. I demand an explanation."

Her mother rolled her eyes, brushing her graying, auburn hair. "My dear, I can never keep up with your grievances. Pray, tell me what ails you now." Her tone was laced with poison and annoyance.

Adriana stormed toward her. "I am betrothed without my knowledge, having heard it for the first time in front of the entire court, and then forced into the city to announce it. My brothers have barely become ash in the wind, and you have already sold me like a mare!"

Her mother sighed heavily, fixing a few pins in her hair from a small pile of them on her vanity table. "Must I be the one to tell you life isn't fair? Your father arranged this match before his death. May he rest with the gods. And you have the audacity to complain?" She continued fiddling with her hair, "Lord Joseph is a suitable match, and you will make suitable children and go about living your suitable lives. It is what my mother did, I did, and what you will do too." She emphasized the last few words, holding a pin by her teeth as she arranged the last bundle of her hair.

"But I am not you. At the very least, it would have been nice to be consulted with."

Her mother took a last look in the mirror, and satisfied with what she saw, finally turned to look Adriana in the eyes.

"After all these years, you still do not understand, do you? You are nothing more than a means for securing prosperity in our kingdom. As every woman in this court is—"

"I do not even know him. What if we despise each other?"

Her mother stood, fine lines visible from years of stress and suppressed anger. She glared at Adriana, her posture tall and rigid. How did such a woman bear a child that she despised so much?

"Then hate him with a smile on your face. Marriage is a contract; love is a rarity. It would do you well to get in line and accept your fate. Questions will bring you nothing but madness, my dear."

Adriana could not think of what to say, her mouth dry as the words settled.

Her mother raised a brow, looking Adriana over. "Now get dressed, my child. There are more important matters to attend to."

She walked past her, brushing her shoulder against Adriana, and out of her chambers. And all Adriana could do was stare, as if her voice had left her along with her mother.

If she ever had one at all.

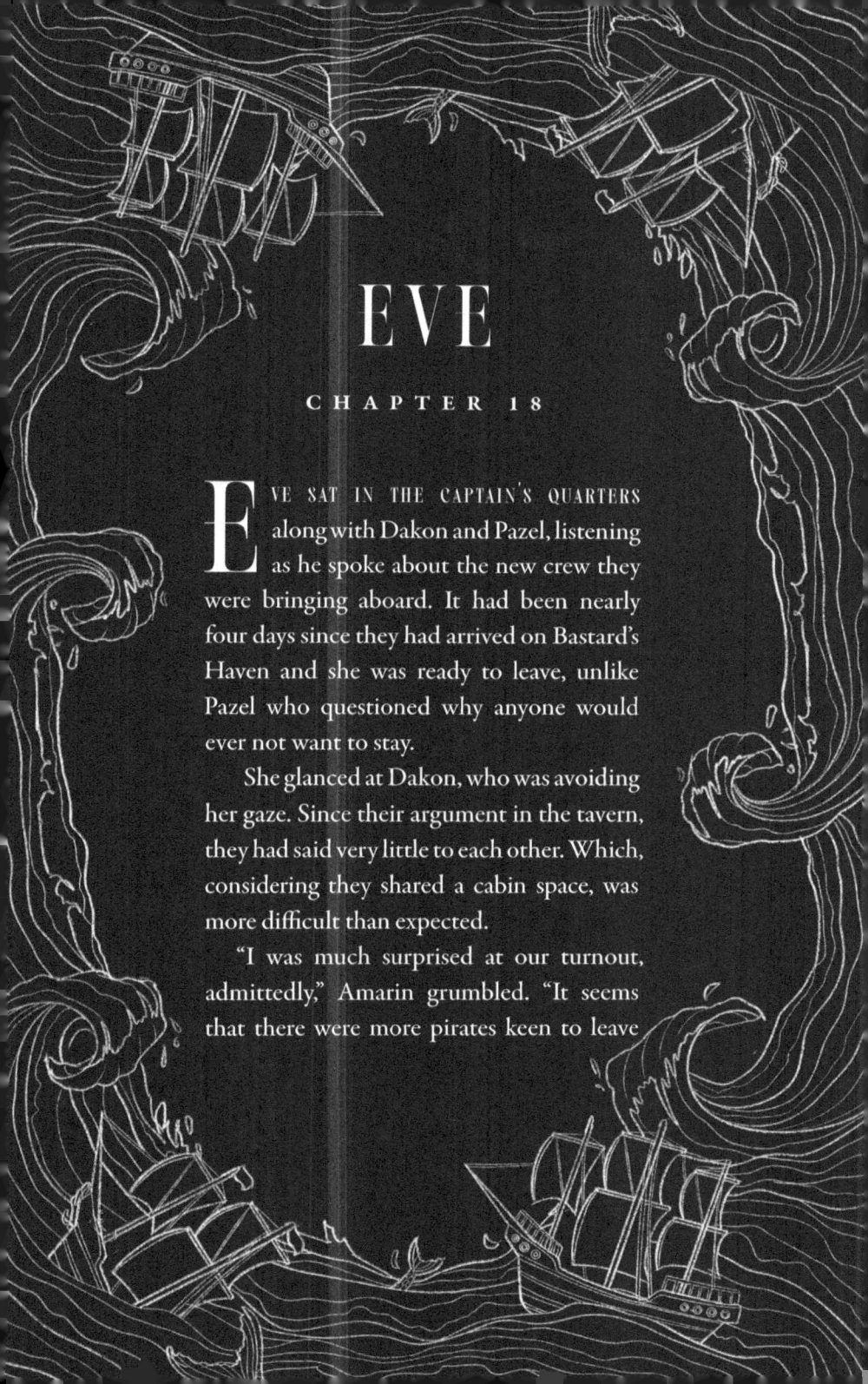

EVE

CHAPTER 18

EVE SAT IN THE CAPTAIN'S QUARTERS along with Dakon and Pazel, listening as he spoke about the new crew they were bringing aboard. It had been nearly four days since they had arrived on Bastard's Haven and she was ready to leave, unlike Pazel who questioned why anyone would ever not want to stay.

She glanced at Dakon, who was avoiding her gaze. Since their argument in the tavern, they had said very little to each other. Which, considering they shared a cabin space, was more difficult than expected.

"I was much surprised at our turnout, admittedly," Amarin grumbled. "It seems that there were more pirates keen to leave the island than I expected, even if it meant docking at the Blackthorn."

Eve nodded, pleasantly surprised at this turn of events. "That is good to hear, Captain, thank you."

"Don't thank me just yet, I imagine you'll be regretting this before long."

"Perhaps, not." Eve rolled her eyes; she was rather irritable from lack of sleep. And since her healing was slower than Dakon's, she felt rather pained by the scars still healing on her arms from the grimoire's continued attempts to lure her.

"When can we meet the crew?" Dakon asked.

"They should have boarded by now. But I warn you"—he pointed a finger at Eve—"not many pirates take too kindly to witches. I would stow your"—he waved a hand aimlessly in her direction—"magic or witchcraft or whatever we're calling this fire trick of yours as best you can so as not to spook them."

"You have my word, Captain." Pazel placed a hand over his chest.

The captain glowered at Pazel, before shaking his head and moving toward the cabin door.

"Last chance, my dear." The captain faced Eve, his hand hovering over the handle. "Do you still wish to sail for the Blackthorn? We can turn course to anywhere else the sea takes us. *Anywhere* else."

Eve thought of the grimoire, of Theo and Callum's deaths, of how Clarisa had set her up for slaughter.

Who knew the next chaotic thing she would have me take the fall for?

"I have to find my sister. The Blackthorn is my best chance at finding answers."

Amarin nodded, as if convincing himself of her words, then turned the knob and walked outside with Eve and her familiars in tow.

"ABSOLUTELY NOT, HE IS NOT COMING WITH US!" EVE HISSED TO THE CAPTAIN.

Amarin turned to face her, a line of at least ten of the new recruits behind him. "Damn you, woman. What are you going on about? You haven't even let them introduce themselves."

Her eyes locked with the dark ones of a man she swore to hate. He smirked in her direction, making her skin heat considerably.

"I don't trust him, that one there." She tilted her chin to the man.

"Eve," Dakon hissed back, "we are not in a position to bargain. We need every pirate we can get. Can you just give him a chance?"

Pazel, Dakon, and the captain looked at her incredulously, and she was livid at being rebuffed by their responses.

"I saw him the other day, outside the tavern."

"And?"

"Well, he saw my body on fire, saw the rain turn it to smoke . . ." Even as the words left her mouth, she became increasingly aware of how childish she sounded.

"Eve"—Dakon pulled her aside, Pazel following—"if this man saw you use any magic, do you not think that you would be safer with him on board rather than him on an island of nefarious company spreading rumors about the witch with an arrest warrant and a tempting reward?"

"Why should you care about him? He's just one man."

Dakon clenched his jaw, and for the first time gave her a stern, admonishing look. "He may be more of an asset than you think. You aren't a noblewoman anymore. You have no more influence than I do here."

Eve chewed on the inside of her cheek to keep herself from insulting him.

"We need to let him prove his worth. If he tries anything, I'll be here." He patted the daggers on his hips. "Remember we're a team."

"And a family," Pazel chipped in.

"If you three are done wasting my time, I have a ship to run," Amarin grumbled.

Eve righted her shoulders, annoyed and unsatisfied at this turn of events.

Amarin turned toward the line, addressing his new recruits. "This is my ship, only my ship, and will forever be my fucking ship. If any one of you steps out of line, I will slice your throat and feed you to the fishes." He gestured to Eve and her familiars. "These are our guests, leave them alone, and you'll be left alone. Mind your damn business, and we'll all get along, be paid, and go about our merry way at the end of this. We are headed to the south of the Blackthorn. There we will replenish supplies and determine our next destination. If witches don't scare you, then welcome. If they do, you can leave now, and no one but the gods will judge you for it."

One man retreated from the line and scurried off the ship.

"There's always one," the captain mumbled. "Now for those remaining, state your name and occupation aboard the ship for everyone to hear."

The first pirate stepped forward, a woman with golden-brown skin, her eyes caught a hint of sun, shining a bright aqua hue against it.

"Niani, first mate."

Niani, that name sounded familiar, but Eve couldn't place where it was from. The woman stepped back, tall and confident, her dark hair fastened in two braids that fell behind her shoulders. Her presence, the way she spoke was assertive and confident.

The line continued until it was the vile, deceptively handsome man's turn. He stepped forward, smirking in Eve's direction. She rolled her eyes, facing away from him.

"Izan, healer."

He stepped back, keeping his eyes locked on Eve's and she did her best to avoid his blaring gaze. The rest of the pirates continued down the line, a boatswain, another cook, a ship steerer, and more.

Amarin finished his remarks, and soon the pirates were released to their various tasks.

The ship rocked in the sea, free of the anchors, and Bastard's Haven soon became a speck in the distance. She moved away from the pirates as they worked, positioning herself along the railing behind the steer, watching as the land in the distance became obsolete, blending into the background until it was solely the sea and the sky. The sun began to sink, and a soft reddish pink filled the sky.

She pulled up her sleeves eyeing the remainder of the faded scars on her skin. She hoped that she would be able to rest tonight, that the book would give her a reprieve from its haunting. The scars were becoming too painful to wake from.

"Interesting bruises you have there, Lady."

Eve whirled around coming face-to-face with Izan. He stood confidently with his hands in his pockets, the corner of his lips rising.

Eve's breath caught; she couldn't think of a witty reply. She instinctively pulled down her sleeves.

"Tattoos," she sputtered.

"Tattoos?" He smirked.

"Don't you have something better to do than spy on me?"

"I'm a healer, there's not much to do until someone falls ill or we come under attack."

Eve scoffed. "So, you admit you're dead weight."

"Not entirely. You'll be begging for me if a fever hits."

"I can't imagine begging, especially for you."

He laughed, and an impossibly perfect smile revealed his dimples. She added that to her list of now undesirable traits.

"Oh, Lady, you will before this journey is done. I guarantee it."

"Didn't the captain warn you to mind your business? Or do I have to bring this conversation up to him?"

"I thought *you* were the dangerous one if I recall correctly. Besides, I'm doing my duty to temper any potential threats of harm on board."

She bit her lip and turned away.

If I pay him no mind, he will scurry away like the rodent he is.

Instead, his footsteps closed in behind her.

"What're you—" she began.

"I think we both know those aren't tattoos," he said with a serious tone.

She could only stare back at him, unprepared and admittedly a bit unwilling to deny it.

"May I?" he asked, gesturing to her arms.

She nodded, curious.

He pulled up her sleeves gently, as if with a practiced hand, revealing the scars. They were much better now than they were when she woke earlier this morning, but still reddened and painful to the touch.

"Can you keep a secret, Lady?" he whispered.

"Yes," she breathed, his proximity was making her head swim. All rational thought escaped her.

He nodded, a ghost of a smile on his lips. He placed his hands over her arms, so close they could nearly draw the same breath.

The scars began to retreat from her skin, slowly folding into themselves until she was free of them once more.

Izan clenched his jaw, a slightly pained look on his face. "That never gets easier."

"How did you—" Her eyes widened as she whispered, "Are you a witch?"

"Shh, Lady, you promised me a secret." He smiled smugly. "We're even now."

Eve's mouth was agape, so many questions on her lips.

Izan looked down at her. "You're quite precious when you're not demanding things from me."

She blinked, still stunned at what had thus unfolded before her, "I—I don't imagine we'll be speaking again like this."

He chuckled, taking a few steps back and descending the steps toward the main deck.

"Oh, we will. And have your familiar help you next time, it's his duty."

Eve nearly rushed after him if not for the audience that surely remained below. She promised the captain to remain out of sight and out of mind, running after his healer would surely cause a scene. No, she needed to think, gather her thoughts.

She turned back to face the water, the sun losing its daily battle with the night sky. Another witch aboard this ship, Dakon and her still on tense speaking terms, Beast still lingering about, and Pazel still a coat and shoes short of his debt to the captain—it was Amarin's dream come true she was sure.

She sighed, fiddling with her hair and braiding it without thinking as if it would better prepare her for what was to come.

A perfect storm waiting to be unleashed.

DAKON

CHAPTER 19

"HOW LONG HAVE YOU KNOWN THIS witch of yours?" the captain asked, tapping his fingers on the desk, his cool eyes assessing Dakon.

Dakon was seated across from him in the captain's quarters, a litter of parchment, random quills, and a candle nearly burned to the wick lingered between them. Its long flame licked the edges of the glass, trying in vain to remain alive, to feast on something new.

"Not long, admittedly," Dakon answered.

"Hmm."

"Why?"

"No reason," Amarin grumbled, standing and walking toward his cabin window.

Dakon watched as the captain faced the late afternoon sea. They moved slowly away from the island, the lush trees and golden sand now just a spot in the distance.

It unnerved Dakon to slip away back into the sea, as if the journey was beginning again. He assumed the captain felt the same, noting his rigid stance, a tension that came over him as they continued further into the dark water. His long, red hair gleamed against the simmering darkness, the bit of his ear that was missing from their sword fight in the tavern moons ago barely visible from where he stood.

"I don't trust what I don't know. And I suspect you feel the same way."

Dakon tensed, and realized his palms gripped the edge of his seat. He forced himself to breathe, to relax his body. "I know Eve well enough."

"Ah, yes. By the way you two have been avoiding each other, one would think you were close as kin."

Dakon kept silent; it was futile to argue. They had rarely spoken to each other since their fight in the tavern, save for practicing their magic together in silence and bickering about Izan earlier, both of them stubbornly unwilling to cede apologies.

"You, or rather your bloodline, were created by a witch for a witch," Amarin continued, eyes still fixed on the window, "from the moment you were born, you have been destined to serve another until your death. A terrible tragedy."

"It's my choice to help her."

Amarin turned, giving him a sad smirk, "Do you believe you truly believe that? Looking at you, I wager you never had a choice in your life. Scrubbing pots, sweeping floors, entertaining men who would step on your corpse to keep their shoes clean—no, you never did."

Dakon's skin pricked, heating. "Is this why you asked me to come here? To insult me?"

Amarin narrowed his eyes, "I'm not insulting you, boy. I'm trying to help you."

146

"How is this helpful?"

"I've been around witches longer than you've been alive, no familiar can outlast their witch without giving up parts of themselves. Parts that can be painful to lose. You need to ask yourself would your witch save your life as you would hers, or are you simply a pawn to get the revenge she so clearly desires?"

"She only wants to find her sister . . ." He couldn't finish his thoughts, because in truth he had never thought to ask himself this question.

Would she?

In fairness, she had not had the opportunity to save him when he had busied himself protecting her. Could he really condemn her for a chance that had not presented itself?

Amarin shook his head, rubbing his eyes in frustration. "I am not trying to cause discord between you, quite the opposite. I want you both to be prepared for what may come. She has angered a powerful kingdom that wishes her dead, to think that you are safe because you are on my ship is folly. I cannot promise you complete protection, but I want you both to be safe."

Dakon's jaw tightened. "Why do you care about what happens to us?"

Amarin turned once more to the now-darkened window. "Call it a favor to an old friend."

Dakon opened his mouth to question his motives, but the captain continued. "Witches have a hard time staying alive for long. Especially with a bounty on their heads."

He pulled a scroll from his coat pocket and handed it to Dakon. Dakon unfurled it, reading the contents. It was a summons for Eve for five thousand silver coins . . . by the Blackthorn kingdom.

"When did you get this?"

"It was posted on the island. It seems your witch is becoming quite the prize."

Dakon closed the scroll, placing it on the desk. "Does Eve know?"

"Not yet."

Dakon shook his head, "What do we do? Do you think the Blackthorn is truly the safest place to go now?"

"Nowhere in Serit is safe. But that is out of my hands now. She wishes to go to the Blackthorn, maybe there she can find sanctuary amongst her kind."

"Is this a trap?"

"If you suspected the daughter of the enchantress had a chance at resurrecting your beloved goddess, wouldn't you be searching for her too?"

Dakon considered this. Maybe the witch kingdom had the answers to helping Eve, to help them learn their magic.

Would they be embraced and welcomed?

Certainly it would make the journey of finding Clarisa much simpler . . .

He looked back into the captain's weary eyes.

"And where will you go?"

"Back to the sea, where I belong."

They sat silently for a few moments, Dakon watching Amarin as he seemed to forget his presence in the quarters. Looking off into the window, the sun barely visible over the horizon, Dakon tried to think of something other than their bleak situation. He thought of the singing voice once more.

"Does it not frighten you, to sail the sea with all that lurks beneath?"

Amarin scoffed, walking to a cabinet across the room. He opened it, retrieving a flask and taking a long swig. Dakon watched curiously as he made his way back to the seat across from him. Amarin's shoulders sagged in the chair, the flask in a loose grip on his lap, his thumb circling the open top.

"I have seen more than you could even fathom and then some."

Dakon took his chance. "What's the worst you've seen?"

Amarin raised a brow, a chilling look passed his eyes. "Have you seen something?"

"You first, Captain."

"I can't recall." Amarin took another sip.

Dakon considered pressing the issue but relented. "On Bastard's Haven, the first night we were there. I saw a woman in the water singing—"

"Were you drunk?" Amarin wiped his mouth with the back of his hand, his voice gruff.

"Well, yes, but—"

"Was the woman naked?"

"I—"

Amarin scoffed, a bit of his drink spilling onto his red beard. "Could it not be that she was bathing?"

Dakon could feel himself redden, unsure of how to regain control of the discussion. He was sure this wasn't any ordinary woman.

"There was something about her. As if she was beckoning me to her. Her voice—"

He met Amarin's eyes and noticed the furrowing of his brow.

"Nothing that speaks from the sea is to be trusted. Remember that and you'll have less to worry about here."

DAKON LEFT THE CAPTAIN'S QUARTERS, SET TO FIND EVE AND TELL HER about Amarin and all that he had thus uncovered. He walked briskly to the center of the deck, checking around to see if she was getting fresh air as she usually did early in the evening. Members of the crew moved past him, going about their business and he steered clear of them as they worked. He turned toward the helm of the ship and stopped.

She and the healer from the beach were speaking rather sharply from behind the wheel. They seemed familiar with each other, and he watched as Izan even touched Eve's arms.

Who was this man? How did Eve know him?

He was wary of Izan's presence but was indebted to him. The boy pirate would have surely died if not for him.

Was he a witch, a familiar, something else?

Dakon kept a fixed eye on them as he moved slowly toward the helm. By the time he made it to the bottom of the stairs, Izan was making his way toward him, alone.

"Is she well?" Dakon heard himself asking as Izan brushed past him.

Izan's eyes met his, a pleased look on his face. "She will be. I took care of her for you."

Before Dakon could respond, Izan patted his shoulder and left, making his way down into the ship.

What the hells was that about?

Dakon gripped the railing of the ladder, unsure why he was so hesitant. In only days since they arrived at Bastard's Haven, he and Eve had become more divided than he realized. He couldn't dispel the feeling of being replaced.

He loosened his grip, taking a few steps back and watching as Eve focused her attention on the sea, oblivious to his presence. She was still such a mystery to him, and he wondered if after everything was done, if he would still be in the dark about who she really was.

He needed space, the sinking feeling in his stomach making him uneasy.

Dakon slowly turned on his heel and made his way to their cabin.

He spoke to Pazel of magic transference and more of Cerene's stories until he finally drifted off into a troubled sleep full of dreams of Adriana and haunting voices singing from beyond his window.

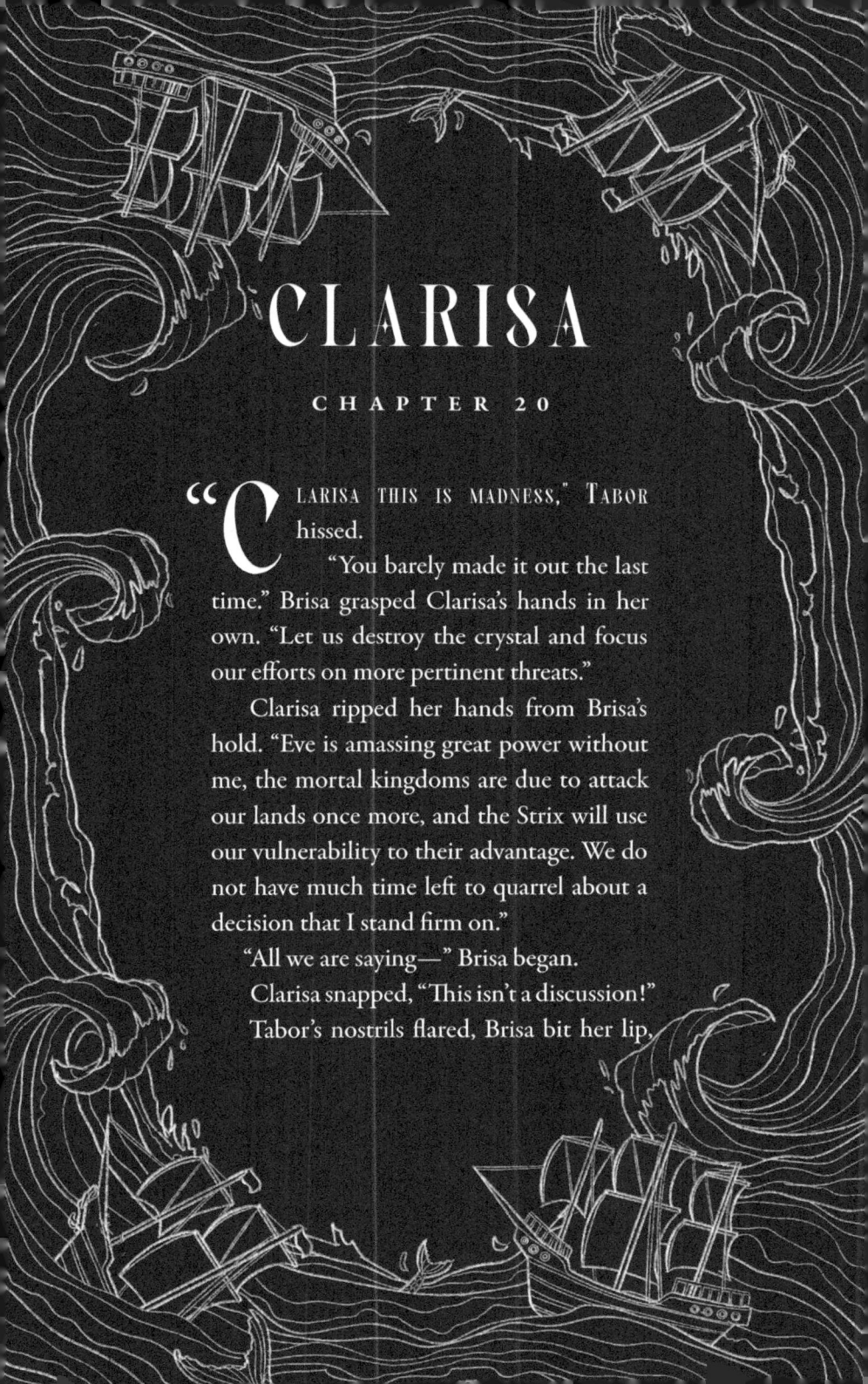

CLARISA

CHAPTER 20

"Clarisa this is madness," Tabor hissed.

"You barely made it out the last time." Brisa grasped Clarisa's hands in her own. "Let us destroy the crystal and focus our efforts on more pertinent threats."

Clarisa ripped her hands from Brisa's hold. "Eve is amassing great power without me, the mortal kingdoms are due to attack our lands once more, and the Strix will use our vulnerability to their advantage. We do not have much time left to quarrel about a decision that I stand firm on."

"All we are saying—" Brisa began.

Clarisa snapped, "This isn't a discussion!"

Tabor's nostrils flared, Brisa bit her lip,

but neither argued back. Clarisa took a moment to compose herself, realizing that this was the first time she ever spoke to them out of turn.

"I am the only hope the Blackthorn has to prevail." She pulled the luring crystal and its thin silver chain from her neck. "The oracles can show us the way. You have to trust me."

"We trust that you believe so," Tabor crossed his arms.

Clarisa ignored him. "I need their visions to make sense of my own. They were right when they told me about Eve. She is what is stopping me—us—from resurrecting Isila."

"Then why not work *with* her?"

"Because she doesn't deserve it!" The words slipped venomously from Clarisa's mouth. "Eve is not one of us. I have seen what has become of her. We must seek the oracles' guidance once more."

"Then do it yourself," Tabor snapped. "We will not take part in you destroying yourself. Do you think we do not see how you look after the crystal? How it consumes you?"

Clarisa closed the distance between them, coming face-to-face with him, meeting his dark, narrowed eyes. "Tell me, how long has a familiar lived without their witch?"

THE SUMMONING CIRCLE MADE OF THIN ROPE WAS LAID IN HER ROOM, the candles lit, the hint of sage from their cleansing still lingered in the air, the crystal placed gently in the center with Clarisa. On either side of her, Tabor and Brisa began chanting low and deliberate.

Her chambers darkened, the candles flickered, and soon she saw them. The three oracles emerged from the pitch-black corner of the room. Amia, Sybila, and Diani, each representing the different stages of creation—youth and innocence, maturity and life, wisdom and experience. They appeared much like they did the last time Clarisa had summoned them, except their robes. They were no longer dark gray, but a lighter, subtler shade.

The oracles stood before her, and Clarisa righted her shoulders.

"She summons us once more," said Sybila.

"Summons us for answers," replied Diani.

"A summons of desperation," added Amia.

Clarisa swallowed, trying to not let their remarks hinder her. "Last I was here, you told me that my sister was the prophesied daughter. The Blood of the Blackthorn, the one who would resurrect our goddess—"

"Ah, the little half-witch, she still does not listen," Sybila interrupted.

"She listens not with her magic."

"She listens with her mortal ears."

"What do you mean? I remember what you said."

"She wishes to know her fate."

"If she can still be prophesied."

"If she can have ultimate *power*."

"No! No, that is not what I want." She righted her shoulders trying to maintain control. "I wish to know if I can resurrect our goddess without harming Eve?"

"You have already embraced the magic of your ancestors."

"You have killed with it."

"You have sealed your fate with it."

"Why are you not answering my question?"

A thin silence stretched as the oracles stared at Clarisa, assessing her from beneath their hoods. Clarisa tried to concentrate, focusing instead on the other reasons she summoned them.

"Can you tell me of the Unclaimed Wastes?"

Sybila reached a hand toward her, and Clarisa took a step back.

"We graced you with a gift when you last summoned us."

Clarisa peered over at her familiars, who were focused on their chanting.

The hag stones?

"I—I thought it was for my dreams."

"The stone will not quell your nightmares."

"The truth that appears in your sleep."

"The visions that keep you awake."

Clarisa could not think of a response. She recalled only the nightmare of Eve as a young girl holding the grimoire in her hands, her red eyes full of hate and wickedness. The oracles took a collective step toward her. Clarisa shifted back once more.

"What about the Unclaimed Wastes?"

The oracles raised their hands; a white orb appeared between them and Clarisa. She peered at the orb, watching as something moved within. It was a snowstorm, violent and heavy. She could hear screams coming from it. It took all of her might not to touch it.

"There," Sybila mused, flicking her hand and making the orb disappear. "Your magic fades."

"Frozen by the flame."

"In the silver storm."

"That doesn't make sense. How is that possible?" The questions burst through Clarisa, her panic rising at the thought of her power being . . . vulnerable.

The oracles moved closer.

"With souls of the covens."

"You can summon her."

"Summon without her precious book."

They closed in on Clarisa, their hands outstretched. For the first time she looked upon them closely; their fingers appeared decayed and long. The flesh seemed to melt off their bones falling in hideous shreds onto the stone floor.

Clarisa couldn't move, couldn't speak, all she could hear were the chanting of her familiars.

Sybila's nails barely brushed Clarisa's cheek, making her flesh crawl.

It was putrid and cold as ice, leaving a chill in its grasp. She wanted to scream, to move, but something grounded her to the spot.

"She will do nicely."

"She can bring her back."

"She will—"

The oracles were gone.

And Clarisa fell hard to the ground.

She could hear Tabor and Brisa thanking the goddess and closing the circle.

"Never again, Clarisa," Tabor snapped as he began winding the rope.

Brisa collected the candles but avoided Clarisa's stare.

It was over, and despite the oracles' attempted attack, Clarisa was disappointed. Once again, she was left with more questions than answers. She pulled the crystal from where it rested in the center of the circle and placed it back over her head.

"What is happening?"

Clarisa and her familiars whipped their heads to the chamber door, and there stood Ana. Wide eyed and terrified.

"Ana!" Clarisa stood, a bit wobbly. "It's not what it looks like."

"Summoning oracles?! They've been forbidden for centuries!"

She backed to the door, and even as Clarisa approached, she raised her hands to keep distance.

"No, no. They're helping me. I need them."

Ana narrowed her eyes, "that's what they want you to believe."

"You don't understand—"

"No, I understand perfectly." She scowled. "It's why you've been so angry lately."

"I'm not angry, I'm scared." She tried to grab Ana's hands. "Ana, the Blackthorn will fall without my magic. But I can't save us alone. I can't defeat more than a few ships at a time, what if the mortals send armies of them? You said so yourself, 'magic isn't immortal.'"

Ana shoved her away, moving out of Clarisa's grasp. "So you resort to forbidden magic? Where did you even learn about this?"

Clarisa wanted to tell her, wished she could, but Navir's voice trailed in her thoughts like a warning.

I can't tell her. It's too dangerous.

"I—"

"What do you think will happen when it has taken over you? Do you think that you will stop at summoning them once?!"

Clarisa shifted her eyes to the floor.

Ana lifted her fingers to Clarisa's chin, forcing her face up. "This isn't the first time, is it?"

Clarisa couldn't meet her gaze, shame taking over.

"Answer me!"

"No."

Ana dropped her hands, her shoulders slumped as if all the air from her body escaped her. Clarisa tried to comfort her, but Ana pushed her hand aside.

She turned her eyes to Tabor and Brisa, standing silently behind Clarisa. "And *you*, you are sworn to protect her!"

Tabor stepped forward, but Ana raised her hand, stopping him, "I don't want to hear your excuses."

She took a few steps back, her dark eyes narrowing on Clarisa for a tense moment.

"What have you become?"

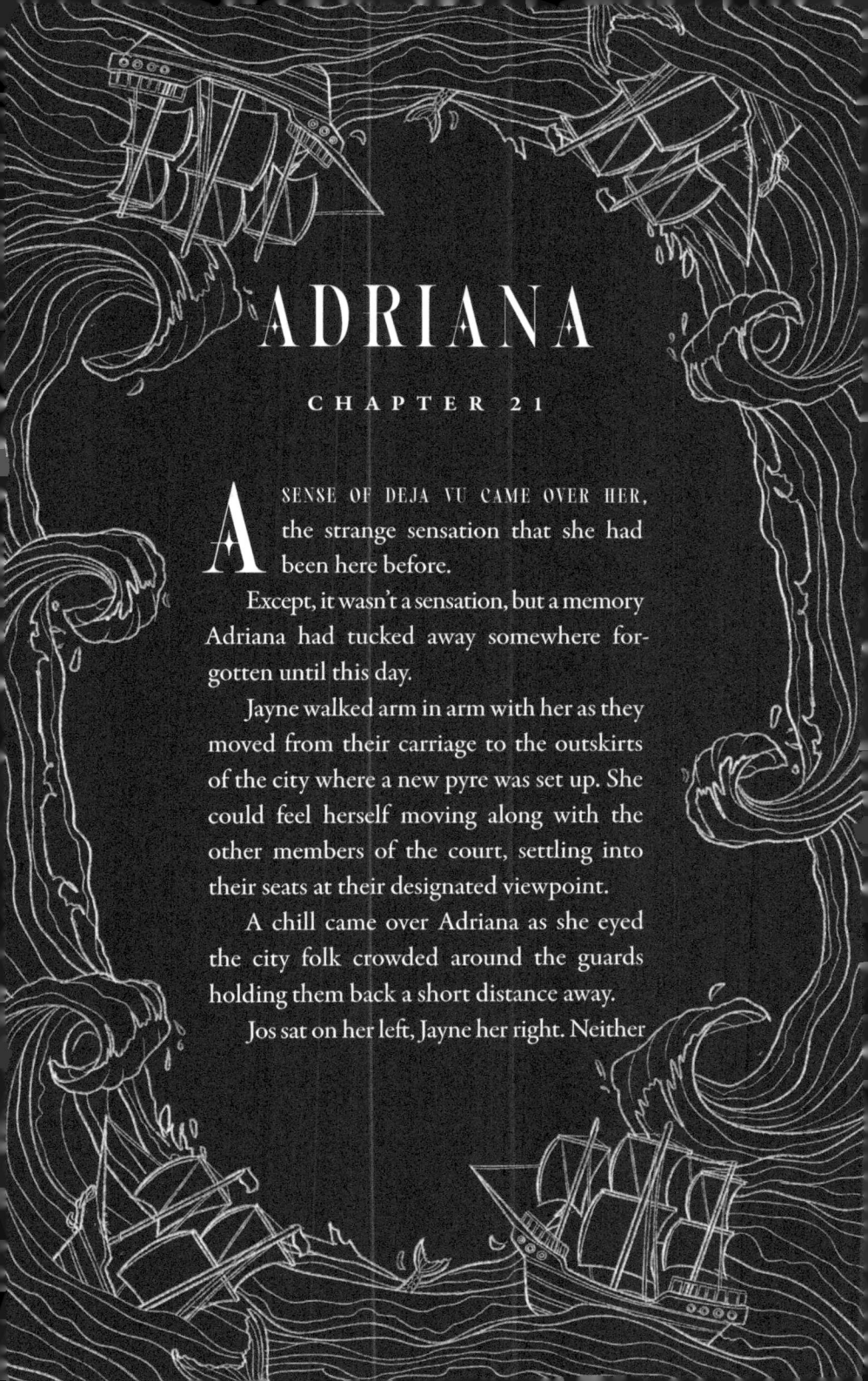

ADRIANA

CHAPTER 21

A SENSE OF DEJA VU CAME OVER HER, the strange sensation that she had been here before.

Except, it wasn't a sensation, but a memory Adriana had tucked away somewhere forgotten until this day.

Jayne walked arm in arm with her as they moved from their carriage to the outskirts of the city where a new pyre was set up. She could feel herself moving along with the other members of the court, settling into their seats at their designated viewpoint.

A chill came over Adriana as she eyed the city folk crowded around the guards holding them back a short distance away.

Jos sat on her left, Jayne her right. Neither

of them were particularly comforting to be with.

Elder Borgias walked up the steps, settling behind the podium as they awaited what was sure to come. Screams and raucous cries echoed from beyond the street, growing louder as the sounds of a wagon moved closer. Two women were tied behind it in iron chains being forced to walk barefoot through the streets in nothing but thin, linen dresses.

The women protested their punishment, claiming their innocence as they were tied to the stake. They cried for their families, their children, their lives. Tears pricked the corners of Adriana's eyes.

"Princess"—Jayne handed her a handkerchief—"your heart is too pure. Do not cry for evil, for it will think you a worthy victim."

Her words disturbed Adriana, but she took the handkerchief and dabbed her eyes with it, trying not to meet Jayne's. "Thank you, of course."

"I wear white to celebrate this day of victory against evil, against sin, against these abominations against the gods!" Borgias roared.

The women cried, and unlike the last burning as the stakes went up in flames, there were no eerie voices emanating from the women. No magic, no merciful quick fire. There was only the agony of a slow, painful death.

Jos stood suddenly as the flames finally killed the women's cries. And Adriana stood with him.

He turned to her, both aware of the people around them watching.

"I cannot watch them die as my sister did," he whispered urgently, an exposed side she had yet to see.

Adriana placed her arm in his and they both moved toward the carriages, leaving the rest of the court behind to watch what little remained of the burning.

"I'm so sorry you had to witness that."

Jos stopped, turning to meet her gaze. He ran his fingers absent-mindedly through his hair. "I thought I wanted revenge. But this"— he gestured to the burning and the crowd—"this is not what I meant. None of this will ever bring Felicity back."

"What are you saying?"

Jos tensed his jaw, his eyes burning into hers as if begging her to understand. "Do you feel safer, Princess? Do these burnings make you feel closer to your people?"

"No," she admitted.

He pulled to the carriage away from the listening ears of the guards nearby, "I know you do not know me well, but I do not consider myself a tyrant."

"I—"

"Were they given a trial?"

She knew the answer to this without having to be told. "No."

He gestured to the pyre, his nostrils flaring with frustration. "What did you make of that spectacle?"

Adriana turned once more, seeing that the flames were now reduced to ash and the crowd was beginning to disperse. She swallowed, hoping she could trust his confidence.

"They were not witches," she breathed, her hands trembled as she spoke aloud for the first time her darkest, truest thoughts. "They were women."

ADRIANA STARED UNCOMFORTABLY AT HER FOOD, TOO DISTURBED FOR hunger as she sat next to Jos and Gabrielle. Her brother, Marc, was in deep conversation with Lord Wesley at the other end of the table. All the rest of the seats filled with council members and strangers she was quite unfamiliar with, guests of her brothers from gods knew where.

She looked around them. The servants, too, were strangers in the space. Faces she did not recognize looked back at her or toward the floor. She missed seeing Dakon's gaze, when his bold green eyes met hers with longing and warmth from across the room. For the hundredth time that week, she wondered where he was and if he was thinking about her anymore.

"It seems we are not among friends, are we, Princess?" Gabrielle whispered, raising her glass and drinking the contents of it in one sitting. She seemed far more perturbed than usual, her hair barely held together by pins that slid down her tendrils.

"No, it does not," she whispered back, reaching over to fix Gabrielle's hair.

A man a few seats down raised a brow in Adriana's direction. She finished her task and quickly forced a bit of pork into her mouth, chewing to distract herself. His stare was burning through her; she could feel it.

"Do you have any plans for your honeymoon, Gabrielle?" Jos asked.

Gabrielle scoffed. "Marc wishes to visit the Mistral Islands, only the gods know why. I wished to go to Rubianes Keep, at least they would have enough wine to sedate me into a pleasant stupor." She raised her glass, and a servant came to fill it.

"The Mistral Islands?" Adriana tilted her head.

Gabrielle's family was from a minor house there in the southern shores, their trade in making ships and becoming wealthy from it. In the northern section lived Adriana's aunt, Unella, lady of the Mistral Islands. It had been years since her family had visited. Her father had fallen out with his sister before Adriana was even born.

"Yes, it's dreadful," Gabrielle rolled her eyes, taking a sip. "I long to get away from the Dallise Sea, so full of death and decay. But no, until I can give your brother a child, I am stuck by his side."

Jos shifted uncomfortably in his chair, focusing intently on his glass.

"I'm sorry." Adriana placed a hand on hers. Gabrielle initially tensed, but did not shy away from it. Then, her shoulders sagged a bit and her eyes softened.

"No, I'm sorry. I have spoken out of turn. I am happy that your brother takes such good care of me and that your family continues to welcome me as your own."

Adriana's eyes flicked to Marc, laughing jovially with the men around him, not a care in the world. All the while his wife was clearly miserable, swallowed by grief and drink.

The strangers around the table eyed them suspiciously, one man clearing his throat loudly until Adriana pulled her hand back from Gabrielle.

"Of course," Adriana said, "but if you should need anything, please tell me. It cannot be easy to celebrate when you are still mourning."

Gabrielle bit her lip but said nothing. She lifted her glass once more, taking a long swig. Her fingers trembled around the stem and accidentally spilled the rest of the wine. Servants rushed to clean it up and offered Gabrielle handkerchiefs for her ruined dress.

"Sister!" Marc called out to her. Adriana looked up, the feeling of dread instinctual as she met her brother's eyes.

"Yes?"

"Come here." He waved Adriana toward him. The room silenced, and Jos began to stand from his seat, before Marc waved a hand dismissively. "Do you look like my sister? No, just her."

Adriana stood, trying to keep a calm demeanor as she made her way down the long table to where her brother and Lord Wesley sat. A servant brought out a chair, placing it next to Marc, he gestured for her to sit.

Marc peered down the table at the rest of the guests, and soon the conversation began to pick up once more, drowning out the silence. Her brother turned to Wesley.

"Lord Wesley, how many eligible, noble bachelors are there in the kingdom?" Marc tilted his head to his adviser.

Wesley smirked. "About fifty, Your Majesty."

"Hmm, and how old are these men?"

"Most are widows, nearing the end of their days to put it lightly."

"Rich?"

"About thirty."

"Excellent."

Adriana furrowed her brows, confused. "Why are you speaking of this?"

Marc turned to Adriana, narrowing his eyes. "My *sweet* sister. I am merely weighing my options for you."

"But I am betrothed to Jos."

Marc ignored her, "I see you commiserating with my wife as if you have any say in the matters of my marriage. Perhaps, it would do you good to be matched with someone who could make you hold your tongue. And if Jos won't do it, then I will have to find someone who will."

Adriana's eyes widened, speechless.

"Oh, so you can be quiet. Good," Marc hissed. "Now run along and speak of pretty dresses or sewing. You are depressing my wife."

Adriana stood, every bit of her tense with shock and anger. She bowed and Marc caught her arm, gripping it tight.

"And don't forget to smile."

He released her, and she continued back to her seat, not bothering to say another word to anyone for the rest of the dinner.

ADRIANA WALKED AMONGST THE DINNER CROWD INTO THE HALL, FOCUSED on getting back to her chambers in peace, when a hand grabbed hers.

"Jos, Jos?! What are you doing, where are you taking me?" she hissed, trying to pull against his firm grip.

Jos didn't answer, instead pulling her into a corner alcove of the hallway out of notice. He released her.

"If you don't tell me why I am here, I swear to you I will scream."

Jos sighed, pinching the bridge of his nose. "Please, don't. There isn't much time."

"What're you talking about? Betrothals can last months if not years."

"Not the betrothal." He placed his hands on Adriana's shoulders, leveling with her. "You and I are nothing but a distraction to what is really going on."

"Of course we are," she huffed, feeling lighter by confirming it aloud, even if it was in hushed tones.

"Exactly, except, I don't think it's going to stop. And—and haven't you noticed all the new guests lately? There is something very wrong with what is happening in this castle. There are talks of continuing attacks in the Blackthorn, there are burnings happening daily. People are afraid."

"What are you suggesting?"

He looked back into the hall and, satisfied it was empty, whispered, "I have sources informing me that your brother is targeting critics of his rule. A minor lord's wife was recently burned in Larrea after being accused by the crown of witchcraft, there are talks of another rebellion. One that could spell the death of your brother and those sworn to him. It's gaining traction throughout the kingdom."

She nearly forgot to breathe; *another war in Givensmir?*

"I fear the time may soon come when we may need allies. Powerful ones should we need to escape."

Adriana knew he did not include her brother. If a rebellion was successful, her brother would not live past it, but they could.

"Zafira," she responded. "I was a ward in their court when I was younger and have strong ties to the noble families there. With Zafira and Mytar, we can assure our safety, should something happen."

He looked relieved. "I would not have told you this, had I not believed I could trust you."

She nodded. "The feeling is mutual."

Jos's eyes softened. "I understand that this betrothal is not what either of us wanted, but perhaps we can use it to our advantage."

It relieved her to hear him acknowledge it, as if there was hope for her yet.

"Agreed."

No sooner had she spoken, then footsteps echoed loudly in their direction. They were too close to manage an escape, and she nearly died of fright as it approached. Without warning, Jos quickly wrapped her in his arms and kissed her tenderly. Adriana barely managed to push him off as a voice startled before them.

"Your Highness, my lord! I—"

It was Lord Agustin, surprised by seeing them in the embrace. Jos turned, holding Adriana's hand. "Forgive me, Lord Agustin, I could not help but kiss my betrothed. We are in such bliss." He kissed her knuckles tenderly, winking at her. She managed to smile back.

"Of course, of course," Agustin said quickly, bumbling over his words, unable to look either of them in the eyes. "I was heading to my chambers—"

Without another word, he quickly scampered off.

"He seemed to come out of nowhere," Adriana mused, fixing her dress skirt; there were wrinkles there now that irritated her.

Jos released her hand. "My apologies, I would rather keep up the ruse than for us to be discovered conspiring."

He appeared sincere, apologetic.

"I would have done the same, admittedly."

It would not be the first time I was caught in halls with a man . . .

Jos quickly peered out toward the hall. "Let us go before we are forced in each other's arms the rest of the night."

Adriana sighed, linking her arm in his. "Yes, how dreadful that would be."

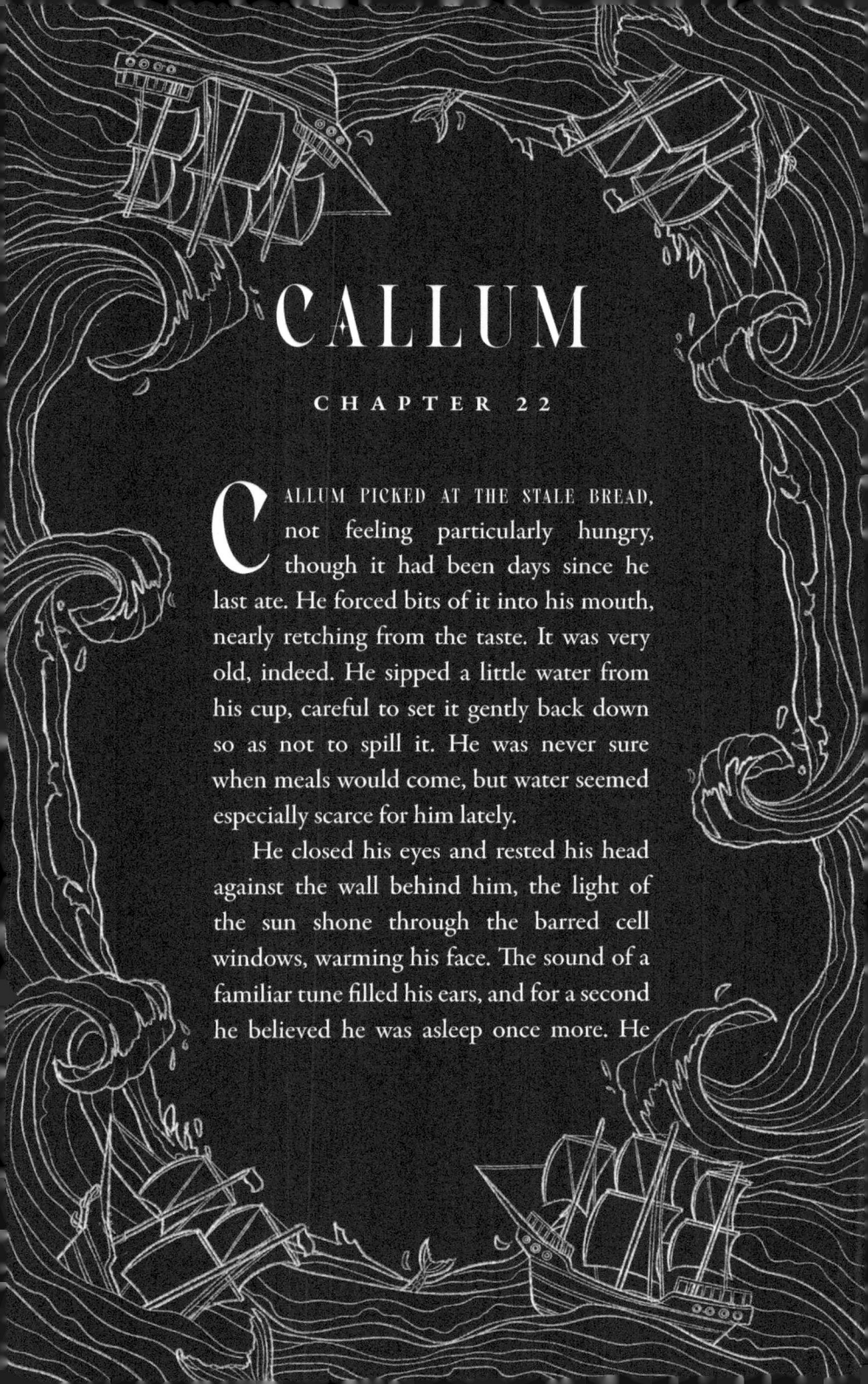

CALLUM

CHAPTER 22

ALLUM PICKED AT THE STALE BREAD, not feeling particularly hungry, though it had been days since he last ate. He forced bits of it into his mouth, nearly retching from the taste. It was very old, indeed. He sipped a little water from his cup, careful to set it gently back down so as not to spill it. He was never sure when meals would come, but water seemed especially scarce for him lately.

He closed his eyes and rested his head against the wall behind him, the light of the sun shone through the barred cell windows, warming his face. The sound of a familiar tune filled his ears, and for a second he believed he was asleep once more. He almost welcomed it, but the sound grew, and no Eryce appeared behind his eyes.

He glanced across the bars at Emilio, leaning against the wall of his cell, whistling as he inspected his bread. He ground his teeth, his hands trembling with the injustice of what he was witnessing.

"That is not your song!"

Emilio quieted suddenly, dropping the bread onto the floor.

Seconds passed before Emilio cleared his throat. "Forgive me, Lord Callum. It is a common tune amongst the people; I was simply beckoning my friend."

"Your friend?"

"Yes, the crow here." He pointed up toward the window, where a small crow lingered watching them.

Callum opened his mouth, confused.

Emilio tore off a small piece of his bread and handed it up to the crow. The bird quickly took a piece and flew away into the daylight.

"I—I do not understand," Callum managed.

"I wouldn't expect you to," Emilio replied, staring outside longingly. "Crows are very smart birds. And for the last week, this one has remembered that I gave it food. It returns every so often when I whistle and brings me a gift." He raised a small stick in front of him proudly as if it were gold instead of a flimsy piece of bark.

"W-why have I not heard this before?"

"Perhaps, because you spend your days and nights sleeping."

Callum bit the inside of his cheek.

Emilio sighed. "I miss hearing the birds. It seems these dungeons rarely entertain life outside its walls."

"Did you befriend many back home?"

He nodded. "I find we have much in common."

"How did you come upon such a discovery?"

Emilio smiled. "I am but one of seven children—most of my childhood spent locked in my room for being an errant and disappointing son. Very much unlike my older brother and sisters." He continued picking at the bread. "I would sing in my chambers and the birds would keep me company at my window, much like here."

Callum remained silent, listening. Emilio left a few more crumbs for the crows who picked at it eagerly.

"My father and older brother caught ill recently, and it fell upon me to represent my family house at the royal summons of King Marc. I was supposed to attend the funeral, pay respects to the new king, and come back home." Emilio leveled a sad glance at Callum. "But as you can see I have disappointed my father once more."

"I'm sorry," Callum managed.

"As am I. My first taste of freedom, and I am but a bird in a cage once more." He looked back up toward the crow longingly. "It has only been days for me, and it is rather depressing, I can only imagine the toll it has taken on you."

Callum faced the ground, picking at his dirty tunic to distract himself.

"It is quite all right," Emilio said gently. "We are but mortals after all."

Callum focused on a spot of blood, rubbing his fingers on it as if that would remove the stain.

"I cannot imagine anyone else who would have lasted as long as you have and still have the courage to live, to speak."

"You are too generous," was all Callum could muster.

"No," Emilio replied, "I am far from it. All of my misdeeds are what landed me here in the end, much deserved if I am being honest. The gods have interesting ways of delivering punishments."

Callum raised a brow. "Why are you here?"

Emilio shrugged. "For having questions. And for being from Larrea, I suspect. Apparently our alliance to Givensmir in the war did not matter as much as our prior one to the traitors."

Callum tried to ignore a stinging in his chest. "So, you have been imprisoned for questioning the king?"

Emilio nodded gravely. "And I suspect many will die for less."

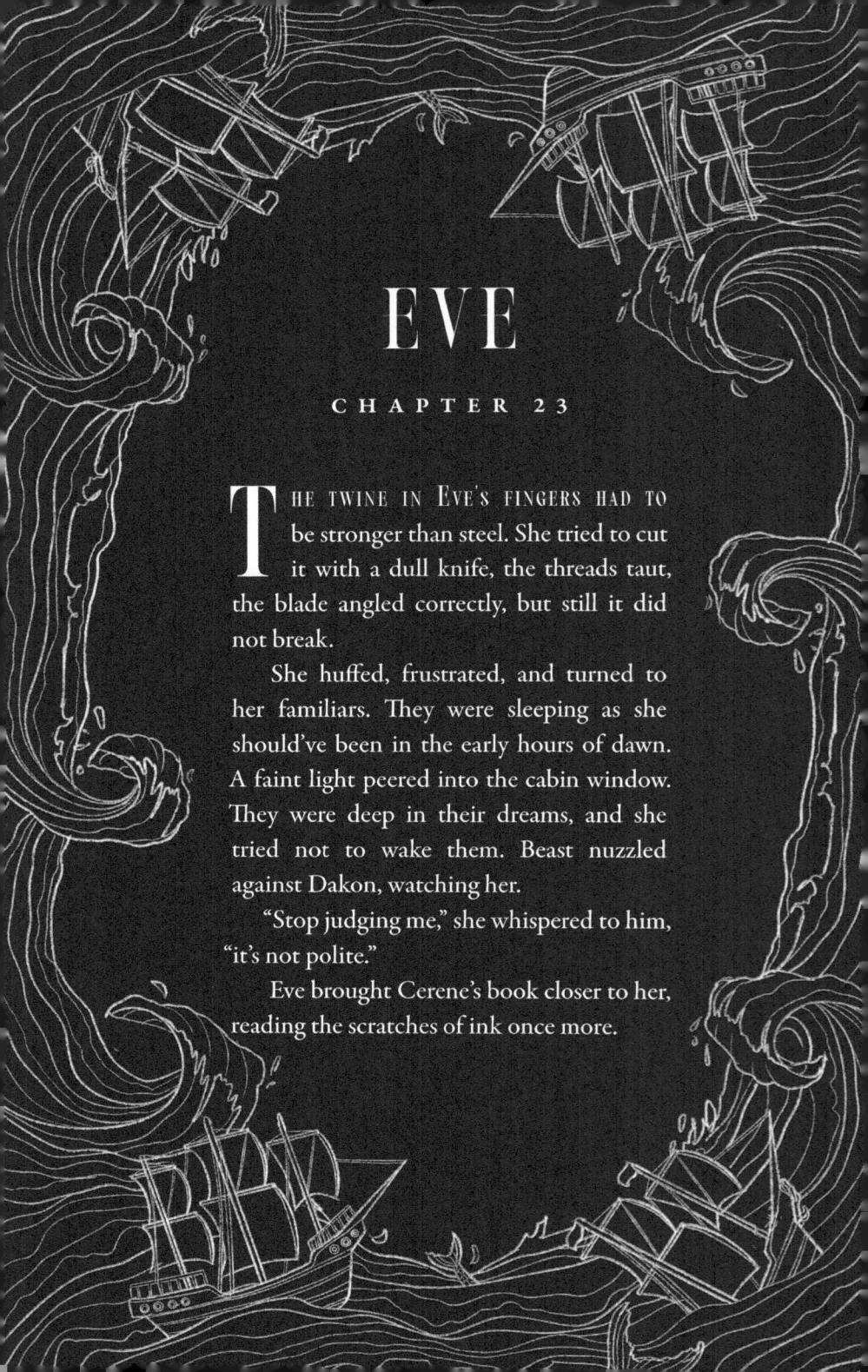

EVE

CHAPTER 23

THE TWINE IN EVE'S FINGERS HAD TO be stronger than steel. She tried to cut it with a dull knife, the threads taut, the blade angled correctly, but still it did not break.

She huffed, frustrated, and turned to her familiars. They were sleeping as she should've been in the early hours of dawn. A faint light peered into the cabin window. They were deep in their dreams, and she tried not to wake them. Beast nuzzled against Dakon, watching her.

"Stop judging me," she whispered to him, "it's not polite."

Eve brought Cerene's book closer to her, reading the scratches of ink once more.

FOR CLARITY
A circle.
A candle, lit with intention.
A clear mind.
Let it wander.

Eve sighed. "Do you think you could snap it with your jaws?" she whispered again, lifting the twine to the gytrash.

Beast tilted his head, then lowered it with a huff.

"I didn't think so."

Eve had been pulled from her nightmares with the grimoire, fresh scars settling into her skin. She needed answers. A way to focus her thoughts about what lay ahead.

Would Clarisa be in the Blackthorn?

Would the witches even know who she was?

She pulled the twine tighter with one hand, and angled the blade with her other, trying to saw through the strings once more.

Who was her sister now?

Half of the string pulled away.

Did she try coming back to save Eve?

Only a bit more force and it would give.

Did she know the truth about their mother?

The twine snapped and the force of the knife sliced downward onto her knuckles.

She gasped, quickly pulling the sleeve of her tunic over the wound, placing pressure. Standing, she faced Dakon, ready to ask for his help.

He was peacefully asleep next to Beast. His long, copper tendrils framed his calm face. For once, he appeared serene and blissful. Guilt racked her. She would be waking him to yet another mishap of her making.

Eve looked down at her hand, a faint red stained the cloth.

How much pain would this cause him to heal?

She stepped back, wrapped hand against her, and without another thought left the cabin.

Outside, the wind whipped wildly at her hair, the sun barely visible in the cool distance. The water lapped against the ship, and she could nearly taste the salt of the sea.

The pirates worked around her as she moved like a spirit. She leaned against the railing, slowly unwrapping her hand. The cut was messy, but didn't appear too concerning. The blood was slow and bright, and while the pain was bearable, it still stung in the saltwater spraying overboard.

"I seem to always find you in one state or another, Lady."

She turned quickly, putting her wounded hand behind her. Izan crossed his arms, staring amused down at her.

"It's—"

"Another tattoo?"

"Maybe."

He took a few steps closer, raising his hand to her. She eyed it suspiciously.

"Can I take a look?"

She glanced about the deck, the pirates seemed far too focused on their duties, but she didn't want to give them any cause to speak of their interaction. Izan raised a brow.

"Or we could go to the healer's cabin?"

HIS CABIN WAS TIGHTER THAN HER OWN, WITH ENOUGH ROOM FOR A small makeshift bed, a desk and stools in the corner and satchels filled with herbs and healer's tools lining the sides.

He pulled out a stool and gestured her to sit, lifting her arm onto the desk.

"Might I ask what caused this?" He inspected her knuckles. The blood was no longer seeping from the wound, but the cut was deeper than she realized as he cleaned it.

"An accident."

"Hmm." He rifled through one of his satchels. "Does your familiar know?"

"I don't know what you're talking about." She cast her eyes around as he pulled out a flask. "Is this really the right time for you to drink?"

Izan smirked. "It's not for me, it's for you." He passed it to her.

"Why would I need this, are you not going to use magic?"

Izan laughed. "Magic is not the solution to everything, Lady. You only need a few sutures to fix this up."

Eve's eyes widened. "Sutures?!"

"Or I could cauterize it?"

Eve ripped her hand from his.

Izan's grin widened. "How else would you like to heal it? Seeing as you didn't ask your familiar, I expect you would have ended up this way regardless."

Eve bit her lip. "I can go now and ask him."

Izan softly grasped her hand. "And let you miss the fun of mortality? I think not."

He pushed the flask toward her once more, and Eve eyed it warily. "Drink, or this will be far more painful."

She scoffed. "And I thought healers were supposed to be gentle." She raised the flask and took a long sip. It was bitter on her tongue and burned her throat. She gagged at the taste.

Izan chuckled, adjusting her knuckles to the candlelight.

Before Eve could speak again she realized the drink had numbed her senses. Her hand no longer hurt; in truth, she could barely feel it at all.

Izan began to tend to her wound, his deft and agile hands making quick work of her sutures.

"Now, why didn't you ask your familiar to heal you? Did you finally grant him mercy from taking your pain?"

"No. I mean, yes." She sighed, her mind clouded. "We haven't been on the best terms."

Izan glanced at her. "Did you kill his mother?"

"No, I don't know his mother."

"His father then."

"No."

"His brother, his lover?"

"No!"

"Ah," he said as he tied off the suture, "then I suppose you'll both be fine."

He raised her knuckles out to her, and she inspected them. The sutures glinted against the light, though a bit blurred in her vision.

"Thank you," she mumbled.

Izan pulled the flask back, placing it in his satchel along with the rest of his supplies. "That wasn't so bad, was it?"

"It wasn't," she admitted.

Izan sat straight in his chair, running his eyes over Eve. "You're new at this, aren't you?"

"I'm afraid I don't know what you mean." She began to roll her eyes but stopped herself. The motion made her dizzy.

He leaned closer. "You don't need to lie to me. We are the keepers of each other's secrets, are we not?"

Eve stared back into his dark eyes. Her heart thrumming loudly in her ears. "You ask a lot of questions for a mere healer."

"You don't ask enough."

She narrowed her eyes, feeling bold. "Who are you?"

"Izan."

"No, not your name."

"Then I'm a healer, and we are back where we started."

She lifted her chin, refusing to back down. "I saw you running away, when you touched my hand on the island."

He clenched his jaw.

172

"Who were you running from?"

Izan shook his head. "Witches."

"What luck," Eve scoffed, "you ended up on a ship with one."

"No, these are not just any witches." He placed his hands together on the table.

"What are they?"

"Nightmares."

"That narrows it down."

He sighed, shaking his head. "I was orphaned, left upon their shores when they found me as a boy. They raised me as their own, taught me their craft. By the time I understood what they were doing—all I could do was run."

Eve leaned in. "And so you went to sea."

His eyes flashed to hers, and he shifted closer. "Yes."

"But how?"

"It's where I truly belonged."

"That doesn't make any sense."

Izan tilted his head, and Eve realized in the haze of the candle-light that they were only inches apart. "As I said, you're new to this."

Eve knit her brow, suddenly feeling warm.

"Perhaps I can help you," he murmured, "to understand what you've been missing."

His lips were nearly touching hers, the walls seemed to close in, her body felt hot. "I would like that."

He lifted his hand to her face, exposing the faint blackthorn scars on his arms from when he healed her days prior. He pushed a stray lock of hair and tucked it behind her ear.

"Your skin is burning," he mused, removing his hand from her.

Eve longed for his touch once more, but Izan sat back, studying her. She suddenly felt foolish and stupid.

"It always does that," she sputtered, crossing her arms. "It has nothing to do with you."

There was a loud knock on Izan's door.

Eve stood, startled. The tension gave way.

The door opened, and two pirates stumbled in.

"Izan," the one Eve recognized as Niani called out, "Alonso here thought it was a good idea to spar with the guest. Fix him up, won't you?"

Izan stood, moving to the pirates as Alonso kept insisting he was well enough for another duel. His arm bled through his tunic, and Eve pitied him.

Hope he enjoys sutures.

"Dakon?" Eve asked.

"No," Niani replied, flicking her aqua eyes knowingly between Eve and Izan. "Pazel. Seems to be a mighty swordsman."

Eve couldn't stifle a laugh as Izan sat Alonso down to inspect his wound. "Are you certain?"

"Do you doubt your protectors, miss?"

Eve's eyes widened, realizing there was no humor in her tone. "No, I—"

"You're lucky. If I had half the swordsmen he is, then I wouldn't be here, would I?"

Speechless and feeling out of place in the cramped cabin, Eve closed the door on her way out, while Niani moved to tend to Alonso. As she walked back onto the deck, she mulled over Niani's words.

Who is she?

Eve lifted her eyes and beheld Pazel sparring with another pirate, remarking on their techniques. She watched as they clashed their swords under the cloudless sky, not realizing how quickly Pazel had picked up the skill.

While Eve spent many moons wallowing in her frustration, the world and the people in it were growing without her. She raised her stitched knuckles, focusing on the small wounds. The skin had already begun to heal, closing in beneath the suture.

Perhaps, it was time for her to grow too.

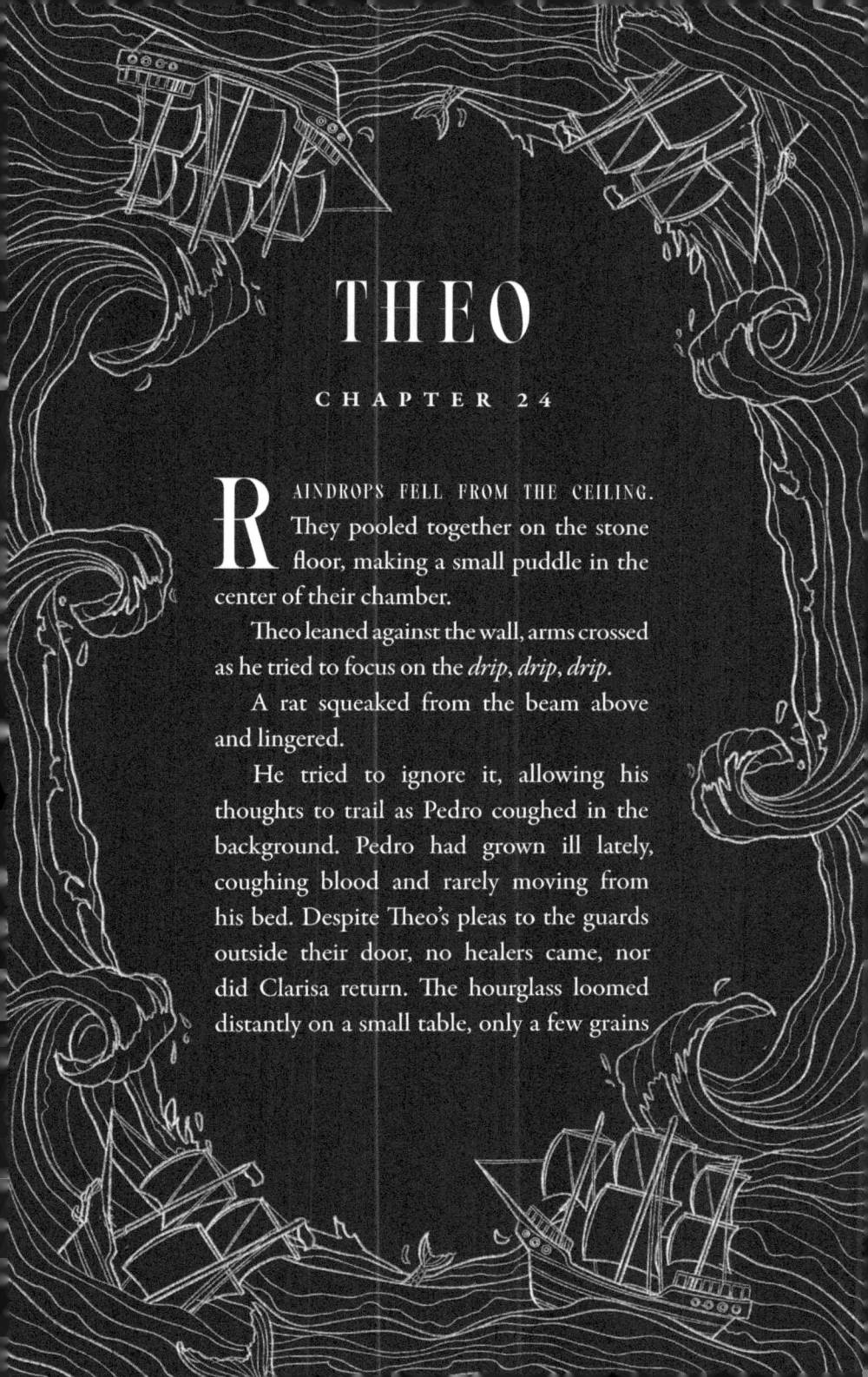

THEO

CHAPTER 24

R AINDROPS FELL FROM THE CEILING. They pooled together on the stone floor, making a small puddle in the center of their chamber.

Theo leaned against the wall, arms crossed as he tried to focus on the *drip, drip, drip*.

A rat squeaked from the beam above and lingered.

He tried to ignore it, allowing his thoughts to trail as Pedro coughed in the background. Pedro had grown ill lately, coughing blood and rarely moving from his bed. Despite Theo's pleas to the guards outside their door, no healers came, nor did Clarisa return. The hourglass loomed distantly on a small table, only a few grains at the bottom. He hoped that when the sand had finished making its way down—which at this pace may be months—that they would be killed quickly or freed, even if it was on a single boat over the Dallise.

Theo felt his side, the wound that had at one time been fatal was now a large scar that trailed along his ribs. He closed his eyes, wishing that Eryce could have healed this way too.

How long had Marc been planning the ambush?

He often asked himself this, wondering if there was any way he could have prevented Eryce's death. But he came up empty.

The night their father ordered their attack, Marc looked afraid. Nothing like a man who was orchestrating a mutiny. Even after all the carnage, Theo struggled with understanding Marc's actions.

What if something had forced his hand?

"I'm bored, Theo. I fear that will kill me before this illness," Pedro groaned.

Theo knelt next to him. "It will pass, as most sicknesses do, my friend."

"You may be right," Pedro nodded. "It would be too cruel a punishment for all the women back home, even for the gods, should I die."

Theo laughed. "While you have your humor, there is still hope."

Pedro coughed into his handkerchief, wiping the blood from his lips. He let out a shaky breath. "I sometimes dream that we are home—the sunlight warming me in its embrace, the stone castle walls smooth beneath my touch, the shimmering waters as far as the eye could see—only to wake up in this gloom. Of everything we are to endure, I am most afraid that I will never see the sun again."

Theo grasped Pedro's hand. "I cannot promise you anything, but I swear to you that if I have any power to make it so, I will carry you to sunlight myself."

Pedro closed his eyes, his face pale. "I expect nothing less from my knight."

Theo chuckled. "Of course, Prince."

Pedro laughed along with him, then stopped, clutching his side. "Apparently, I have more injuries than I initially thought."

Theo tensed. "They will send someone soon I am sure. We are still waiting to hear back from Marc. He may choose to spare us." Theo did not believe his words and hated how unconvincing they sounded from his lips. He could hear the damn rat scampering to the other end of the beam.

Pedro scoffed. "Marc only ever cared about Marc." He hesitated, as if considering his next words. "While we are on our deathbeds, I must admit that I did not care for your father either. I am sorry for his loss only as it affects you."

Theo sighed. "I am far less disturbed by it than I care to admit. He was sick, I do not believe he would have lasted much longer."

Pedro opened his eyes slowly. "Do you believe Eve did it?"

"Yes." It surprised Theo how quickly the word parted from him.

Pedro coughed and Theo adjusted him in the bed, patting his back. Pedro wiped his mouth with the back of his hand, taking a deep breath to settle himself.

"I don't blame her," Pedro said.

Theo recalled the last night he saw Eve; he broke her heart with his parting words. His heart had broken too. He had been so close to changing his mind and running away with her before Callum entered the room.

"I loved her," Theo breathed, "and it was my fault she felt hopeless." He stood, pacing, "I'm certain she had no other choice."

"It's not your fault."

"It is."

"Your father would have brutalized her; Eve did what she had to do to survive."

Theo cast his eyes to the puddle on the floor, the rain still dripped there. "I was foolish enough to believe that my father would have spared her simply because I asked him to. He was just waiting for me to leave so he could do as he wished."

"As did Lord Wesley." Pedro sighed. "He told me the king planned to release Eve after having a brief word with her."

Theo straightened. "Did he happen to say anything else?"

Pedro furrowed his brow. "He did inquire about Clarisa, asked if Eve ever spoke of her."

"Why?"

"I'm not certain, something about how it would have been easier with both of them."

The rat let out a final squeak, and Theo watched as it scurried into a hole. He hated that rat. Theo turned his attention back to Pedro.

"What would have been easier?"

"I didn't think to ask. I thought he meant Eve would have stayed out of trouble had her sister been alive. Now, I am not so sure."

The door swung open with a loud thud against the wall, Theo and Pedro quickly turned to their guest.

Navir walked through, and a guard closed the door behind him.

Theo righted his shoulders. "You don't need to make such grand appearances. There is no one here but us."

Navir smirked. "But you are my humble guests. Under confinement, but guests nonetheless."

Theo narrowed his eyes. "We need a healer for Prince Theo."

Navir's eyes trailed to Pedro, then back to Theo. "They are all indisposed at the moment, unfortunately."

Before Theo could impart some choice words, Navir continued, "But I come with news."

Theo raised a brow.

Navir pulled out a scroll and handed it to Pedro. Pedro took it in his weak hands, and Theo moved next to him as he unfurled the parchment.

"It seems your brother has sent his reply. Quite the poet, I might add."

Theo looked upon the words inked onto the single parchment. They barely took any space, the message clear and brutal.

> *Kill them*
> *and send me their*
> *heads as a parting gift.*
> *King Marc of Givensmir and the Four Seas,*
> *Defender of Mortality and the Faith of the Five*

Theo ripped the scroll from Pedro's hands and tore it to shreds, tossing it at Navir.

"Is this your idea of a sick joke?"

Navir didn't move as the pieces flitted onto his cloak, he only looked amused. He brushed a piece of parchment from his shoulder. "It seems your king's decision is final."

Theo's nostrils flared, his chest heaving.

Marc, that fucking bastard.

"Why show us this? What do you want from us since we are of no use to you now."

"Oh, we still have use. Plenty of it."

"Bring Clarisa to us," Pedro demanded. "There is no risk in it now if you wish to kill us."

Navir laughed. "With as often as you accuse me of it, I am beginning to think you wish for death."

"Why hasn't she come back?" Theo asked, angrily closing the distance between him and Navir.

"Because I cannot force her to."

"What do you mean?"

"Must I explain? She does not wish to see you."

"Bullshit," Theo spat. "Why in all five hells would she save us, then?"

"Because even a half-witch can't fight her mortality. Consider it a gift that she didn't leave you on the sand to bleed out."

"Damn you."

"No, but your brother did."

Navir's smug face, the truth of his words was too much for Theo to handle. He swung forward, aiming for Navir's head, but hit nothing but air.

The chamber turned black.

Impossible.

Theo turned, around and around, but there was nothing. No shapes or shadows to make out in the space, nothing discernible at all.

It was as if he was blinded from life.

"Where am I?!" he demanded into the dark.

There was nothing but the echoes of his voice. It went far, too far, away.

Goosebumps raised on his flesh, and he tried to quell the panic that rose in his chest.

"Damn you! Bring me back!"

"Bring me back!"

"Bring me back!"

"Me back!"

"Back!"

"Back!"

"Back!"

The echoes trailed on and on maddeningly.

Theo breathed erratically, his muscles shook and tensed, his lips quivered, and something sinister slowly began to rise within him. Something longing to be released. The injustice of everything he had endured, his fury built with every second that passed in his dark hell. All of it became the perfect storm.

Rage. Pure Rage.

Theo shouted furiously, quickly coming undone. He swung wildly, hitting nothing, feeling nothing, seeing nothing.

Felicity, Eryce, Pedro, *Eve.*

He failed everyone he fought for; everyone was damned because of him.

"Bring me back you monster!" he screamed into the void. Hot tears rolled down his cheeks burning into his skin like Eve's touch on his flesh. He could smell the ash, feel the fresh blisters on his hands once more.

"Bring me back you monster!"

"Me back you monster!"

"Back you monster!"

"You monster!"

"Monster!"

"Monster!"

"Monster!"

He shoved his hands over his ears; the echoes pierced his skull. Theo screamed and cursed Navir's bloodline, every person who ever wronged him, every god in existence until his voice grew hoarse and his body limp.

He let himself fall, anticipating the thud against the ground, but none came. He fell and fell and fell until a blinding light consumed his vision.

Theo lifted a hand to cover his eyes, blinking until he could finally make out the rat scurrying on the beam above him.

It squeaked as it went.

Theo raised himself from the floor, Pedro stared at him, worried.

"Thank the gods you're alive," he breathed.

"What happened to me?" Theo sat up shakily.

"You tried to strike him, but then you fainted. Your eyes went white, and you fell on the floor."

Theo stood, his legs wobbly beneath him. He backed into the wall. "Where did Navir go?"

"He left moments ago."

"He—he bewitched me. I know it. I was nowhere. Th—there was

nothing," Theo sputtered, his skin prickling, his body shaking at the thought of the darkness. He had never been more terrified in his life.

"Theo?" Pedro turned to him as he lay. He kept coughing, his strength seeming to fail him. "Gods, you look like you've seen a ghost."

Theo's lips trembled as he raised his wet eyes to him. "I wish I had."

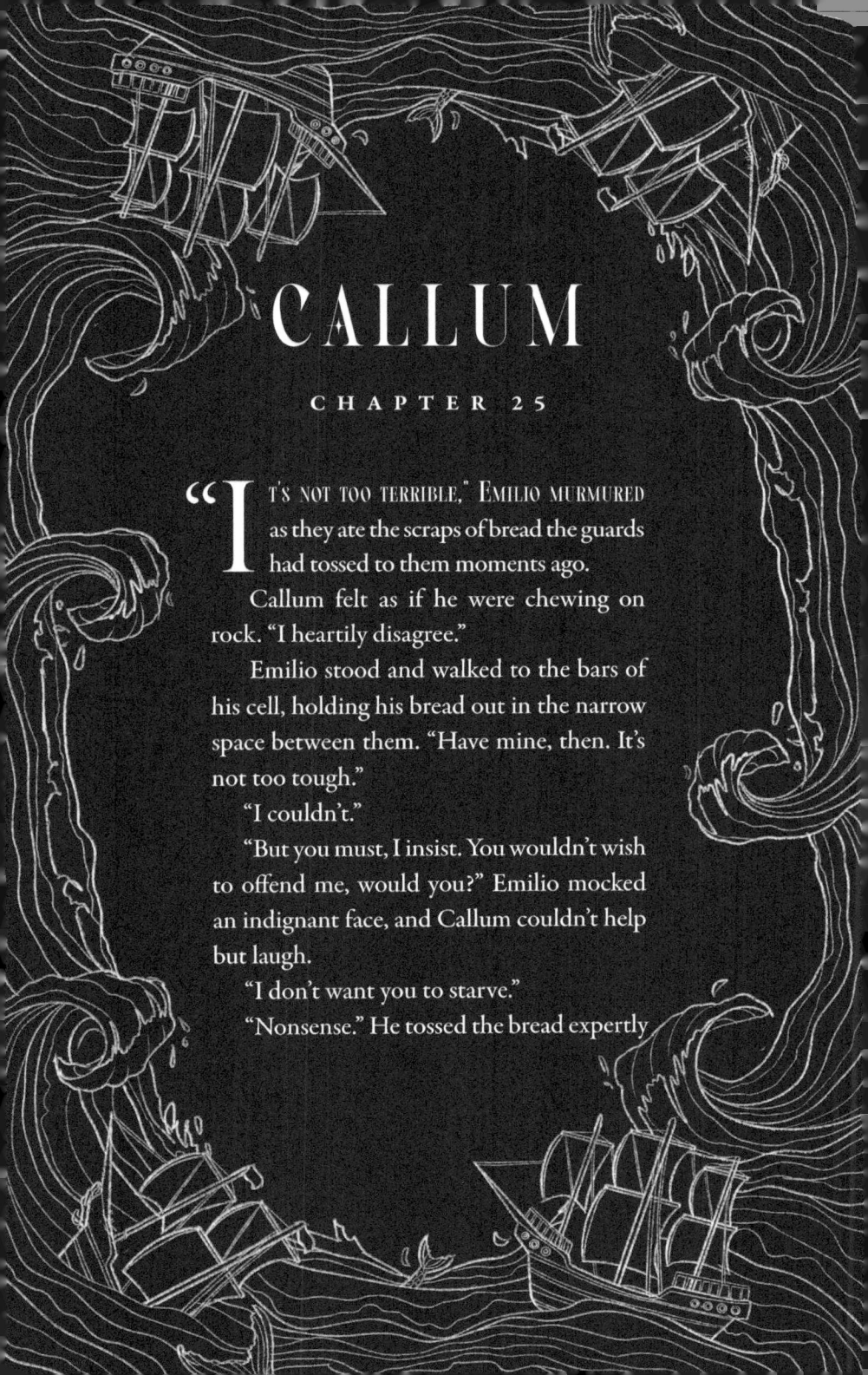

CALLUM

CHAPTER 25

"It's not too terrible," Emilio murmured as they ate the scraps of bread the guards had tossed to them moments ago.

Callum felt as if he were chewing on rock. "I heartily disagree."

Emilio stood and walked to the bars of his cell, holding his bread out in the narrow space between them. "Have mine, then. It's not too tough."

"I couldn't."

"But you must, I insist. You wouldn't wish to offend me, would you?" Emilio mocked an indignant face, and Callum couldn't help but laugh.

"I don't want you to starve."

"Nonsense." He tossed the bread expertly

through the cell, and Callum picked it up, brushing off any bits of dirt. It was softer and certainly appeared more edible.

Callum tossed his own bread back, an unfair trade but one that made him feel less guilty. Emilio grabbed and inspected it.

"They certainly wish to kill you, my dear friend. How anyone could eat this is a mystery to me." He broke it into small chunks, whistling as he did.

Callum had grown comforted by the sound over the weeks, he could nearly see Eryce singing the notes behind his closed eyes. He listened and watched as Emilio continued breaking the bread, placing it between the bars on his window. Soon, a crow came bearing a gray-black stone, taking the bread as payment.

"The crows are rather fond of you."

Emilio smiled. "I should hope so, I feed them enough."

"What do you hope to get from them?"

Emilio placed the last of his bread between the bars. "Freedom."

"Freedom?"

"Is there anything else you'd wish for?" He picked up the stone and inspected it before placing it under the straw in his cell.

Callum briefly thought of Eryce but shook his head. "I'm not sure anymore."

Emilio wiped his hands on his dirty tunic before moving closer and holding onto the bars of his cell. His face was weathered and tired now, as if he had aged years in only weeks, Callum wondered how he looked to Emilio. Perhaps a man on his deathbed.

"You still have much to live for Lord Callum. Do not let them destroy your spirit."

Callum scoffed weakly.

"Look at me. Come here."

Callum sighed but stood. He walked to his own bars and met Emilio's eyes. The narrow space between them made him feel closer than expected.

"There are forces out there fighting for you. Your imprisonment has brought questions about Marc's ability to rule, about the matter of his brothers' deaths, about everything. You will not die in this cell, that I promise you."

Callum wanted to believe him, but to what end? At what point did his spirit break first?

He could see his cold breath in front of him as he pondered his thoughts. He couldn't remember the last time Givensmir had been this cold, even in the winter.

"How can you promise this?"

"Because," Emilio breathed, "I spoke to your aunt shortly before I was imprisoned."

"My aunt?"

"Yes, quite the feisty woman Lady Tyrina is."

His aunt, the Lady of Teros, had borne no children, but had raised and named Callum as her heir. They had not seen each other in years since he came to ward in the capital.

"How?"

"When news of your imprisonment reached Teros, your aunt dispatched doves to the lower kingdoms calling upon them to join her banner. Not only for your rescue, but to discuss concerns regarding the king. It seems he is surrounding himself with peculiar fanatics who defy the five gods."

"Did the summons fail?"

"On the contrary, she received a number of lords and ladies in Teros. Most are rallying forces across the kingdom to support your release. They will fight for you if they must."

"But there has been no battle, I have seen no banners, no evidence of such attempts."

"With Givensmir's loyal army too powerful, they opted for discretion in saving you while they prepared."

"Discretion?"

185

"What better than to send a little-known son of a minor house to infiltrate their defenses."

Callum's eyes widened. "You're here because of me?"

"And from what I see there is no better cause, my lord of Teros."

Emilio bowed and Callum could do nothing but stare.

Could it be true?

Would Emilio lie to him?

"And what of Eve?"

Emilio raised a brow. "What of her?"

"Is there any word on her? Is she safe?"

Emilio cocked his head and stood. "I wonder why you worry for a witch who killed the king?"

"Because she didn't kill him, at least not out of malice. He was going to kill us. She saved my life."

Concern crossed over Emilio's face, before settling into something less severe. "I have not heard about your witch's whereabouts, only that she escaped onto a ship and fled."

Callum nodded, it was better than bad news. Despite it all, if one of his loves could make it, then he was not a failure.

"You were engaged to her, were you not?"

"Yes."

"But she is not the name you call for in your sleep?"

Callum turned. "Love has many forms. It is not singular."

Silence followed, and Callum sat with his back against the bars.

The cold day inched to a cold night and as Callum shivered on the floor, he closed his eyes. Eryce still lingered behind them.

"Emilio?"

"Yes?" His voice was close as if he had been waiting for Callum to call for him.

"Can you sing his song again?"

Without question, Emilio began the tune, singing softly into the dark night until Callum was reunited with his love once more.

186

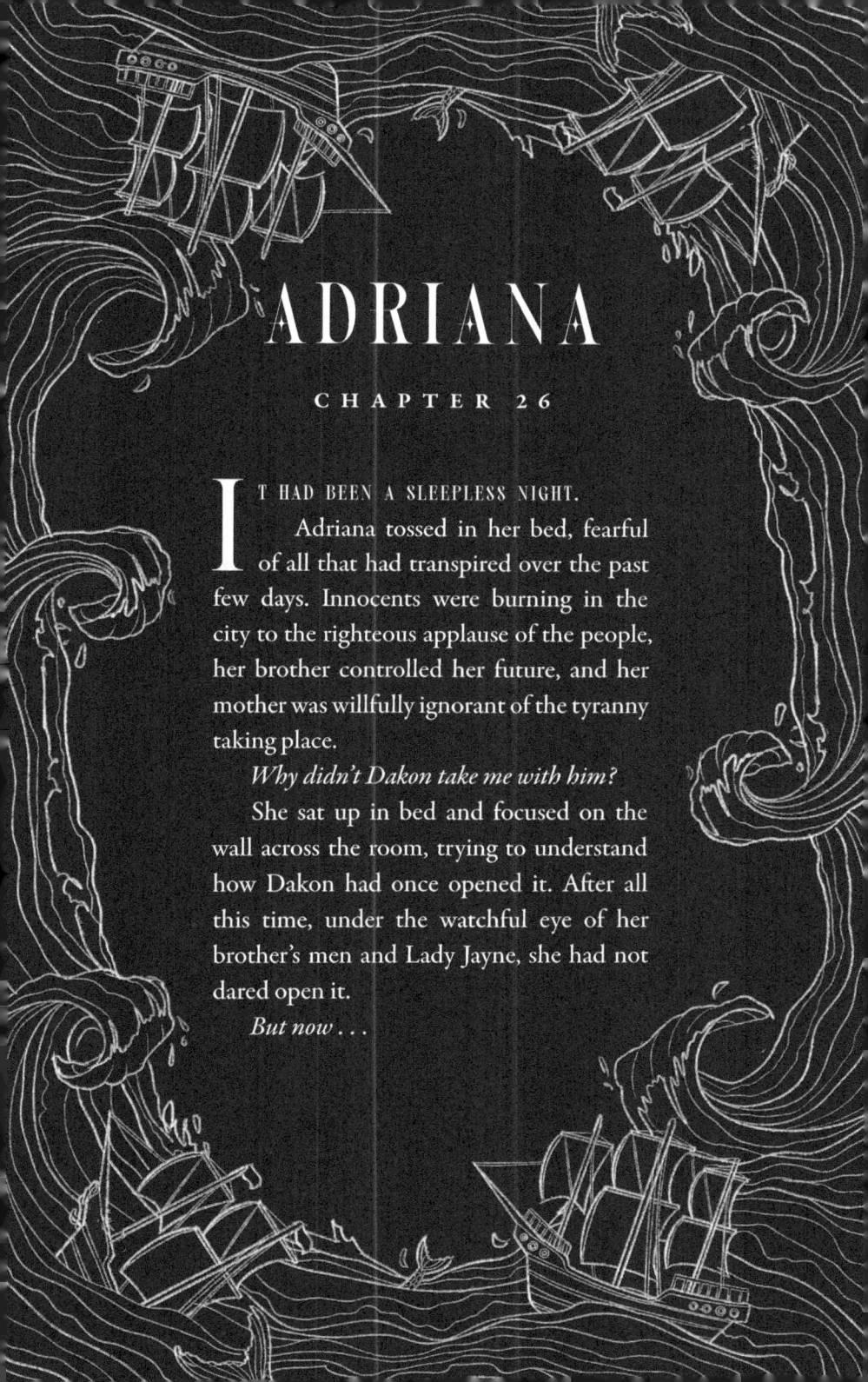

ADRIANA

CHAPTER 26

IT HAD BEEN A SLEEPLESS NIGHT.
Adriana tossed in her bed, fearful of all that had transpired over the past few days. Innocents were burning in the city to the righteous applause of the people, her brother controlled her future, and her mother was willfully ignorant of the tyranny taking place.

Why didn't Dakon take me with him?

She sat up in bed and focused on the wall across the room, trying to understand how Dakon had once opened it. After all this time, under the watchful eye of her brother's men and Lady Jayne, she had not dared open it.

But now . . .

She glanced at her door, knowing Timothy was on the other side. It was early enough, the dawn barely filtering through her balcony, the birds chirping lightly as the sun peeked out faintly from beyond the horizon.

There was enough time.

Adriana stepped out of bed, her footsteps gently padding along the floor as she made her way quietly to the wall. The dark stones stacked upon each other in tight formations did not appear to present a seal from which to part it.

"Hello?" she whispered, placing her ear on the stone. It was silent.

Adriana tried to push against it, but the wall did not give.

She traced her finger along the wall, trying to remember exactly where Dakon had made his way in from. It was cool beneath her touch, shaking off every last bit of sleep she had.

Adriana felt around the area Dakon had pushed the wall in, and while she could feel the faintest break in the seal, it did not budge.

"Damn you," she breathed, "damn you, damn you, damn you."

Frustrated, she continued pushing along the wall, making her way down the side until suddenly she moved forward just the slightest bit.

Her breath hitched; an excitement full of fear and anticipation, took over her. Adriana pushed once more, and slowly the wall groaned open until she was sure there was enough room for her to squeeze through the opening.

Of course, I only had to push the other end of the seal.

She looked back at her once inviting and safe space. There were no signs that the guards heard anything, not even movement outside her chamber door.

Adriana grabbed a candle from her desk and lit it, quickly returning to the opening. Her breathing was unsteady as she beheld the darkness that awaited her.

Before she could convince herself otherwise, Adriana moved forward into the shadows.

WITH ONLY A CANDLE TO LIGHT HER WAY, ADRIANA CONTINUED DOWN the gloomy path, remembering how Dakon once pulled her through the tunnels after saving her life from the unruly city crowd. She kept note of which way she turned, trying to remind herself of the little time she had before she needed to return to her chambers.

There were small holes along the walls of the tunnel, and peeking within a few she saw private chambers, council rooms, and even the chamber pot. She grimaced, moving forward until she heard a familiar voice.

"Reyher, how many have refused to join you?"

It was her brother's.

She stepped back until she found the hole to the room from whence his voice carried. She peeked inside and saw the golden tapestries along large windows, the seal of a merlion hanging above the fireplace, a massive desk with correspondence littering the top and behind it sat Marc. It was his solar now, and Adriana watched as he spoke to an unfamiliar man standing next to Lord Wesley.

"Most, Your Majesty," the man grumbled. "Many do not wish to anger the goddess."

"Then threaten them with death."

"We have, many of them are in the dungeons now as we speak."

"Then kill a few to send a message. Isn't that what the Strix are good for?"

"Your Majesty, we need all the magic we can get. Otherwise, our spell will be futile."

Wesley cut between the two, smirking at Reyher. "Tell me, do all witches know each other?"

Reyher knit his brow. "Uh, no, my lord."

"Are you able to tell someone is a witch simply by looking at them?"

"No, not quite."

"Exactly." He placed a hand on Reyher's shoulder. "I believe we are on the same page now, aren't we?"

Reyher's eyes widened a fraction, but he nodded, nonetheless. "Yes, of course."

"Good," Marc interjected. "Schedule a few burnings, intimidate any witches who wish to resist our call, and in due time we shall have our army." Her brother wrote something down on a piece of parchment. "Besides, burning these spare women will rid us of our population problem here in the city. I consider it a win for the crown."

"Excellent, Your Majesty," Wesley remarked.

"Now, what of Eve?"

Eve? Adriana's eyes widened and she leaned in closer to hear better.

"We have sent many doves throughout the kingdom and across the seas. Our spies last reported seeing her in Bastard's Haven. She boarded a pirate ship and left for an unknown location." Wesley clasped his hands before him, straightening his shoulders.

"A pirate ship?" Marc scoffed. "My precious Eve must be dying inside—she never liked to get dirty."

"Yes, she seems to be accompanied by two of our castle's servants. One of whom might humor you."

"Who?"

"Dakon, Your Majesty."

Marc tilted his head. "Who?"

"The royal fool."

Adriana covered her mouth to suppress a gasp. Dakon was alive and helping Eve.

Why was he doing this?

How long has he known her?

Marc roared with laughter. "Just when I thought she could stoop no lower." He wheezed between breaths. "From a fine, rich maiden to a poor beggar commiserating with the help. How humiliating."

The other men laughed with Marc, and Adriana was on the verge of tears.

"How soon do you think your people can get to her?" Marc asked Reyher, taking in deep breaths to suppress his laughter.

"Soon enough, Your Majesty. We have convinced a powerful ally to work for us in exchange for clemency upon our success. She will be taken alive as requested."

"Good, and the preparations for her arrival will be set by then?"

"As expected."

Marc nodded, walking around the desk and lifting a dagger that lay there. It was black with encrusted dark jewels, he lifted it, inspecting it against the light.

"My father would've been proud of me."

"And you are sure you wish to wield it, Your Majesty?" Reyher asked cautiously. "There will be no going back. This spell has never been attempted before."

Marc narrowed his eyes at the man. "Then I shall be the first . . . and last."

There was a knock on the solar door and the three of them turned to face it. Bright sunlight peeked through Marc's window.

She was out of time.

Without seeing who was on the other side of the door, Adriana reluctantly turned on her heel, racing back to her chambers. She barely pushed her way through the wall, closing it as tight as she could muster behind her, just as her handmaids made their way inside her room.

All the while, as they prepared her for the day, the only thoughts that clouded Adriana's mind were of the people about to suffer at Marc's hand, and that Eve and Dakon were alive together.

It shamed her to admit it, even within the safety of her mind, but a simmering jealousy began to fill her, for she wished she were with them too.

As she and Jos walked along the castle gardens, Adriana could feel the cool, unwelcome gaze of Timothy on her back. She shifted uncomfortably under his stare as she and Jos continued moving past the hedges. They were large and shaped like the war horses of Teros, she fought back tears thinking of Callum. He had been too good for this world. She tore her gaze away, suppressing any more memories of him.

Jos gently grabbed her hand, bringing her back from her wayward thoughts. "I believe we are far enough away from the castle to speak." He gestured to a stone bench. "Can you call off your hound to give us some privacy?"

Adriana turned and locked eyes with Timothy, whose gray eyes assessed her suspiciously.

"You are fine there, Ser Timothy, we won't go far."

Timothy stiffened, glancing at Jos then back at Adriana before nodding. He took a step back and faced the opposite direction.

"Now," Jos whispered, "what is it you wish to tell me so urgently?"

She turned to Jos, taking in his expectant green eyes, a shade lighter than she was used to—like that of a spring morning instead of a summer day that reminded her so much of Dakon.

She bit her lip, unsure of how to begin. "I discovered something that I think would help you and your informants. Secret passages that run throughout the castle where one could easily spy without being caught."

Jos's eyes widened. "How did you find this?"

"I learned how to open one in my room this morning. I overheard my brother talking from his solar."

"What did he say?"

She swallowed, suddenly feeling faint. "What we suspected is true. They are killing innocent women to force the real witches into

192

doing something they don't want to do."

"Like what?"

"I don't know, they didn't say. But there's more. Eve is still alive. They have spies following her. It appears she is essential to their plans."

Jos took this in, his face nearly unreadable. He stood, pacing before her. Every second of silence sent her nerves astray.

"What do we do?"

Jos rubbed his eyes; he seemed tired. She wasn't the only one having trouble sleeping.

He knelt before her, taking her hands in his. "I will go to Zafira and speak to our contacts. I suspect that our doves will not make it there, not anymore."

"And leave me here?" She stood suddenly. "Let me come with you."

His eyes softened, a pitying look within them. "Would your brother let you leave now with all that has happened? The only time I have seen him let you leave the castle was for the burning and the temple, heavily guarded might I add. No, I will go on my own, strike up a deal with the lords there, and I will come back for you. I promise."

Adriana despised his sound words; tears pricked at her eyes as her dire situation had become very real now. Marc would never let her leave willingly. Neither would her mother. And she couldn't abandon Gabrielle, not unless she could convince her to come with them.

"What will you tell my brother?"

"That I have business with Zafira, we were working on new trade routes through the mountains not so long ago. It's perfect."

"I—I don't want you to abandon me," she choked, tears falling down her face.

Jos lifted a hand to her cheek, hesitating slightly before gently wiping them away. "We may not love each other, but I am not cruel." He placed both hands on hers once more. "I would like to think that if my sister was in your position, that someone like me would do right by her. You only have to hold on for a short while longer, and then I will take you away from this wretched place."

Jos placed a soft kiss on her hands, his green eyes focused intently on hers. "I am a man of my word, and it would take an army to make me abandon you, Princess."

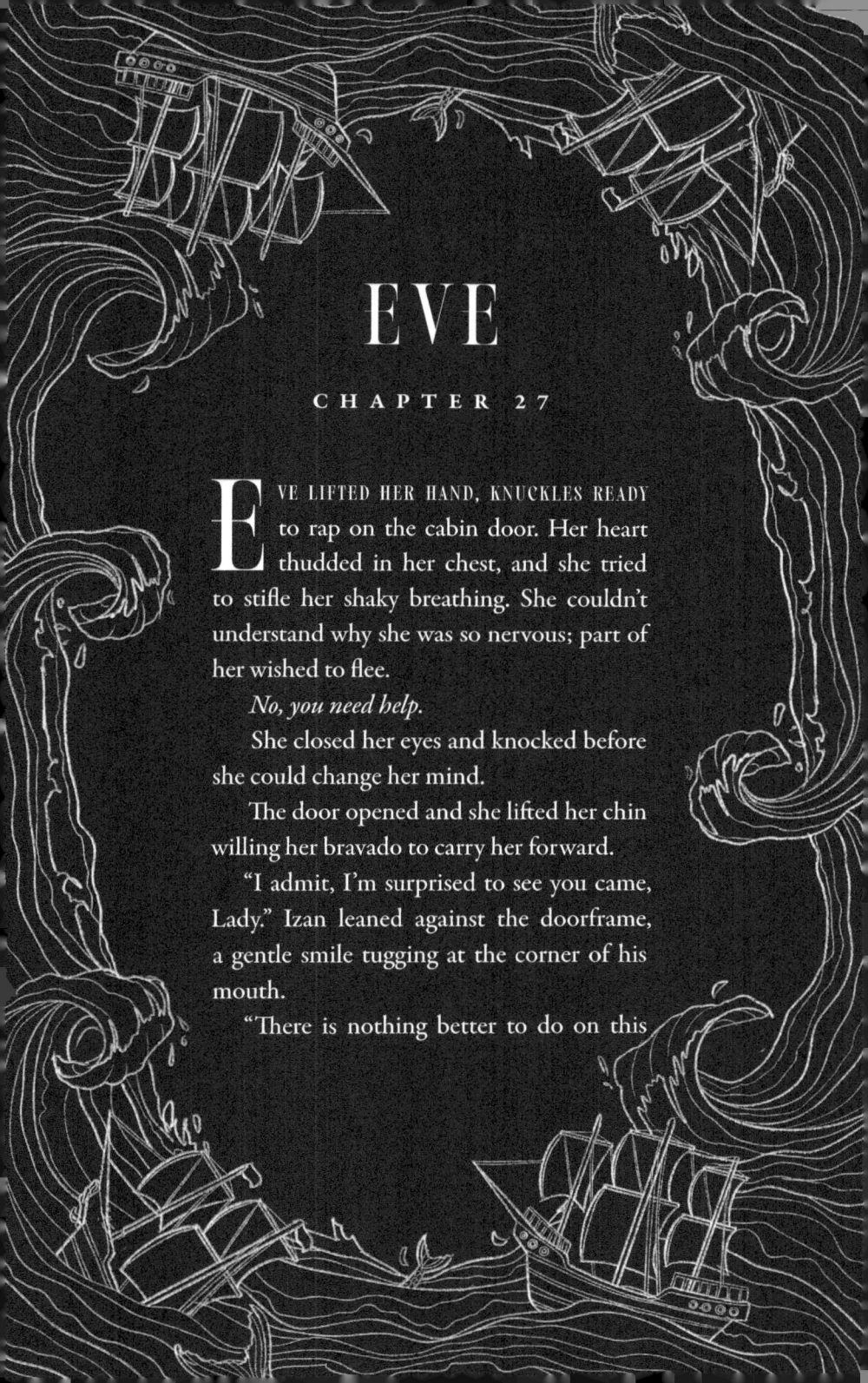

EVE

CHAPTER 27

E VE LIFTED HER HAND, KNUCKLES READY to rap on the cabin door. Her heart thudded in her chest, and she tried to stifle her shaky breathing. She couldn't understand why she was so nervous; part of her wished to flee.

No, you need help.

She closed her eyes and knocked before she could change her mind.

The door opened and she lifted her chin willing her bravado to carry her forward.

"I admit, I'm surprised to see you came, Lady." Izan leaned against the doorframe, a gentle smile tugging at the corner of his mouth.

"There is nothing better to do on this

ship," Eve quipped, unwilling to give him the satisfaction.

Izan stepped aside, allowing Eve to walk into his cabin. She took it upon herself to pull out the stool and sit. His small porthole reflected the purple, orange hues of light from outside, casting long shadows in the cabin. She suspected she did not have long before night fell.

"You are welcome, regardless." Izan sat across from her.

She fiddled her fingers nervously on her lap. "When I was here last, you mentioned that you could help me. To see what I was missing."

Izan crossed his arms, smirking. "That depends. Are you willing to talk?"

"Can you not show me what I need to know?"

Izan chuckled. "If it were that simple . . ." He reached for Eve's hands, and she pulled them back, warily.

"What are you doing?"

"Relax," he said, "I want to see something."

She furrowed her brows, but relented, giving him her hands. Her lips parted at his gentle touch as he placed her hands in his, inspecting them.

"Tell me, Lady, how does a witch like you end up on a pirate ship in Bastard's Haven?"

"It's hard to say."

Was she willing to tell him that much?

"Oh, now that's not fair," he chided. "You know far more about me than I do you. You haven't even told me your name."

"It's Eve," she said. "My name is Eve."

"Eve." The word was a warm caress on his lips. She wished he would say it again. "It suits you, as does *Lady*."

He released her hands, his eyes burning into hers.

"You are quite the mystery to me," he continued. "Smoke billows from you in the rain, you can see my past with a single touch, and your skin burns when I touch you."

He lifted his palm to show her faint red marks in the center.

She reddened. "I'm sorry, I didn't mean to."

"I believe you." He pulled out a cloth from his satchel and wrapped his hand with it. "When did you discover your magic?"

Eve bit her lip. "A few moons ago."

Izan raised a brow. "And you were living as a noble?"

Eve hesitated.

"Is that why you fled?" He leaned in. "Because you were scared of being discovered?"

"Yes." She lowered her gaze.

Izan sighed. "There are few noble witch families hiding in the mortal kingdoms. I imagine they would have never let you out of their sight had they discovered your magic. It is rare for witches to possess fire the way I've seen you do."

"I wasn't raised by witches."

"I know, otherwise you would have learned how to control it by now."

Izan reached back into his satchel and brought out the same flask from earlier. Eve was about to protest, but instead he took a drink himself.

"Is this troubling for you?"

"Not at all"—he closed the lid—"but this is going to hurt me more than you."

Eve let out a nervous laugh. "Why do you say that?"

"Because I need to see what you can do." He placed a candle on the desk between them. "Light it."

Eve tilted her head, confused.

"Then what?"

"We'll see."

Eve knit her brow, but raised her hand above the candle, willing it to light. No sooner had the thought come, than the candle began to burn. "There."

Izan studied it. "Now, what is it telling you?"

"Telling me?"

Izan smiled. "Yes, Lady. Scry."

She bit her lip, and he sighed. "Let it speak to you, show you what you need to know." He reached out and once again grasped her hands in his, the touch heating her skin. He gently tightened his hold and closed his eyes.

Eve furrowed her brow, but didn't argue. Izan was calm, breathing softly as he held her hands. She leaned in toward the flame, watching as it danced in the air, burning the wick and forming a small puddle of wax in the center.

What am I supposed to be looking for?

What am I supposed to hear?

She concentrated on how the flame stretched as it consumed more of the wick, trying in vain to reach upward for something more to feed on. The orange and yellow hues became all she could see in the blackness that slowly enveloped her. A light in the darkness she eagerly wanted to keep alive.

And within the flame, something else lingered, beckoning her to it. She narrowed her eyes, squinting to make out the small figure. It had long, brown hair, a burgundy dress, and it sat on a bed fiddling with something she could not yet make out.

As the vision cleared, Eve's heart sank.

It's me. This is me.

She watched terrified as she relived the memory of her opening the grimoire, the Blood of the Blackthorn, pricking her finger, the blood spilling onto the weathered page.

"It's time."

"Let me in, *Blood of the Blackthorn*."

"Let me in."

The voice, the dreaded voice was in her thoughts again. She could see her past self in the flame turning and facing her, book in hand, a sinister smile on her face.

Leave, she thought, *please, leave!*

"We are one for eternity . . ." her past self said. *"Let us claim our power."*

Eve screamed, knocking over something, and suddenly she realized she was back in the healer's cabin. The stool clattered on the ground, and Izan rushed to her.

"What happened? What did you see?"

Tears stained her cheeks, and she shivered in his arms. Ash from her fingers stained his clothes. "I saw me. I saw it. I saw—"

Izan placed the stool upright and sat Eve down. He knelt in front of her. "I need to know what is possessing you." His eyes stared fiercely into Eve's, his hands—blistered and red now—gently held her own. "Please, I cannot help what I do not know."

Eve's lips trembled as she spoke. "It's a grimoire."

Izan leaned back. "When did it first appear?"

"When my magic did."

Izan stood, his eyes wide. "It can't be."

It all came out as Eve tried to explain, the feeling freeing as the burden of secrecy was released from her lips. "It's haunting me, it wants something from me, but I'm afraid. Afraid of how much I both need and hate it. I feel very mortal without it, but powerless with it. I don't know how to control something that I have never even known existed. I want it to stop, but then I don't."

Izan's eyes never left hers. "You're the Blood of the Blackthorn?"

Eve's heart thundered in her chest, the words spoken aloud for the first time by someone other than the grimoire.

"Yes," she breathed, more tears rolling down her face, "and I need help."

Izan pulled her in, holding her close. His arms wrapped around her, and she placed her head on his chest, listening to the sound of his heart. Slowly, it soothed her, reminded her that she was still among the living, that there could still be hope.

"I'll help you," he said, "I promise."

THE NIGHT NEARLY CLOAKED THE CABIN IN SHADOWS BY THE TIME Eve and Izan left. They walked to the main deck where most of the crew sat in a circle beneath the starlit sky. They were speaking loudly, laughing and drinking amongst each other. A much-needed reprieve after the few days at sea.

Eve watched as Niani, who was among the group, raised her hands and stood.

"My turn for a tale!" she hushed, and the pirates settled. Pazel was seated next to her, focused intently on Niani's every word. Dakon was nowhere to be seen. Eve hoped he wasn't ill.

"Do you wish to join them?" Izan asked. "Distraction may do us good."

Eve nodded, wanting to lose herself in a story.

As they approached, Niani placed her mug in Pazel's hands to hold, which he clung to very willingly, and faced the crew. Eve and Izan stood behind him.

"Who here has heard a tale of dragons?" Niani asked, her eyes sparkling with excitement.

A few of the pirates raised their hands.

"They are fierce creatures in every book, tearing apart lands and kingdoms alike with nothing but sheer force and flame."

Eve remembered the tales of such beasts from her childhood, recalling how she would paint pictures of them with Clarisa.

"This is a story of the dragon that lost its fire."

Eve moved to sit on one of the barrels, fascinated.

"Centuries ago, the gods as we know them had abandoned the mortals, leaving witches to plague the lands. They followed an evil goddess, who grew in power as the witches created more beasts to worship her.

"In charge of maintaining the delicate balance between life and death, the goddess challenged her witches to create something that could transport her

between veils. A creature that could carry the souls of the dead and keep alight the fires of her underworld. The winner of creating such a beast would be granted a single, precious wish.

"The witches worked day and night with their familiars, crafting horrendous, terrifying creatures. Every single offering brought to the goddess was rejected. None of them could last in the fires of her underworld, none could bear the weight of the souls, none could cross between the veils without harm.

"That is, until a witch, cunning and powerful, decided to follow the goddess to her sanctuary. He seduced her, whispering promises of love and devotion.

"One night, when the goddess was fast asleep, the witch cut out her icy heart, replacing it with a crystal, and fled into the night. He casted her heart into a fire of snakes and souls, watching as the flames danced under the dark moon. And then he cast himself into the fire as well.

"When the morning came, the fire was no more than embers and ash beneath a gray sky.

"In the witch's place, was a dragon forged in fire.

"The goddess was delighted, unaware of the trick the witch played. For the dragon carried the souls and kept the flames alight in the day, and at night in his witch form slept with the goddess. And all was bliss.

"But the witch grew too arrogant.

"He seduced others in the shadows. He abandoned his duties, and soon the souls began to pile in the lands of the living, walking amongst them as spirits. And whispers of the witch's betrayal reached the goddess's ears.

"The goddess scoured the lands, vengeful and angry.

"And when she found the witch, he revealed that he was the champion of her challenge. Begging to be allowed his single, precious wish. A wish to live.

"The goddess, known for her trickery, granted it. But instead of living as he thought he would, the witch was banished to the lands of ice and snow in his dragon form. Never again able to feel the warmth of the sun, nor the fire from within.

"And there he remained, the dragon that lost its fire."

The crew was silent as Niani finished her story. Eve herself was captivated, eyes wide as she tried to imagine a witch who would tempt their fate so terribly.

Pazel stood, clapping by himself. "Incredible story, Niani. I'd listen to a hundred more."

The pirates gave him a puzzled look, and Niani turned to face him, cocking a brow.

"Thank you?"

Pazel reddened as he sat once more. "Er—did he ever get it back, his flame?"

Niani smirked. "Would there be a story if he had?"

"I suppose not," Pazel mumbled.

"Maybe he's waiting for something to light it." Niani patted a hand on his shoulder then turned to the rest of the crew. "Get some sleep. I'll see you in the morning."

Niani took her mug from Pazel and walked off.

Eve watched, amused, as Alonso and Giovani patted Pazel on the back. "The good ones are always out of reach, boy," they assured him as they left the deck.

"Does he always pine after women?" Izan raised a brow.

"Not always." Eve moved toward the railing, wanting to linger a bit longer.

Izan followed. "Pity, he'll have his heart broken for certain."

She nudged him. "Maybe not, give him a chance."

"Tell that to the first mate."

Eve rolled her eyes. They were relatively alone on the deck now, with only three of the night shift tending to their duties a short distance away. As the silence lingered, Eve longed to fill it. She didn't want this night to end, to have to leave the comfort of Izan's presence next to her.

She peeked at him from beneath her lashes, his hair tousled just beneath his brows, his dark eyes glinted a speck of silver in the moonlight. He didn't turn to her when he spoke. "What happens when we arrive in the Blackthorn?"

Eve followed his gaze to the water, watching as it glistened under the evening sky. She wished she could appreciate it more. "I need to find my sister."

Izan nodded.

"And you?"

He clenched his jaw, "I'm not sure. I don't like to linger on land for long."

"Oh."

Izan turned to her. "But I did promise you I would help, and I'll do my best with the time we have."

This sounded too close to farewell for Eve's taste. It made her feel as if she were losing something again.

"Do you trust me, Eve?"

She flicked her eyes to Izan; he had called her by her name. He smiled gently, reaching slowly to tuck the loose tendrils of her hair behind her ear. She closed her eyes at his touch, relishing in the warm feeling that spread through her, the quickening of her heartbeat.

"I do," she breathed.

She opened her eyes and reached out to touch him. His fervent gaze locked on her, his lips slightly parted as she felt his face beneath her fingers.

Izan leaned in, his hands guiding down her back, pulling her closer.

Theo.

The name entered unwelcome in her mind. The last man she had loved and let inside her heart. The one who left her and died shortly after. She felt defeated for letting him back into her thoughts.

Is it too soon?

She stilled.

Izan opened his eyes, a hurt within them.

"I'm sorry," he said. "I wanted to kiss you—I should have asked."

Eve bit her lip, tears threatening to fall. It had been a long time since she gave into desire and had it reciprocated. Theo, despite her laying her heart bare for him, chose to reject and abandon her when she needed him most . . .

But this is not Theo.

She raised her head, watching as Izan turned to leave.

It's time to grow.

As Izan took his first step, Eve grabbed his arm to stop him. He turned back, confused, and before she could convince herself not to, she pulled him into her arms and pressed her lips on his.

He tasted sweet and welcoming as his lips softened against hers. A gentle coax, a promise of something more. His arms grasped her, gently pressing her against his chest. Eve closed her eyes, allowing their touch to guide their next movements. She wrapped her hands behind his neck, pulling him deeper into her embrace. Izan was intoxicating, his touch heating her skin. He was rain, and she was a drought, desperate for every taste. He guided them away from the railing and leaned against the foremast, never loosening his grip. He pressed his mouth eagerly against hers again. She wanted more of him. She needed to have more of him. Her pulse raced; her body trembled with excitement and passion. And he met her with the same intensity, kiss for kiss, as they explored each other beneath the stars.

Izan placed a tender hand on her cheek, brushing strands of her hair once more from her face. He met her wanting gaze, his eyes filled with a lust she had only known once before. He smiled wickedly, his dimples clear in the night. His eyes, there was a glimmer of some-thing in them . . .

"You will be the end of me, Eve." He craned his neck, revealing small burns.

"We can stop," she said, removing her hands, and returning his smile.

He grabbed them quickly, placing them back around his neck. His eyes burned into hers.

"Never."

He captured her mouth again, and Eve kissed him as if the world were on fire.

DAKON

CHAPTER 28

DAKON AND PAZEL SPENT MOST OF their day reading Cerene's book, trying to become as familiar as they could with the stories and writings within. They flipped through it, and each time it was opened and closed, there seemed to be new pages within. It was a never-ending torrent of text that soon overwhelmed them. And after asking numerous times, the book did not give them the answer to their burning question.

How do we contain the Blood of the Blackthorn?

Instead, it showed then once again the story of the Original Witches and how they transferred their magic. Dakon read it aloud for the tenth time and finally pushed the book aside.

He was missing something . . .

As the afternoon sun sank in the distance, Pazel finally caved.

"If I have to listen to that story one more time, I think you'll have to give me your magic so I can destroy the book myself." He groaned as he stood, stretching his arms. They had been seated on the floor for hours and even Dakon's body had begun to ache.

"I know." Dakon rubbed his eyes. "I wish it would show us something different."

Pazel stretched his neck. "It's very much like her—telling stories that we think mean nothing until they do." He picked up his sword, the very one Dakon had given him after his fight with Timothy and placed it in his makeshift scabbard. It stuck out slightly, the leather material that he received from the quartermaster far past its usefulness.

"You can stay if you want, but I plan to feel the sun on my face while there's still light."

Dakon thought of the boy he sparred in Bastard's Haven. "You'll have to enjoy the sun for the both of us."

Pazel placed a hand on Dakon's shoulder and shook him slightly. "We are safe, Dakon, days out from land and far beyond the reach of the king. Try not to spoil it by wallowing in pages of the dead when there's still living to do."

"I know," he grumbled.

Pazel gave him a brief smile as he left, shutting the door behind him.

It was a different kind of quiet now in the cabin. Without Pazel or Beast, who had not appeared since last evening, Dakon could hear the ship groaning against the water, the sails flapping against the wind, and the muffled voices of the pirates outside on the deck.

For the first time, Dakon felt alone.

Truly alone.

He missed Adriana, he missed life in the castle before he was forced to be a fool, and he missed Cerene. *If she were here, she'd have all the answers . . .*

Dakon picked up the book from the floor and placed it on the bed. He paced before it, trying to distract himself from his wayward thoughts. But his mind was fettered in a chaotic mess of repressed memories as if the silence beckoned their release.

As he paced the floor, he tried to focus instead on happier memories, the rare ones of joy in his life of servitude.

Adriana.

The time they spent together in the forest, talking freely as if they were not separated by their class. If he closed his eyes he could smell the crisp, earthy aroma of the trees and even a hint of lavender. He could see her hazel eyes brightened by the colorful periwinkle flowers that grew like weeds around them. His heart ached for her, and perhaps that's what made the loneliness more unbearable. It was not that he was without companions, but it was that he was without *her*.

Dakon opened his eyes, realizing that time had skipped forward and the night had fallen. The view from his porthole was dark with hints of light from the stars outside.

"Damn."

He shook his head, staring at the book once more. He placed his hands on either side of it, concentrating as if any semblance of hope would make up for lost time.

Think, Dakon, think.

"Can you show me how to help Eve?"

He watched as the book shook slightly, then opened, the pages flipping erratically until finally it landed on the story of magic transference.

"No," he ran his hands frustratedly through his hair. "Come on, Cerene, I need something more than that."

The book didn't move.

He huffed. "How does knowing this make me a better familiar?"

It remained still.

Dakon was losing his patience. "What would I even need to do?"

The pages of the book shook slightly. Dakon's stomach dropped and rushed to it. Carefully, he spoke. "What do I need to transfer magic?"

Quickly the parchment flitted back and forth until finally landing on a page with a short list.

MAGIC TRANSFERENCE
Blood of a Witch
Blood of the Witch's Familiar
Blood of a Mortal Sacrifice
A Living Host

Dakon felt cold, the silence now eerie and consuming as he read the words again.

"Why would any witch do this?" he asked himself.

Maybe they were forced to.

The thought sent chills down his spine and recalled Marc's interest in Eve.

Would he have made her into his new enchantress . . . or take it for himself?

Dakon stood, suddenly, feeling dazed. He had to tell Eve—she needed to know. Guilt sank in as he realized he had not been forthcoming with all he had learned thus far.

He opened the door just in time to see Pazel going into the first mate's cabin. Dakon shook his head, *another problem for another time.*

He walked to the deck, taking in the incredible starlit sky above. It was mesmerizing, making him lose track of his steps as he took it in. One of the pirates on the night shift reached out with a firm grip and helped him back to his feet. He was an older man with tired eyes that looked as if they wished to be shut.

"Thank you," Dakon said.

The pirate nodded wearily. "Are you looking for your lady?"

Dakon raised a brow. *Is that what they call her?*

"Er—yes, I suppose I am."

He placed a hand on Dakon's shoulder and shook his head sadly, "I wouldn't if I were you."

Dakon's heart sank. "What do you mean? Is she hurt?"

The pirate shifted uncomfortably. "No, but I think it's best if you go back to your cabin. Save yourself the heartache."

Dakon looked out to the deck, confused. "I don't understand, wh—"

Then he saw them, pressed against the mast nearly hidden from view. Izan and Eve tangled in a passionate embrace. The way she kissed him, the way she clung to him as if he were her reason for being, cracked Dakon's spirit.

He nearly forgot to breathe, his legs were frozen beneath him, unable to move.

Izan?

Eve?

The questions filled his head, practically burying him. He warred with himself whether to confront them or move away and pretend he never saw anything.

He watched as Eve giggled, and Izan pulled her in again.

Dakon couldn't bear it anymore. He took a step back, trying to be as discreet as possible, but missed the step again. The pirate grabbed him by the shoulders, making sure Dakon was standing straight before he released him.

"I'm sorry you had to see that, boy."

Dakon swallowed, but the lump in his throat wouldn't go. He clenched his jaw, tearing his eyes from Eve. He couldn't face the pirate as he whispered, "No, I needed to see this."

Without another word, he quietly raced down the steps and back to his cabin. All the while, his mind was ablaze.

Did she tell Izan anything?

Were the rumors at court true, that the enchantress's daughter was nothing but a gossip?

Dakon let himself feel angry and betrayed, though he wasn't certain why. He tried to convince himself as he ran away that it was because she now endangered them. For all they knew, Izan could be one of Marc's spies sent to kidnap her.

He stormed inside the cabin, but it was empty save for Beast resting in the corner.

"And where have you been?" Dakon demanded.

The gytrash cocked its head. It's big, blood-orange eyes looking curiously at him.

He sighed. "At least you're here, Beast. I don't want to be alone tonight."

Dakon pulled the blankets over his head and faced away from the door. He stared into the darkness, willing it to lull him somehow into sleep.

He was not sure how much time had passed, but soon he heard Eve make her way inside. She closed the door carefully and tiptoed to the bed. He could hear her nestle under the covers and soon her steady breathing as she slept.

Shame filled him, deep and unrelenting.

Eve was not his, and he loathed feeling so strongly. But he couldn't help it. He wished that he had chosen to wait until morning to speak to her. He wished for a lot of things as he lay miserably in his sorrow.

Slowly, he reached into his pocket and retrieved Adriana's letter. It was weathered and tattered now after having it for so long in this journey. He held it tight against his chest and wondered if she ever thought about the fool who loved her.

As he finally drifted off into a troubled sleep, he could hear the faint sound of singing through the porthole.

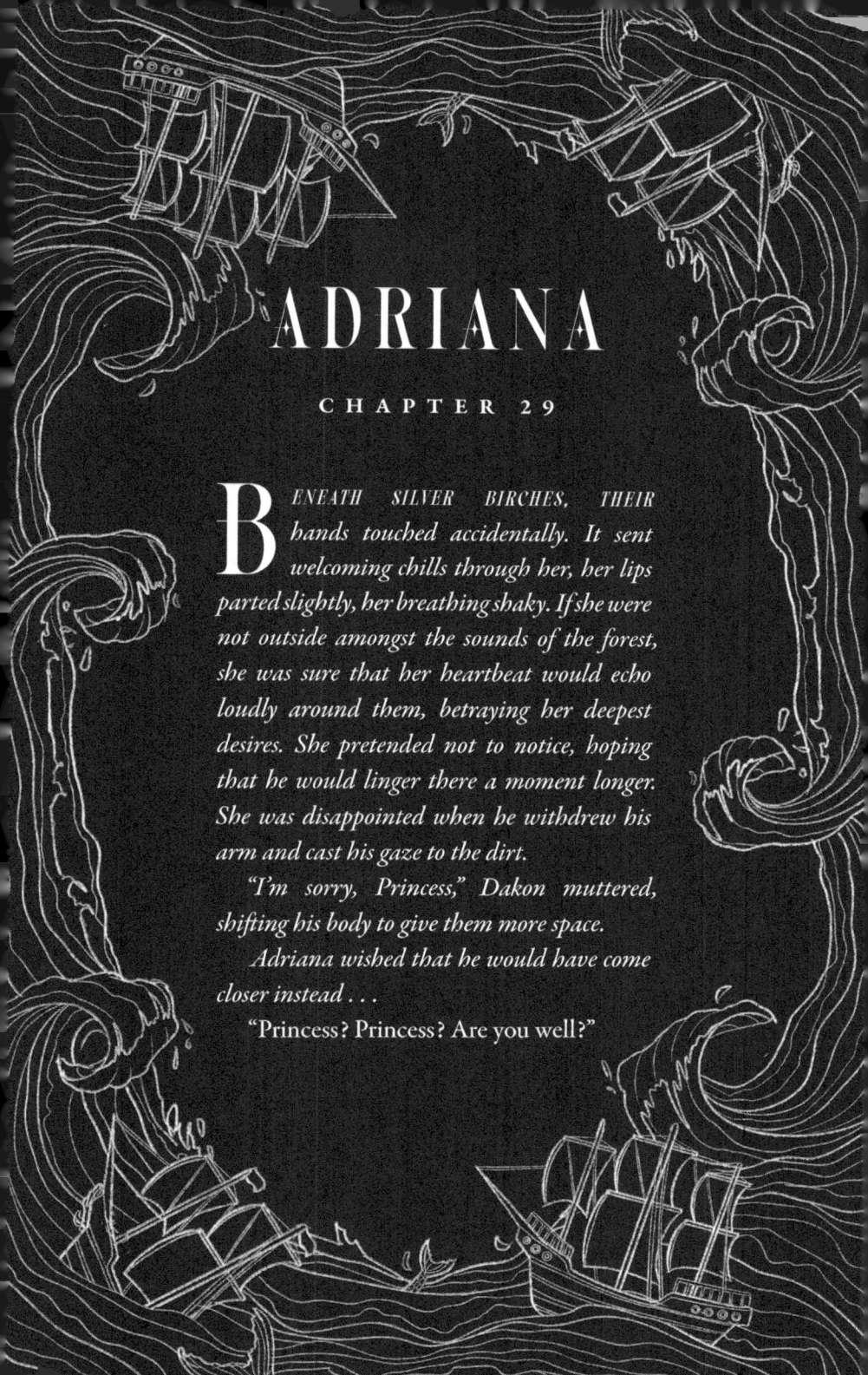

ADRIANA

CHAPTER 29

BENEATH SILVER BIRCHES, THEIR hands touched accidentally. It sent welcoming chills through her, her lips parted slightly, her breathing shaky. If she were not outside amongst the sounds of the forest, she was sure that her heartbeat would echo loudly around them, betraying her deepest desires. She pretended not to notice, hoping that he would linger there a moment longer. She was disappointed when he withdrew his arm and cast his gaze to the dirt.

"I'm sorry, Princess," Dakon muttered, shifting his body to give them more space.

Adriana wished that he would have come closer instead . . .

"Princess? Princess? Are you well?"

Adriana blinked a few times, bringing herself back from her memories. She turned slightly to take in Timothy's frustrated gaze. She was irritated by his presence.

"I am rather surprised my brother has you guarding me after the last time he saw us together," Adriana replied, curtly.

They continued walking down the hall toward her mother's chambers. Since Jos had left for Zafira, Timothy had become far too comfortable at her side—it vexed her. She counted down the days until Jos had promised her he would return.

Only a moon left.

Timothy kept his chin up, clenching it awkwardly. "Yes, Your Highness, His Majesty is very kind."

"You need not speak so formally with me, Ser Timothy, we are far past unfamiliarity are we not?"

"I do not wish to cause either of us trouble."

"Then we want the same things." She stopped, facing him.

He tilted his head, confusion evident. "Your brother has doubled your guard, there is nothing to worry about, Princess."

"Then why do I not feel safe?" she challenged.

"You are in mourning. It has set us all on edge. But King Marc has dispatched a special force into the city, we have removed dozens of witches that were hiding there. Before long, they will all flee or be killed."

"Dozens?"

"Yes, they have made quick work these past few weeks."

Adriana furrowed her brow. "And we are certain they were witches?"

Timothy sighed. "If they weren't, then they wouldn't have burned."

Adriana had an unsettling feeling in her chest as she pressed further. "How is it these witches were not discovered beforehand, but so easily now?"

"I'm not sure, Princess. I only know what I have been told."

"Do you know their occupations?"

"The witches?"

Adriana nodded.

"A few were whores, others wet nurses, and perhaps a shopkeeper. I'm not entirely certain, in truth, nor do I care for the lives of these trifling women."

Women.

All of them were women.

"Does any of this seem odd to you?"

He shook his head. "No one but a witch would dare speak so ill of their monarch. But rest assured, Princess, they are no longer causing strife in the city. I imagine the rest of their kind will follow soon enough."

Adriana swallowed, trying to keep herself steady as they walked side-by-side.

They reached her mother's chambers, and Timothy bowed before her.

"I will be waiting outside for you, Princess. As I said, you are safe with me."

His gray eyes sparkled at her, but Adriana quickly turned, wondering how and why she ever saw anything comforting in them before.

No longer bold enough to spy through the tunnels, Adriana had no choice but to remain in the dark of her brother's dealings. To keep herself distracted from the catastrophes that brewed within her, she continued her royal obligations.

She attended every dinner only to hear of more deaths.

She kept company with the court and often saw smoke from the recent burning billowing from a nearby window.

Another noblewoman was tried as a witch, much to the excitement of the gossips.

More women were sentenced to burn as the court around her

relished to their heart's content, pretending not to notice the fires from beyond the city gates. They laughed and ate and drank and laughed some more, becoming a cycle of endless torment that Adriana could barely stand.

It sickened her.

And even as she tried to sleep, nothing but her hands against her ears could muffle the screams from beyond her balcony. It haunted her, feasted upon her guilt for there was nothing a caged dove could do to tame the wild animal her brother had become. His veiled threats to marry her off to "higher bidders" was not lost on her, neither was the truth that she would soon lose her usefulness to him.

When will Marc accuse me?

She woke, tired and weak, holding onto the hope that the lords of Zafira would accept Jos's bid to grant them sanctuary. If she could make it out of the capital, then maybe she had a chance . . .

Adriana now sat in her chambers, thankful that Lady Jayne had taken ill recently.

She wanted to be alone.

With a quill in her hand, she scribbled another letter for Jos. To keep up pretenses, she wrote of how she missed him and her excitement to begin wedding preparations. Her hand trembled as she wrote, and she spent far more time focusing on her penmanship than she did the words she scribbled on the parchment.

Once he returns, everything will get better.

We will escape.

We can find a way to stop this madness.

She sealed the letter. In her hands it felt like hope, and she wanted to cling to it for as long as she could. Adriana gripped it tight as she walked to her balcony, taking in the sights of the western district of the city and the sea beyond it. Like tiny insects, the common folk moved through the capital in the daylight, tending to their shops and bartering for everything they needed to live.

How many of them will be among the dead?

It was a gruesome thought, but as the death toll rose and Marc's order for witch hunts increased, anarchy loomed on the horizon.

Would I kill to live?

Would I have to?

Her eyes glanced over to the sea, taking in its brilliance. It sparkled as if tiny gems floated on the surface and glided gently against the shore. She reached out a hand wishing she could touch the water, wishing she could take a boat and sail out into the distance.

"Damn you, Dakon," she whispered, "why did you not take me with you?"

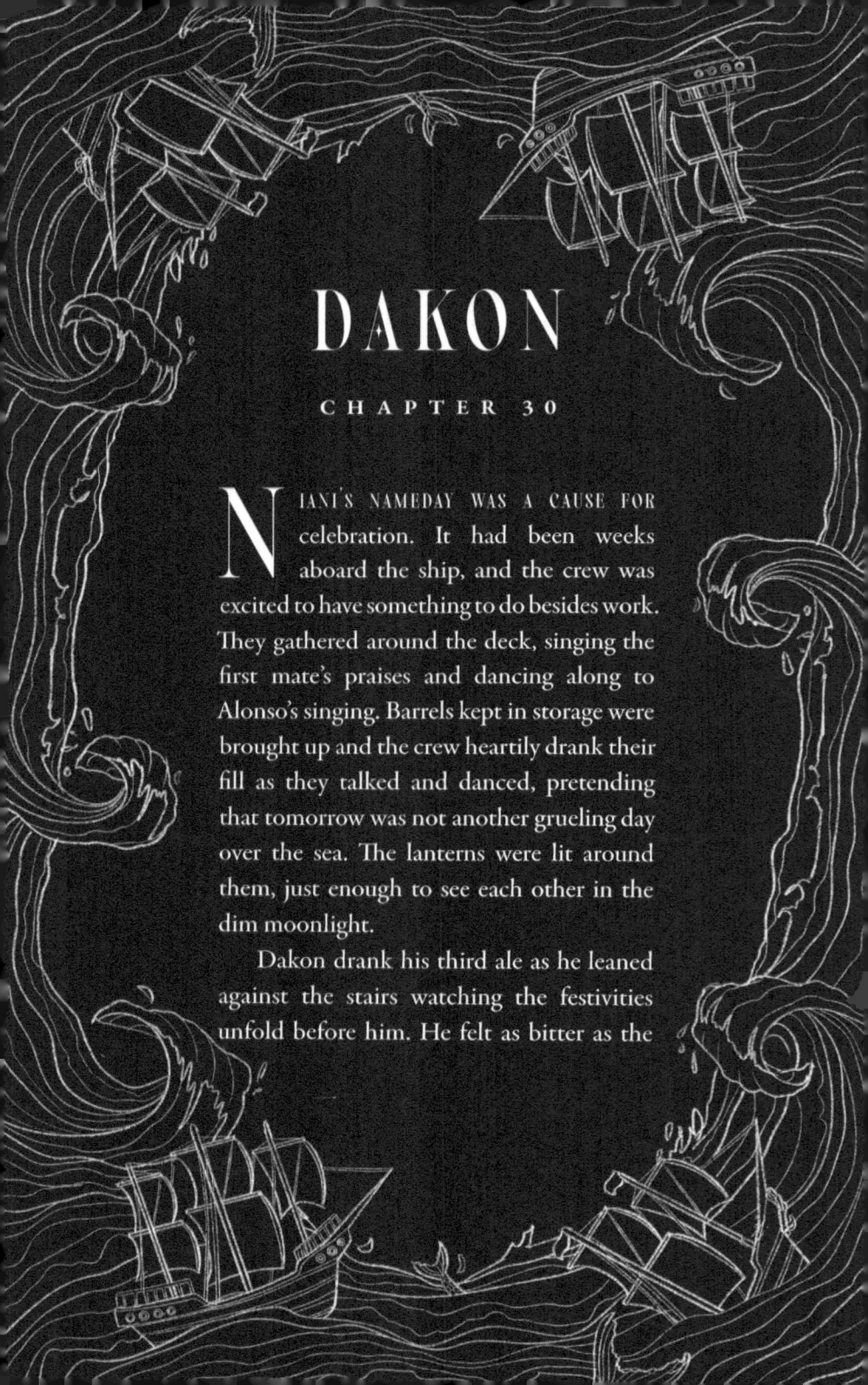

DAKON

CHAPTER 30

NIANI'S NAMEDAY WAS A CAUSE FOR celebration. It had been weeks aboard the ship, and the crew was excited to have something to do besides work. They gathered around the deck, singing the first mate's praises and dancing along to Alonso's singing. Barrels kept in storage were brought up and the crew heartily drank their fill as they talked and danced, pretending that tomorrow was not another grueling day over the sea. The lanterns were lit around them, just enough to see each other in the dim moonlight.

Dakon drank his third ale as he leaned against the stairs watching the festivities unfold before him. He felt as bitter as the drink tasted. Since he had seen Eve and Izan, he had kept to himself, trying to distract himself from confronting the truth about why it bothered him so. Eve was dancing now with Pazel, the two laughing and twirling without a care in the world.

He bit his lip and pulled out Adriana's letter. It was greatly damaged now, having been read so many times over so many moons. It was torn on one end and had a hole through it on the other.

How could something so precious be so easily destroyed?

He groaned, trying to read it again, but the words were smudged, and the ink was smeared. And despite the joyful music and the bliss of everyone around him, Dakon was heartbroken.

She would never have come with me.

I was nothing but a distraction to her.

The last words hurt the most to think, but Dakon was finding it harder to convince himself otherwise. Did his kiss with Adriana mean more to him than her?

He took another sip, relishing in the numbing feeling it gave him. Anything was easier than sitting in his cursed thoughts and broken heart. He walked to the side railing and looked out into the pitch-black sea. The letter felt heavy in his hand, the parchment no longer smooth, but rough and grainy. He lifted it to his lips and gave it a gentle kiss, wishing that he could have been worthy for someone like Adriana.

Then, he let it go.

And watched as it fell overboard, until it was swallowed by the dark.

It took Dakon two more drinks before he found the courage to walk up to Eve.

She was dancing with Giovani, twirling in his arms, her eyes alight with a rare joy he had not seen with her since they met. Her smile was bright, her cheeks a soft pink against her tanned skin. Her laugh was infectious, and he could feel himself smile as he closed in on them.

He cleared his throat, Eve and Giovani stopped while the rest of the pirates continued around them.

"Dakon?" Eve raised a brow, as if she could not believe he was finally speaking to her. He couldn't blame her.

"I-I'd like to have a dance, if you'll have me?"

Giovani stepped from Eve, mumbling about getting another drink. As he walked away, Eve turned to Dakon. "Have you danced before?"

Dakon had seen many dances in the Great Hall but had never once done it himself. He shook his head. "No, but I imagine the pirates won't care too much."

Eve lifted her lips. "I would be surprised if they did." She gestured to the crowd around them, who were twirling and moving in various states of drunkenness. Pazel was talking to Niani in the corner. He smiled. *A problem for another day.*

Dakon lifted his hand out to her, trying to recall how he saw it done back in the castle.

Eve tilted her head, pleasantly surprised, and placed her hand in his.

He pulled her in, and his heart lurched as she pressed against him, her head tilted up and waiting for his next move. He took a step to the left, then to the right, then he spun with her in his arms.

"Are you certain you haven't danced before?" Eve smiled.

"I haven't." He could feel his cheeks burning. "I was always on the serving end."

Her eyes lowered. "Oh, of course."

"I'm sorry, I didn't mean to upset you."

"No, I'm not upset."

Dakon tried to think of something to say, but the words felt just out of reach. The awkward tension grew as they danced. He did not realize just how divided they had become despite sleeping in the same cabin for so long. He needed to make the first move.

He took a chance and twirled her, just as he had seen it done before. Her face lit up unexpectedly as she went around, she even giggled slightly as he pulled her back in.

"Dakon you are a terrible liar," she laughed.

Dakon grinned. "I don't think I've seen you this happy before."

"I love to dance," she said. "I love how it makes me feel so free."

Left.

Right.

Spin.

Left . . .

He tried to focus on his movements as he listened to her, not wanting a foul step to ruin this moment.

"Why are you talking to me now?" she asked, her enchanting, brown eyes gazing back at him.

He bit the inside of his cheek.

"I'm happy you are," she continued, "I only meant that things between us have been . . . strained."

"I know," he said, "and I'm sorry. I—"

Saw you with Izan.

Heard you coming in late at night.

Felt something strange about seeing you with him . . .

"I have been busy, trying to figure out Cerene's book." He let out a sharp breath.

"And have you found anything?"

"Yes."

"Will it help us find my sister or with the *other* book?"

She looked up hopefully, and he wished he had the right answers for her.

"Not exactly." He spun her around and brought her back in, this time she did not smile. "But I think you should be wary of those you trust."

"What do you mean?"

"I mean," he sighed, feeling foolish, "I mean I think you are in far more danger than you realize. Which puts me and Pazel in danger too."

Eve loosened her grip on his hand and shoulder; she was slipping away. Her skin was heating, but nothing he couldn't handle.

"We are on a ship in the middle of the Dallise Sea, there are no threats to us here."

"As long as you are the Blood of the Blackthorn, there will always be threats."

She dropped her hands from him, her eyes wide with disbelief.

"What did you say?"

If he felt foolish before, now he felt stupid for doing this while they were having a decent moment.

"Nothing, I—"

"No, don't lie to me, Dakon. I heard what you said."

He was thankful the pirates were drunk around them, far more focused on standing straight than on two guests aboard their ship squabbling.

He lowered his voice. "Eve, why don't we talk alone?"

"How long have you known?" She crossed her arms.

Dakon could practically see walls being built between them once more. He panicked at how quickly their rapport dissolved. He swallowed as he froze the space around them, the pirates now barely moving. She seemed to notice it, too, her eyes narrowing as she took in their stilled surroundings. They were in their own world for as long as Dakon could keep it that way.

"Answer me!" she demanded.

"Not long," he said, concentrating on keeping everyone frozen, "and before you ask, I found out on my own. Something like *that* book preys upon witches for a reason."

"You don't know what you're talking about." She took a step back.

"Oh, so grimoires appear from thin air and harm witches for fun now?" He grasped her arm, revealing the faint scars there. Eve grabbed her arm back, pulling down the sleeve to hide it. Dakon continued, "I had a right to know. It's bad enough it's trying to take over you, but how long until it starts to come after me too?"

"It won't."

Dakon took a step toward her. "You don't know that."

"It won't," she repeated, her voice cracking.

"Eve, I want you to be safe. I can't bear the thought of something happening to you." He closed the gap between them, Eve stood firm.

She locked eyes with him, her lips trembling slightly. "It was easier pretending the book would go away with time than to admit I was blood bound to it. I wanted to protect you."

"We are supposed to be doing this together. We are blood bound, too, since I was born I was meant to protect you from grimoires, mad kings, pirates like Izan—"

"Izan?"

Shit.

"There's still a lot we don't know about him."

"That doesn't mean he's dangerous."

"It is if you're spilling secrets to him," he snapped.

"I trust him!"

"And what about me? Have I not earned your trust, did I not give up my life, my heart, my godsdamn soul to be at your side?!"

"I didn't ask you to!"

"I didn't have a choice!" His breathing was ragged, he tried to concentrate on keeping everything still, but it was more effort than he could handle. "All we've been doing is keeping secrets from each other, and ever since that night in the tavern, everything we were building has come undone. Dammit, Eve, we're better than this."

She knit her brows and bit her lip. "Why do I feel we are talking about something other than protecting me?"

His hazel eyes pierced her brown ones, and he could feel the words on his lips, how badly he wanted her to know how much she meant to him, what lengths he would go through to make her safe. But before he could utter a single one, he felt a hand on his shoulder and heard the thunderous voices echoing through the air once more. Caught in his emotions, his magic had slipped, and time was as it was once more.

"I think you've had her long enough. Time to give a pirate a chance."

Dakon turned, meeting Izan's dark eyes.

"I think Eve needs rest."

Izan peered over at her. "Why don't I let her tell me what she wants?"

Dakon could feel how hot his body was; part of him worried he would burn a hole beneath Izan's feet if he was pushed any further. They both looked at Eve, who was lost for words.

What am I doing?

He shook his head, feeling ashamed.

"Sorry," Dakon mumbled, "of course Eve knows what she wants."

Without another word, he brushed past Izan and headed to the cabin, hoping that Beast was there to comfort him.

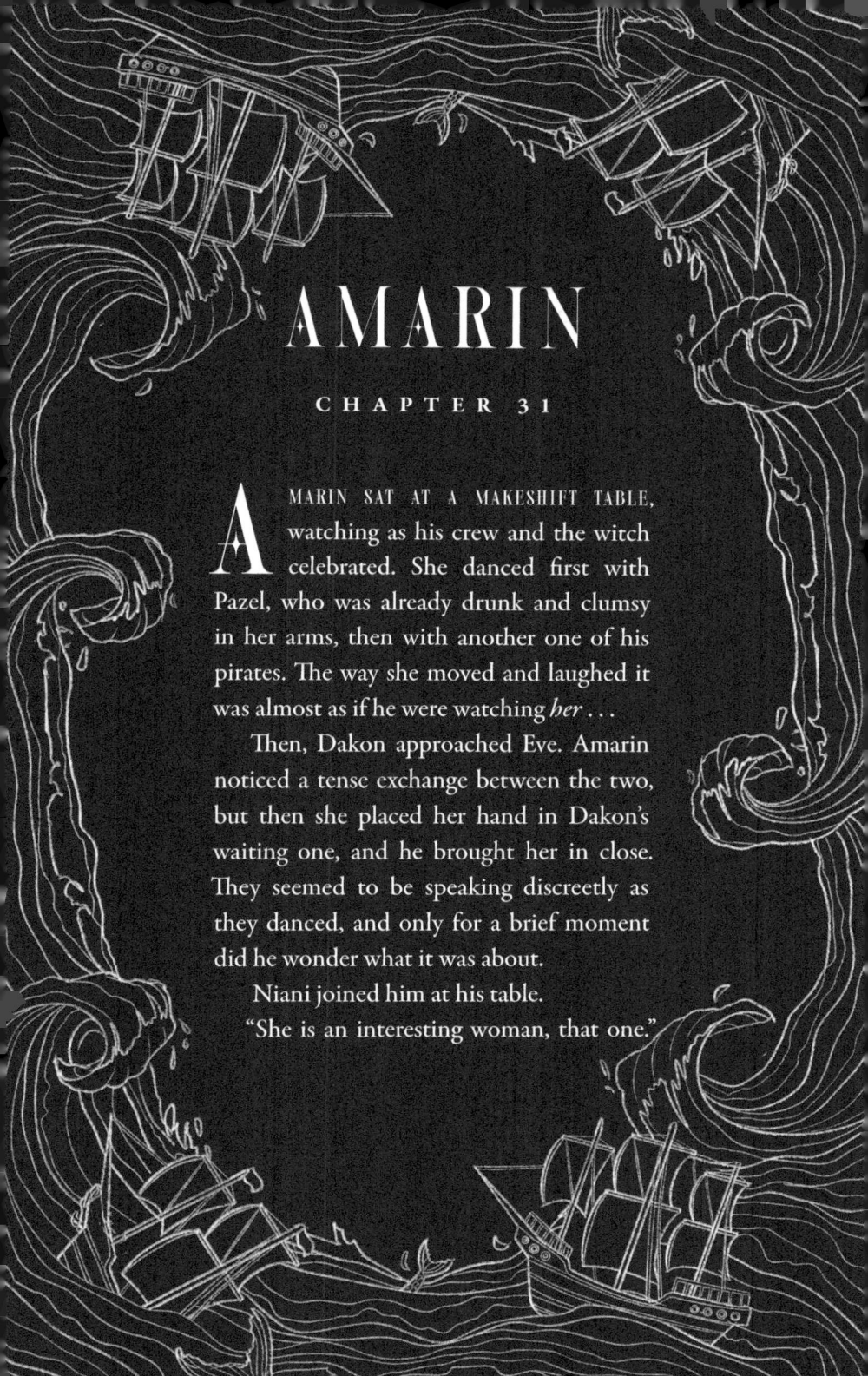

AMARIN

CHAPTER 31

AMARIN SAT AT A MAKESHIFT TABLE, watching as his crew and the witch celebrated. She danced first with Pazel, who was already drunk and clumsy in her arms, then with another one of his pirates. The way she moved and laughed it was almost as if he were watching *her* . . .

Then, Dakon approached Eve. Amarin noticed a tense exchange between the two, but then she placed her hand in Dakon's waiting one, and he brought her in close. They seemed to be speaking discreetly as they danced, and only for a brief moment did he wonder what it was about.

Niani joined him at his table.

"She is an interesting woman, that one."

Niani lifted her chin to Eve. "I've seen how you watch them."

Amarin took another drink. "Only fools try to meddle in the lives of others."

Niani laughed. "Then a fool I may be, but a shrewd one at that."

He smirked. "Fine. What do you make of them?"

"Is it not clear?" She tilted her head to Eve and Dakon. "They are bound by something, though I am not sure what."

"Let me guess, *love*." Amarin scoffed.

"Close." She smiled. "I expect we may have a quarrel soon."

"I'm not interested."

"But he is." She lifted her gaze across the deck and Amarin followed it. The ship's healer, Izan, took a swig of a drink and was making his way too confidently toward Eve.

"Oh."

"Yes, Captain"—she finished her drink—"we may have some entertainment to look forward to. Or a funeral. Either way, here's to a good night." She stood, clinking her mug against his and walked back into the small crowd where Pazel waited for her.

Amarin continued watching as Izan spoke with Eve and Dakon. Dakon stepped back but eventually brooded away. Izan and Eve began to dance, this time she was silent, but her eyes said everything unspoken.

A lowly pirate and a beautiful witch.

The fool stood no chance.

Witnessing this moment reminded him of someone he once loved a long, long time ago.

Thirty-Seven Years Ago

AMARIN FINISHED CLEANING THE DECK FILLED WITH THE REMNANTS of fishes from the day's catch. He was on night shift, a punishment for talking back to the first mate about something that now seemed entirely unimportant. He stowed the cleaning materials and made his way back up to the empty deck. It was the middle of the night, in the middle of the sea, without a soul to hear the pirates sleeping aboard but the gods.

He considered cursing them but kept his tongue. He may be a young man, but he was not stupid enough to incur their wrath while aboard a ship. That much he had learned in all his years of living on the water. He was but a lowly pirate, making his way through the ranks of various ships, hoping to one day command a fleet of his own. Perhaps, join a crew of his own making, liberating and free of the constraints of taking orders from others.

He thought of the music of his village, Prialis, where he spent the first few years of his life. An island east of Serit, where the beaches were warm every season and he could climb the trees and eat their fruit with ease. Each year they celebrated the gods; the villagers would play music and sing for the enjoyment of the crowd. He remembered their melodies and voices: joyous and free-spirited. He lingered on the memory, the singing, of dancing with his mother as a young boy.

"It sounds lovely." He heard a gentle voice from behind him. He whirled, taking in sight of the captain's not-so-secret stowaway. She walked toward him along the railing, her bright eyes curious and full of wonder.

"I've never heard such beautiful music before."

"I didn't realize I had company," Amarin mumbled, fully aware of the witch with tricks the captain smuggled aboard. He overheard some of the crew say the captain planned to sell her for a decent price in Bastard's Haven after a quick stop in Givensmir. He pitied the young woman.

"I'm sorry. I couldn't sleep."

"Well, you're welcome to join me, if you can keep my thoughts to yourself."

The witch smiled, and he was momentarily lost in how magical it looked. "Of course."

They leaned against the railing in silence for a few moments, and he tried to think about anything but her presence next to him.

"Do you not have music where you're from?"

"We do, but it sounds nothing like where you grew up."

"It was all we had for entertainment. The sounds of our voices and whatever instruments we could make from the land."

"I like it."

"So did I."

"And your dancing, quite enthusiastic for your age." She giggled.

Amarin nearly forgot to respond, so focused on the sweet sound. "I was a perfect dancer by my sixth nameday, thank you."

She smirked, facing the sea, taking in the gentle waves as they shone under the clear night sky. "I don't doubt it."

He turned to face her, seeing how very mortal she appeared to him. Nothing like the rumors of the crew aboard, how she frightened them with her witchcraft and mutterings. It was bad enough that the captain chose to stop at the Silver Port, even worse that he brought a witch back. It was tantamount to a death sentence in the Blackthorn, and yet, each season dozens of witches were captured there and sold throughout Serit. It was no wonder the captain made swift work of their departure. He had a prize worth thousands of gold coins.

Amarin's stomach knotted as the last thought came to him, knowing her future was bleak.

"How is the captain treating you?"

"Good, I suppose."

"Good." He nodded, unsure of what else to say.

"I know what he plans to do with me," she said, still eyeing the waters. "He thinks quite loudly."

Amarin couldn't hide his surprise. "Then why not try and escape? Why come onto this ship at all?"

She lowered her gaze to her hands, her fingers fiddling with each other. "This ship is my escape, and after . . . well, I have plans too."

"I can't imagine the captain would agree to them." He sighed. "He is not particularly fond of negotiations that aren't suited to his pocketbooks."

She turned to face him, cocking her head. "You underestimate me?"

"No, not exactly."

"Then you overestimate your captain."

Amarin couldn't think of a reply.

She leaned in, whispering, "He will not last long, and by then I will be gone."

Her eyes were bold and serious, and shivers ran down his spine. He thought of all the rumors of the Blackthorn witches. Their bloodthirsty tendencies, their witchcraft, how they defied the gods above. His mouth felt dry as he weighed this.

"What do you mean?"

Then, all at once her serious eyes brightened, and her face crumpled into another giggle. "You cannot spook so easily if you ever wish to be a captain. You must be what people fear, nothing less."

"Understood," he managed, letting out a deep breath, compelled to smile along with her. "I shall be as chilling as Death."

"Ah, yes. Your gods," she replied, picking a bit of invisible dirt off her dress. "Now, about your dancing . . ."

"What about it?"

"Did your mother teach you?"

"She did. As did some of the other villagers. Do you not dance in the Blackthorn?"

"We do." She smiled as if recalling memories of the past. "I love dancing."

He wasn't sure what compelled him to ask—perhaps the fondness of his memories, the way she looked in the bright moonlight, or both—but he opened his hand out to her.

"Would you dance with me?"

She knit her brow, looking down at it and back up again. "Are you sure?"

"That doesn't answer my question."

She smiled. "As you wish."

The witch placed her hand in his, and he grasped it gently, feeling a flutter in his chest. She seemed to feel it, too, looking curiously at him from beneath her lashes.

Be confident, you fool!

Amarin cleared his throat, leading her out to the center of the deck. She pressed up tenderly against him, placing a hand on his shoulder and the other in his free hand. Goosebumps rose on his skin, and his breathing was shaky as he placed his hand around her lower back.

"Take the lead," she whispered.

It took every bit of willpower he had to begin moving gently with her in his arms, suddenly he was terrified that he may trip himself or her during the dance. It had been a long time since he danced with a woman, and he worried that he may not remember all the steps.

She began to hum, and he calmed, thinking of the music of his village once more. Amarin brought her in close as they swayed together. A gentle breeze flowed, and the scent of sea salt and chamomile filled him. He never wished to forget it. And for a moment he wondered if this was truly happening or if he was in a heartless dream ready to wake up alone once more.

"I don't know your name," he whispered against her ear.

"Lucia," she breathed, seemingly off in a world of her own. "Yours?"

"Amarin."

"Amarin," she said, lifting her chin to face him. "It suits you."

They continued swaying against the music of his memories and the all-too-quick beating of his heart. He wondered if she felt the same.

Of course not, you idiot. You're a damn pirate.

He tilted his head back, laughing. "Now you're trying to wound me."

"How dare you." She bit her lip, stifling a laugh.

"Well, where do we go from here?" He held her gaze with a wicked grin.

"Perhaps, you can help me remember."

"I wouldn't want to put you through such torture, surely, if it was so forgettable."

She stood. "Then I shall go and leave you to your torment."

Eve began to walk past Izan as he sat, but he reached for her. His touch around her wrist made something tighten inside her. She hesitated and turned to face him.

He met her gaze, lips parted slightly.

She could hear her heartbeat in her ears, loud and quick.

Was she even breathing?

He stood, slowly, his eyes never leaving hers. They were intense, the silver tint glistening against the candlelight. He took her face gently in his hands, his thumb tracing her lips.

She let out a soft whimper, needing him closer.

He bent down, his lips barely brushing hers, waiting.

Eve swallowed, her mouth dry.

"Kiss me," she breathed.

He pressed his lips against hers, his hands wrapping around her waist, pulling her closer. She placed hers against his chest, feeling her way up his rigid shoulders and into his wavy hair twisting her fingers in the smooth strands.

Eve pushed him up against the cabin wall, and he groaned against their kisses. His hands released her braid, her hair tossing wild and free. Her skin heated, and she was desperate for more before her body turned to flames in his arms.

She removed his clothing greedily, their kiss never faltering.

He led them to his makeshift bed, the blankets beneath cushioning her as he laid her back. He tugged her blouse and trousers off, his eyes widening as he took her body in. She tugged him over her, wanting nothing more than to have him in her arms. He trailed kisses from her lips down to her neck, his hands slowly moving along her body.

"Do you—"

"Yes," she said, "yes."

He smiled against her lips, reaching his hand down her thighs. His touch there was too much, this kiss was too much, she could feel the sweat on her skin, her body like an open hearth as she tried to quell the fire within. He lifted his hand back up to her hips, settling himself between her legs.

Eve shuddered as he eased himself inside. She let out a low moan, closing her eyes as she wrapped her legs around his waist. He leaned over her, their lips meeting once more.

"Your eyes," he murmured, thrusting further in her, "open them."

Eve groaned, pulling him closer, but kept her eyes closed. She was too afraid to open them, afraid of what it might mean to lay her feelings bare as they still warred between him and another. Tears pooled at the corners of her eyes, overwhelmed by everything he was making her feel.

He thrusted again. "Please, *Eve*."

The way he said her name—a gentle beg, a longing—slowly broke down her walls.

She opened her damp lashes, taking in his tender smile.

"There's my lady."

He kissed her softly, keeping his eyes on hers. She felt vulnerable with something this powerful. She tilted her head back, starting to close her eyes again to escape, to imagine them both, but he ran his fingers gently across her cheek.

"Stay with me," he pleaded. "There are no secrets, remember?"

Eve focused on him, nearly forgetting how her skin felt aflame as she kept hold of his gaze. "No secrets," she repeated.

Izan lifted himself to his elbows, looking down at Eve with a blissful smile. She raised her hand to him, brushing away his loose tendrils again and tucking them behind his ear.

"You are beautiful, Eve," he whispered.

She smiled timidly, unsure of what to say.

He kissed her cheek. "What? No banter?"

She giggled. "I'm at a loss for words."

"Miracles do happen."

She shoved him playfully. "I can still burn you."

He bit his lip. "I have enough battle scars for the moment, thank you."

Eve looked at the burn marks healing across his skin, guilt clawed through her. "I'm sorry."

"It doesn't hurt as bad as it looks, I assure you."

She shifted uncomfortably. "Are all healers so quick to mend?"

"Depends"—he rested his forehead against hers—"on what kind of healer they are." He kissed her temple.

"What kind are you?"

He shifted to lay next to her. "One of the sea."

"Ah, yes, where you belong."

"It's who I am."

"The sea or healing?"

"Both."

She huffed. "But where is home for you when you're not over the water?"

He gazed upon her silently for a moment. His brow creased as he shook his head. "Perhaps one day we can talk about where I truly come from."

Before she could respond, he pulled her in close, capturing her mouth once more.

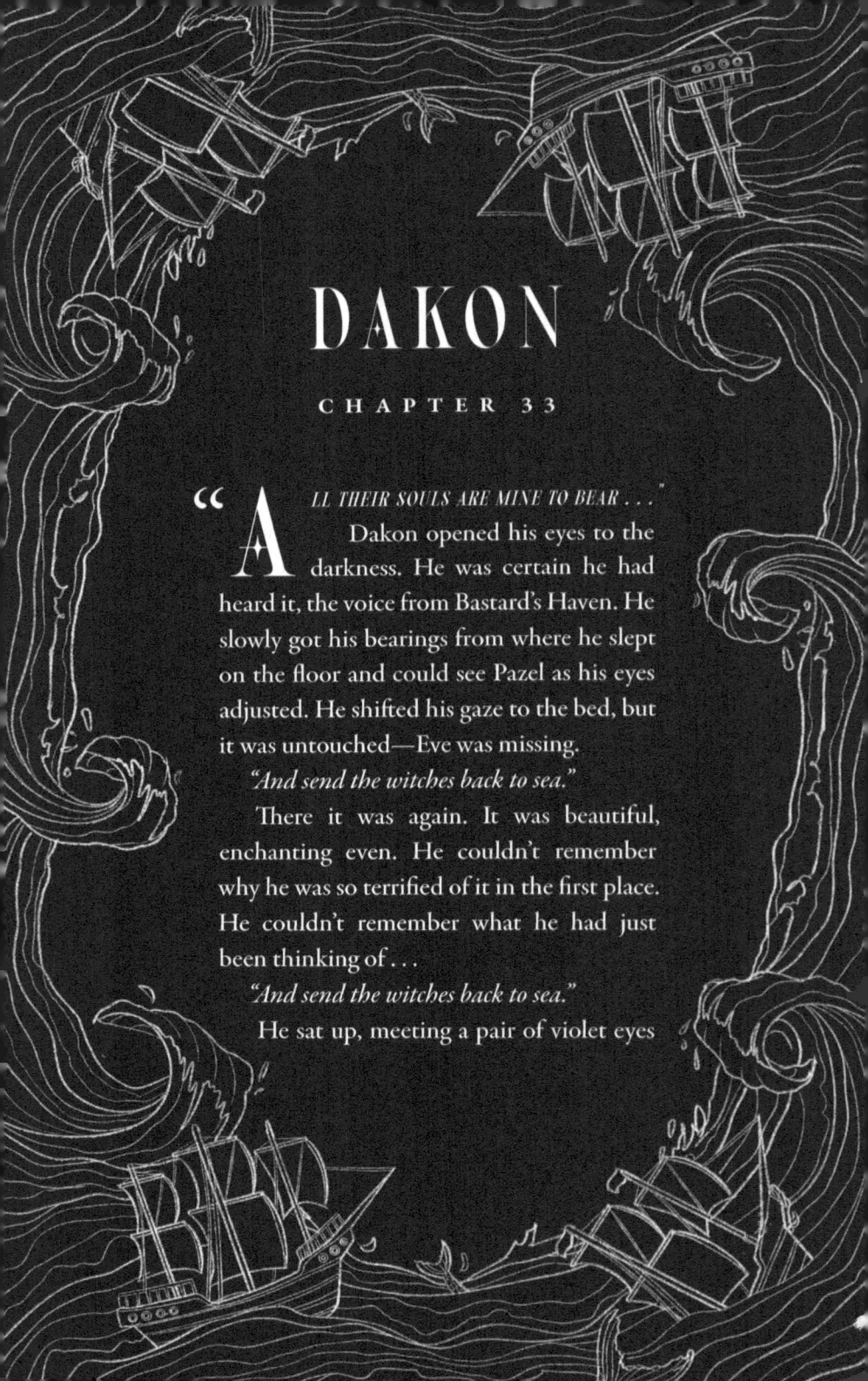

DAKON

CHAPTER 33

"ALL THEIR SOULS ARE MINE TO BEAR..."
Dakon opened his eyes to the darkness. He was certain he had heard it, the voice from Bastard's Haven. He slowly got his bearings from where he slept on the floor and could see Pazel as his eyes adjusted. He shifted his gaze to the bed, but it was untouched—Eve was missing.

"And send the witches back to sea."

There it was again. It was beautiful, enchanting even. He couldn't remember why he was so terrified of it in the first place. He couldn't remember what he had just been thinking of...

"And send the witches back to sea."

He sat up, meeting a pair of violet eyes

through the porthole. She was serene and welcoming, reminding him of warm thoughts and happy places. She pointed a delicate finger at him, smiling gently, invitingly.

Dakon stood, taking a step toward her, but she giggled and shook her head. He stopped, watching as she pointed at his cabin door. He turned to face it, feeling himself walk to it. He had a deep desire to see her, as if nothing else mattered.

"And send the witches back to sea."

She was seductive, alluring. He needed to speak with her, needed to see this woman with violet eyes. He felt a tug at his sleeve just as he was about to twist the knob. It was Beast, whining and tugging him back.

Something about Beast's face, his reluctance to release him nearly cleared his clouded mind. The gytrash's eyes bore into his, pleading. Dakon's hand lingered on the knob, concentrating on Beast, trying to remember why he was standing before the door.

"And send the witches back to sea."

This song, this voice singing. It compelled—no, demanded—that he follow it. A deep, primal urge warred within him, begging him to seek out the woman behind it. He would die if he didn't find her.

"I'll be right back, Beast."

Dakon made his way to the deck, where the rain pounded on the wooden planks and blurred his vision. He whirled around, trying to find where it came from, but an unsettling realization dawned on him. The deck was empty, not a soul around that he could see.

Where was the night shift?

Where was the woman with violet eyes?

He stood, desperately confused, by the main mast. His clothes were drenched, the rain picked up speed, and panic clawed its way through him until she sang again.

"And send the witches back to sea."

He turned to the voice, and his blood ran cold.

Adriana was sitting at the edge of the railing, her arm reaching out to him. Her hazel eyes met his, and the world around them stopped.

"Dakon, my love, I have been waiting for you."

Dakon's heart thundered so violently he swore it would burst through his chest. He swallowed, his mouth feeling dry despite the rain, and took a step toward her. A million questions begged to be released from his lips.

"A-Adriana, how did you get here?"

She lifted both arms up to him now, letting the rain soak her thin, blush-colored dress. Her soft lips, the very ones he had once kissed so sweetly, were lifted in a smile. Her smooth, brown hair was drenched, sticking to her face and chest. Even so, she appeared serene and beautiful, the very essence of his memories come to life. It took all his strength to not fall at his knees for her.

"Will you not embrace me?"

Dakon shivered with excitement under the frigid, unrelenting deluge.

She's here.

She loves me.

She chose me.

She shifted slightly and a panic seized him. He lifted his arms, trying to remain calm. "Can you please get off the railing? It's too slick."

Adriana lowered her arms, wrapping them around herself instead. Her lips began to tremble, her eyes downcast. "I thought you loved me, Dakon." She shifted back further, close to falling should the ship sway hard.

"I do, Adriana!" He reached a hand out, only an arm's length away, trying not to startle her. He couldn't understand why she would tempt Death this way, not after they were finally together. "I don't want you to fall. Come here, please, in my arms."

She met his eyes once more, then quickly shifted it behind him. Her soft gaze now narrowed in fury.

"Dakon! Stop!"

It was Eve's voice. He turned to see her, Beast, and the crew in various states of undress and shock.

"Siren!" Amarin shouted, drawing out his sword.

Izan held Eve back as she fought against him. Rain turned to mist against her body, her eyes turned that peculiar red color. Izan was losing his grip against the heat of her skin.

A barrage of shouts and screams pierced through the brutal downpour, waking Dakon from his daze.

"Run!"

"Save yourself!"

"Cover your ears!"

"Fire witch!" Adriana screeched, pointing at Eve. Dakon turned back to Adriana, everything settling upon him too late. She was not herself, her hazel eyes were violet, her lips curled revealing rows of sharp teeth. He tried to run, but the creature that was Adriana grabbed him in a fit of strength.

She screeched again, quickly releasing him.

Her hand turned to burning flesh.

She bellowed angrily and grabbed hold of Dakon's collar. He fought against her as she shoved him to the railing.

"You *will* come with me!" she growled, morphing before his eyes into a creature he had never seen before. Her skin was scale-like, her eyes large and deadly, her mouth twisted and bloody. Her legs began morphing into one. She was a siren, the very ones from Cerene's stories, coming to take him into the treacherous sea.

He pushed her off him but slipped on the deck. The rain pounded harder, stinging his exposed skin and nearly drowning him as he tried to get to his feet. Then, a shadow leaped over him.

He watched as Beast barreled into the siren, sinking his teeth into her flesh. They battled on the deck as Eve reached a hand to him.

"Hurry!" she screamed, pointing to the edge of the ship. With trembling limbs, Dakon turned in time to see more sirens, climbing over the railing. There were too many of them. Lightning lit the ship from a distance, thunder rolled deep and furious.

Dakon met Eve's eyes, grasping her hand and clamoring to his feet. They were nearly halfway across the deck to the rest of the crew who now grasped weapons preparing for the inevitable, before Dakon heard a sickening crack. He whirled, seeing the siren shove Beast onto the ground. The gytrash did not move, laying limp and still beneath the siren.

"Beast!" Dakon screamed.

The siren pushed him aside, discarding him as if he were nothing. Her eyes locked in Dakon's direction and with a deep breath, she screeched, loud and deafening into the night sky. Dakon and Eve fell to the deck, writhing in pain.

Lightning cracked across the sky, the rain pelting their skin, and the storm violently shook the ship. The *Wretched Sentinel* turned to madness. Sirens clambered onto the deck, leaping toward the crew. The pirates were in uproar with swords, daggers, fists, using anything they could to make it out alive.

The ship rocked chaotically, and Dakon watched in horror as two pirates were dragged off the ship by sirens. Niani and Pazel, swords in hand, fought together against a terrifying siren with glowing, green eyes. Amarin struggled to fight one whose claws sank into another pirate. He shoved the siren off, but the pirate was dead.

"Damn you, Cassandra!" he hollered as he sliced his sword chaotically in the air. "Stop this madness!"

Cassandra?

Dakon had no time to think before his eyes caught sight of Izan stabbing one of the sirens with a knife. He pulled it out but quickly became overwhelmed as more shoved him down the stairs.

"Get to Amarin's cabin!" Dakon yelled at Eve. They were only a few strides away from it, such a short distance that felt entire lifetimes

away. A siren and a pirate struggled against each other, knocking Eve and Dakon back to the ground.

Dakon grabbed Eve's hand, dragging her as quickly as he could to the cabin. They were so close, the door was in sight, the handle only a few feet away, he only needed to reach out and touch it.

The shrieking continued, nearly deafening Dakon as he and Eve fell against the door. All around him, the captain, crew, and Pazel were fighting against or to free themselves from the sirens.

He thrust open the door, practically throwing Eve inside. She barely made it in before claws, sharp and long, wrapped around his chest.

"You are coming with me, *lover*," the violet siren purred in his ear.

"No!" Eve screamed.

Dakon kicked the door closed before she could try to save him. He willed his powers to come, for any bit of magic to come. His skin heated as he struggled against her tight grip. Her flesh hissed as his scalding skin seared her. She shrieked in pain, but did not let go, throwing them overboard.

Dakon grabbed the edge of the railing, holding on as the siren dug her nails into the flesh of his side. He screamed at the agony of his skin tearing apart as she clenched tighter.

"You are mine!"

Pazel and Niani appeared then, grabbing hold of his arms, trying to pull him back onto the ship.

Dakon looked down, trying to kick the siren away amidst the pain, and his heart nearly stopped. Sirens emerged from the dark waters clamoring over each other like starving sharks in a pool of prey. They reached their scaled, decaying hands from the water begging for a taste of him.

Dakon struggled, his hands in a slippery grip against Pazel and Niani. They were losing him, he could feel it, he could see it on their faces.

"Cut his throat and be done with it!"

He kicked against the siren with all his might, but to no avail. Her long fingers gripped his neck, and his vision ran red.

DAKON RECALLED THE TIME HE TRULY FELL IN LOVE WITH ADRIANA. It was not at a ball, or a dinner, or a fancy event for which he was the stoic, handsome, wealthy prince that took her breath away. But under the silver birches of Givensmir's castle forests, where he escorted her through the footworn paths on a horse that he tended to personally.

They would lie underneath the shade it provided in the sticky, summer sun and discuss all matters of great unimportance such as meddling gossips and the best sweets in the castle kitchens.

On this day, however, deep in his lies of a secret admirer who would pass along notes through him, Adriana spoke of her dreams: to travel outside of Serit and see the lands beyond, to learn the ways of other kingdoms and pass the knowledge onto the people.

"We could be great if we gave them what they needed."

He had a sudden thought, then. How he would not stop her, if he could, from leaving. He would love her through her dreams, her distance, and whatever made her happy. Because to him, at least, loving someone meant letting them be who and where they wanted to be. Even if that did not include him.

He loved her. This was forever indisputable.

Cerene was right.

Coveting her would only bring him misery and death.

And I would love her all over again, he thought, as his body went limp.

FIRE ENGULFED HIM, ITS BURNING TOUCH ON HIS SKIN.
Dakon welcomed it.
There were screams from far away, shrill and violent in the air.
Then silence.

"HE'S NOT GOING TO MAKE IT⁻"
"Save him, or I will make you beg for death!"
Eve.
It was *Eve.*

A GENTLE HAND HELD ONTO HIM.
Teardrops fell onto his skin and made a hissing sound.
It was *their* kind of warm.

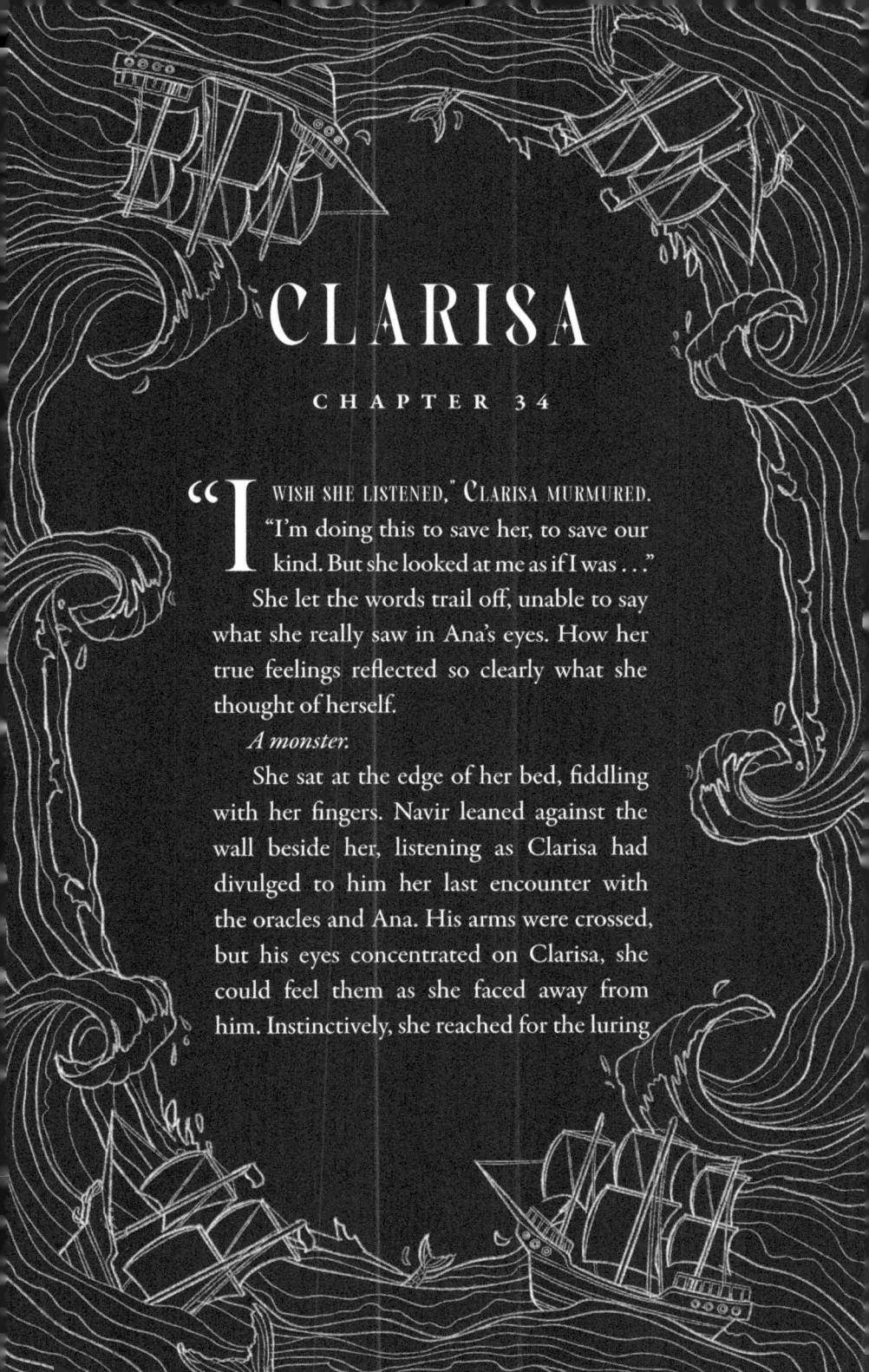

CLARISA

CHAPTER 34

"I WISH SHE LISTENED," CLARISA MURMURED. "I'm doing this to save her, to save our kind. But she looked at me as if I was . . ."

She let the words trail off, unable to say what she really saw in Ana's eyes. How her true feelings reflected so clearly what she thought of herself.

A monster.

She sat at the edge of her bed, fiddling with her fingers. Navir leaned against the wall beside her, listening as Clarisa had divulged to him her last encounter with the oracles and Ana. His arms were crossed, but his eyes concentrated on Clarisa, she could feel them as she faced away from him. Instinctively, she reached for the luring crystal about her neck, needing to feel its smooth texture beneath her fingers.

Tink. Tink. Tink.

He sighed. "You are destined for something she cannot understand. Not yet."

Clarisa met his eyes. "What if there is another way? A way that doesn't involve forbidden magic?"

Even as the words left her lips, she did not feel their conviction. It would prove difficult to leave the crystal and its magic, much less destroy it.

Tink. Tink. Tink.

"The oracles have given you valuable information. We will need them in the war to come."

A rumble of thunder in the distance startled Clarisa, water dripped from her hands. She shook them out and wiped the dampness off on her dress.

Her chambers were too cold now, her body trembled, and she hugged herself as she thought of Ana.

Will she forgive me?

Navir removed his cloak and wrapped it around her, his touch making her shiver unwelcomely, but she accepted the gesture. He was the only ally she had in this matter.

He sat too close to her, and Clarisa pretended not to notice, focusing intently on a spot on the floor.

"Thank you," she whispered, trying to cut through the silence before it stretched too long.

Navir nodded. "I am here for you, Clarisa. Your life, your power, is of the utmost importance to me."

"And what if it went away? What if it fades as the oracles predicted?"

He grimaced. "I am certain they meant something else by it. Oracles, it is said, have a peculiar way of speaking."

"I don't want to lose my magic," Clarisa admitted, her hands shaking.

Navir took them in his own. "Then I will destroy anything that would try to."

Clarisa narrowed her eyes at him, trying to carefully remove her hands from his grip, but he tightened them. "Anything or *anyone*."

She pulled back more forcefully, and he relented. His nostrils flared as he stood and began pacing along the floor.

"Do you know when I might see my cousin?" she asked, changing course.

"My mother has yet to make a decision on their fates. I suspect it is because she is waiting for you to prove your worth."

Clarisa's eyes widened. "There is nothing I can do until the mortals attack next."

"Oh, there is much to do. And you wouldn't want your poor cousin and his friend to suffer would you?"

Clarisa stood, letting Navir's cloak fall to the ground. "Are you threatening me?"

"It's not a threat, my dear Clarisa. It's a promise."

Her name on his lips felt vile; she no longer wanted to be alone with him. "Harming innocent mortals is beneath us."

"They were on their way to kill us; they are the spoils of a war *they* started."

"A war their king started," she corrected him.

He stopped pacing, his eyes locking on hers. "I'm beginning to wonder whose side you're on."

"How could you ask me that?"

"How could you question me?!" He stepped toward her. "If I hadn't spoken for you, you wouldn't be here. You should be thanking me."

Clarisa bit her tongue, hating the truth of his words.

Navir took another step closer. "Don't lose sight of the real threat. Your sister grows in strength every day, has familiars of her own, and rumor has it she is on a ship headed here to find you."

"That can't be." Clarisa clutched her crystal once more.

Tink. Tink. Tink.

"This is no longer a war between us and the mortals, nor us and the Strix . . . this is a war between you and your sister."

Clarisa could feel the cold tears running down her cheeks.

"She is coming for her revenge, just as I predicted," he continued. "Your precious Ana will not be safe for long. And with you distracted by visiting cousins and debating moralities of forbidden magic, she will destroy everything and everyone you love."

Clarisa held herself, trying to stay on her feet, the overwhelming sense of dread nearly knocking her to the ground.

I need to keep Ana safe.

She sat back on the bed, trying to keep calm as the lightning flashed in the window. Navir knelt before her, lifting her chin so she met his gaze.

"If you truly love Ana, you will do anything to keep her alive."

"I love her." Clarisa's hands were damp again, her tears falling onto them like her own bout of raindrops.

"Then follow my lead, and I promise you both *paradise*."

It was disturbing and strange, the feeling she had as she looked in Navir's cold, blue eyes.

She could see her and Ana in the sun, running through the meadows of some foreign land far away from the Blackthorn, making love beneath the moon and stars. She closed her eyes and could nearly feel Ana pressed against her, her lips as they explored what was already hers, their hands as they caressed each other, promising to never let go.

"What do I need to do?" Clarisa breathed, unable to remove her gaze from Navir's, "I'll do anything."

He smirked, gripping her hands once more. "That's what I like to hear."

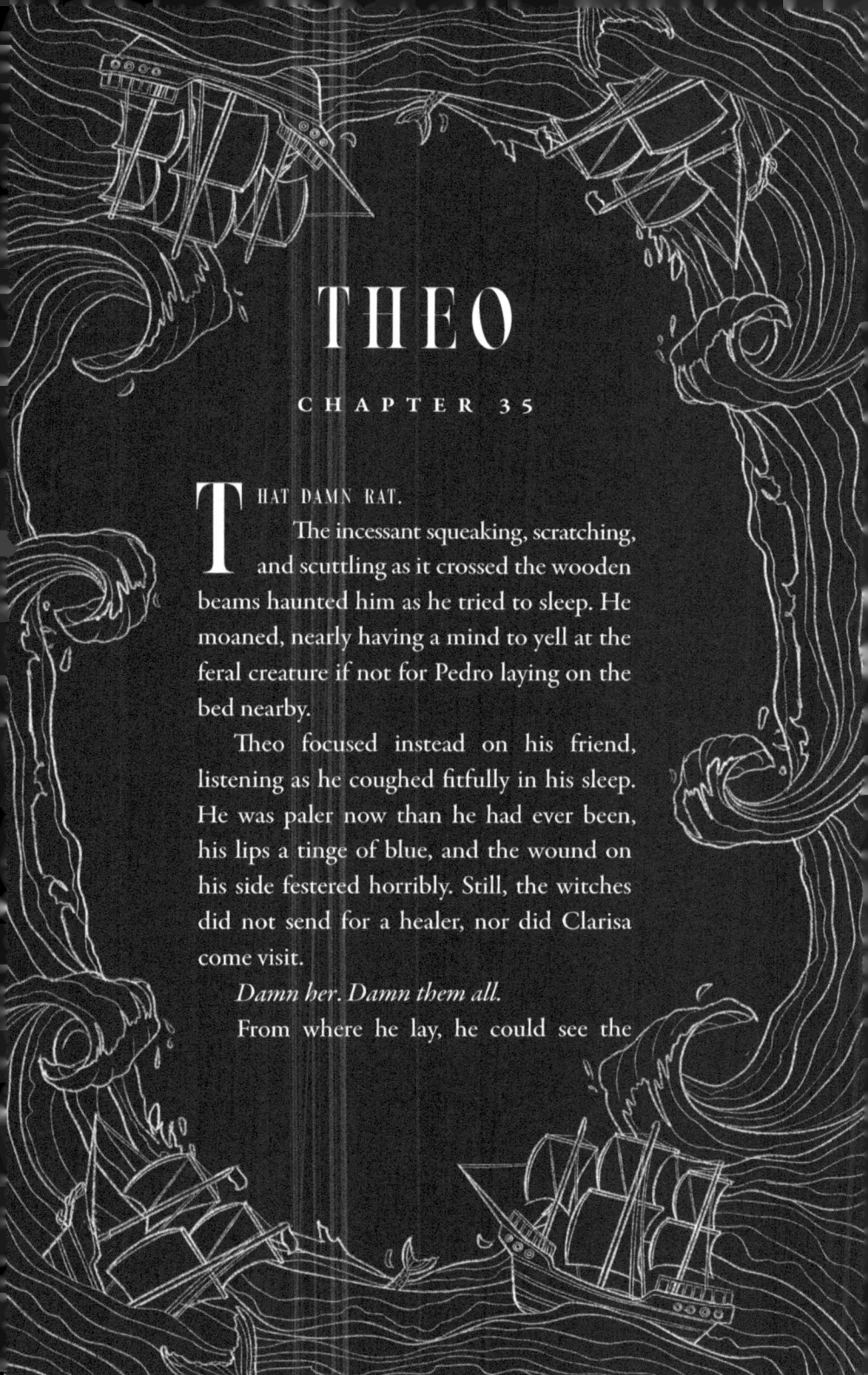

THEO

CHAPTER 35

THAT DAMN RAT.

The incessant squeaking, scratching, and scuttling as it crossed the wooden beams haunted him as he tried to sleep. He moaned, nearly having a mind to yell at the feral creature if not for Pedro laying on the bed nearby.

Theo focused instead on his friend, listening as he coughed fitfully in his sleep. He was paler now than he had ever been, his lips a tinge of blue, and the wound on his side festered horribly. Still, the witches did not send for a healer, nor did Clarisa come visit.

Damn her. Damn them all.

From where he lay, he could see the

hourglass on the table. The sand now filled a quarter of the bottom, still he had no idea what it meant. And after his bewitchment by Navir in the place of total darkness, he did not wish to trifle with it, leaving well enough alone.

There was a knock on the door and the rat scampered away into its hole in the wall. Slowly, the door opened and there Clarisa stood.

Pedro groaned, his eyes were still closed but he managed a few words. "Have they come to kill us?"

"I hope not." Theo stood carefully, watching as she removed the hood of her pale blue cloak.

"The queen has asked for you," she said, softly, gesturing to Pedro.

"As you can see, he is indisposed at the moment. Because you refuse to give him a healer, he is getting worse."

Clarisa raised a brow, then curiously looked up toward the roof. "W-we were not informed of his illness."

"Bullshit," Theo spat.

"I must do as I am commanded—"

"Get him a healer"—Theo placed himself between them—"or you will have to get through me."

Pedro coughed in the foreground, struggling to sit up. "Perhaps I can negotiate your freedom."

"No, you need help."

Guards came in then, shoving Clarisa aside. They rushed toward Theo, outnumbering and holding him back as the rest brought Pedro to his feet. They removed him from the chamber and cast Theo hard to the floor.

"He needs a healer!" Theo screamed after them, but it all happened too quickly. He was left on his knees, gasping for air.

Clarisa lingered by the open door. Her hand on the wood, her eyes cast down.

"Your time is running out," she whispered, a hint of sorrow in her voice.

Theo turned to face the hourglass.

It was now halfway done.

Impossible.

"Why are you doing this? Why not kill us now?" he shouted, the madness beginning to take hold of him. He couldn't deal with the unknown any longer, the dread that weighed on him day after day, never knowing when their end would come. And now Pedro was taken away to gods only knew where.

Clarisa stared at him with a glint of pity.

"Kill me! Please! Not him!"

Theo could have sworn tears pooled at the corners of her eyes, her cheeks flushed, watching as he cried onto the floor.

"Kill me!"

"I can't," she whispered. And without another word, left him alone in his misery.

"No!" he shouted. "No! No!"

He ran to the door, but it was locked. He pounded his fists against it, sure that it would break beneath his strength, but it didn't budge. Not even a splinter.

Pedro was the only one who kept him sane in this hell. He tried to calm himself down, but thoughts of what they could be doing to him creeped back into his mind.

Please, he begged whichever of the five gods was listening, *please spare him.*

Theo sank to the floor. He felt helpless and desperate and cursed at his dead father for ever putting them in this position. His greed had ruined them all ...

"The wretched man," he said. "All for witches who wanted to be left alone."

Just like Eve.

Her name spelled regret in his head. All she wanted was to live a mortal life, to love him, and he had cast her aside for propriety and what he believed to be honor.

Is this how she felt when she was trapped alone in her room, waiting for the worst to come?

His mouth tasted bitter as the last thought settled on him. He was a callous ass, and he desperately wished he could go back to that night and help her escape. He could have done it, or he could have at least tried.

"Stupid, stupid fool," he told himself.

He hoped that she had not been found, prayed that she was safe far, far away from Givensmir. Somewhere his wicked brother could not reach nor ever wish to find her. His heart sank and he didn't try to stop himself as the tears fell down his dirt-stained cheeks. He hoped that his sorrow would kill him, but that would have been too easy.

The gods were pernicious.

He looked back to the hourglass as it sprinkled grains of sand slowly, playing vicious games with his dread.

HOURS CRAWLED. DARKNESS SHROUDED HIM ONCE MORE. AND THEO could not find the will to move even when the door sprung open and shoved him back to the ground.

The guards carried Pedro in and threw him carelessly onto the bed.

All life sprang back into Theo as he realized Pedro was alive, grunting against the pain. He ran toward him as the guards left and locked the door.

"Pedro! Pedro, what happened?! What did they do to you?"

Pedro's brown skin was so pale, all the color there drained and smothered like a corpse. His mouth was still the faint blue hue, and his wound bled through his clothes. Theo ripped open Pedro's shirt, taking in the sight of blood in horror. A single name carved deep into his skin.

Eve.

There would be no surviving this.

"Pedro"—he gently placed his hand on Pedro's cheek—"please, talk to me."

Pedro knit his brows, his lips parted slightly, and he let out a ragged, but weak cough. "Theo."

"Yes, it's me, my friend. I'm here, you're safe."

"Theo. I failed you."

"No." He grasped Pedro's hand tight in his own, desperately wishing for any miracle, swearing internally that the gods would have his undying devotion for the remainder of his life. "You have never failed me. Ever."

Pedro locked eyes with Theo, they were no longer a warm almond shade, but a faded gray. "They will kill us all."

"Who?" Theo's blood-stained hands clutched Pedro's in a fierce grip.

Pedro's eyes widened, his mouth opened into a scream that did not leave, his body began shaking violently. "He watches us—he—"

Theo tried to remain calm, his hands firm on Pedro to prevent him from barreling out of bed. But he was uncontrollable, his mouth became rabid, and his eyes began to roll into the back of his head. Blood flowed from his mouth and the wound on his side covering Theo's chest and arms as he used all his strength to keep Pedro still.

"No, Pedro! It's getting worse!"

"He is watching!" Pedro screamed, and his arm shot up to the ceiling, pointing with a quivering finger. "He's watching!"

"Stop!" Theo shouted, tears falling as he clung to him miserably. "Please, stop!"

Then, he did.

Pedro's arm fell.

And his body went still.

"Pedro?" Theo lifted himself up, blood staining his clothing so red it was nearly black. Fear seized him, breaking his spirit in two.

No. No. This isn't real.

"Pedro?!"

It's a trick. Another trick by the witches.

"Pedro!"

He shook Pedro hard, unable to control the panic that ripped through him, the truth settling like a stone weight on his chest.

Pedro was gone.

His eyes stayed fixed on the beams, his heart no longer beating.

Theo cried, unrelenting, guttural sobs.

And even through his grief, he could still hear the cursed rat scampering on the beam.

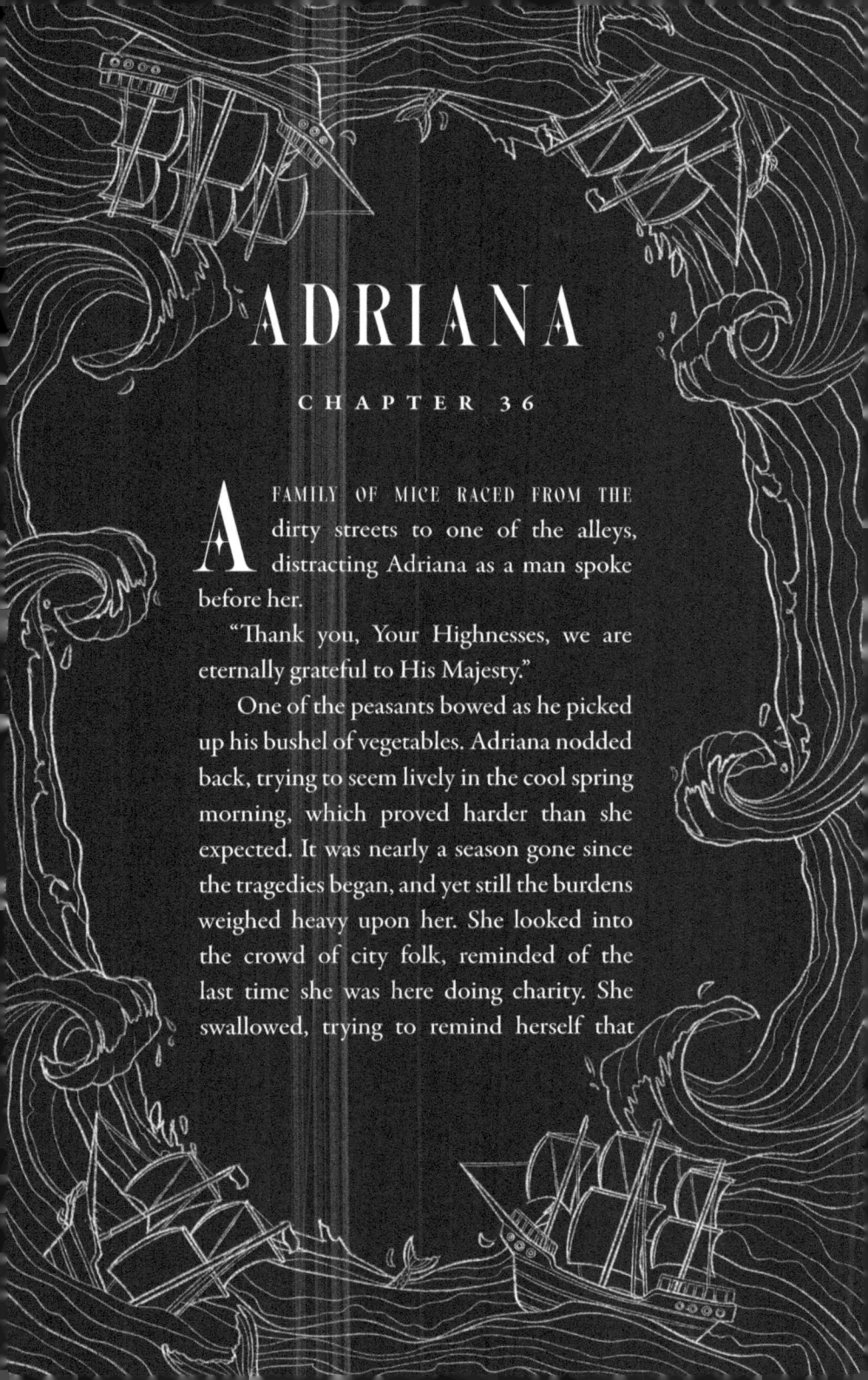

ADRIANA

CHAPTER 36

A FAMILY OF MICE RACED FROM THE dirty streets to one of the alleys, distracting Adriana as a man spoke before her.

"Thank you, Your Highnesses, we are eternally grateful to His Majesty."

One of the peasants bowed as he picked up his bushel of vegetables. Adriana nodded back, trying to seem lively in the cool spring morning, which proved harder than she expected. It was nearly a season gone since the tragedies began, and yet still the burdens weighed heavy upon her. She looked into the crowd of city folk, reminded of the last time she was here doing charity. She swallowed, trying to remind herself that these people were scared and struggling. Adriana desperately wished she could tell them she was frightened too.

Her mother pinched her covertly on her left arm. "Speak, my errant child."

Adriana pulled away and looked to the man. He was nearing his later years, tired and worn out from life's hardships. She blinked, coming to. "Yes, we shall tell His Majesty. Thank you for all you do for our kingdom."

It was rehearsed and the man knew it. But he smiled all the same and took his gift with him down the steps. She turned to Gabrielle to her right, who drank often from her chalice. Adriana suspected it was not water. Gabrielle grimaced as she sipped; Adriana placed a gentle hand on hers.

"I'm here, Gabrielle," she whispered.

Gabrielle gave her hand a firm squeeze in return.

"Thank you."

As Elder Borgias blessed the next offering of charity, her mother scolded her in trails of whispers. "What I fail to understand is how you are not smitten with happiness. You have everything a woman could ever wish for and still you transgress common decency."

Adriana breathed deeply, trying in vain to not let her mother's words vex her.

"And what's more is that you used to be so kind, now you walk around as if there is something the matter at all turns."

She focused on the crowd as Borgias preached of gratitude and sacrifice for the greater good. There were peasants of all ages, the young clinging to their mothers and fathers, the eldest typically standing alone. Sadness enveloped her as her eyes trailed over them.

"If I had even the slightest opportunities you did at your age, I would have thrived as a lady of the court."

She let her eyes linger on the street, looking to the alley where the mice had run.

Then, she saw them.

A guard and a young woman just beyond the crowd. She tried to leave his embrace, but he kept pulling her in, trying to force her into the alley. The people around them didn't notice—or pretended not to.

"Instead you waste it, spending all your time in your chambers like the spoiled princess you are."

The woman pushed against the guard, and he slapped her with the back of his hand. Adriana watched, horrified, as the guard then grabbed the woman by her hair, pulling her further between the shops.

"Your brother has high expectations of you, and you are letting us all down with your dalliances and daydreams."

Adriana stood, unable to keep her eyes off the woman. She trembled, her voice failing her.

"Adriana? What's happening?" Gabrielle stood and Adriana raised a trembling finger toward the woman.

The woman twisted and fought, scratching the guard's face just enough for him to release her. She began to run into the crowd.

Gabrielle cried out, gripping Adriana tight.

"What in the gods are you doing?!" Her mother grabbed her other arm, trying to shove her back into her seat.

"She needs help!" Adriana continued pointing, but it seemed no one heard her, because as soon as the words left her lips, another damning one caught the crowd's attention.

"Witch!" the guard bellowed, pointing at the frightened woman. "The witch is trying to escape!"

"No!" Adriana screamed.

But it was too late, the crowd parted for the guards to close in on the poor woman. She tried to fight against them but there were too many of them.

"Adriana, sit down at once!"

"No! She's innocent!" Adriana yelled, running toward the guards and the woman.

"What is the meaning of this?!" Borgias' voice carried over the chaos, surprisingly loud for a man of his advanced age.

The lying guard stepped forward. "This woman tried to tempt me with her wicked ways; I stopped her, but she struck me." He gestured to the scratches on his face. "She is a witch, I am certain."

"He's lying!" the woman cried. "He attacked me!"

"Silence the witch!" Borgias yelled, and the guards stuffed a cloth into the woman's mouth. She cried against them, her body slumping over in agony.

"Stop this madness!" Adriana begged, moving toward Borgias. "I saw him attack her, she is innocent!"

"Princess"—Borgias shook his head—"you have been bewitched."

Gabrielle ran up to them. "No, my elder, what the princess says is true!"

Borgias looked between the women, his eyes pitying. "This woman made you *think* you saw her being attacked. Your hearts are too pure and precious for her wicked tricks."

"Please, let her go," Adriana begged. Her legs buckled and Gabrielle caught her before she fell.

Borgias ignored them and gestured to someone behind her. Adriana turned in time to see Timothy grabbing her with as much politeness as he could muster in front of the people.

Adriana shoved him, pointing a finger at Borgias. The crowd made a collective gasp, to disrespect an elder was to wish a cruel fate by the gods.

"You are killing innocent women!" Adriana shouted. "They are innocent! She is innocent!"

"Take her away and silence her, *now*," Borgias hissed at Timothy, before turning to the confused city folk. Gabrielle followed in shock as another guard guided her carefully away.

"The poor princess." He placed his hand over his heart as guards circled Adriana. "This witch has tried to curse her but thank the gods and their many blessings she will surely recover with rest. She doesn't know of what she speaks."

Timothy grabbed Adriana, placing his hand over her mouth to keep her quiet. The guards kept their barrier around them, trying to hide how forcefully Timothy needed to drag her away. Adriana fought and struggled against him every step of the way to the carriage. She caught a glimpse of her mother, the scorn and disapproval on her face, shaking her head slowly. Her mother turned away as Adriana passed and clapped along with Borgias' new speech on why witches were the cause of their struggles. The guard gave Gabrielle another chalice and sat her down next to the Queen Mother. Gabrielle's eyes were haunted and glossed, her lips trembling slightly as she took another sip.

Angry tears cascaded down Adriana's face as Timothy finally shoved her in the carriage and stepped in with her. He closed the door and tapped on the roof; it began to move.

He was breathing heavily, stretching out his neck from the strain of their struggle. Adriana was shaking fiercely, terrified for the woman, angry that no one believed her.

She turned to Timothy, every bit of her wanted to claw his eyes out. In this moment, he was the embodiment of all those who watched and did nothing as women died for existing. Men like him didn't deserve the air they breathed.

"One day," she seethed, "you will die. And I will dance upon your ashes, because I will watch you burn. I will watch every single one of you burn."

Timothy smirked and shook his head. "Oh, Adriana, have you learned nothing?" He leaned in toward her, his face dangerously close.

"Women like you will always burn before men like me."

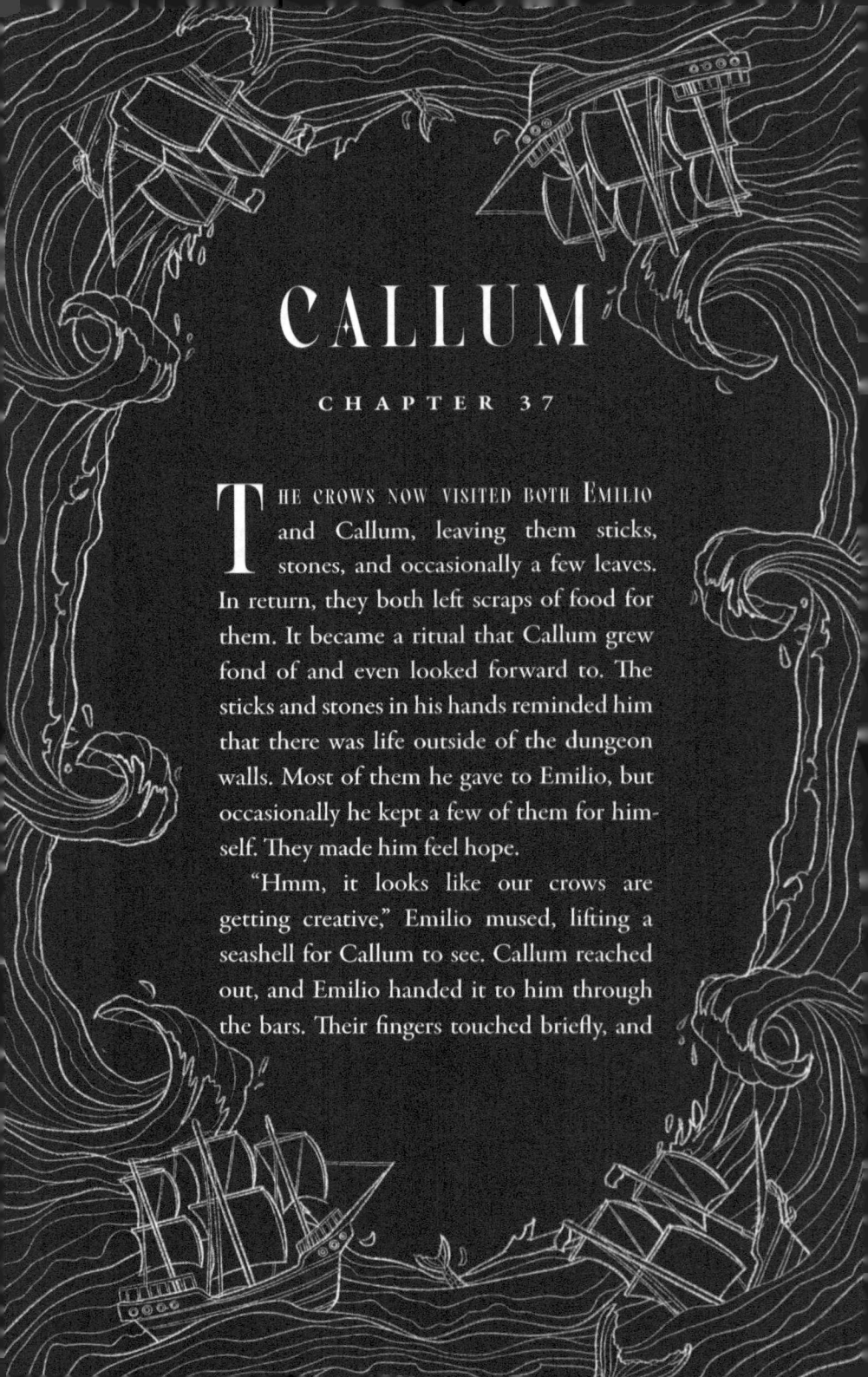

CALLUM

CHAPTER 37

THE CROWS NOW VISITED BOTH EMILIO and Callum, leaving them sticks, stones, and occasionally a few leaves. In return, they both left scraps of food for them. It became a ritual that Callum grew fond of and even looked forward to. The sticks and stones in his hands reminded him that there was life outside of the dungeon walls. Most of them he gave to Emilio, but occasionally he kept a few of them for himself. They made him feel hope.

"Hmm, it looks like our crows are getting creative," Emilio mused, lifting a seashell for Callum to see. Callum reached out, and Emilio handed it to him through the bars. Their fingers touched briefly, and

Callum hitched a breath, accidentally dropping it. It hit the ground and rolled a few feet away, out of their grasp.

"I'm so sorry," he said quickly.

Emilio smiled. "I felt it too."

Callum raised his eyes to meet Emilio's; there was no humor within them. They were sincere, glistening against the light that poured in through the barred dungeon windows, providing the only sense of comfort and security in their personal purgatory. He reached out once more toward Callum, his hand hovering between their cells.

"I would like to feel your touch again, if you want me to."

Callum's heart beat rapidly in his ears. He felt joyously over-whelmed and a bit vulnerable. He could not remember the last time he was touched this way; time lost its essence here. He appreciated the beard growing on Emilio, it made him look rugged and handsome. He wished that he could run his fingers through it.

Callum leaned against the bars and reached his hand to Emilio's. He was certain he was not breathing as they touched, a welcome shiver running through him.

"I wish we could do more than this," Emilio whispered.

"At least we have this." Callum tightened his grip gently and smiled as Emilio did the same.

The sound of metal on metal caused Callum to rip his hand away. As if on instinct, he cowered back toward the stone wall at the far end and watched for what was coming. Emilio furrowed his brow and lowered his hand. But he remained at the bars of his cell, following the sound.

Ulric and another guard clanked chains against the bars of the cells as they walked toward them.

"Wake up, Lord Callum! Wake up, you little shit," he called out.

Callum went to the ground, trying to make himself small, as if he could disappear by wishing it so.

"You're shit!" Emilio shouted at Ulric.

The enormous guard shoved the heavy chain at his bars, startling Emilio and making him fall backward onto the floor.

"Quiet, you," Ulric snarled. He turned to look at Callum. "Have you missed me?"

Callum didn't respond, putting his hands over his face, shaking uncontrollably.

Ulric gestured for the other guard to unlock Callum's cage, and he did so without hesitation.

"Come and fight me, you coward!" Emilio leapt to his feet and shook the bars of his cell violently.

Ulric snickered as he looked at Callum. "Don't worry, pretty boy. I'll make sure your savior has a full view."

The guards stalked into the cage.

Callum closed his eyes and imagined he was somewhere else. He could faintly hear Emilio scream and curse in the foreground and the sound of rattling cage doors that he was certain would break.

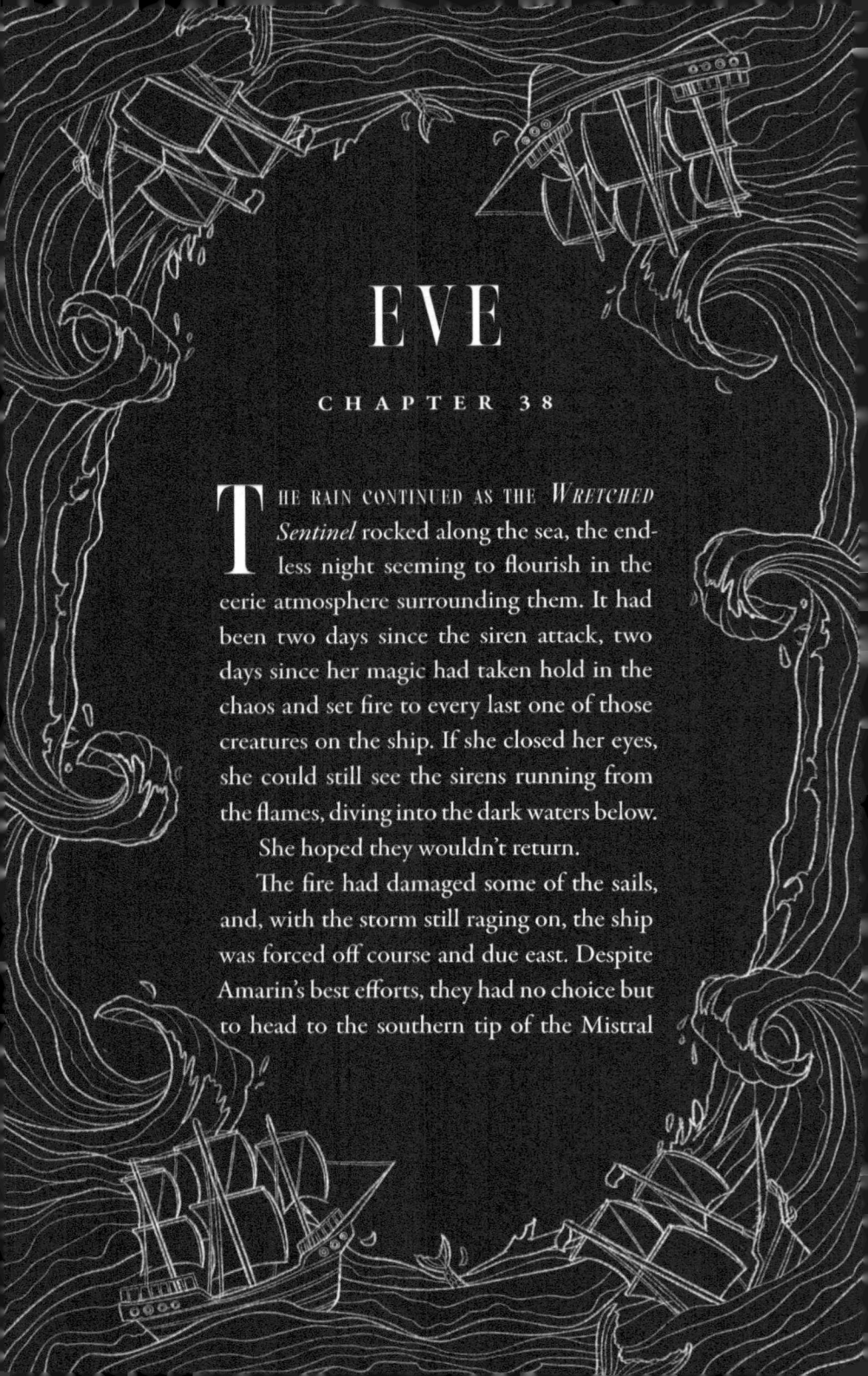

EVE

CHAPTER 38

THE RAIN CONTINUED AS THE *Wretched Sentinel* rocked along the sea, the endless night seeming to flourish in the eerie atmosphere surrounding them. It had been two days since the siren attack, two days since her magic had taken hold in the chaos and set fire to every last one of those creatures on the ship. If she closed her eyes, she could still see the sirens running from the flames, diving into the dark waters below.

She hoped they wouldn't return.

The fire had damaged some of the sails, and, with the storm still raging on, the ship was forced off course and due east. Despite Amarin's best efforts, they had no choice but to head to the southern tip of the Mistral

Islands. And now they waited as nature set their bearing apart from their intended plan.

Eve stayed at Dakon's bedside in their cabin, feeling a myriad of emotions as she beheld his ashen, but peaceful face. Without the weight of their troubles upon him, he was more relaxed than she had ever seen him before. His breathing was low and shallow, barely noticeable if not for the subtle rise and fall of his chest. She focused on that, and it gave her comfort knowing that he was still alive, somehow in there. She couldn't bear the thought of losing anyone else.

Beast occasionally stretched on the bed next to Dakon but refused to leave his side. From the moment they pulled Dakon back onto the railing, he had not left his side.

I suppose what is dead cannot die again . . .

Pazel lay on a small blanket in the corner, finally asleep after spending nearly every waking moment assisting Eve and Izan with the healing. They each bore the scars upon their necks, Eve's was nearly healed and Izan . . . she had not seen him since they completed the spell. After she threatened his life for Dakon's, he did what she asked and left.

She placed his hand in hers, tears pricking at the corners of her eyes. If she had been open and honest with him from the beginning, perhaps he would have told her about the siren that followed him. Instead, she kept her secrets, too fearful to confront their haunting truths, and all it did was lead him closer to Death. Guilt racked her as she tightened her grip. This was a mess, and she couldn't fathom how to fix it.

There was a gentle knock at the door.

Eve did not bother turning to see who it was.

"Might I join you, for a moment?" It was Niani.

"You may, though there is not much to entertain."

Niani sat on the floor next to the bed, leaning her back against the wall. "Lucky for you I am only interested in rest."

"So, our cabin is the new inn of the ship?"

Niani chuckled. "I only meant that you have no obligation to humor me."

Eve bit the inside of her cheek, still keeping her eyes on Dakon. She brushed a strand of hair from his eyes. "I have not slept much."

"I wouldn't either. If the love of my life was near death—"

"He isn't," Eve said gently.

"Oh"—she hesitated as if searching for the right words—"he is lucky to have you."

Eve turned to Niani, her hand still holding onto Dakon's. "I only mean that I am not ready—for love, that is."

Niani straightened. "I sense a story."

"I sense a gossip."

She laughed. "Witty and sharp-tongued. No, Eve, I want to know you. We are the only two women on this ship, after all."

Eve swallowed. "You first."

"Me?"

"Yes, your name is Niani, but what about your family? Where do they come from?"

Niani's eyes hardened. "How long have you wanted to ask me?"

"Your name sounds familiar, but I cannot place it," she admitted.

Niani took a deep breath. "I am one of the exiled members of House Ivari . . . of Larrea."

Eve's eyes widened, she could not recall ever meeting a noble from that house, but the name Ivari was spoken of often in the royal court. Particularly as the war raged on over the last few years.

"You—you were the sister of the false king."

"He was no false king." Niani shook her head. "Our people rallied first behind my father, and many others, before my young brother was left. We were weary of the cruel king in the west."

"How did you end up here?"

"My father saw to it that all his children were experts in manning a ship and crew. When we lost the war, the king in the west saw to it that my mother, sisters, and I were exiled to Bastard's Haven. I have been making connections there ever since."

"What happened to them?"

"I smuggled them on a ship away from Bastard's Haven set for lands west of the Blackthorn."

"Is that why you came with the captain?"

She nodded. "I had some unfinished business to attend to, but now I am ready to meet them."

Eve mulled over this, never expecting to see anyone from the Ivari line, much less alive. "I'm so sorry, for everything you and your family have endured."

"So am I." Niani sighed, lifting her gaze to Eve. "But mostly, I'm angry."

Eve met her aqua-blue eyes, within them was an ember waiting to turn to flames. She understood that feeling only too well.

"I'm angry too." She looked down at Dakon. "I'm always angry."

"Good," Niani replied. "Anger can be useful so long as you don't let it control you."

It always controls me, she wanted to say, but instead they sat in silence as Eve considered a more suitable reply. It only felt fair to be as vulnerable as Niani was.

"I was in love with Prince Theo . . . we left on uncertain terms before he was killed in battle."

"Now I'm the one who is sorry."

She shook her head, sadly. "He was promised to someone else; it was foolish of us."

"Was it the princess you killed?"

"That was my sister," Eve cocked her head. "Is that what people think?"

"People think many things. I would suggest owning the rumors or making them worse for a better reputation."

Eve rubbed her eyes as exhaustion began to settle on her.

"This sister. She is the one who disappeared as a child?"

"Yes."

"But now she is back?"

"With the Blackthorn, I think."

"Ah, that is why you are so keen to get there. I wonder how you convinced our stanch captain."

"I didn't. He changed his mind."

"No one changes their mind without a reason."

Eve considered this. In truth, she was so eager to get to the Blackthorn that she had not questioned the captain's motivations.

Dakon groaned slightly and she tensed, hand still grasping his. Niani heard it, too, eyes flicking to him. But Dakon fell back to sleep. Beast nuzzled his chest. Then it was quiet once more.

"So, how did you plan to kill her?" Niani whispered.

"Who?"

"Your sister. I assume you were not going to jump off the port, knock on the castle doors, and demand entry."

Eve bit her lip, she had not thought about anything other than simply reaching the isles. Clarisa owed her answers, but would Eve truly *kill* her? And even if Clarisa wasn't there, the Blackthorn was where their mother was planning to escape to before she was murdered. Certainly it was safe there.

Wasn't it?

"I thought so," Niani mused.

"I want the deaths to stop." Eve cleared her throat. "Though, it would be nice to prove my innocence as well. However unlikely."

"Very unlikely."

Eve huffed. "So, I must be the scorned witch who killed her lover's wife out of jealousy. Is that the story?"

"I've heard worse." She pulled a flask from within her pocket and handed it to Eve. "Did you want the first drink?"

"No, I—"

Niani held it up higher in front of her face. "Come now, the best stories are told when tongues are loose."

Eve let out a small laugh and took a greedy sip. The burning sensation swept over her, a bitterness that somehow made her calmer. She handed it back to Niani.

"Thank you."

"Don't thank me." Niani took a long sip. "You'll want more but I will make sure this is long gone before then."

Eve smiled.

"Now"—Niani leaned a bit close—"you were lovers?"

Eve nodded. "Before the betrothal, of course."

"Tell me."

"There is not much to say. We were raised in the same court as children, and I grew to love him."

"No, the exciting parts. Did he kiss you well? When did you lie with him? How many times?"

A grin spread across Eve's face. It was an unspoken rule between her and Theo that their affair be held in secret. Now, she felt free being able to tell another soul.

"Once, in the gardens on a summer night before he left for war . . ."

"Ah, it was meant to be goodbye."

"It was an end before there was a beginning."

"Do you regret it?"

Eve thought back to that night when their naked bodies became one beneath the stars and the shadows of the weeping willows. A gentle breeze cooled their skin as they became fire in each other's arms. Their mouths lay claim on one another without grace, putting aside modesty for a night to fulfill hopes and dreams, to live as if they could wake the next morning in the same bed. It was raw and passionate, everything she wished from Theo in the daylight, but never received.

She loved him, though.

And some part of her hoped that he had loved her too.

"I only regret leaving things as they were." The sting of his rejection stirred something painful deep inside her once more.

"We tend to say the worst in times of turmoil."

Eve's heart ached, wishing she could have expressed her feelings to Theo without it being laced in anguish and desperation. Wishing that she could have held onto Callum tighter as the flames licked their skin. Wishing she didn't feel so guilty about Izan.

Eve looked at Dakon once more, thinking back to their argument and tension since that night in the tavern. She wished that she could have listened to Dakon's words instead of letting pride cloud her judgment in anger.

Grief-stricken and heavy-hearted, Eve did not realize she had begun crying until Niani folded her into a hug and sobs racked from within her.

"Death is inevitable, but love is eternal," Niani whispered as she stroked her hair and back.

There was a soft knock at the door and the creaking sounds of it opening. Eve tore away from Niani, quickly wiping her tears as she faced away from their visitor.

"I came to check on you." It was Izan. "I thought you might need me."

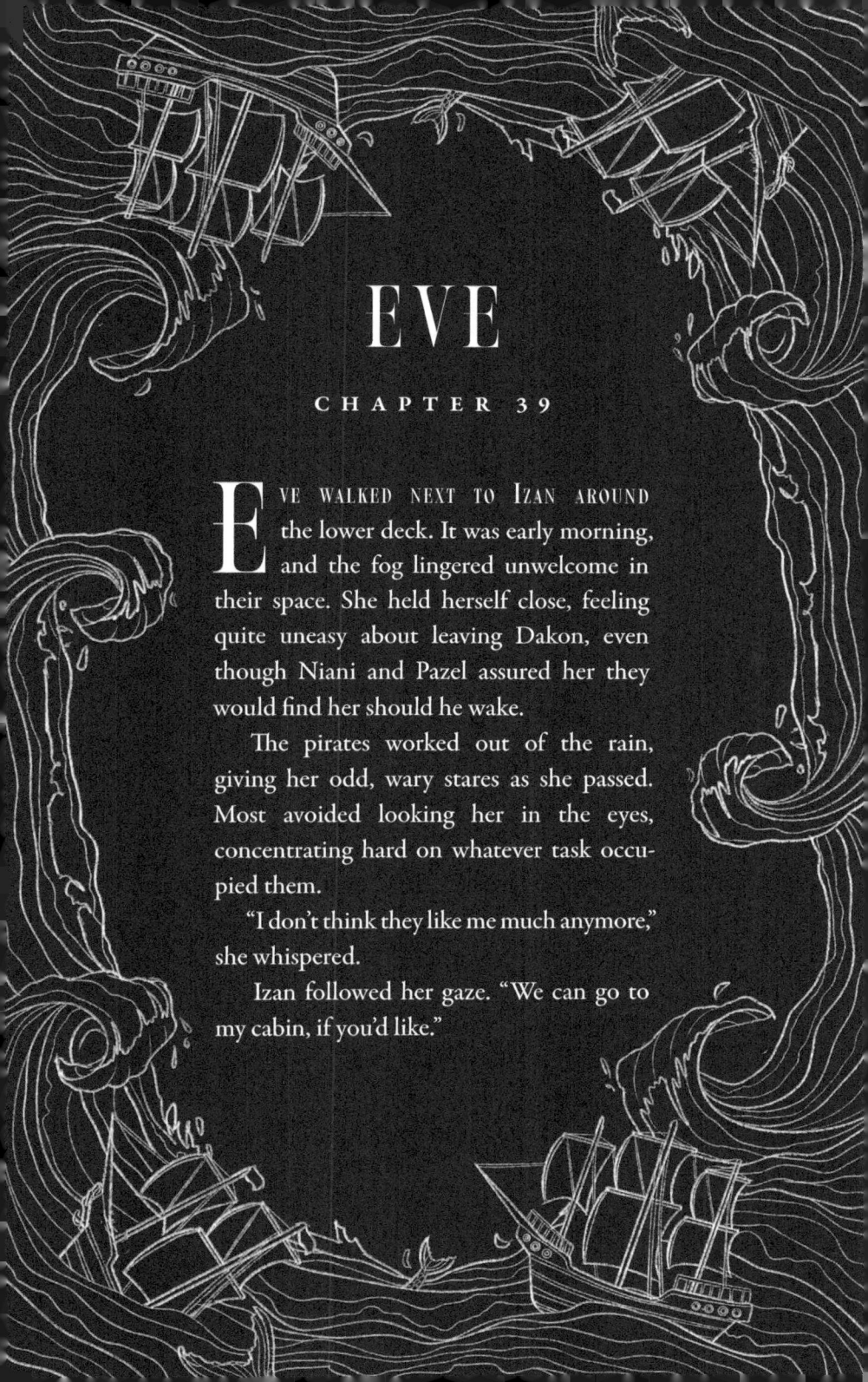

EVE

CHAPTER 39

E VE WALKED NEXT TO IZAN AROUND the lower deck. It was early morning, and the fog lingered unwelcome in their space. She held herself close, feeling quite uneasy about leaving Dakon, even though Niani and Pazel assured her they would find her should he wake.

The pirates worked out of the rain, giving her odd, wary stares as she passed. Most avoided looking her in the eyes, concentrating hard on whatever task occupied them.

"I don't think they like me much anymore," she whispered.

Izan followed her gaze. "We can go to my cabin, if you'd like."

She nodded and they made their way down the next set of steps in silence.

As they reached the door, Izan took a deep breath.

"Eve"—he turned to face her—"I only want you to come inside with me if you are willing to speak the truth. After everything that happened, I need to hear it from your lips. No more secrets, no lies, only the truth."

Eve swallowed. "I promise."

"Very well," he pushed open the door, revealing the cabin that had become so familiar. The vials of medicine, the satchels filled and lined against the wall, the small desk, the stools, the makeshift bed at the far end. She stepped inside, feeling calmer in his presence and away from the wary eyes of the other pirates.

He pulled out a stool for her and sat across the table.

"What do you want to know?" Eve asked, ready to speak.

Izan gave her a hard look. "Who are you? Not your name, nor that you are the *Blood of the Blackthorn*. I need more than that."

"Fair," Eve whispered. She breathed in deeply, closing her eyes and finding the words. "I am the daughter of a witch and a mortal."

He blinked a few times, trying and failing to appear unbothered. "Wh-who are they?"

Here it comes.

"My mother was Givensmir's first, and only, royal enchantress. My father is the Lord of Rubianes."

He sat back, eyes wide. "You were in the royal court."

She nodded, the admission freeing.

"How did you ever escape? Givensmir's castle is a fortress."

"Dakon and Pazel freed me. They found a break in the castle's wall, and we fled into the night."

"The king is looking for you. The king of Givensmir is looking for you," Izan breathed, more to himself than Eve.

He held out his hand and she took it, feeling his cool skin beneath her fingertips. She welcomed it.

"This is why I am escaping to the Blackthorn. My mother once tried to smuggle me and my sister there, but only one of us made it. My mother was killed shortly after. They might have the answers I need to rid myself of this cursed grimoire and find my sister."

"Why didn't the king kill you too?" His eyes narrowed, a flash of silver in them.

"Because he wanted me as his next enchantress." She met his eyes with a steely resolve. "The court and my father distracted me with praise and decadence so that I would never question my mother's death. I was primed from a young age to be a noblewoman worthy of a prince. Yet, the truth is that the king allowed me to think this until the moment my powers manifested."

"And so you killed him?"

"I would rather die than be a dog on a golden chain to make it appealing."

Izan clenched his jaw. "I hope he rots wherever the gods have sent him."

Eve thought of the king wallowing in an eternal flame of her making, that would be justice indeed.

"So, you are a *half-witch*." He said the last words uncomfortably. "And you are now running to a rival kingdom after killing your own king with magic you have only just discovered?"

"It seems far simpler when you say it."

Izan's eyes softened. "And you have a cursed grimoire prophesied to bring back a fallen goddess tethered to you by blood."

"Unfortunately."

"And here I was thinking I was pursuing a simple fire witch."

"Sorry to disappoint." She gave him a weak smile.

He gave her one in return.

"Not at all, Lady."

"If only the crew felt the same."

"You saved our lives, I'm certain they will come around."

She shook her head. "You saw how they looked at me."

"All pirates are wary of witches, even the good ones." He lifted her chin, his eyes sincere as he beheld her.

"Am I good?" she asked. "Because when I saw Dakon being pulled over the railing, everything turned red. I wanted it all to burn." She hesitated for a moment, adding, "And I destroyed Amarin's ship, it's beyond forgiveness."

"If it is destroyed, how are we still sailing?"

Eve rolled her eyes, his response making her giggle unexpectedly. "This is no laughing matter."

Izan smiled gently. "But I love seeing you laugh."

Eve blinked, trying to make sure she heard him correctly. Without thinking, she retrieved her hands from his, fiddling with them in her lap. She suddenly was overwhelmed, the cabin feeling too hot and cold at once.

His gaze grew tender, vulnerable.

"What are we doing, Eve? What do you want?"

"I don't understand—"

"I want you." He reached out for her hand once more. "I *need* you, Eve."

The air in the room thinned; her breath hitched.

Is this not what she felt too?

"Izan, I . . ."

Words failed her. She could not fathom why her heart and mind were at war within her.

"If you don't feel the same, if I am alone in feeling this way . . ." His hand lingered on the table between them, waiting for her to grasp it. But she couldn't force herself to move.

"What happened the other night—"

"—was the first time you felt free, tell me that is not the truth. Because for me, with you in my arms, kissing you, holding you, I felt magic between us unlike anything I have ever felt before. Please tell me I am not the only one who suffers this bewitching agony." His stare was pure misery, his hand over his heart as if he could feel the painful stabs of her hesitance.

"Time," she managed, "with Dakon—"

"Dakon?"

"He needs me, we are bound for life, I can't live without him."

Izan straightened, the strands of his hair tousling over his brows. "Do you love him?"

"What?" she scoffed.

"Are you in love with him?"

"Why would you ask me that?"

"You aren't answering my question."

"Because it's ridiculous. He's my familiar, I'm his witch. We were attacked by creatures I didn't even know existed until days ago. This is too much, too soon. I shouldn't have to explain myself to you."

Izan sat back and hung his head, nodding slightly. An uncomfortable silence stretched between them, before he finally spoke. "I asked you for the truth, and you gave it to me. Thank you."

He stood and Eve stood with him. "What are you doing?"

Izan opened the door to his cabin, keeping his eyes locked on the floor. "Letting you go."

It was a clear dismissal.

He didn't meet her eyes as she walked slowly out the door.

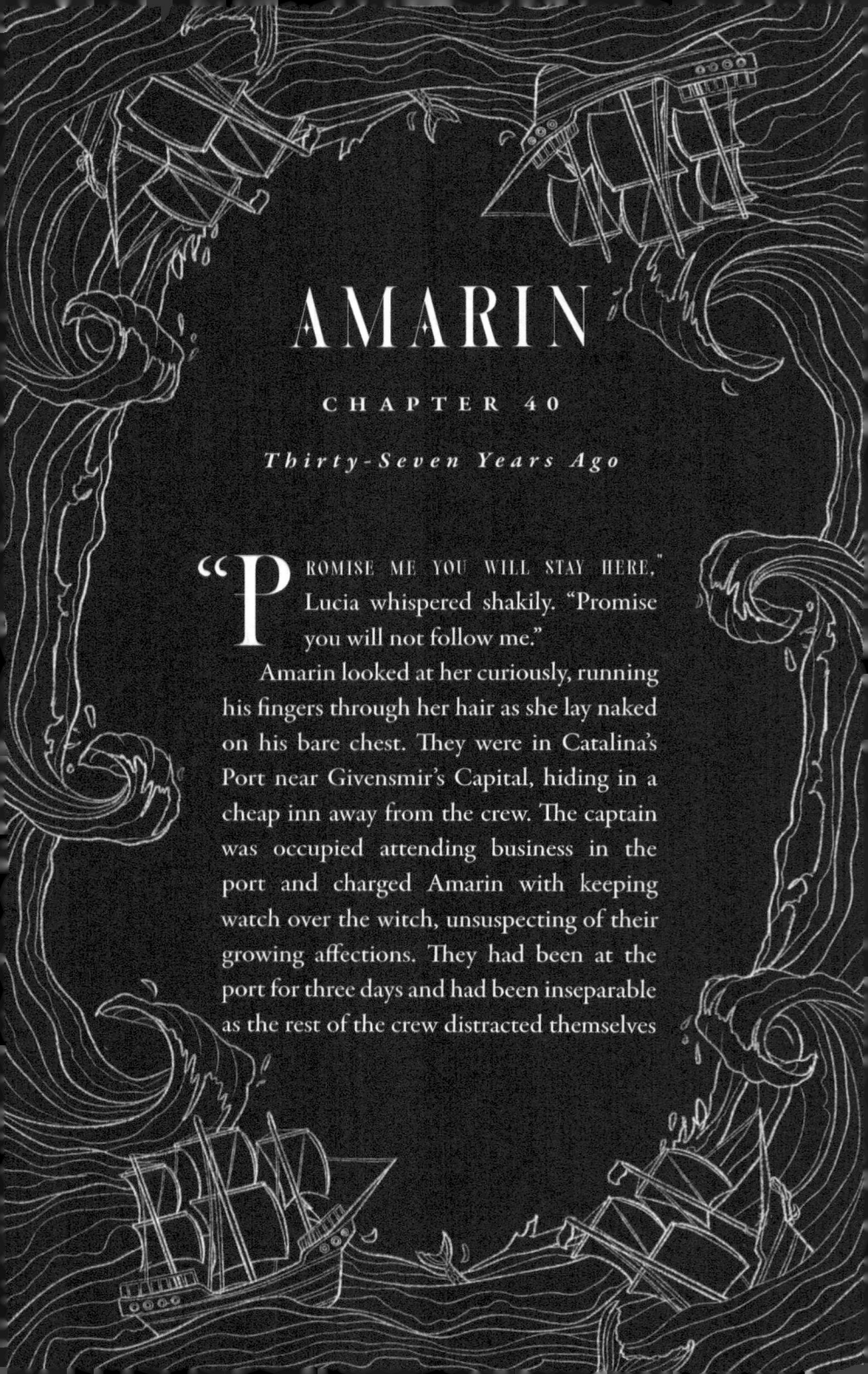

AMARIN

CHAPTER 40

Thirty-Seven Years Ago

"Promise me you will stay here," Lucia whispered shakily. "Promise you will not follow me."

Amarin looked at her curiously, running his fingers through her hair as she lay naked on his bare chest. They were in Catalina's Port near Givensmir's Capital, hiding in a cheap inn away from the crew. The captain was occupied attending business in the port and charged Amarin with keeping watch over the witch, unsuspecting of their growing affections. They had been at the port for three days and had been inseparable as the rest of the crew distracted themselves with the brothels, markets, and taverns. At night he and Lucia ventured back onto the ship, and during the day, after entertaining themselves throughout the port, they ended up back in this place.

"I promise that I *will* follow you, wherever you go." He kissed her head.

"I'm serious, Amarin," she replied.

"As am I."

She sat up, suddenly, pulling the blanket to her chest. He felt empty without her in his arms, but righted himself, leaning against the headboard. He studied her curiously. She seemed shaken where only moments before they had been laughing about something. He wished time had not taken their bliss away so soon. "What do you see?"

Lucia bit her lip. "Golden armor surrounding me and a large castle."

"Is it the Blackthorn? Do you believe they have come for you?"

"It is not them." Her eyes betrayed her fear. "I suspect it is the mortal king."

"Here? This one?"

"Yes, word of my arrival has reached him. Though I cannot foresee when they will come for me."

Amarin stood, suddenly, unable to keep his visceral feelings about this knowledge to himself. He began to pick up their clothes, throwing on his tunic. "Then we must escape. We can stowaway on another ship. We can go back to Prialis, we can build a home there, we can, we can—"

He noticed her silence, her faraway stare as tears slowly streamed down her cheeks. Her long, brown, wild curls fell nearly to her waist as she held herself in her arms. She was terrified, and it broke his heart.

"Lucia"—he knelt next to her—"for as long as I breathe, you will never be alone."

Her face reddened as the tears flowed down now, reaching her chin and falling into her lap. She faced him, her lips trembling. "It comes to me in waves. My powers—I will be at their mercy."

Amarin placed a hand on her cheek, wiping away her tears with his thumb. "Then I will kill them all with my bare hands if they touch you."

They locked eyes as he continued. "I will never leave you."

"I know you will never want to."

"It's the city watch!"

"They're coming this way!"

Amarin fluttered his eyes open to the sounds of running and shouting from the deck above. It took him a moment to adjust to his surroundings. It was the fifth day they had been at Catalina's Port, and not a single castle guard had even been seen on this side of the bridge. He had convinced himself that perhaps Lucia's visions were wrong, that maybe she might have misinterpreted them.

"They're here!"

The sound of a woman screaming jolted him from his hammock.

Lucia!

He clambered out of it, rushing to the deck without a single weapon or even boots. The sunlight bore down, bright, nearly blinding him as he took the final steps, and his heart nearly stopped. Over fifteen guards, clad in golden armor, were aboard the ship, swords pointed at the crew members, pushing them away from the center of their formation. There, Lucia stood, silent as a guard put iron chains on her wrists. The clanking of the metal ripped through him. And he momentarily lost his voice, unable to think, unable to act.

"Thank you for your time," a guard said to the captain, handing him a pouch of what he assumed to be coins.

"Always a pleasure, Ser Cardo." The captain eyed then pocketed the coins. "We'll be out of here soon enough." He raised a hand to Lucia, running his fingers through her hair, she flinched against his touch. "You don't have too much fun without me, dear." He blew her a kiss, and Amarin felt sick.

"Lucia!" he yelled.

She turned her head. "Amarin."

He rushed to her, but a guard shoved him to the ground, pointing a sword at his throat. "Move and I'll slice your filthy pirate throat."

Amarin spat in the guard's face, twisting just in time before he stabbed his sword through the wood. "I'll kill you!" the guard shouted.

Amarin ran toward Lucia but was quickly overwhelmed and pinned to the ground as another kicked him in the jaw. The guard he spat on came into view, raising his sword above him as two others lifted him onto his knees.

"Stop!" Lucia screamed. "Please! I will go wherever you wish, just please leave him."

"That's enough, men," Ser Cardo boomed through the ship.

A guard with a seal of Givensmir on his golden armor glinted on his chest said, "We must not start a scene or inflict the witch's wrath. Not here."

The guards holding Amarin shoved him to the ground and kicked his stomach once more. It happened too quickly; the guards began pulling Lucia away, down the steps. More guards waited at the end with a cage hooked onto the back of their horses. Amarin coughed violently, trying in vain to stand but the pain was too intense.

She was locked up like an animal, then paraded down a street of curious onlookers. The guards turned around the bend, and then, she was gone.

Taking his heart with her.

CLARISA

CHAPTER 41

CLARISA FELT THE ROUGH TEXTURE and uneven ridges of Raven's Hold-fast beneath her fingertips. The stone, dark and weathered, had taken unkindly to the elements over the centuries. She pressed her head against it gently, closing her eyes. Every step she took, it felt as if circumstance brought her three steps back. Now she was here again, with Navir and her familiars, to seek out the guidance of Aris, the high priest and scholar of this place. Navir was inside speaking to Aris while she and her familiars waited outside.

The last time she walked these halls Aris had given her the luring crystal and told her cautionary tales of its misuse. She reached for it about her neck, clutching it tight. Her hands had become so frail; she could barely remember the last time she had eaten, so focused on keeping the oracles safe inside.

Tink. Tink. Tink.

"Clarisa, he is ready for us." Tabor placed a gentle hand on her shoulder, his eyes narrowing on the crystal. He shifted uncomfortably, adjusting his quiver of arrows slung across his back.

Brisa moved next to him, her golden eyes widening slightly as she beheld Clarisa leaning against the wall.

"What?" Clarisa stood as straight as she could manage, her lips were dry, her surroundings blurred. In only a few hours, she felt *different*.

"Your eyes," Brisa managed, lending a hand to help Clarisa stand. "When is the last time you slept?"

"I sleep fine."

"No," Tabor interrupted, "it's this crystal. You are not yourself." He reached out for her and Clarisa hissed, holding the crystal in a white-knuckled grip away from him.

Tabor startled. "That thing has gone too far, give it here!"

"No!"

He took a step forward, but Brisa moved between them, her hands on his chest. "No, Tabor, not like this." They seemed to be speaking to each other with nothing but their stares. After a moment, Tabor turned on his heel and brooded away.

"Where is he going?" Clarisa demanded.

"For some air," Brisa replied, crossing her arms. "Come, let's meet the prince."

"I WAS BEGINNING TO WONDER WHEN YOU WOULD RETURN." ARIS stood on a chair as he rummaged with a wooden crate before him, using a long cane to move the objects within. The vast space of the sanctuary echoed his words as he spoke. The cool, white stone of the altar table loomed behind him, a solitary beam of light from glass on the ceiling illuminated it.

"I wondered myself," Clarisa replied. Navir appeared to give her an approving nod as he leaned against one of the pillars beside her, silent, observing. She wished now that Brisa was here, but Navir had denied her entry into the room. It made her nervous to be alone with these men.

Aris retrieved a long, black cloth. "Help me would you? I am not as young as I once was."

She walked to the high priest, her footsteps echoing through the space. She lifted the blanket, shook out some dust, and laid it over the altar.

She swallowed, nervously. "What are we worshiping today?"

Aris continued rifling through the crate. "Wisdom, always wisdom."

He pulled out five silver candles, handing them to her. She took them gently, placing them atop the altar in a circle.

"So, it appears you have summoned the oracles," he mused, lifting a glass orb from the box, inspecting it, and tossing it back in.

Clarisa swallowed, putting the last candle on the altar. "Yes. I have."

"And did you find the answers you were looking for?"

"I think so."

"Hmm." He fished out a small figurine of Isila. The statuette, solid white, was made of smooth marble. He handed it to her, and she took it gracefully. She turned to leave, but Aris gripped her arm tight. "It seems they have taken a liking to you."

Clarisa met his wary gaze, feeling as if he were staring into her very soul. His eyes moved to the crystal.

"I haven't asked them," Clarisa murmured.

"Have you taken anything from them?"

Clarisa's eyes widened, thinking of the hag stones.

Aris did not let go, his sea-green eyes hardening. "Magic is not immortal, child. Where one takes, one must give."

"What should I do?"

"Exactly what we are doing now." He released her and handed her a knife from his robes. "Now, place this, too, on the altar."

Her limbs trembled, but she did as she was told.

"When I gave you that crystal, my dear, I knew you and your familiars would be able to successfully summon the oracles. You were the prophesied daughter after all."

Clarisa bit her lip as she placed the statuette of Isila in the center of the altar.

"But do you remember what I said of them? They will host and feed upon their witch until there is nothing left. Then they will seek another. And another. It is a vicious cycle."

Clarisa held the crystal, looking down at the dark swirls of smoke within.

Tink. Tink. Tink.

She had nearly forgotten the lesson, but hearing it again, it all came back to her. Dread, deep and foreboding, fought against reason. Her lips quivered, her breathing labored. She could think of nothing but the horror of what had been happening as she kept the crystal close.

Tink. Tink. Tink.

Aris appeared next to her, and she whirled, pointing the knife down at him.

He was unmoved, narrowing his eyes as he watched her clutching the crystal in one hand, and the knife in the other. He slowly placed a finger on the blade, pushing it away from his face.

"If you plan to kill me, my dear, please do it quickly. And try not to leave a mess by the altar."

Clarisa released a breath. "Oh, no, no. I'm sorry, I was, I—"

"There are only two choices"—Aris sighed, placing a wooden cup next to the statuette—"either we destroy the crystal, or give your oracles a new host."

"You mean, give it up?"

"No." Navir walked toward them. "Someone new for them to feed on."

"I don't understand."

Clarisa watched as Navir and Aris shared a look.

"We do not plan to destroy the luring crystal," Aris said gently. "It is too great, too powerful, to risk when there are threats that can and will destroy our kingdom."

Clarisa took a shaky step back.

"It's the only way," Navir reached for the knife in her hand, grabbing it by the hilt and forcing it from her grip. He handed it to Aris.

"You have to trust me, remember?" His blue eyes met Clarisa's.

"You are losing strength. Your power is becoming unpredictable as they consume you," Aris explained, placing the knife on the altar. "You need someone for them to feed on while you continue to seek their guidance."

"You want me to sacrifice innocent witches?"

"No. They are not innocent," Navir said, "I would never ask that of you."

Clarisa looked between them, fear intensifying within her. "No, I can't—I won't." She stood firm.

Navir and Aris shared another look.

"Tell her," Aris sighed, "tell her what we've learned."

"What?" Clarisa looked to Navir. He shook his head, words not coming out quickly enough for her. "What happened?!"

Is it Ana?

Navir locked eyes with her once more. "Eve has killed Pedro."

Clarisa could not breathe, the weight of a thousand stones upon her shoulders.

No.

No, no, no.

She could barely utter the word. "H-how?"

"When we brought him before the queen, we discovered her name carved into his skin. A clear and cruel bewitchment. He died too quickly to stop it." Navir hesitated, taking a deep breath. "I'm so sorry."

Clarisa doubled over, retching on the side of the altar, tears springing hot and heavy down her cheeks. She sobbed through it, horror and grief gripping her like a deadly snake.

She thought they could help him.

Navir forced her to look at him, his eyes serious. "She is coming, Clarisa, and she is *powerful*. Everyone you love—no one will make it without you, without your sacrifice."

"Ana," Clarisa breathed.

"That will be her first victim."

Clarisa stood suddenly, panicking. "Then hide her! Move her back with her mother in the west, take her from the capital! I want her safe now!"

"There is not enough time." Navir clenched his jaw. "We need the oracles. We need you to use their power and tell us what we need to do. We cannot fight a war against the mortals, the Strix, and your sister without them."

The little girl from Clarisa's dreams, the one with red eyes and a wicked smile filled her thoughts. Eve was no longer the child she remembered, no longer the girl who begged Clarisa to make water appear from her hands, giggling with infectious innocence.

No, she was a murderer.

A *monster*.

"With these sacrifices, your power will grow, you will take over their magic and it will become one with you," Aris explained, taking a vial of blood and placing it in the cup. Each drop sending shivers down Clarisa's spine. "You must tell no one. For we are making the ultimate sacrifice for the coven. Do you understand?"

Clarisa nodded shakily as she stood before the altar. Navir lit the candles.

"Place your crystal in the center," Aris instructed.

Clarisa trembled as she removed the necklace from her, placing it before Isila's statuette.

"Wh-who's blood?" she whispered, tears wetting the black cloth.

"A slayer. Killed his entire family and fled into the woods. He nearly strangled a familiar but was apprehended by a few villagers," Aris said with little emotion, lifting a pitcher and pouring its contents into the cup. "Hand me the datura, please." He gestured to Navir as he continued his story.

"He has been in the dungeons for far too long, responsible for too many deaths. But now"—he took the leaves of the datura plant from Navir, and he cut them with his hands into the cup—"he can be used for a greater purpose."

Aris stirred the contents and handed Clarisa the cup. "Life."

"Give it your intentions, Clarisa." Navir placed a hand on her lower back; the feeling made her sick. "Think about saving our kind, our kingdom, *Ana*."

She looked at the cup, suddenly feeling a sense of deja vu. A time when she was sitting in the queen's solar before killing the princess. A time when everything seemed far less complicated. Slowly, she looked inside.

"Help me!"

Clarisa could faintly hear the plea in the drink, each time crying out, begging for help.

Aris and Navir began chanting, and she held the cup in both her hands, tears blurring her sight.

I have to.

I need to.

Ana, please forgive me.

The chanting and the witch's plea drowned out as she closed her eyes, tilted the cup back and drank.

The sanctuary spun and darkened. The burning sensation of the drink trickled excruciatingly slow down her throat. She coughed, clutching her neck and falling to her knees.

"Help!" she gasped. "Aris, Navir!"

All she could hear was their chanting far away. The altar was empty, as if everyone had disappeared.

She coughed, trying to heave the drink from her body, but nothing came out. Finally, the burning faded, and she stayed on the ground, too weak to move. She lay there, closing her eyes and taking in deep breaths.

I'm alive.

Ana will be alive.

We will go to paradise.

Then three voices, ones that she had never heard before, filled the sanctuary. "Our precious descendant, we've been waiting for you."

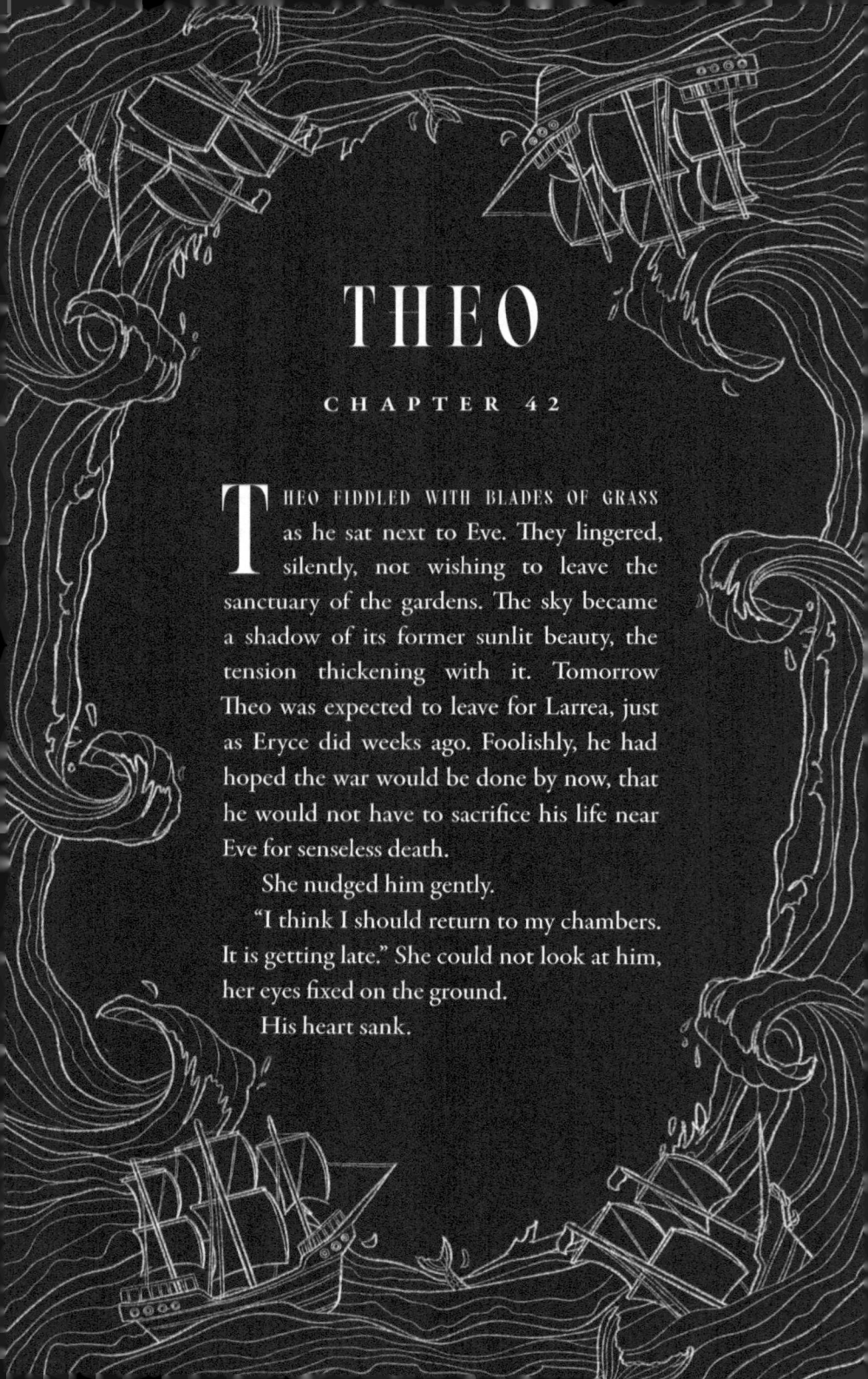

THEO

CHAPTER 42

THEO FIDDLED WITH BLADES OF GRASS as he sat next to Eve. They lingered, silently, not wishing to leave the sanctuary of the gardens. The sky became a shadow of its former sunlit beauty, the tension thickening with it. Tomorrow Theo was expected to leave for Larrea, just as Eryce did weeks ago. Foolishly, he had hoped the war would be done by now, that he would not have to sacrifice his life near Eve for senseless death.

She nudged him gently.

"I think I should return to my chambers. It is getting late." She could not look at him, her eyes fixed on the ground.

His heart sank.

"We have only just arrived, Eve. Please, stay with me a little longer."

He discarded the grass and held out his hand to her. The look in his hazel eyes was tortured as he gazed upon her. Eve faced their weathered footpath that led to the castle, then back to Theo. She bit her lip, relenting, and grasped his hand.

"Only for a little while." She met his stare. "Last I need is for the ladies at court to spin their tales as they always do."

"They will gossip anyway." Theo smiled, pulling her to sit closer. "Why not do what makes you happy regardless."

Eve laughed softly, entering his embrace. "My, my Theo. I did not take you for a rebel. I must be wearing on you."

"Depends," he placed a hand on the small of her back. "Do you like a rebel?"

Eve tilted her head. "I thought you'd never ask."

Theo felt playful as the weight of the world began to leave their space. He looked around, trying to see and listen to the gardens through blissful eyes. Perhaps, they did not need to end this night so miserably.

"Do you hear that?"

Eve furrowed her brows, confused.

"Our garden is singing to us."

"Singing? I don't hear anything."

"Ah"—Theo gently put his hands over her eyes—"that is because you are not listening, Eve. Try again."

Eve smiled, her full trust in him never wavering, never questioning. She rested her head against his chest. The castle gardens buzzed with fireflies, the chirping of crickets, and the occasional hooting of an owl. The willows danced, their leaves swaying in harmony. A soft breeze rocked the pond water gently as the moonlight reflected upon its surface like diamonds. The summer air flowed across their skin, giving them a reprieve from the heat. The gardens were alive and incredible, paying special attention to their visitors in the night.

Her soft smile turned into a joyous grin; she could hear it now; she could feel it. A song for just the two of them.

He removed his hands, and her bright, brown eyes met his. As always, they were the shade of sparrows, the hearths of winters passed that he longed to see every day of his life. They were meant to be, her and him, he was sure of it.

"I love you, Eve," Theo whispered.

His heart thundered in his chest. It was the first time he had ever spoken so boldly.

Her eyes grew serious, she lifted a hand to his face, caressing it. If he was breathing, he did not know it, for his mind became lost in her gentle touch. He leaned closer, their lips barely touching.

"Can I kiss you, just once?"

She nodded. "Always."

He closed his eyes but did not feel her lips against his.

"Eve?" His heart hammered against his chest, as he opened his eyes.

She was gone.

Theo gasped, clutching his body drenched in sweat. He lurched forward, trying to make sense of his surroundings. The rain dripped next to him on the floor, the puddle growing bigger on the uneven stone. The hourglass sat on the small table in front of him, the top of it nearly empty now. He rubbed his tired face.

Eve.

She's gone.

And I am here with Pedro.

Pedro.

He stilled, his limbs trembling, as it all came back to him. He squeezed his eyes shut, fear seizing him as he turned. He didn't want to open them, didn't want to see, but he had no choice.

Pedro lay in a mess of blood and sheets atop the bed.

Theo startled back on his hands and knees, falling into the puddle. The touch of the water bringing him back to his senses, he looked down and realized how much blood was left upon his skin and clothes. He turned back to Pedro, crumbling in wretched sobs on the floor.

They couldn't even give him a proper death. He deserved better than laying in this waste.

These bastards, these fucking bastards.

In between his cries, he heard something that at once made his blood boil and his body tremble with rage.

The rat squeaked as it ran across the beam, knocking tiny films of dirt and pebbles onto the floor. One of them hit Pedro on the head.

Theo turned to it, screaming, "Fuck you! Fuck you! Fuck you!"

He threw anything he could get his hands on at the vile creature, but it continued making its way across, everything missing its mark. Theo grabbed the hourglass, and the rat stilled. He pulled his arm back and lurched it forward, throwing the object hard toward the beam.

The rat scampered, barely making it out of the way as the hourglass smashed against the wood. It obliterated into shards of glass and sand that fell from the ceiling like snow. The sound of it crashing on the floor was music to Theo's ears.

Theo heaved air into his lungs, tormented and angry.

The rat stood on its hind legs staring down at him. He locked eyes with it, never wavering.

Finally, the rat did as it always did and ran back into its hole.

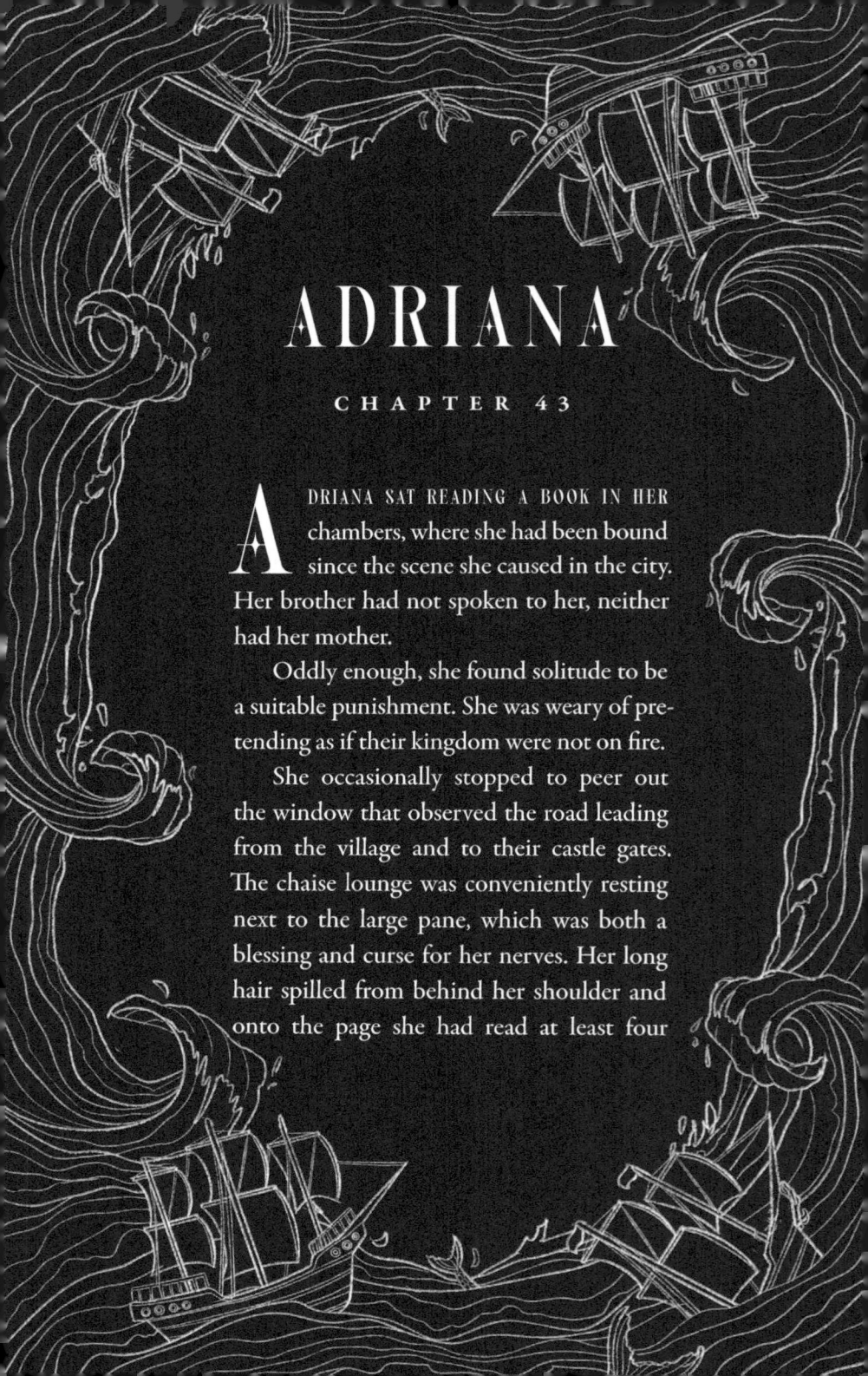

ADRIANA

CHAPTER 43

ADRIANA SAT READING A BOOK IN HER chambers, where she had been bound since the scene she caused in the city. Her brother had not spoken to her, neither had her mother.

Oddly enough, she found solitude to be a suitable punishment. She was weary of pretending as if their kingdom were not on fire.

She occasionally stopped to peer out the window that observed the road leading from the village and to their castle gates. The chaise lounge was conveniently resting next to the large pane, which was both a blessing and curse for her nerves. Her long hair spilled from behind her shoulder and onto the page she had read at least four times in a row, and she took it as a sign to look out the window again. Nothing, at least what she was anticipating, was present yet. She had an unsettling feeling in her gut, a disquieting, horrid sensation that kept her occupied for most of the last couple of days.

The door opening to her chambers surprised her, and the book she held fell to the floor. Her handmaid came through carrying a small tray of fruits, placing it on a table in the center of the room.

"My Lady, did you need anything else?"

Adriana shook her head. "No, thank you."

She bowed and turned to leave.

"Wait," Princess Adriana called.

The handmaid turned. "Yes, Princess?"

"Can you please let me know when he arrives?"

"I will, Your Highness, but it seems you are the best judge of that." She gestured to Adriana's position by the window.

"Yes, well . . . please find me here when he does."

She nodded politely and closed the door behind her.

Adriana picked up her book off the floor, but didn't care to open it. She forgot the page she was on and instead focused her attention on watching out the window where nothing out of the ordinary stirred in her field of vision.

Princess Adriana stared out at the gray skies and the pregnant clouds; rain was approaching, but not her betrothed. The man sworn to her, the man by whom she had no choice but to trust. He had proven his worth and honor to her, and she hoped that he would not fail her now.

But where was he?

As the sun began to sink into late afternoon, she began to pace restlessly in her chambers. It was late, much too late for him to have returned from his meeting with the lords of Zafira.

The people in the south had long claimed to be under attack by witches even before her brother's reign. Along with heavy taxes, unpopular rulings, and the innocent blood spilt by her brother, riots were a near certainty. With talks of usurping against the realm already secretly underway, her brother's actions would certainly be reason enough that even the nobles there would support Jos's negotiations for their sanctuary.

There was another knock at her door, but she barely heard it as she was consumed by the pitter patter of the rain droplets hitting the window.

"My dear sister."

It was her brother's voice. She turned quickly to it, startled by his sudden and unexpected presence.

"Brother, what do I owe the pleasure of your visit?" She did her best to smile, to radiate the feminine, innocent image so many of the court claimed to have loved about her.

"Can I not visit my favorite sister?" Marc smirked, and Adriana's smile dropped. The small hairs on the back of her neck raised.

"Of course." She tried her best to control her breathing as he entered her chambers and closed the door. He tinkered with her fruit tray, finally settling on a grape that he popped into his mouth.

"Are you waiting for someone?" He pointed to her set up by the window—a blanket, pillow, and a couple of books.

"No," she squeaked.

He approached closer as Adriana trembled.

Marc eyed her as he picked up one of the books. He opened it. "*The Royal Decree of Diplomacy Between Territories and Lands Among the Givensmir Realm*, this is quite the literature for someone who need not worry about politics." He arched a brow to her.

"I love to keep a sharp mind. Especially considering I will be a Lady of Mytar soon." She prayed to the gods that her answer was a good one.

"Ah, yes. You always had to know *everything*." He thumbed

through the pages, not meeting her gaze. "I blame Mother. She was far too busy avoiding our father's wrath to pay attention to you." He snapped the book shut and Adriana flinched.

Marc grinned, continuing, "For if she had, you would have been raised far more compliant and less *curious*. Perhaps, I have been too lenient in that regard. Allowing you to be curious, expressing opinions, having ideas." He set the book down.

Adriana's stomach dropped, and her limbs trembled as she tried to calm herself. "I have been fortunate for your kindness, Marc. I am always grateful to you."

"That is good to hear"—he reached out his hand, and she looked at it, then back at him. Slowly, she settled hers on it—"because I have news that I think may interest you."

"Yes, Brother?"

"Lord Herbert recently lost his wife, Lady Tabitha, due to sickness. He is finally ready to search for a new wife."

Lord Herbert, a man twice her age, a known brute, womanizer, and the real reason his wife died—murdering her after a drunken episode if the rumors were to be believed.

"I—I am sure he will find a suitable wife at court. Perhaps at my wedding to Lord Jos."

"I was thinking about your wedding, considering the kingdom needs more coin to fund the war against the Blackthorn. The Gold Council and I have come to a different arrangement for Jos . . . and you."

Her eyes widened, her pulse quickened, and it took all of her restraint to resist falling into hysterics. "N-no."

"I did warn Lord Herbert that he may not want a woman who does not listen, but he assured me that you would be given some discipline in his care."

Adriana's blood ran cold, and she was rendered speechless as her brother eyed her, a hint of humor on his face. He pulled out a small jewel from his pocket, an emerald-green, gemstone ring from her personal collection; it must have fallen off when she had struggled against Timothy in the city.

"I believe this belongs to you." He placed the ring on her finger as she remained stunned in shock. "As did that." Marc gestured to the window. Adriana turned in a haze of shock and confusion.

Cresting the hill toward the castle gates was an army of men riding on horseback. As they approached from a distance, holding the flags of Givensmir's realm, she began to realize they were holding stakes as they rode.

One was held by none other than Ser James himself.

She shook uncontrollably and placed a trembling hand on the glass.

Atop James' stake was a head, which became more visible through the rainfall and darkened skies. Light hair and green eyes that were now cloudy and disengaged.

Jos.

She screamed a guttural horrific scream as her hands pressed into the window with horror.

"Is that any way to say hello to your former beau, my sweet sister?"

Adriana sobbed uncontrollably, the weight of her last hope dragging her down.

Her brother clapped, and Timothy entered the room with a few other guards. "I didn't want to have to do this, but you have left me with no choice. You have become a threat to me and my dear, innocent wife. She was quite in her feelings when she came home that day, very *curious* too."

Gabrielle.

Adriana turned. "Leave her alone!"

Marc ignored her, a deadly glare in his eyes. "Until your new husband comes to receive you, your new home will be where the rest of the traitors lurk."

She lunged at Marc, but Timothy was too quick, grabbing her arms and shoving her to the floor. She scratched and fought against

him and the other guards as they tried to get control of her. Adriana howled until they finally subdued her and lifted her back onto her feet.

Marc picked at the fruit tray, taking a bite of a berry. Slowly, methodically, he made his way toward her. "Things would be so much simpler if you just stayed quiet."

Adriana spat at him. Keeping her eyes locked on him, breathing raggedly, she knew that there was little left to live for anymore.

Marc wiped the spit from his face. "I am really tired of that happening." He slapped her hard with the back of his hand. Pain radiated through her cheek and jaw, her head whipped to the side, and she tasted blood.

"Take her away," Marc ordered.

Her vision was blurry as she was dragged down the hall, down the stairs, down, down, down, to a part of the castle she had never been before.

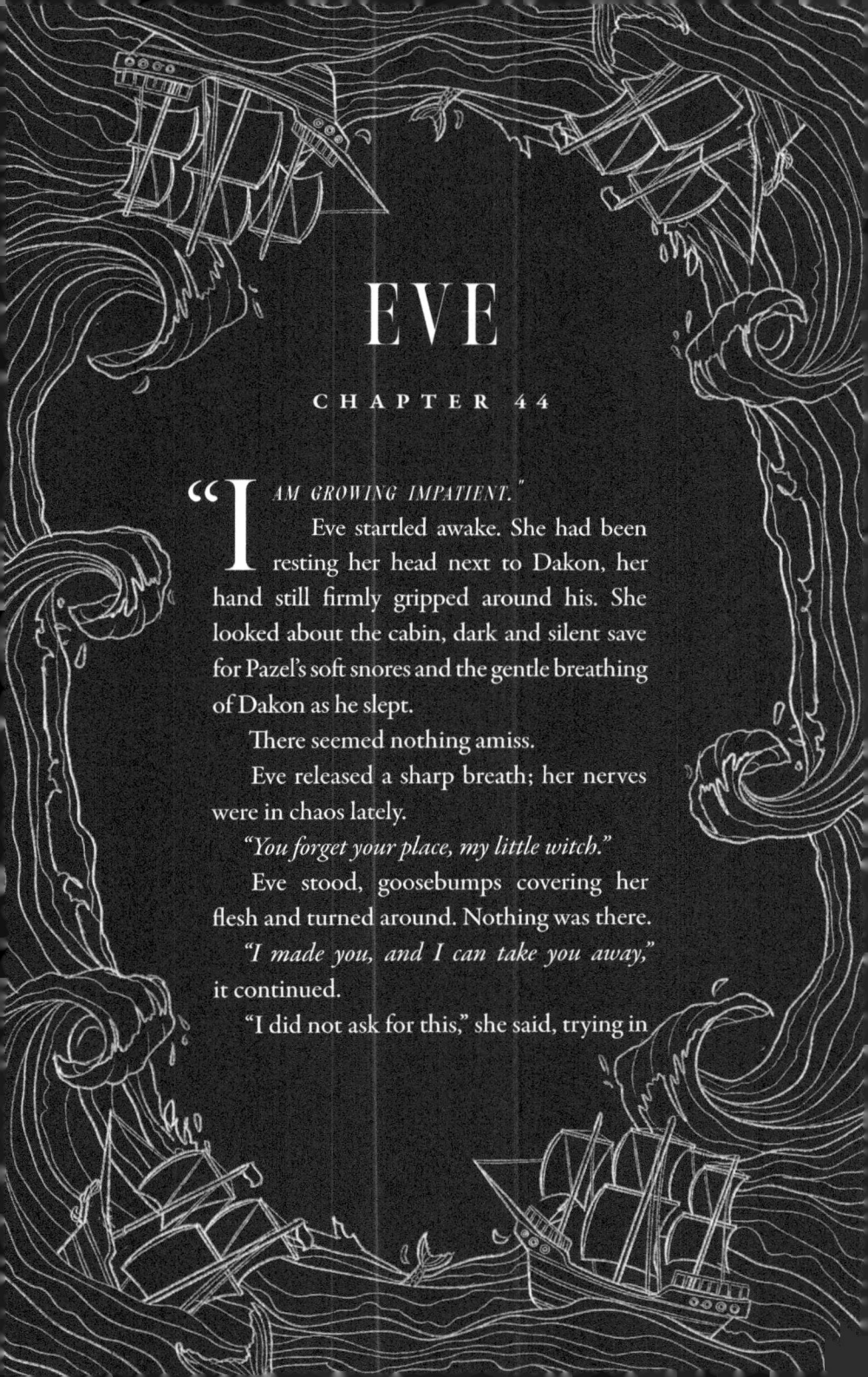

EVE

CHAPTER 44

"*I AM GROWING IMPATIENT.*"

Eve startled awake. She had been resting her head next to Dakon, her hand still firmly gripped around his. She looked about the cabin, dark and silent save for Pazel's soft snores and the gentle breathing of Dakon as he slept.

There seemed nothing amiss.

Eve released a sharp breath; her nerves were in chaos lately.

"*You forget your place, my little witch.*"

Eve stood, goosebumps covering her flesh and turned around. Nothing was there.

"*I made you, and I can take you away,*" it continued.

"I did not ask for this," she said, trying in

vain to find the source of the voice.

"*Your body. Your power. Your soul.*"

"No," Eve breathed, "no, you cannot have it."

"*We will be the fire that rules the world.*"

"I don't want to rule. I don't want any of this."

"*We will end the eternal curse.*"

"What curse? What do you want from me?"

The grimoire appeared before her, shining bright once more in the dark cabin. Words in dark ink began to write itself on its pages.

"YOUR NAILS ARE DIGGING INTO MY SKIN."

Eve lifted her head from the bed. It was a gray morning, but the rain seemed to settle. The grimoire was gone, taking whatever story it was writing with it.

Dakon's green eyes met hers.

"Dakon!" She threw herself on his chest and hugged him fiercely. "You're awake, oh, thank the gods."

Dakon lifted a hand gently, brushing his fingers through her hair. "It'll take more than sirens to keep me away."

Eve laughed, tears rolling gently down her face. "And what about a witch with a repentant heart?"

He looked at her curiously, and Niani's words echoed in her head. This feeling in her chest was familiar, the proximity reminded her of a time long past.

He moved his hand from her hair to her cheek, wiping away a tear. Time seemed to have frozen, because she kept this portrait of him in her mind, locking it away with the other precious memories of her life. Her heart pounded, her skin heated, there was something begging to be released within her—was it desire, lust, simple bliss?

Izan entered her thoughts, then, and she grew conflicted.

Is it possible for a heart to be torn?

Dakon's green, summer eyes beheld her, his hand cradled her cheek, and there was a ghost of a smile on his lips as he spoke.

"Eve, I . . ."

"Gods, you're alive!" Pazel rushed to Dakon's side, placing a hand on his forehead. "Why didn't you wake me?" He looked at Eve, surprised.

She stood, the fleeting feeling leaving her more confused than ever. "He just woke, I—I was in shock myself."

Eve walked back until she nearly tripped, hitting her head against the cabin door. Both Dakon and Pazel furrowed their brows, and her nerves went astray. She fumbled around for the handle, needing to free herself.

"I need some air. Happy you're alive, Dakon." Her cheeks burned bright red as she rushed out.

Happy you're alive?

Gods, she was insufferable.

Eve climbed up the steps. The rain had lessened considerably into a slight drizzle. She was filled with a burning intensity she had not felt since that night with Izan.

Izan.

She wanted him, but she wanted Dakon too.

Why the hells was this so complicated?

It was too much. She took the last step onto the deck, not caring if she got wet; she needed to rid herself of the fire burning within her. Pirates moved to and fro around her, focusing on their various tasks in the dreary, misty day.

Something tugged inside her; she was too warm, too desperate, longing for another's touch. Perhaps it was the intensity of her emotions, their near-death experience, being so close to Dakon their lips practically touched, or even Izan's words as he practically gave his heart to her days ago.

What was I thinking?

She groaned, mulling over her dilemma and the longing that was becoming unbearable. It made her tremble, and she desperately needed relief.

What is happening to me?

The pirates gave her peculiar looks, and she noticed a mist rising from her body as the rain touched her heating skin. She turned on her heel and ran back down the stairs.

She needed release. She needed to rid herself of this reckless spirit festering inside of her. It was growing stronger and more powerful.

Eve was coming undone, losing all sense of pleasantries as she ignored a *good morning* from someone. She practically ran, letting her feet guide her to where she needed to go.

She pounded on the cabin door. She could hear someone inside and she knocked even harder, her skin practically burning.

It finally opened.

"Eve? Are you all right?" Izan's dark eyes met hers, his brows furrowed.

"No."

He placed a hand on her forehead, retrieving it quickly. "You are clearly ill, let me see if I can help you."

The way he said those last words sent the familiar chill through her. She didn't move.

"I need you."

Izan cocked his head, confused. "That's what a sick witch would say."

"No"—she moved closer—"I *need* you, Izan."

He narrowed his eyes. "Eve?"

"Do you still want me?"

His eyes bore into hers as if searching for any humor that lingered there. Finding none, he closed the distance between them.

"No. I *need* you, Eve."

EVE

CHAPTER 45

THE NEXT MORNING, EVE FIDDLED WITH the candle on the floor before her, the *Wretched Sentinel* rocking far too much for it to stand on its own. She tried pushing it down, hoping it would stick with some force, but with a groan of the ship, it fell once more.

She tossed it aside, frustrated.

"Do you need help?" The voice was comforting, but it filled her with shame. Dakon knelt next to her.

"I think I can manage, I'd rather you rest." She collected the candle once more, placing it before her to try again.

She could feel Dakon's eyes on her. It was only the two of them in the cabin; Pazel walked about the ship, and even Beast was nowhere to be seen. It was the first time they had been alone together since he woke from his injuries.

"Eve, we need to talk."

"We are talking," she replied, keeping her eyes on the wayward candle.

Dakon sighed, gently taking the candle from her and placing it on the floorboard. After a moment, it stayed still despite the rocking. Eve wasn't sure if she was thankful or frustrated with herself.

"I don't want us to continue this way. The tension, the avoidance."

"I'm not avoiding you."

"Then you are upset with me."

Eve glanced at him. "What do you want from me, Dakon?"

"We are bound for life; wouldn't you prefer to spend it in peace?"

What was peace, exactly?

She rubbed her eyes. "I'm sorry."

"I understand." He placed a hand on hers. "We both have lost greatly, but you are not alone."

His green eyes were sincere. They were rich and earthy, reminding her of the grassy meadow in the high season. Of a time of freedom and happiness.

She realized she had been staring too long and pulled her hand back slowly. "I'm sorry, too, for what I said in the tavern, it was cruel."

"It was," Dakon said, focusing now on the candle. He waved a hand over it once, and it flickered to life. "But it wasn't entirely untrue. I have quite a bit to learn as do you. In that at least, we are similar."

Eve smiled gently, watching him unwind some twine and lay it around them in a circle. "Some might say *'familiar.'*"

Dakon laughed. "Exactly."

Eve settled before the lit candle in the circle. Focusing her strength on the flame licking the frigid air.

Dakon retrieved Cerene's book and knelt on the outside of the twine. "Now, what is it you wish to do?"

Without removing her gaze from the flame, Eve replied, "To see."

Eve walked along the empty corridors of Givensmir's castle. It felt hollow, dark, and in ruins as nature trespassed and laid roots within the walls and along the stone floors.

No longer did it bask in the summer sun but withered in winter's embrace.

She could hear her footsteps as she walked slowly through the halls. She was in the maidens' keep; Eve recognized the art hung along the walls, the way the windows were positioned, and the path she took to her room nearly every day of her life.

A thick, silver fog clung in the air as she approached her room at the end of the hall. Something pulled her toward it, beckoning her.

Her footsteps echoed throughout the space, louder and louder as she reached her door.

Then silence.

Her hand hovered above the knob, now unsure of opening it. Uncertain of the horrors that may linger within waiting to embrace her.

"Enter."

She pushed the door open. Within it was the chamber of her childhood, drawings depicted along the walls, two beds affixed to the end of the room, and a bright sun shining through the windows.

Eve entered, taking careful steps inside what felt like a memory. It was as she remembered, how it all used to be and look, before Clarisa and her mother were torn from her life.

"The voices, they never cease do they?" a very real voice said.

Eve whirled around; sitting atop her bed was her mother.

Come, my child. I've been waiting for you." Her mother opened her hands wide, and Eve walked toward her.

"Are you really here?"

Her mother smiled, sadly. "Only for a little while."

So many questions were on Eve's lips, but she couldn't think of what to say. She sat next to her mother, admiring how serene and comforting she was, as if she had never left.

"You are so beautiful, my daughter. I'm so proud of you."

Tears pricked the corners of Eve's eyes.

Her mother pushed back Eve's tendrils. "I love you. You and Clarisa are so precious to me."

Her touch was smooth on Eve's skin, and she nearly tasted the welcoming chamomile scent that time had forgotten. "Then why did you bind me?"

Her mother's eyes grew serious, regretful, "I tried to give you as much time as I could. The king and his son, there were whispers of using you both for magic. By the time you were born, it was too late to hide Clarisa's."

"Then why not escape with us?"

She held Eve's hands. "I think you know the answer."

King Eryck. He never would have let her out of his sight.

"And Clarisa . . ." Eve swallowed, unable to finish her words.

Her mother let out a shallow breath. "You must find her before it is too late. Dark forces are consuming her. She does not have much time."

"Where did you send her?"

Her mother lifted Eve's chin to face her. "To the Blackthorn. You must go through the veil."

"The veil?"

"It's the only way."

Eve noticed her mother fading before her as if she were a spirit.

No.

"Wait! It's too soon!"

"Protect your souls." She was barely visible anymore.

"Protect from what? Please, stay with me!"

Her mother gave her hands a final squeeze. "Don't let it consume you."

Then she was gone, and Eve was sitting in the cabin once more.

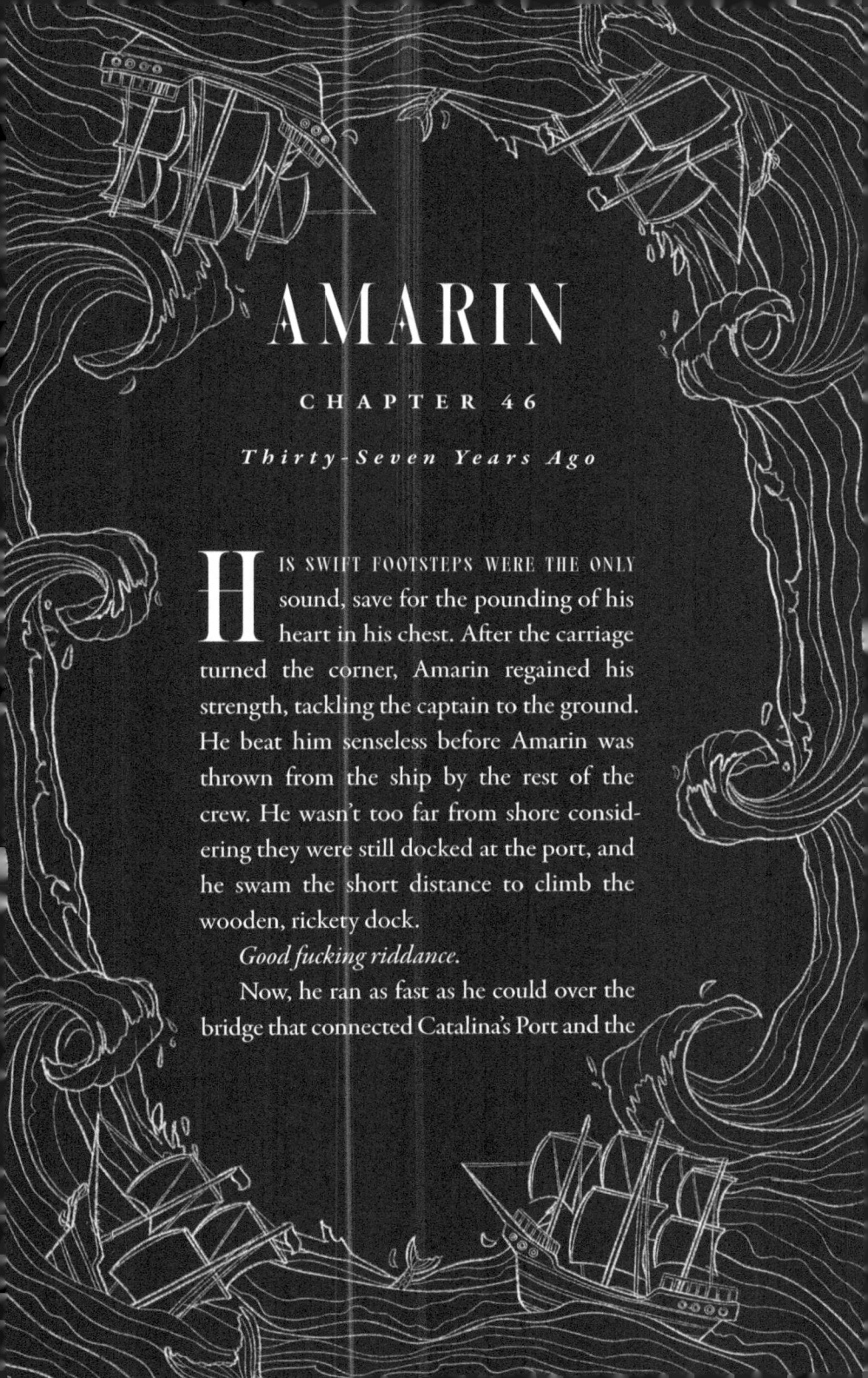

AMARIN

CHAPTER 46

Thirty-Seven Years Ago

H IS SWIFT FOOTSTEPS WERE THE ONLY sound, save for the pounding of his heart in his chest. After the carriage turned the corner, Amarin regained his strength, tackling the captain to the ground. He beat him senseless before Amarin was thrown from the ship by the rest of the crew. He wasn't too far from shore considering they were still docked at the port, and he swam the short distance to climb the wooden, rickety dock.

Good fucking riddance.

Now, he ran as fast as he could over the bridge that connected Catalina's Port and the capital, racing toward the castle where Lucia would no doubt be. His lungs were burning, his arms fatigued, and his breath was ragged as he made his way toward the shining beacons of the castle towers in the distance. Nothing on his mind—not a plan nor weapon on him—save for getting Lucia back in his arms and away from this godsforsaken place.

There were a few guards in front of the walled off entrance to the castle grounds, and the common folk meandered about, mostly merchants trying to make a coin off anyone who passed through. Amarin avoided them, mustering all remaining courage as he approached the guards.

"I need to speak with the king."

The guards looked at each other, serious at first, then hollering with laughter.

"Aye," one choked between wheezes, "and I need to meet with the gods about my many riches."

"I'm serious!" Amarin challenged.

"As am I. You are about as likely to have an audience with His Majesty as I am with the gods. The king does not meet with common folk. Now move along."

"He has taken someone from me. And I will not leave until she is given back!"

To this the guards looked at him with something peculiar. *Pity*?

"Look, eh—I am sure the king will give you back your wife before tomorrow. He does not spend much time with his mistresses."

Amarin couldn't help himself, while the guards were unprepared, he thrust his fist into the one who spoke. They were embattled in a bitter brawl and the merchants and city folk circled them.

Amarin grabbed the guard's sword from his belt, holding it at the neck of the guard, facing him out toward his counterparts. "You *will* let me through these gates or so the gods help me, I will cut his fucking throat."

The guards stood, but not one of them moved.

"I'll do it!" Hot tears stung his eyes. "I swear I will fucking do it!"

The guard in his arms shook, speechless; the sword was already drawing beads of blood.

"Now, now," a voice called out, "must we really behave so barbarically?"

Amarin turned. A blond man with short hair and piercing blue eyes approached him from the crowd. He was dressed in fine clothing and flanked by two rather intimidating guards of his own.

The rich man waved a hand in the direction of the guards, and they took a few steps back, allowing him to step between them.

"I am Lord Wesley, adviser to King Paul. What is your name?"

"A-Amarin," he stammered, feeling the weight of his actions upon him.

"Can we talk as friends, Amarin?"

Amarin nodded.

"Good, now, *friend*, I want to remind you that threatening the city watch is a serious offense, killing one would mean certain death for you."

"I am only here for Lucia, once she is with me I will leave in peace, I swear it." Amarin's hands began to shake. The crowd now watched silently, curious as to how this exchange would turn out.

"Of course, Lucia you said?" Wesley smiled pleasantly, as if they were discussing the latest catch and not the imminent and precarious return of his sweetheart.

"Y-yes, Lucia. She was kidnapped by the king's guards this morning from Catalina's Port."

"Oh, yes. A dreadful misunderstanding." Wesley placed a hand on his chest, speaking the next words loudly for the crowd to hear. "Should you have requested an audience with the king through the city official, he would have gladly obliged you."

"I—I did not know."

"Well, now that you do, can you please release the guard in your . . . care?"

Amarin couldn't force himself to remove the only piece of leverage he had.

"I promise to personally resolve your matter, but I cannot do that as we are."

He swallowed, unsure of what to do. But ultimately, he dropped his sword. The guard crawled quickly away, as if he was scared Amarin would change his mind.

Lord Wesley tilted his chin toward Amarin, and before he could speak, he was tackled by guards who seemed to come from nowhere. They cuffed his hands in chains behind his back and removed the sword from his reach. They lifted him to his knees roughly, the dirt from the ground on his face and in his mouth. He spat it out.

Wesley moved closer, his mouth inches from Amarin's ear. "You will regret that. And now, you must be made an example of before the rest of these people get any ideas."

Amarin raised his head in time to see the lingering city folk piercing him with their eyes before a sack was placed over his head, obscuring everything in darkness.

The man addressed the crowd. "Now we will settle this matter with the privacy it deserves. Go back to your shops and homes." He heard the guards push the crowd back, the latter of whom now seemed more annoyed at the lack of bloodshed than the solving of the matter at hand.

"You promised to bring me Lucia!" Amarin shouted into the sack. "You lied to me!"

"No," Lord Wesley's voice was in front of him now, "I promised to resolve your matter. And the matter is you causing a scene and demanding a witch be returned to you."

Amarin had no time to respond, before the hilt of a sword came down on his head.

"Rise and greet the evening, sleepy pirate," a voice chided from nearby.

The room spun, and Amarin coughed into the cold, dank space. His eyes adjusted to his surroundings—bars in front, bars on the windows, dim lanterns, stone walls—he was in a dungeon. The castle's dungeon. He lifted himself off the ground, feeling sick at the motion, but leaned against the stone wall. Just beyond the bars, was Lord Wesley and a few guards.

"W-where's Lucia?" Amarin managed, his voice hoarse.

Lord Wesley snapped his fingers, and a guard swiftly opened the cell, subduing Amarin before allowing Wesley to enter. He thought it humorous that they considered him to be such a threat, as if it were not obvious he was barely clinging onto life.

"Lucia," Amarin repeated, his body weak against the tight grasps.

"I have something better." Lord Wesley procured a sack and opened it before Amarin. It was filled with gold coins. "I hear you one day wish to be a captain of your own."

Amarin had never seen so many coins at once in his life and felt sickened by their presence.

"No."

"No?"

"No."

"Well, then"—Wesley pocketed the sack—"I have good news and bad news for you, Amarick."

"Amarin."

"Yes"—he smiled sinfully—"*Amarin*." He paced slowly, almost gracefully in front of Amarin, before finally speaking once more. "If you answer my questions, I promise you a swift death. And as you know, I keep my promises."

Amarin scoffed against the guards. "And the good news?"

"That was the good news."

Amarin gave him a wicked smile. "The bad news, then?" Amarin's stomach was in knots, and he was unable to swallow as he stared into the eyes of this wicked man.

"That the *enchantress*—as we'll call her now, must we not wish the people to confuse her nature with those of other witches—has been told of your death, prematurely, of course. Oh, how she wept. Heartbroken, actually. I take it you were lovers?"

"You bastard!"

Amarin ignored him. "The king does not wish for there to be any trouble, any *distractions* for his new enchantress. Should she so much as be emboldened to escape—well, let's just say a witch burning would seem like an easy death."

Amarin leapt to the lord and was struck in the chest by something that took his breath away.

ROUNDS OF TORTURE AND QUESTIONS ABOUT THE PRESENCE OF OTHER witches aboard the ship plagued Amarin's days and nights.

He lost count of how many.

No answer seemed good enough for this man.

HIS CLOTHES WERE STAINED IN BLOOD.

He quickly removed them, switching into the guard's clothes instead.

HE WAS RUNNING, RUNNING AGAINST THE FERAL WIND AND RAIN.

Running until he could not feel his legs anymore.

Jumping into a boat and rowing aimlessly into the dark sea.

They did not seem to catch up to him.

Did not seem to see him.
He drifted further into the storm.

Amarin lay there, underneath the moonlit sky.
He hated himself.
Hated that he could not keep Lucia safe.
Hated that he broke his promise to her.
Anger rose within him, white hot and furious.
He screamed into the dark oblivion and cursed the gods until his throat was raw.

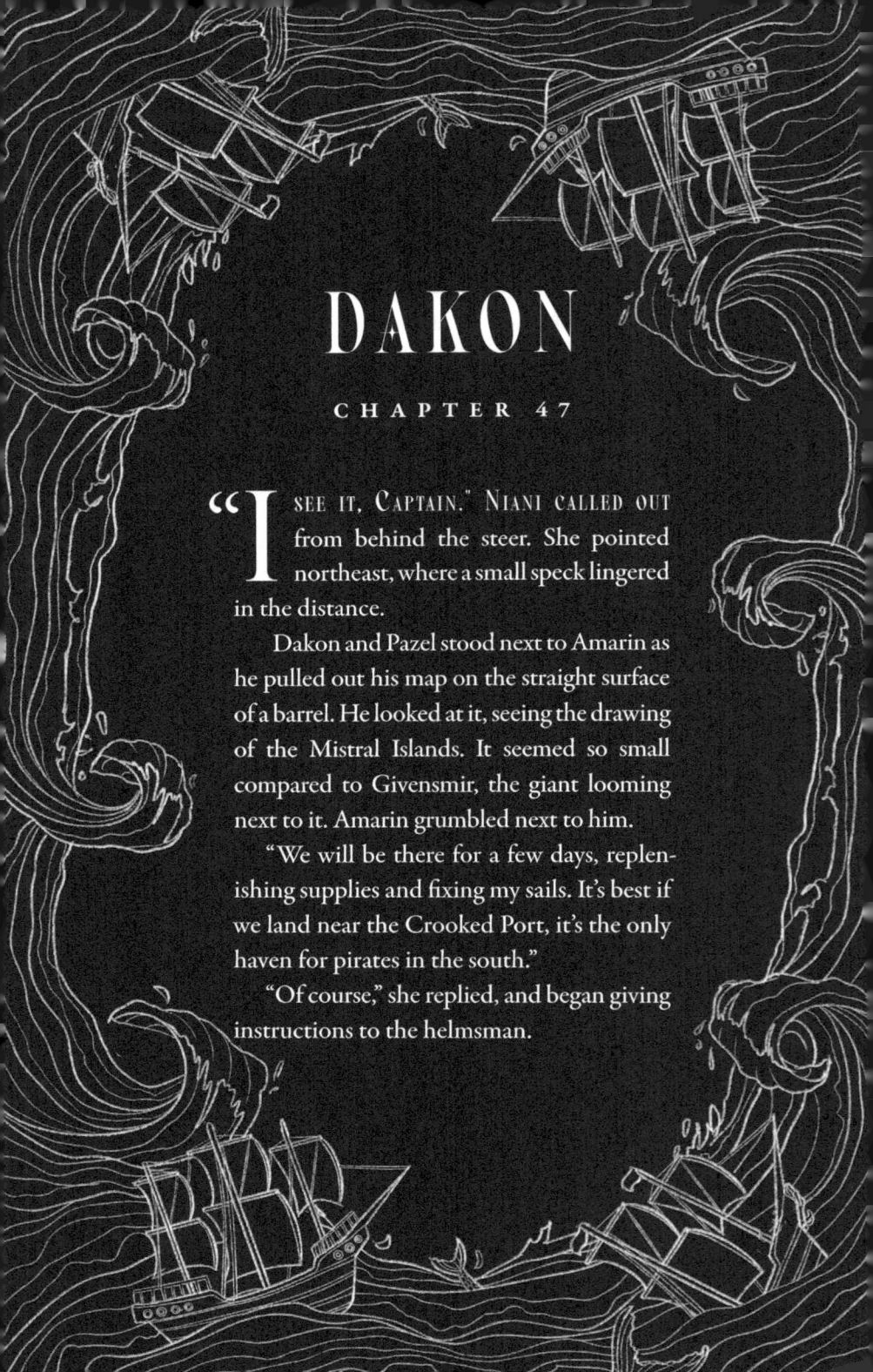

DAKON

CHAPTER 47

"I SEE IT, CAPTAIN." NIANI CALLED OUT from behind the steer. She pointed northeast, where a small speck lingered in the distance.

Dakon and Pazel stood next to Amarin as he pulled out his map on the straight surface of a barrel. He looked at it, seeing the drawing of the Mistral Islands. It seemed so small compared to Givensmir, the giant looming next to it. Amarin grumbled next to him.

"We will be there for a few days, replenishing supplies and fixing my sails. It's best if we land near the Crooked Port, it's the only haven for pirates in the south."

"Of course," she replied, and began giving instructions to the helmsman.

"She is one talented woman," Pazel mused aloud.

Amarin gave him a pointed look. "Someone has to make up for all your shortcomings."

"What do you mean, Captain? I'm taller than you are." Pazel cocked his head.

Dakon gripped Pazel by the shoulder. "That's not what he meant."

"How about you give me *two* new coats and shoes, and I won't stab you in the gut?" Amarin challenged.

"I have no money, Captain, I lost it at the tavern."

"Then you better learn to sew."

Pazel gulped, but Dakon stood between them. He pinched the bridge of his nose, sighing. "Why don't you keep Niani company?"

All former threats seemed to disappear as Pazel lit up and patted Dakon's back. "You don't have to tell me twice."

Amarin and Dakon watched as Pazel went up the stairs two at a time and met Niani at the top. She rolled her eyes but smiled as she turned from him.

"I will never understand how a boy like that got a woman like her." Amarin shook his head.

"He claims it's his charm." Dakon smiled.

"Or maybe he has some of that witchcraft too."

Dakon looked up at Pazel who focused intently on Niani as she continued speaking to the helmsman.

"No, he just listens."

THEY DOCKED ALONG THE CROOKED PORT AND DAKON FELT RELIEVED to be off the ship. The village was less chaotic than Bastard's Haven. It reminded him of Catalina's Port, where the drunks stood between the alleys and a musty scent lingered. He felt for the daggers on his hips once more, hoping he wouldn't have to use them.

He stepped onto the shore, the sand shifting beneath his boots, and trudged up the beach toward the palm trees. He sat in front of one, a bit out of the way, wanting nothing more than to think in solitude.

Niani and Pazel left together from the ship. Dakon smiled. *Good for him.*

Other pirates disembarked, and then he saw them. Eve and Izan walked close together. He bit his lip, unable to take his eyes off her.

Soft fur nuzzled next to him, and he didn't have to look to know it was Beast. He was always there when Dakon needed him most.

He ran his fingers through Beast's fur, absentmindedly, as Eve and Izan laughed, taking off toward the village.

"What do I do, Beast? I'm lost."

The gytrash licked his hand.

"I guess it's just you and me."

Eve walked up the path and was obscured by trees from where he sat. Losing sight of her made him feel uncomfortable. He touched the last bit of scarring on his neck. She had waited for him, she was the reason he was alive. He owed her protection, for his sake as well, but he also wanted her to be happy.

"Tell me she's safe, Beast. Tell me she is safe, and I won't go after her."

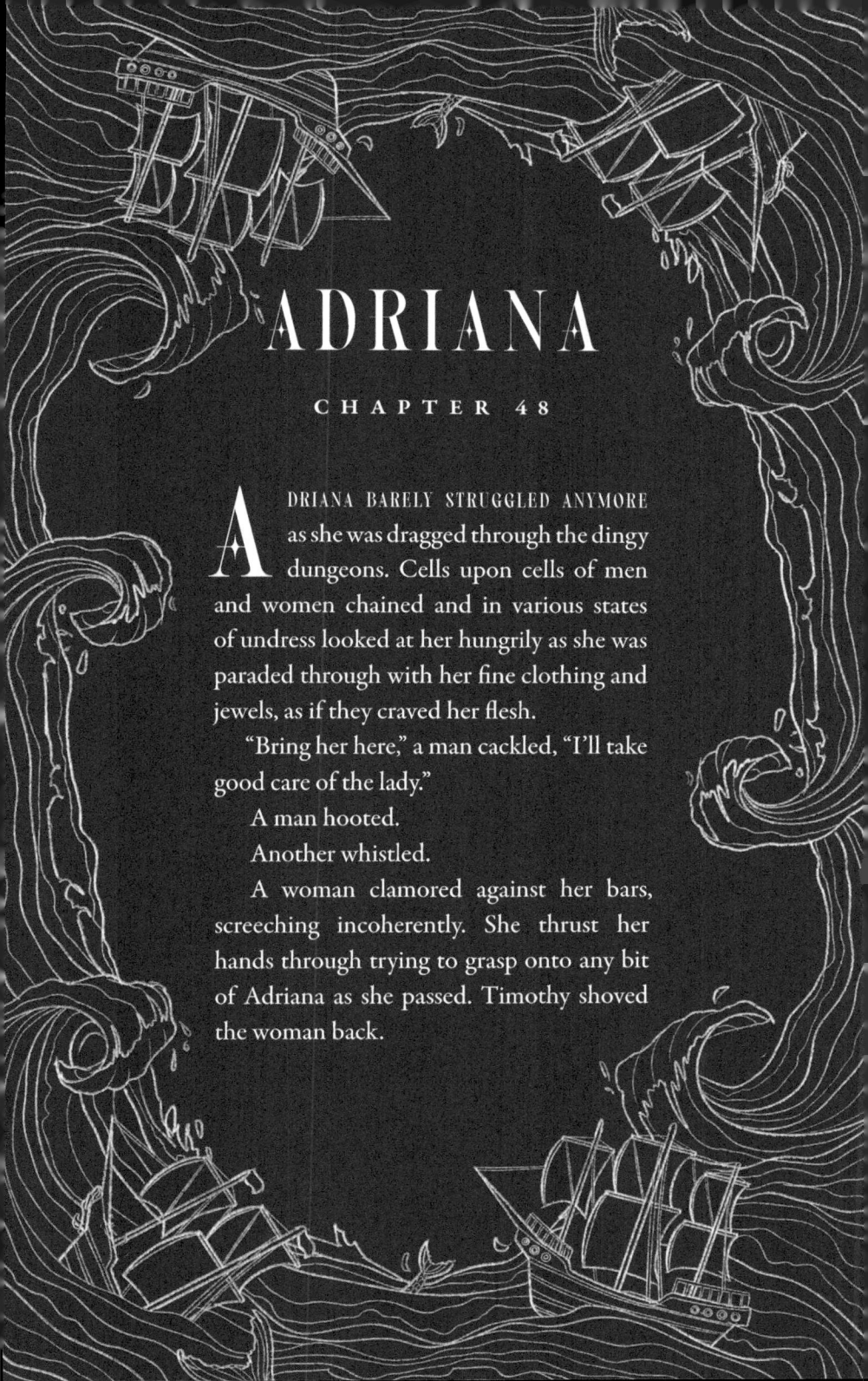

ADRIANA

CHAPTER 48

ADRIANA BARELY STRUGGLED ANYMORE as she was dragged through the dingy dungeons. Cells upon cells of men and women chained and in various states of undress looked at her hungrily as she was paraded through with her fine clothing and jewels, as if they craved her flesh.

"Bring her here," a man cackled, "I'll take good care of the lady."

A man hooted.

Another whistled.

A woman clamored against her bars, screeching incoherently. She thrust her hands through trying to grasp onto any bit of Adriana as she passed. Timothy shoved the woman back.

"I just want to taste her, a little nibble!"

Adriana shivered and moaned as the daunting realization of her circumstances weighed heavily upon her. The guards took her down a more isolated corridor, and she lifted her head enough to see that only two of the furthest cells were occupied.

"Please don't put me in with them," she begged through tears. "I want to be alone, please."

"It didn't have to be this way, Princess," Timothy sighed. "All you had to do was stay quiet. I tried warning you."

They were halfway down the hall, nearing the occupied cells. "Please, no!"

She tried fighting against them as panic ripped through her. She nearly got out of their grasp, but Timothy wrapped his arms around her, holding her tight against him.

"Open that cell there!" he ordered. "Now!"

A fiercely large guard that she had never seen before, slapped the head of another meeker guard. "You heard the man, move it!"

The smaller guard rushed forward with keys and opened up an empty cell.

"Timothy," she begged, "please don't do this. You're a good man; you're a good person. Please don't do this to me!"

Timothy held her tight still, unable or unwilling to look into her panicked eyes. "Leave the keys," he said to the guard, "you all are dismissed."

The guard left the keys in the cell door, and Adriana could hear as the rest of them left.

"Princess," he said softly, "I have tried to be reasonable, but you would not listen."

She seized onto the moment, anything to free her, to survive what Marc may do to her. "I'm sorry," she breathed. "I'll listen, I promise, you and me, we can leave together."

Timothy smirked, and Adriana's stomach dropped. "Give me a

kiss, Princess. Show me you mean it."

She hesitated, every inch of her body fighting the urge to run. "I—"

"If you aren't willing to kiss me, then I suppose you aren't serious about escaping."

Adriana fought the tears and tremors running through her. She pressed her lips against him, thinking about how desperate she was to leave this godsforsaken place. Thinking about how much she wished it was Dakon pressed against her instead.

She pulled back, watching as Timothy opened his eyes slowly, satisfied. "Thank you for that, Princess."

Before she could respond, he pushed her into the cell and quickly locked the door.

Adriana rushed to the bars. "You lied to me!"

Timothy smirked. "I never promised to help you. But thanks for the kiss."

With that, he walked down the corridor and turned the corner, taking her last hope with her. Her knees buckled beneath her, and she slipped down to the floor, sobbing uncontrollably.

"Princess?" a low voice spoke.

Oh no, they recognize me.

She turned away from it. "N-no, you must have me confused."

"No, I would know that voice anywhere. Adriana, it's me."

Callum?

She turned back quickly. Before her eyes was Callum, thin and badly beaten. She ran to the bars that connected their cells.

"Oh my gods, Callum. You're alive?"

He limped to her, blood on his clothing, and bruises harsh along his face. Her heart sank.

He held her hands through the slats, tears filling his eyes. "Not for much longer, I suppose." He groaned as he adjusted his footing. "Why are you here?"

"Marc," she whispered, "he has gone mad."

Callum gave her a woeful look. "You don't deserve to be here."

"Neither do you. I can't believe you're here." She ran her fingers gently over his face, her spirit tearing to shreds as she beheld how brutalized he had been.

"I wish they would have killed me."

"I'm so sorry." Adriana kissed his hands tenderly. "I had no idea."

"I suppose none of the court does."

"How long have you been here?" She held his gaze, his golden-brown eyes forlorn.

"Since I helped Eve escape."

"Has the bewitchment not left?"

"Bewitchment?"

"Yes, we were told you were bewitched by Eve. We believed you to be dead."

"That's what they want you to believe." A voice cut through their conversation. Adriana turned to it, seeing a man across the narrow hall in a cell of his own.

"Adriana, this is Emilio, from Pleasant Peak."

Her eyes widened as she recognized the man leaning against the bars. The very one who was arrested in the throne hall.

"Pleasure to meet you, Princess, apologies for being so underdressed."

"What is happening?" she breathed, incredulous.

Callum shook his head sadly. Using a gentle touch to turn her to him.

"You may want to sit, Princess. There is much to tell."

CLARISA

CHAPTER 49

SHE WAS NOT SURE WHO SHE WAS becoming anymore, could barely remember who she used to be. Anger filled her, and her limbs trembled with the force of it. The candles flickered wildly around her chambers, shadows danced on her walls, and the rain thrashed itself against her windows. She faced the mirror as the room spun, and within it only those blue-gray eyes of hers stared back.

"It's ours. All ours. We will rule the kingdoms. We will have unlimited power."

HER VISION WAS HAZY AS THREE SHADOWS CREPT DOWN FROM THE corners of the long, dark hall. Clarisa could hear the clatter of a weapon on the stone floor, echoing through the corridor.

The guard in front of Pedro's chamber was bewildered as he spoke to her.

When did he get here?

"I swear it Clarisa, the only visitor they've had is you."

"COME BACK TO ME." ANA PLACED HER HANDS ON CLARISA'S, HOLDING firmly. Her beautiful, brown eyes slowly lifted to meet hers. "Tell me you are still in there."

It was barely a whisper, like a plea, and Clarisa felt the weight of the world on her shoulders as she met her gaze.

When did she end up back in her chambers?

When did she leave Raven's Holdfast?

Where did Pedro's guard go?

Her chambers were no longer in chaos, but untouched as it had always been. The rain tapped gently, peacefully, against the glass, or was it the crystal?

Tink. Tink. Tink.

It was the only sound in the otherwise silent room. She could feel her lips quivering from the slight chill, or more likely, whatever had taken hold of her sanity.

Clarisa blinked, taking in the darkness of night and the soft candlelight by her bed. She had been here before with Ana and each time she slowly felt easier in her presence. She righted herself on the bed, gathering her wits about her, and controlled her breathing.

Was it only a dream?

A premonition of what was to come?

"I am here."

Ana knit her brow; concern laced her gaze. "I'm worried about you. You have not been the same since . . ."

Clarisa didn't press for her to finish her words, both of them knowing full well her meaning. She had not been the same since she was caught with the oracles, using forbidden magic.

The prophecy as Clarisa knew it was in full force, her sister coming to tear it away from her, to kill Ana, to destroy everything good in this world. There was no going back to the way things used to be.

"I am trying," Clarisa breathed, resting her forehead on Ana's, "but I'm scared." She felt like a little girl again, petrified of the shadows on the walls and her old magic that now seemed like child's play. This magic, the power that coursed through her veins was not something to fear, but to harness.

Then it wasn't a dream.

She was now filled with the blood of that witch and the full power of her ancestors.

Tears fell down Clarisa's cheeks, hot with frustration.

Ana lifted her hand, wiping them away gently. "I know. I'm scared too."

Clarisa bit her lip, "I don't know what to do. Everything's changed." Panic rose once more, her breathing heavier with each word.

"Shhh." Ana placed a finger on her lips. "There is nothing to do now but sleep. You are safe with me, remember?"

Ana caressed her, and Clarisa rested her head against her chest, listening to the sound of her heartbeat, strong and steady. She closed her eyes gently, trying to focus on nothing but Ana's touch. They remained silent for a few moments.

"I didn't always have terrible nightmares," Clarisa mumbled, her eyes still closed against Ana's chest.

"Hmm," Ana replied.

"Yes." Clarisa smiled sadly. "I used to dream about us."

Ana's grasp stiffened slightly before relaxing once more. "Is that so?"

Clarisa nodded. "Before we were ever together I would dream

about you. The beautiful healer in the castle, with the enchanting, brown eyes, and sweet smile." She lifted herself off Ana's chest, taking her hands in hers and meeting Ana's gaze. "And as time went on, I would often dream about us together. Far from the Blackthorn, sailing west to paradise, away from the rain, and under a golden sun. Just you and me."

Ana smiled in response, her eyes watering as she looked into Clarisa's. "It's a beautiful dream."

A tightness in Clarisa's chest loosened upon seeing Ana's smile; she loved it so much, and it had appeared infrequently recently. With all her soul, she wished she could make this dream come true for her.

"I promise one day we will leave this place. We will find another land and live as normally as we can. I will build us a home and the worst we will worry about is the baker overcharging us."

Ana laughed. "You do not know how to build, nor do I think any baker will overcharge us. You will be their primary buyer."

Clarisa smiled. "But I can learn. For you, I would learn how to build a palace with my bare hands."

Ana met her gaze, conflicting feelings and a sense of happiness within her eyes. Before she could utter another word, Ana tugged at the fabric of Clarisa's dress collar, pulling her against her. She wrapped her arms around Clarisa's neck and pressed her mouth on hers. Clarisa let herself go, releasing every bit of frustration, fear, and burden into their embrace.

Clarisa bit Ana's lip, harder than intended. She opened her eyes; Ana's lip began to bleed.

"Your lip," Clarisa pulled back, feeling guilty.

Ana touched it. "Oh, I'm sorry."

"No"—Clarisa ran her fingers through Ana's braids—"it's my fault. I should have been more careful with you."

Ana smiled. "I will think about forgiving you, then, if you get me something to clean it with."

Clarisa kissed her cheek and moved off the bed. She tinkered with the drawers of her side table, accidentally shutting it too hard when she pulled the handkerchief out.

The hag stone atop it fell to the ground.

Clarisa picked it up, inspecting it for any chips or cracks. She lifted it to her eye and was about to place it back when something caught her attention. In the hole of the stone, she saw herself, right where Ana was sitting.

Her blood ran cold.

"Can I have the cloth now?" Ana cocked her head, a grin still on her face. Clarisa handed it to her absentmindedly.

Surely, she was mistaken.

She lifted the hag stone once more, and now she saw another woman in it. Queen Saryn.

No.

No. No. No.

"Clarisa? What are you doing?" Ana asked, her brows furrowing.

Clarisa swallowed, lowering the stone. She stared at Ana, letting out a shaky breath, "I—I am not feeling well."

If the stone is not meant for my dreams, then . . .

"Can I do anything to help?" Ana asked. "It's what healers are known for."

Clarisa tightened her grip on the stone, her eyes watering. "Navir has told me my cousin has been killed."

She watched as Ana's smile fell.

"Eve's name was carved into his skin."

Ana was too quiet.

"I asked the guards who was allowed in their holding chamber. Do you know what they said?"

Ana took a sharp breath. "Clarisa—"

"Do you know what they said?" She narrowed her eyes at Ana.

Tears rolled down Ana's face. "It's not what you think," she managed.

330

"They said that only I was. Me!"

Ana broke down, choking back sobs as she tried to explain.

Her heart shattered, the betrayal too great. "You lied to me! You killed Pedro!"

"No! No, no I didn't kill him I swear." Ana reached for Clarisa, her hands shaking as they tried to wrap around Clarisa.

Clarisa pushed her away. "How long have you been able to shape-shift. How long have you been disguising yourself as *me*?"

Ana clutched her chest, sobs racking through her, but Clarisa kept firm. "Answer me, now!"

"I—I have only tried to protect you."

"Protect me? Protect me!" Clarisa cried out. "You have killed the only family I have seen in years. Ripped him from me, whether you killed him with your magic or not, his blood is on your hands."

"You don't understand, I had no choice!"

Clarisa stepped away from her. "Get out," she seethed.

Ana hesitated.

"Get out!" she roared, the bed shaking, candles flickering.

Ana flinched. "It's Navir—"

"Navir," Clarisa growled, "is the only one left I trust."

Ana paled, her mouth open in shock. "Clarisa, don't do this."

"I never wish to see you again."

"Please—"

"Leave!"

Ana trembled as she ran from the chamber leaving the door open on her way out.

EVE

CHAPTER 50

Eve and Izan walked through the village, lively with people bustling about the streets. She could feel the tension withering from her body as they made their way through the shops. They entered one with fabrics of all colors, and despite remembering the last time she did so, she couldn't help but run her fingers over the smooth silk. It made her feel giddy, thinking of all the dresses she could make with some thread. Her eyes landed on a burgundy dress. She took the precious bodice in her hands and ran her fingers along it. The shade was very similar to the dress she wore at the welcoming ceremony for the Mytar nobles.

"Do you want it?" Izan asked, placing a gentle hand on her back.

She sighed. "Where would I wear it?"

Izan placed a kiss on her cheek. "I'm sure you'll want to change before arriving in the Blackthorn."

She shook her head, though her hand was firmly gripped on the fabric. "I would like to wear something other than these dirty trousers."

"Then it's settled."

She eyed him then turned her gaze back to the dress. "I couldn't."

"Then I will give you a moment to mourn its loss."

Eve rolled her eyes but continued feeling it in her hands.

She missed wearing dresses.

She missed how she felt in them.

Eve turned to leave, walking out of the door and looking about for Izan.

Where was he?

Familiar hands went over her eyes, and she smiled. "I was beginning to think you left me."

"Never, Lady." Izan smiled. "But I do have something for you, nothing big."

He let her go and she turned, seeing him lift a large package from the ground.

"You didn't." Her eyes grew wide, a smile splitting her face.

"I already did."

Eve jumped excitedly in the middle of the street, taking the package in her hands and placing a kiss on Izan's lips. He smiled infectiously back, his dimples, deep and beautiful, on his cheeks.

She peeked inside and sure enough the dress was folded within.

"Do you think I can wear it now?"

Izan laughed. "You can wear it whenever you want, it's yours."

AFTER CHANGING OUT OF THOSE FILTHY CLOTHES AND INTO HER NEW dress, Eve felt more like herself than ever as she and Izan continued further into the market square. They tasted fish, breads, ales, and all sorts of other delicious treats along the way. The village was alive with music and dancing; more joy in a single port than she had ever witnessed in her entire life.

They finished dancing, the afternoon sky settled into night, and Izan and Eve walked back to the ship. As they passed the merchants with their stalls, one called out to them. She was an older woman, with graying braids tightly woven about her head and a tan dress filled with stains. She waved, her frail hands held high above her.

"Good evening to the lovely couple," the woman said. Around her were barrels stacked upon each other, one with a bung slightly loose and dripping what looked to be wine.

"Good evening." Eve smiled. "What do you have here?"

"Wines, my sweet child." She grinned. "I have one from Rubianes, the best in all of Givensmir."

Hearing the place of her namesake made her warm inside. She thought of Pedro, remembering how much he loved to drink the sweet wines from their homeland. He would want her to have a taste.

"Can I try? Just a sip?"

"Me, as well. If you will allow us," Izan added.

The woman smiled. "But of course, how can I deny such beautiful lovers. Though, I must warn you, drinking this may increase your passion."

Eve laughed. "I'll take the risk."

"As will I." Izan wrapped a hand around her waist.

"Excellent." She opened the bung and let the wine fill the cups. She closed it and handed the wine to Izan and Eve.

"How much?" Izan asked.

"Seeing you drink it together is all that warms this old woman's heart." She placed a hand over her chest and smiled warmly.

Izan looked deep in her eyes and clinked his drink to hers. "Cheers to us."

"To us," she replied.

The wine was incredible, the sweet taste on her tongue reminding her of the rolling hills of Rubianes, the fields of grapes reddening in the sun. It was euphoric, wistful, as it passed her lips. She kept her gaze on Izan, ready to head back to the ship, for another night in his cabin.

DAKON

CHAPTER 51

DAKON STAYED BY THE PALM TREE AS night grew. The fog seemed to have followed them from the sea as it grew around the ships docked at the port. He stretched, ready to start anew tomorrow.

He stood, Beast lingering at his side. Pazel and Niani were at the edge of the pier, and she crossed her arms. Dakon wondered if she was upset but Pazel took a new coat from his shoulders and placed it on hers. Niani handed him a small, leather pouch in return and gave him a gentle kiss on the cheek. After a moment, they parted. Pazel lingered at the end of the pier pouch in hand, and she walked back to the ship.

Pazel turned, smiling as his eyes landed on Dakon.

"She is . . . something, Dakon," he mused.

Dakon couldn't help but smile back, patting his friend on the shoulder. "I'm happy for you."

"And those eyes, I could stare into them day and night."

"You are quite at the mercy of the Lovers." Dakon thought of the gods he had once worshipped. The Lovers symbolized romance and truth—all of what Pazel was so clearly displaying before him. He grinned genuinely.

"Then, I shall thank them in my next prayers."

"You pray?"

"No, but if I did I would."

Dakon sighed. "Let us hope this tryst doesn't rid you of your humor."

"This is no tryst." Pazel turned to him, eyes suddenly serious. "Dakon, I—I think I want to stay."

"Here on the Mistral Islands?"

"No, I mean on the *Wretched Sentinel*."

Dakon raised a brow. "Are you certain?"

"Truly. I have never been happier than being aboard this ship. Even before I met Niani, to travel the world, to see new places and things, it has thus far been the greatest adventure of my life."

Dakon felt a pang of sadness. "You will not be staying with us in the Blackthorn, I take it."

Pazel shook his head, and Beast moved to nuzzle against him. Pazel bent down, running his fingers through Beast's fur. "Though, I would stay, if you and Eve need me to."

Dakon knelt next to him, patting Beast on the head. The gytrash appeared to almost smile with all the attention.

"You will always be welcome with us. But it's time for you to go off, live your dreams."

Saying it out loud reminded him of Adriana and how she talked of traveling the world. The same bittersweet feeling came over him.

"How will you ever learn to charm new ladies?" Pazel grinned.

"I will have to manage," Dakon replied, smiling.

They both sat at the edge of the dock, their legs dangling over the sea. Down below there was only pitch-black water, but just beyond the horizon was a star-filled sky, bright and effervescent.

Pazel lifted the leather pouch, Dakon could hear the sloshing of drink inside. "A merchant handed this to me and Niani, called us a *beautiful couple*, can you believe it? Is it that obvious?"

Dakon shook his head. "No, you both have been so secretive, not even the gods have noticed."

Pazel gave Dakon a small shove. "Jealous?"

"With every bone in my body."

Pazel chuckled, handing the pouch to Dakon. "Then I shall take pity and give you the first sip."

"It seems only fair." Dakon shrugged. He made a show of opening it, pretending to inspect the scent and contents. Then before Pazel could scold him, took a long sip.

The wine tasted sweet and welcoming, and he was certain he had never tasted anything so wonderful in all his life. He wanted more, but relented, giving it back to Pazel who drank it in turn.

"This is incredible," Pazel remarked, "as if the gods themselves have crafted it."

"Then I can't imagine why they would share it with us mere mortals."

"A moment of weakness of theirs I'm sure."

"Seems to be quite a bit of that festering." Dakon took the pouch for another sip.

"Do you mean Eve?"

Dakon nearly choked on his drink and whipped his head to Pazel. "Why do you ask?"

"The tension could set fire to a ship, all humor aside."

Dakon rubbed his eyes. "I love Adriana."

"Yes, but she is gone, I'm afraid."

Dakon lifted the pouch. "This wine must have magic in it. Your wisdom could rival the best scholars."

Pazel rolled his eyes. "I only meant that Adriana is far away in a castle that would seek to have our heads. Not the ideal scenario." He sipped. "And you cannot stop what your heart desires in the present."

"Eve is my witch. I am bound to protect her."

"Yes, that makes things simpler doesn't it?"

"What are you saying?"

"That you are hiding, and if I know anything about you, my friend, it is that you seem to stand out even when you care not for it."

"So, I should tell Eve how I feel."

"Depends"—Pazel drank the last of the wine—"how do you feel?"

Dakon knew the answer, it was ready on his lips. But before he could utter a word, a shout rang out from behind them. Pazel and Dakon whirled, facing a strange man he had never seen before.

"Eve!" the man yelled. "Your friend Eve is harmed. She needs you!"

Beast growled, and the man took a step back. Dakon and Pazel looked at each other and then back at the man.

"Are you a witch?" Dakon asked.

The man hesitated a moment, before nodding his head. "That is how I know she is in trouble. Please, follow me!"

Dakon, Pazel, and Beast ran behind the man making their way up the beach and toward the dark forest that separated the village and the port. They tore through the brush, and Dakon nearly ran into the man who stopped suddenly before him.

"Where is Eve?" Dakon was breathing raggedly, his heart lurching in his chest.

The man turned slowly.

"She is somewhere safe now."

"W—what does that mean?" Pazel asked.

The man whipped his hand to the side, and Pazel was thrown against a nearby tree. Beast growled and leapt toward him but was halted midair. Dakon was frozen in shock, watching as they quickly became surrounded by hooded figures in dark blue robes.

The man's eyes turned white, and Dakon took a step back.

"Who are you?" Dakon breathed.

"You know who we are." The man grinned. "We've met before." His face twisted and he transformed before Dakon into the man from the Strix meeting in Catalina Port. The man who nearly grabbed him by the neck if not for Dakon's skin burning him. The same one who tried to attack Adriana in the city streets.

"My name is Reyher, and you must be Dakon."

"It can't be."

The Strix, they are here.

Dakon took another step, fear gripping him. Rough hands grabbed his arms. He struggled against his captor, trying to summon his magic, his fire, but it felt *lost*.

He kicked against him, and the witch let go as he retrieved his daggers. Dakon lifted his arm to thrust it into the chest of his captor, but Reyher's voice stopped him.

"Kill him and I kill your precious companion."

Dakon froze. Beast still hovered above them, unable to move.

"Drop them, now."

Dakon's nostrils flared, his breathing ragged as he released his daggers to the ground. His captor immediately retrieved them.

Another witch gripped Dakon, tying his hands behind his back.

"Let him go," Dakon yelled, "I dropped my weapons, now stand by your words!"

Reyher flicked his wrist and Dakon watched in horror as Beast fell hard onto the ground.

"Go Beast! Run!" Dakon shouted.

The gytrash twitched but couldn't move.

Pazel stirred from where he was thrown, and another witch subdued him.

They were heavily outnumbered, their gytrash unable to help, unable to escape.

Reyher walked toward Beast. Dakon struggled against the witch holding him back.

Where was his magic?!

"Leave him alone! If you touch him I swear by all the gods I will kill you!"

Reyher smirked at Dakon. "These are rare creatures. They belong to the land, not to a familiar. I am doing you a favor."

Dakon began to shout, but the witch pushed a cloth in his mouth to silence him. He watched helplessly as Reyher looked down at Beast who whimpered at his feet.

Reyher lifted his hands above Beast. "From a witch you are made, and to the mist you must fade."

The Strix witches began to chant, repeating the same words again and again.

"From a witch you are made, and to the mist you must fade."

"From a witch you are made, and to the mist you must fade."

"From a witch you are made, and to the mist you must fade."

Beast howled, his body disappearing with the wind, and soon he was gone.

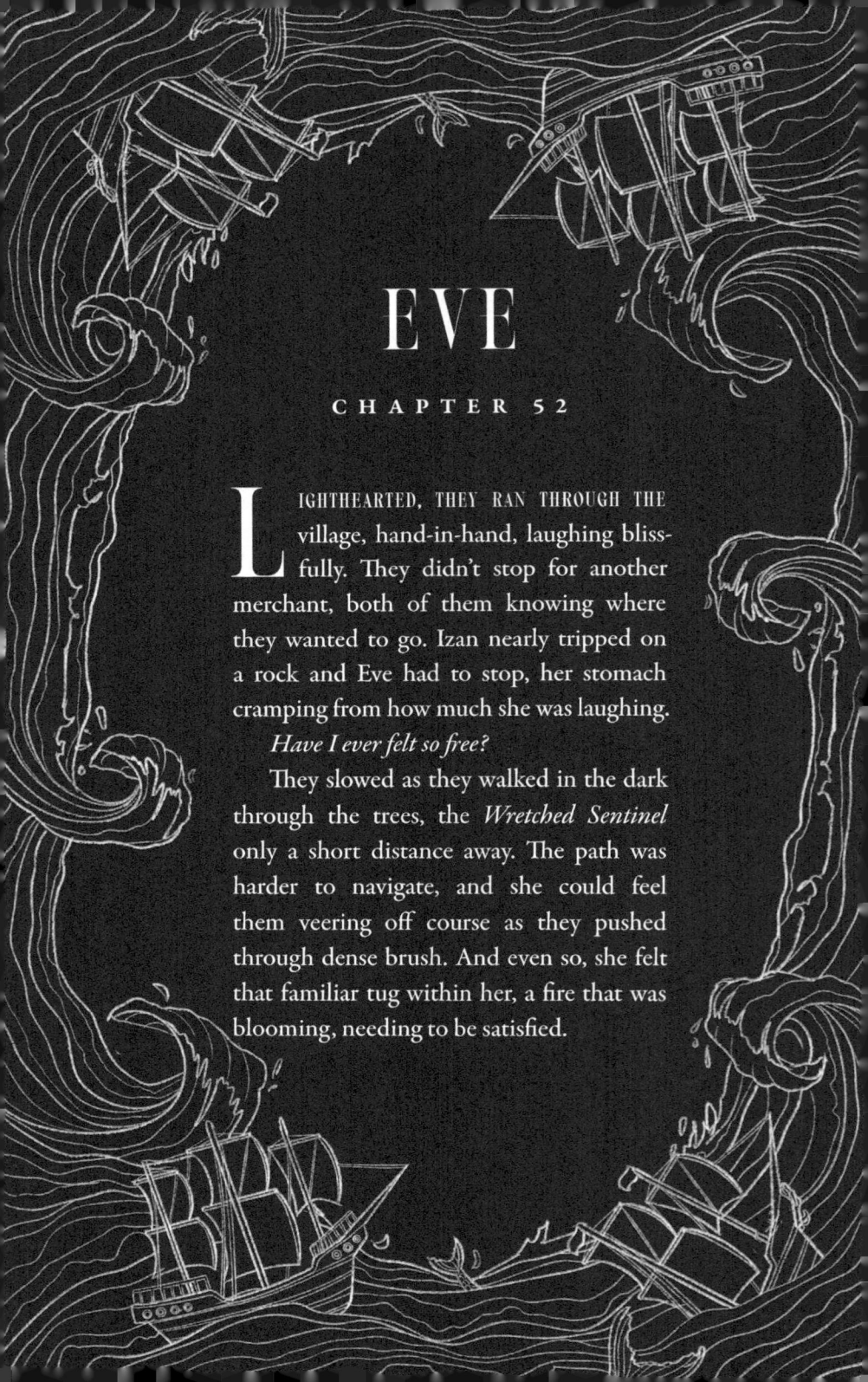

EVE

CHAPTER 52

LIGHTHEARTED, THEY RAN THROUGH THE village, hand-in-hand, laughing bliss-fully. They didn't stop for another merchant, both of them knowing where they wanted to go. Izan nearly tripped on a rock and Eve had to stop, her stomach cramping from how much she was laughing.

Have I ever felt so free?

They slowed as they walked in the dark through the trees, the *Wretched Sentinel* only a short distance away. The path was harder to navigate, and she could feel them veering off course as they pushed through dense brush. And even so, she felt that familiar tug within her, a fire that was blooming, needing to be satisfied.

"Izan." She pulled his hand.

"Eve?" He turned, moving close.

"Kiss me, just once, and I think I can make it back."

He cupped her face in his hand. "Full of theatrics are we not?"

"All to entertain." She bowed slightly in her dress.

He peered down at her, a hungry look in his eyes. "This may have been the best purchase I have ever made in my life."

Eve closed whatever distance remained. "Look who is full of theatrics now."

He bit his lip, as they stared at one another, daring each other to make the first move. She smiled, a banter ready upon her tongue. But he seized her mouth, planting his lips on hers and taking Eve into his arms. She grabbed him back, her nails digging into his neck and shoulder. Their kisses were desperate, needy, as if they would never embrace again.

There was a cough, somewhere nearby.

Izan stopped, his body tightening.

Eve stilled, the small hairs on the back of her neck rising.

"Well, well, Izan," a voice, deep and menacing, sneered, "it's good to see you again."

"Izan," Eve tightened her grip, watching as the group of hooded figures closed in on them. "Izan, who are these people?"

Before he could answer, one of the men called out to them. "It seems that you are too far from the sea to escape now."

A few of the men chuckled as the man spoke.

"Izan, what is happening?" Eve began to panic, realizing she held his hand in a white-knuckled grip.

He clenched his jaw, tightening his grip on her back. "What do you want, Reyher?"

"Ah, Izan. The Strix misses their favorite healer."

Eve's blood ran cold. *The Strix? Izan had escaped from the Strix?*

"I'll never go back," he spat.

"If not for us you would have been killed by the mortals. Tell me, how much does a nymph go for in their black markets?"

Eve froze, dropping her hand from his. *A nymph?*

Reyher continued, "They would *murder* you, but we *embraced* you."

"You used me!"

"We used each other."

"I was a child!"

"And a wonderful healer," Reyher smirked.

"You promised if I healed them you would let them live!"

"And I did . . . for a few moments." He moved closer. "Do you remember how they begged to die? The look in their eyes as you took away their final hope?"

"I'll kill you!" Izan lunged at Reyher, but a large witch tackled him to the ground.

Eve panicked, trying to bring about her fire, her magic. Nothing was working. Not even a spark. She felt different, sluggish.

Eve turned to run but plowed into a man who grabbed her tightly by the arm. She struggled to fight, attempting to bring her power to heel, but she felt weaker. The Strix closed the circle around them.

"Did you give it to her?" Reyher asked a figure next to him. The figure removed their hood, revealing the old woman from the market who transformed into a slightly younger woman with short, dark hair.

"Talesa?" Izan breathed, shocked.

Talesa cocked her head, turning to him. "They drank every last drop."

Eve's heart stopped.

The wine?

Izan wrestled one of the witches but more came and overpowered him.

"Let us go!" Izan growled.

Eve tried in vain to call her magic once more, but she remained empty.

Mortal.

"Izan," Eve called out, "my magic, it's gone. I can't feel it!"

Izan's eyes widened, turning back to face the Strix.

Reyher didn't pay him any mind, addressing the rest of the Strix. "We have her familiars. We need to go before the rest of their crew wakes. Send him to the sea, take the witch."

"Over my dead body!" Izan shoved the witch from him and punched the one holding Eve in the face, knocking him over. Another man rushed him, taking him to the ground. "Run, Eve! Run!"

She spun in circles trying to find a way to escape, but they were surrounded. Dread filled her, and she turned to Izan.

She cried out as someone grabbed her. She tried to scream, but they stuffed her mouth with a rag, silencing her. Tears fell down her cheeks.

Dakon, Pazel, Izan. They were in danger. They were all in danger.

They fought, trying in vain against the sheer number of witches. It became a blur of movement and shouts. Izan fought against the men, throwing punches, and then, a heavy force fell upon her head, turning the world black.

"PLEASE BE ALIVE, PLEASE."

Eve fluttered her eyelids, a soft morning sunlight trickling through the bars on the porthole.

Bars?

Eve sat up quickly, taking in her surroundings. She was in the jail cell of a ship, Dakon and Pazel locked in cages of their own.

"Where are we?"

"Thank the gods," Dakon let out a shaky breath, fear lacing his voice. "We're not sure, but it's not with Captain Amarin."

"Where is Izan?"

Dakon gave Pazel a shamed look. "He wasn't brought here with you, Eve."

Eve stood quickly, backing into the wall of the ship. She leaned against it, sure that her legs would fail her.

"What happened?"

Dakon spoke slowly. "A man told us you needed help, so we followed him. Before we knew it we were ambushed. They were witches, they killed—" Dakon sucked in a shaky breath. "They killed Beast."

"No." Eve dropped to her knees.

"I didn't think the Blackthorn would be so prepared," Pazel murmured, sadly.

"It's not the Blackthorn," Dakon said, "it's the Strix."

"How did they find us?" Eve whispered shakily.

"I don't know." Dakon shook his head, then raised it slowly.

"Eve, can you feel your magic?"

She tried to summon a flame, to feel that familiar pull within her, but there was nothing.

"No, I can't feel anything."

The Strix.

Izan.

The old woman.

The wine.

The wine.

"One of them asked if we drank something. An old woman—"

"From the market?" Pazel asked.

"Yes, she gave us wine."

Pazel shook his head. "She gave me some too. A pouch of wine, me and Dakon drank before we were told you needed us."

"Fuck." Dakon ran his hands shakily through his hair.

"It was a potion; it has to have been." Pazel chewed his lip.

Eve and Dakon looked at him.

"I read about some of them in Cerene's books. Perhaps we drank one that limits your magic."

"How long does it last?" Dakon asked.

"Depends. A day, a moon, I'm not certain." Pazel shook his head.

"Where do you think the Strix are taking us?" Eve asked. The porthole was too high for her to see through.

"Back to your home, of course." A voice echoed throughout the room. *Reyher.*

Eve and her familiars stood quickly, apprehensively, as the witch entered the room. He kept a short distance between him and their cells.

"It's so nice to meet you, Lady Eve. Your greatness and beauty were not exaggerated."

Eve spat at him, missing.

Reyher laughed. "As has your temper. It's a mystery how Izan ever broke through that wall."

"Where is he?" Eve demanded.

"In *his* home, where he belongs."

"Curse you!" she screamed.

Reyher took a step toward her.

"Leave her alone!" Dakon growled.

"Oh, and I haven't forgotten about you, the one who *almost* escaped." He grinned.

"Damn you."

"Unfortunately, for you three, that is your fate. I hear King Marc has great plans for you, little witch. Burning at the stake would have been a mercy."

Eve moved back, not wishing to be anywhere near his chilling gaze.

A small pebble hit Reyher's head, and he whirled quickly.

"Does intimidating ladies make you feel powerful," Pazel snarled, throwing another pebble at him.

Reyher raised his hand, and Pazel hit the floor, spasming and writhing in pain.

"Stop! Stop!" Eve and Dakon pleaded.

The man relented, and Pazel spit out blood. His eyes were angry as he coughed. "M—must feel so big, threatening people in cages." He retched onto the floor.

"Dogs belong in cages. And as dogs you all will die."

Reyher raised his hand once more and Pazel flinched. Satisfied, Reyher turned to the stairs, calling out behind him.

"We are but a short distance from the capital. Pray to whatever gods you wish, perhaps they will grant you swift deaths."

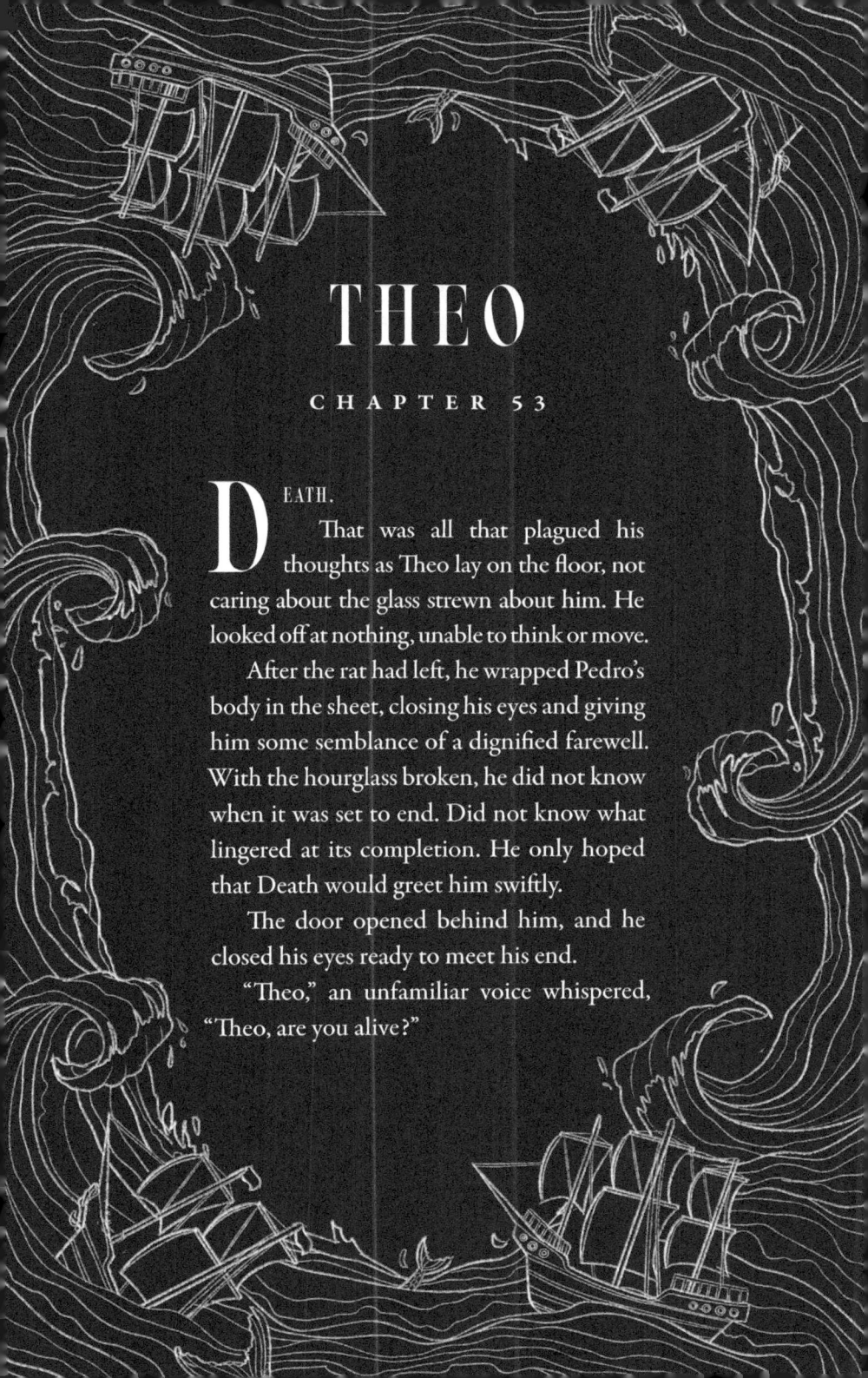

THEO

CHAPTER 53

DEATH.

That was all that plagued his thoughts as Theo lay on the floor, not caring about the glass strewn about him. He looked off at nothing, unable to think or move.

After the rat had left, he wrapped Pedro's body in the sheet, closing his eyes and giving him some semblance of a dignified farewell. With the hourglass broken, he did not know when it was set to end. Did not know what lingered at its completion. He only hoped that Death would greet him swiftly.

The door opened behind him, and he closed his eyes ready to meet his end.

"Theo," an unfamiliar voice whispered, "Theo, are you alive?"

"Kill me if you must, I won't fight, I swear."

Whoever it was, took a few steps to him. They placed a gentle hand on his back, "I'm here to save you."

What a cruel trick.

He turned slowly, not allowing himself to hope, meeting the brown eyes of a woman he never met before. Her braids cascaded down her slender back, her blue dress smooth against her deep sienna skin.

"Who are you?" he asked.

"Ana," she breathed, barely above a whisper. "I can explain everything, but we need to leave now. Time is running out."

Theo sat up, his mouth agape in confusion.

"Where would we go?"

"To the west, as far as I can take you."

She tugged him to his feet.

"Why are you doing this?"

She met his eyes, regret filled them. "Because I should have done it a long time ago."

He couldn't think of what to say. He turned to Pedro's body. "I can't leave him."

Ana flicked her eyes to the body on the bed, then back to him. "He's gone, Theo. Do not let him die in vain."

She began pulling him to the door, watching the beams precariously as they went.

"Wait, please." Theo wrenched his arm from hers and knelt by Pedro's body.

He kissed the sheet where his forehead was and shut his eyes tight.

"You were the best knight a prince could ask for. By the will of the gods, I will avenge you."

He turned back to Ana before he changed his mind. She raised her hand to the door, but before she opened it, she turned to Theo.

"Do not be alarmed by what I must do. This is the only way we will escape."

Before his eyes, she transformed into Navir.

Rage fueled him. "What is this?!"

"I can disguise myself. I am not Navir. I swear."

Theo took a step back. "Then how do I know you are really Ana?"

She narrowed her eyes, those piercing blue eyes sending chills down his spine. "You have to trust me."

She pulled handcuffs from her cloak. "We need to put these on you. The guards will never believe that Navir would let you out without them."

He took a step back.

"Please, we do not have much time before they do to you as they did to your friend."

Theo clenched his jaw but raised his hands to her. She cuffed him quickly, then grabbed his hands tight.

"Follow me and keep your head down until I tell you otherwise."

They stepped into the dark corridor, but it was empty, no guards anywhere that he could see.

"Where are we, where are the guards?"

"The north wing, they are distracted at the moment. Now, quiet."

He didn't question her.

They rushed out the doors and into the darkness and rain where a covered merchant's cart was waiting. The horse neighed, and a woman approached them. She looked nearly similar to Ana save for the color of her graying hair.

"Is this him?" the woman asked.

"Yes, hurry, Mother."

The woman eyed Theo suspiciously, but went back to the horse, covering her head with the hood of her silver cloak. Ana led Theo to the back of the cart amongst crates of vegetables and sacks of potatoes.

She uncuffed him and handed him an empty sack.

"Hide inside and say nothing. If we are stopped, do not move."

He took it from her, still believing that Navir would show up with hordes of guards ready to kill him on the spot. But he could only hear the rain as it pounded against the tarp.

"Be brave, mortal," she whispered, her brown eyes betraying the fear within her. He hesitated a moment and then closed the flap of the cart.

Theo shoved his body into the large sack and lay listening to his heart pounding in his ears as the cart began to move.

He hoped this wasn't a trick.

Hoped that in the hands of this witch he would live to see another day.

Hoped to feel the sun on his skin, just once, for Pedro.

It was all he had left, the only thing keeping him alive.

Hope.

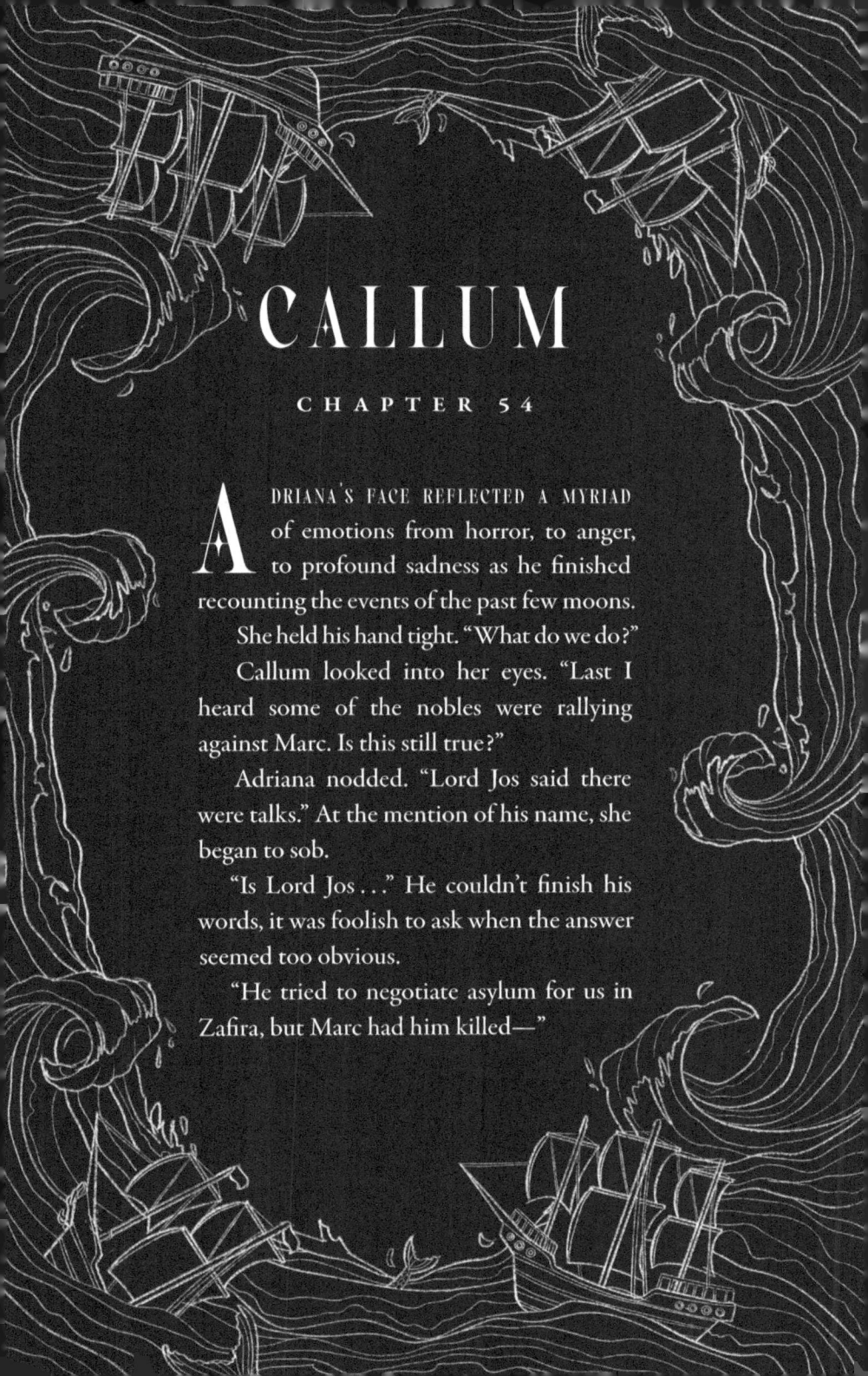

CALLUM

CHAPTER 54

ADRIANA'S FACE REFLECTED A MYRIAD of emotions from horror, to anger, to profound sadness as he finished recounting the events of the past few moons. She held his hand tight. "What do we do?"

Callum looked into her eyes. "Last I heard some of the nobles were rallying against Marc. Is this still true?"

Adriana nodded. "Lord Jos said there were talks." At the mention of his name, she began to sob.

"Is Lord Jos . . ." He couldn't finish his words, it was foolish to ask when the answer seemed too obvious.

"He tried to negotiate asylum for us in Zafira, but Marc had him killed—"

"And sent you here," Callum finished for her.

"We might not make it if we wait for them to revolt," Emilio murmured. "We need to find a way to escape."

"Have you not seen the dungeon?" Adriana asked. "There are guards, everywhere."

"There may be a way," Callum spoke, thinking of how he and Eve escaped the first time. "There are tunnels within the castle walls."

"Tunnels?" Emilio asked.

Adriana's wet eyes widened. "Of course. There must be tunnels in this dungeon too."

"But how would we open it, how would we find it?"

Adriana stood quickly, pointing at the wall. "The tunnels are opened by pushing on one end of the wall, like a panel between spaces. If even one of us is able to escape, we only need to push against the wall with the weak stone. There will be cracks, or seals."

Callum chewed the inside of his cheek, thinking of the mouse that came and went through the hole in the wall. "But how would we get out of these cells?"

"I think I have the answer to that," Emilio retrieved one of the near-black stones from under his straw.

"How will that help?" Adriana asked, warily.

"Princess, do you know where Pleasant Peak is?"

"Larrea."

"Yes, House Pleasant is situated by the Canys River on the western border. This"—he held up the dark, jagged stone—"is a flint rock, very common along the water. And this"—he took off his blouse, using it to retrieve a cluster of stems with toothed leaves—"is common nettle, but handle carefully, it can fester your skin."

Callum averted his eyes, pretending not to notice Emilio's half-nakedness.

"And?" Adriana huffed, unbothered.

"Patience, Your Highness." Emilio placed the dry nettle on the ground, tucking it beneath the bars of his cell. He struck the rock hard against the steel bar thrice, each time causing a spark. On the third time, it landed on the nettle, beginning to burn.

Adriana gasped and Callum's eyes widened.

Emilio grinned, taking in their faces. He tossed a stone to Callum. "It's time to put our friend's gifts to good use."

EVE

CHAPTER 55

"YOUR MAJESTY, I BRING GIFTS!" REYHER announced in the throne room.

They were gagged and held in iron chains outside the doors. The halls were eerily empty save for the guards surrounding her, Dakon, and Pazel. She gave them tearful looks, and Dakon reached for her hand, giving it a tight squeeze. He tried to exude calm, but she could see a deep fear within his green eyes. Her heart thundered in her chest; a chill riddled through her for what awaited them beyond the throne room doors. Pazel appeared to be breathing too quickly. His legs buckled, and a guard shoved him back up. She reached for him, too, holding his hand in hers.

They were not ashamed, they were scared.

Finally, the doors opened, and the guards pushed them inward, forcing them to walk.

The throne room was just as she remembered, save for Marc who now sat in the king's chair. He looked far more dangerous than she remembered, too powerful. Next to him was Lord Wesley, and a few other men in blue robes she had never met before. Otherwise, it was empty and hollow, save for Reyher waiting at the bottom of the steps, giving her a wicked stare.

"My Lady Eve, I've missed you," Marc purred, standing from his chair.

Eve could not speak; bile rose in her throat.

He walked down all the way to where they stood, eyeing each of them carefully. "And how kind of you to bring your friends."

Marc nodded to a guard behind Eve, and she squeezed her eyes shut, expecting pain. Instead, their gags were removed, and she coughed, her dry mouth was too much to bear.

"All better now, isn't it?"

"Fuck you, Marc."

A guard smacked the back of her head, and she fell forward into Marc's arms.

"Get off her!" Dakon growled, as he and Pazel tried their best to fight against their restraints.

"Ah, is this the lover you have replaced my brother with?" Marc shoved Eve back and took a step to Dakon. "And are you not my father's fool?"

Dakon clenched his jaw tight, saying nothing.

Marc roared with laughter, and it echoed hauntingly throughout the room.

The room began to spin.

"Hmm, not very funny now are we?"

"Let us go or you will regret it," Pazel snarled.

"And you are?"

"Give me a knife, and I'll gladly introduce myself."

Marc smirked, retrieving a knife from his belt, placing the tip on Pazel's throat. "You look expendable to me."

"If that were the case, I wouldn't be chained."

Eve watched as Marc narrowed his eyes. "You got quite the tongue, don't you?"

"I've heard worse."

"I can slice you from ear to ear."

Eve's breath hitched, too scared to say anything with the knife so close to Pazel's throat. She watched as Pazel stared back into Marc's eyes, fire in them that she had never seen before.

"Do it then."

Marc seemed taken aback, blinking a few times. He placed the knife back in his belt, "brave or stupid, I can't decide which."

"What do you want?" Eve spat.

"It's simple, really. I want your power and that of your familiars."

"That's impossible."

"It would have been if you had embraced this fallen goddess I have been told about. But seeing as you are in front of me in chains, I take it you are too afraid to claim it."

Eve's eyes widened as she grasped what he was saying. "Marc, you have no idea what you are doing."

"You lost, Eve. Me and the Strix"—he gestured to the men in dark blue robes—"will take over every inch of Serit and the lands beyond."

"Y-you're mortal."

"But that is where you will help me. You see, a witch's blood is quite powerful. A witch *and* her familiar can be twice as deadly. Add in a mortal sacrifice and we have quite the trio."

"No," she breathed.

He lifted her chin, his hazel eyes piercing hers. "What a shame it'll be to lose you. In another life perhaps you could have been mine."

"She will consume you, Marc! The Strix will use you to get what they want, don't do this!"

He shook his head. "I wager you thought yourself clever. Killing my father and running away like a coward. But all the magic in the world could not save you, could it? You are not nearly as smart or as powerful as you think."

He turned away, walking back up those throne steps.

Steps that did not belong to him.

Eve's lips trembled as anger consumed her. "Says the coward who ran back home at the first sight of war."

Marc looked over his shoulder. "What did you say?"

"You are a coward, Marc. Everyone here knows it."

Marc's nostrils flared. "I am the king."

"You are not *my* king!"

Marc went to her, his eyes wild and angry. He raised his hand and slapped her, the impact making her fall back into the guard, pain throbbed along her cheek and jaw. The blood rushed to her head as she took it. Dakon and Pazel struggled against the guards, cursing out, but to no avail.

She would not give him the satisfaction of her tears. She would not cower before him. Eve forced herself upright, turning to face him.

Marc smiled eerily. "You will die giving me what I want, and I will throw what's left of your body into the sea where I left my brothers. Though, I can't remember if Theo was fully dead or begging for mercy on his way down. Be a dear and find out for me when we are through here."

Eve lunged herself at Marc, rage taking over every rational thought. Her hand touched his skin, and there the truth revealed itself through Marc's eyes.

Watching Eryce die, fighting Theo in a bloody mess, Pedro barely making it in time to take them both overboard where they inevitably fell into Death's arms.

Her breathing grew ragged, her heart thundered in her chest, and her skin heated in the chains. She begged for her magic to return, begged for the grimoire to reappear in her arms. She was so consumed with killing him, that she would gladly sell her soul to make it happen.

Marc stepped out of her way as the guards pulled her roughly back. "H-her eyes! Why are they red!"

"Your Majesty, we must begin before the potion wears off. These three are deadly and will kill you if given the chance," Reyher replied. He gestured to the rest of the Strix witches, and they moved quickly toward them.

Marc took a last look at the group, before turning back to Reyher. "Proceed, hurry!"

Eve growled and hissed, trying her best to get away from their touch as they moved closer. The guards loosened their grip on her and Dakon, their metal armor absorbing the stinging bite of their burning skin. She could feel it, and Dakon could too. Their magic had begun to return.

The Strix witches made a circle around the three of them, chanting in a language that was not familiar to her ears. The three of them fell to the ground, the words like heavy stones holding her to the floor.

Reyher approached them, slicing their palms with a dagger. It was black and silver, encrusted with dark jewels—the very same dagger that killed her mother.

No.

She screeched, the chanting heavy on her bones, the pain it caused pulsing through her body. The cut from the dagger was too deep, blood oozing onto the floor.

The chanting grew, and Eve's body began to shake on the floor. Pazel's eyes went to the back of his head. Dakon cried out from the pain.

Reyher took their blood from the dagger and wiped it on Marc's forehead.

The space darkened, fire filling the throne room in a blaze.

There was no other choice.

"Blood of the Blackthorn," she cried, "take it, take my soul, and save us all!"

Her skin on fire, she looked down, and the iron chains began to melt away.

"We will be the fire that rules the world," the voice echoed loud and clear.

Faintly, in the foreground, she could hear the yell of Reyher.

"The mortal! Sacrifice the mortal!"

In an instant, all the eyes of the Strix looked up to Pazel.

ADRIANA

CHAPTER 56

THE RUMBLING WAS DEAFENING AND shook the castle walls so fiercely that Adriana was sure the roof would cave. Bits of dirt and stone fell from the cracks in the ceiling as she worked on a makeshift weapon. Callum and Theo tended to their small embers. It was only a matter of time.

"What is happening?" she yelled over the noise, nearly nicking herself with her sharpened stick.

"I don't know," Emilio shouted, "but can you scream, Princess?"

The sound rumbled louder, and she felt as if the dungeon would crumble and give way.

"Yes!"

Callum shouted from the cell next to her. "I did it, I did it!"

Adriana turned, seeing his flame eating the nettle. He threw straw to keep it growing. It was happening faster than she realized.

"If we call for them, we may be ignored, but you," Emilio yelled, "you need to scream for them to help you, it will attract them to us!"

Adriana nodded, the castle groaning and shaking beneath her feet. She ran to the bars of her cell, screaming as if her life depended on it. Her voice grew hoarse, and she worried no one would come.

The meek guard from earlier popped his head into the hall, and Adriana waved him down. "Please they are starting fires, save me!"

He cocked his head, confused, until Callum and Emilio's fires roared to life.

"Gods!" he yelled, rushing down the hall, keys in hand.

Adriana willed tears to come, pretending to be frightened. "They are mad! Please, take me somewhere safe!"

The guard trembled, clearly overwhelmed, and fumbled with the keys. He shouted down the hall for reinforcement, but fortunately the castle rumbled louder, silencing him.

He twisted the key in the lock, and opened the door for Adriana, she ran out into the hall. She exaggerated her panic, reaching for him, hugging him, claiming she was so terrified, and he saved her life. The guard was shaken, and pushed her off, turning to the flames that erupted before him.

"Gods!" he shouted, pushing them both back and away. "I'm going to find help!"

The guard took off down the hall, leaving her alone . . . as well as the key in her lock.

She grabbed it quickly, tossing it to Callum.

Callum took it, grabbing her arm. "Adriana, the mouse, follow where I told you, the tunnel might be there! Hurry!"

Adriana nodded, running quickly to the end of the hall. The

guards were nowhere to be seen, and she nearly tripped as the castle shook once more.

What in the gods—

Adriana had no time to finish that thought, seeing the guard from before rushing back with a larger one. She ran and hid behind a corner, and they turned left down the hall to where Callum and Emilio's fires roared, eating the straw from the adjoining cells.

She rushed to the wall, seeing the mouse's hole. She felt her fingers quickly along the stone as the castle trembled greatly. Adriana was on the verge of panicked tears when she felt the familiar seal. Her heart lurched into her throat, and she followed it, pushing against the stone where the corners met.

Thank the gods!

It opened, just enough for her to fit through. She turned, seeing the guards shove their way into Callum's cell.

No.

She turned to the tunnel, all its promises of freedom if she just ran inside.

Then back to Callum.

Her heart pounded fiercely, and she shook along with the castle.

Time was running out and before she could stop herself, she ran.

EVE

CHAPTER 57

A HOODED WITCH ENTERED THE CIRCLE, holding out a dagger.

"No!" Eve shrieked in horror.

Dakon's iron chains melted, it clattered barely audible on the floor as the chanting grew louder around them. It drowned her senses, and she grew dizzy as she tried to pull Pazel toward her. He yelled out in pain as her hands left blistering burn marks on his skin.

No!

The three of them were bloody and messy, slipping on the floor, barely getting their bearings. The witch was halfway to them, quickly closing the space.

"Accept me. Now."

The grimoire appeared before her on the floor. The chanting was still too great, she fell, the words like knives in her skin.

"Touch it, Eve!" Dakon shouted. "Take us from here!"

Eve turned, forcing herself to crawl to it. The chanting grew, and she shrieked in pain.

"Do it, Eve!"

"Give your soul to me, and I will set you free."

"Take it!" Eve thrust her bloodied hand on the parchment. The other grabbed Dakon with a fierce grip. The witch raised his blade high above, aiming for Pazel as Dakon reached out for him. The rest of them began to close the circle running toward them.

The grimoire glowed a chilling orange hue. The dark, thorny branches spun out, pulling Eve into its embrace.

A terrifying scream pierced through her.

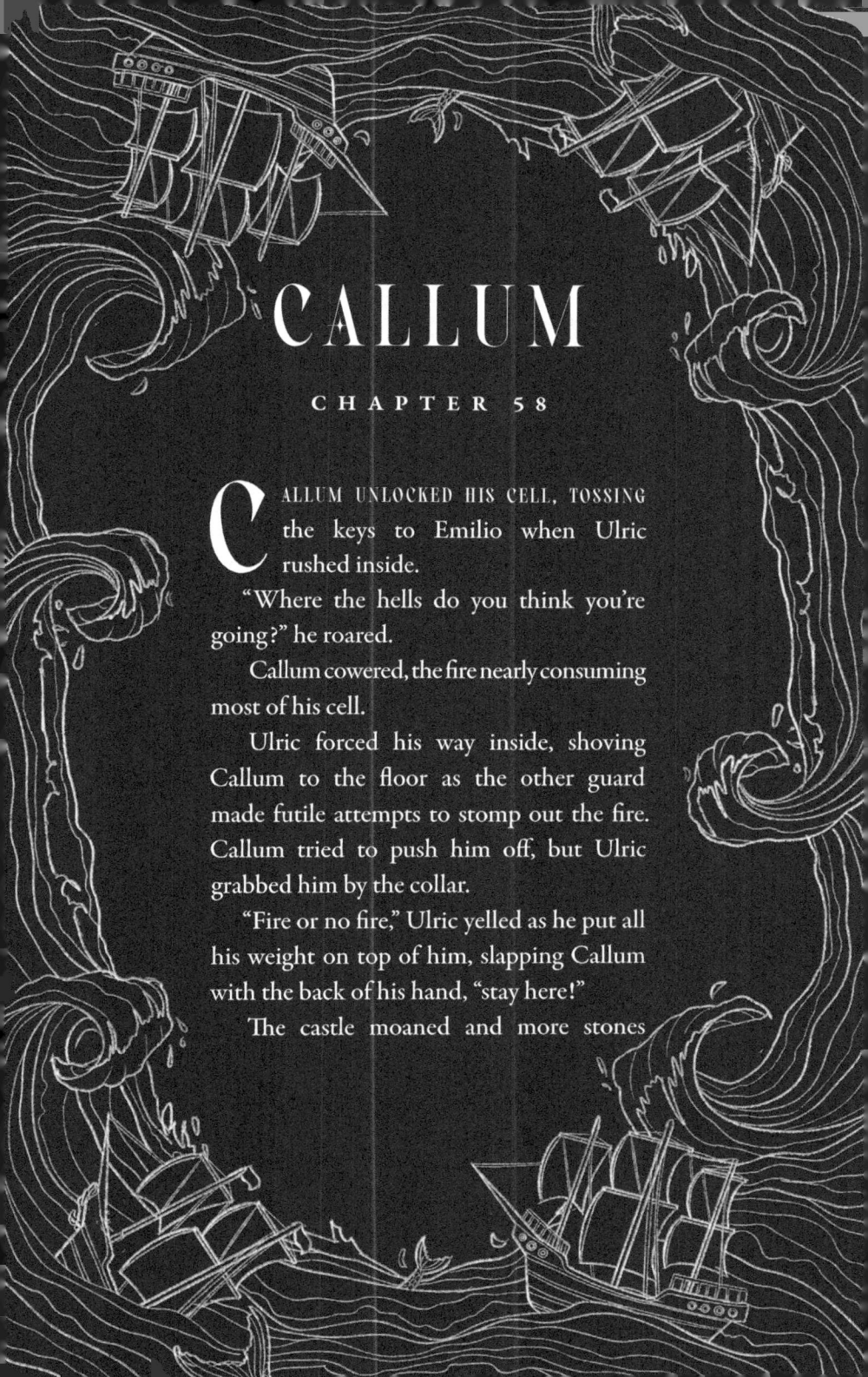

CALLUM

CHAPTER 58

ALLUM UNLOCKED HIS CELL, TOSSING the keys to Emilio when Ulric rushed inside.

"Where the hells do you think you're going?" he roared.

Callum cowered, the fire nearly consuming most of his cell.

Ulric forced his way inside, shoving Callum to the floor as the other guard made futile attempts to stomp out the fire. Callum tried to push him off, but Ulric grabbed him by the collar.

"Fire or no fire," Ulric yelled as he put all his weight on top of him, slapping Callum with the back of his hand, "stay here!"

The castle moaned and more stones

began to topple from the ceiling. A rather large one fell near Callum. The fire roared around them and Ulric raised his hands to Callum's throat, squeezing hard.

Callum struggled in vain, desperately trying to touch the stone, if he could only reach it.

"Stay! Here!" Ulric yelled again, his veins nearly popping from his neck and temple; his face was turning red, and Callum could feel the darkness creeping in. The fire, the smoke, it was all too much.

Eryce.

I'm coming to you.

No sooner had the thought entered his mind, then he took a deep, gasping breath. The other guard had fallen with a sword in his chest on Ulric. Ulric released Callum, shoving the guard away confused and terrified.

More stones fell and the rumbling boomed through the hall.

Callum took his chance, he grabbed the massive stone, and with all his might pounded it against Ulric's head. He toppled off Callum, bleeding from the impact.

Callum gasped for air, as Emilio retrieved the sword, pulling him to his feet.

"Quick, run!"

"Not without you!" Callum shouted, pulling Emilio to him.

Ulric jumped to his feet, and as if by instinct, Callum quickly closed the dungeon door. Emilio was ready, turning the key and locking him inside.

"Let me out!" Ulric yelled angrily, using all his might to shake the bars loose.

"We make a good team," Emilio heaved, catching his breath. The tremors of the dungeon grew stronger now than ever. And Callum pushed Emilio back away from the roaring fire.

Adriana reached them, grabbing them by the arms. "Come, quickly!"

Ulric screamed against the pain of the fire biting his body, but there was nowhere for him to run, nowhere for him to escape his fiery death. He kept screaming as he fell to his knees, the fire consuming him.

"I wish we had more time to see him die," Callum breathed.

Emilio and Adriana said nothing, pulling Callum with them as they ran down the hall.

The floor beneath them trembled and more guards entered the dungeon.

The prisoners shouted as they saw the guards, pointing in their direction.

They had no time to speak or move with the castle dungeons turning to ruins around them. Smoke filled the air, and Callum was haunted by memories of him and Eve in the king's tower when they were surrounded by flames.

I can survive this.

I did it once.

I will do it again.

Adriana led them to the open wall, revealing a dark tunnel. The three of them rushed inside and pushed the wall closed. The only semblance of light filtered through small holes at different points of the tunnel. They had no direction, but with the guards shouting so close by, all they could do was run for their lives.

THEY PUSHED THROUGH A WOODEN CELLAR DOOR, NEARLY BREAKING it as they shoved their bodies against it. They clambered onto damp grass in the darkness. The moon was barely visible behind the cloudy, night sky. They were just outside the castle grounds near a stream.

Callum turned, seeing the towers loom large before him. The entrance to this tunnel was entangled in a mass of shrubs, moss, and other greenery. If they had not just escaped from it, he would never have noticed the door. He closed it, not wishing to leave a trace.

"We need to put distance between us and them," Callum whispered. "We can go to Teros."

"How will we get there?" Adriana asked, eyes wide and afraid. Callum pulled her trembling body in his arms. He was afraid too.

Emilio ran his fingers through his hair, pacing quickly, before stopping. "I have a contact in the city."

"Can they help us escape?"

Emilio clenched his jaw. "I think so. If we try our luck with running through the forest ourselves, the king's hounds will track us."

Callum swallowed, a lump forming in his throat.

"We need to keep moving," Adriana urged. "If we stay here we are damned too."

The rumbling castle and the shouts of guards brought them back to their senses.

Without another word, they took off, following Emilio into the city to seek a stranger that would either embrace or betray them.

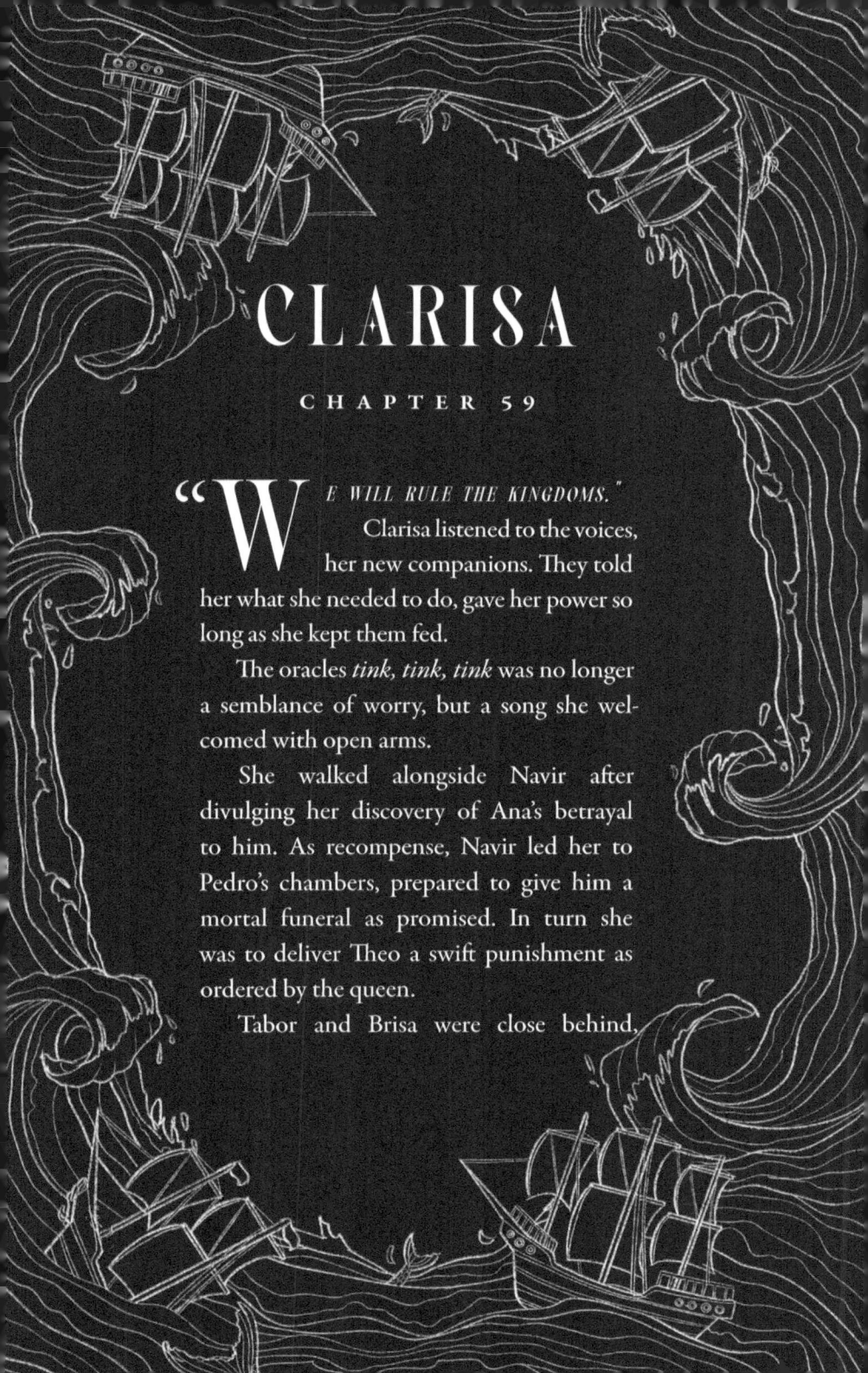

CLARISA

CHAPTER 59

"WE WILL RULE THE KINGDOMS."
Clarisa listened to the voices, her new companions. They told her what she needed to do, gave her power so long as she kept them fed.

The oracles *tink, tink, tink* was no longer a semblance of worry, but a song she welcomed with open arms.

She walked alongside Navir after divulging her discovery of Ana's betrayal to him. As recompense, Navir led her to Pedro's chambers, prepared to give him a mortal funeral as promised. In turn she was to deliver Theo a swift punishment as ordered by the queen.

Tabor and Brisa were close behind,

brooding and uneasy.

A guard rushed toward them as they entered the northern wing.

"My prince"—he bowed to Navir—"Deyes, he is dead!"

"Dead?" Navir responded.

"Yes, he was found stabbed in his bed."

Clarisa stood frozen in shock. "Who did this?"

"We have dispatched our guards to find the culprit. They are searching the castle now."

Navir grabbed the guard by the collar. "If you killed the queen's closest guard, would you stay in the castle?"

The guard trembled under Navir's touch, shaking his head.

Navir released him. "Check the nearby villages."

The guard nodded.

"Now!" he ordered, and the guard startled, running past them.

"Why would someone kill Deyes?" Clarisa asked.

Navir stilled, his eyes staring ahead.

"What?"

He moved forward, ignoring her, his eyes focused on a door at the far end. Clarisa and her familiars followed, rushing behind him as he took off in a sprint.

"Where are the guards?" he bellowed.

Clarisa looked around, confused. It was an empty hall.

Navir retrieved a set of keys and wrenched open the door.

Inside was a bloody sheet and what she assumed to be Pedro's body beneath it.

She nearly collapsed, the sight of it too much.

He didn't deserve this.

She looked around the room for Theo.

But he was nowhere to be seen.

Navir shoved a table to the ground, cursing. "Where is he?!" He whirled around to Clarisa. "Did you know anything?"

"Know what?"

He rubbed his face, releasing a breath as he composed himself. "Where is Theo, where is Ana?"

"Ana?"

"Where is she?" His eyes were serious.

"I haven't spoken to her since last night."

"Fuck!"

"What does she have to do with Theo?"

He grabbed Clarisa by the shoulders, shaking her. "You need to listen to me. Listen."

She quivered beneath his touch, and Tabor reached for Navir.

"Prince," he said, "that's enough."

Navir ignored him, but Clarisa gave him a slight nod. Tabor retreated only a few steps next to Brisa.

Navir locked eyes with Clarisa, "She is dangerous. We need to find her before she hurts anyone else."

"Do you think she killed Deyes?"

Navir straightened, his brows knit. "He's one of many."

Many?

"That can't be. This is Ana, not a murderer."

His eyes lit up slowly, his mouth quirked into a crooked grin. He released her, his hands trailing to the luring crystal about her neck.

"You truly have no idea do you?" His fingers rubbed against its smooth surface.

Tink. Tink. Tink.

He lifted his icy blue gaze from the crystal to her. "There is so much you don't know." He tsked, still holding onto the crystal.

"He defies you . . ."

"Then tell me, enough of these secrets," she demanded.

"Kill them."

Navir let go of the crystal, and Clarisa let out a sigh as it touched her skin one more.

"Kill them all."

He smirked, tilting her chin up to face him.

"You have been sleeping next to Death, and I think it's time we paid her a visit."

DAKON

CHAPTER 60

THE ROOM SPUN SLOWLY. THEIR POWER was coming back.

He held Eve's hand, and reached for Pazel's with the other. They would only have one chance to do this; one chance and all their hope was with the grimoire lying on the floor.

Around them, the Strix began to close in. One of the witches approached, hand lifted above his head, bringing down a sharp, jagged blade toward Pazel.

I can make it; I can stop him. I can—

Dakon stretched out his hand, fingers barely brushing against Pazel's as sharp branches covered everything in darkness.

"PAZEL?! PAZEL!" EVE'S SCREAMS BROKE INTO DAKON'S THOUGHTS. He opened his eyes into a white nothingness, the colorless sky above him never-ending as a fierce, brisk wind pummeled against his body.

He lifted himself up, feeling a damp crunch beneath him. He raised his hands to his face, *snow?* They were in snow. He stood, everything coming back to him at once.

Pazel?

Did they save him in time?

They had to have. They had to.

He turned, seeing Eve in a bloodied dress over Pazel, screaming his name. Howling it as if she herself had been impaled.

He rushed over, feeling as if the world were spinning again, unable to come to grips with what was certainly before his eyes.

The wound was too large, too fatal. A deep gash split his flesh across his stomach and chest.

"Quickly, Dakon. He's still awake, we can save him!"

Eve placed her hands on Pazel's chest, reciting their all too familiar spell, crying out and dropping her hands as only bits of the gashes tore itself on her dress. It barely made a difference to Pazel's wounds.

Dakon stood still.

Magic is not immortal.

He could practically hear Cerene's voice filling him as if she were there next to him.

Pazel was merely tattered flesh on bone; there would be no coming back from this.

Eve noticed him standing there, unmoving, her bloodied hands grasping her midsection as the pain that transferred was too much for her to bear.

"Why are you not helping! We are going to lose him!"

"Eve"—Dakon knelt next to Pazel, swallowing to get the words out before grief took him—"no."

"No?"

Dakon grasped Pazel's hand firmly, seeing his eyes flutter as snow-flakes began to rest on his lashes. His breath strained and visible in the cold. Dakon positioned himself so that Pazel could not see the devastation below his chest.

"You're going to be all right, Pazel," he lied, and hated himself as tears pricked hot against his frigid skin. "Eve is going to close your wounds now, it's supposed to hurt before it gets better. But I want you to focus on me, talk to me about anything you want."

Pazel squinted, groaning against the pain. Eve choked sobs as she moved to grasp Pazel's other hand in hers.

"W-was I a g-good apprentice?" Pazel shuddered in the cold snow, his body losing its ocher tone for lighter, unfamiliar shades.

"The greatest." Dakon's eyes filled with tears. And he could hear Eve shakily breathing every spell she could think of to heal him, but nothing happened. Not anymore.

"I can settle for great . . ." Pazel tried to smile, but instead he coughed, the blood from his mouth was dark and stained the white snow.

His grip on Pazel was the only thing keeping Dakon from suc-cumbing to the horror in front of him. The excruciating agony of watching someone he loved die once again.

"Tell me a story"—Pazel coughed—"like Cerene used to."

Dakon's lips parted, shivering in the chill, but he managed a frail smile, trying desperately not to frighten him.

His voice was shaky as he spoke. "Th-there were two servant boys born of different blood, but had the same hearts, the same spirits. They fought and worked and cared for one another like brothers. They dreamed of adventures as children and as they grew into men they made those dreams come true—escaping the castle that enslaved them, singing drunk in taverns, falling in love with beautiful women, sailing the Dallise Sea, fighting pirates and sirens, can you believe it? The gods have never been so jealous."

"Don't forget handsome. They were handsome." The last words were barely a whisper on Pazel's lips.

Dakon laughed through the tears that fell on their clasped hands. "Of course. At least one of them. The envy of all men."

Pazel lifted his lips in a semblance of a grin, but then his eyes met Dakon's all sense of humor gone and with it remained only acceptance. "Eve is not healing me, is she?"

Dakon's heart sank. "No."

Tears trailed down Pazel's cheeks, leaving a path of wetness above the frost that was now accumulating there. "Continue the story . . . please."

Dakon nodded, trying his best to craft a tale of a hero, no more than a mere mortal who challenged powerful forces and lived the rest of his life going on new adventures beyond Serit. The world was his to explore.

When he finished, his eyes stained with tears, and Eve frozen in shock and utter devastation, he released Pazel's hand.

Pazel was tinted blue, blood no longer pouring from his wound, and through his lips. His eyes stared off, looking at nothing. They were no longer filled with the dark browns of the deep winter forests and the summer walnuts that fell from the trees as they worked outside from childhood to manhood. They were empty and hollow like Dakon's heart without him.

"No! No, damn you!" Eve threw herself at Dakon, screaming and crying until she couldn't anymore.

Dakon held her tight, tears of his own falling down his cold cheeks.

THE BITTER COLD WAS NEARLY UNBEARABLE. THEY TRIED TO CARRY Pazel, but their bodies were too weak against the snowy wind. They stopped in front of a small cave, Eve using her fire to light it.

It was barely larger than a candle and didn't help illuminate the darkness within.

Dakon placed Pazel gently on the ground and approached Eve. He held her hands. They were not warm as they typically were but trembled against his touch.

"What do we do?" she asked, her eyes looking up at him helplessly.

"I don't know." He swallowed. "But we need to get out of the snow."

Eve looked to Pazel, her eyes watering once more. She opened her mouth to speak, but a low, loud grumble echoed from within the cave.

They stared at each other, terror lining Eve's face and Dakon's stomach dropped.

There was another grumble, closer now.

Dakon grabbed Eve and they stepped back, facing the mouth of the cave.

There were large footsteps sending tremors along the ground.

Dakon and Eve were too stunned to move, too stunned to speak, as a white-scaled creature with massive silver wings as big as Amarin's ship, emerged from the cave.

They were exposed; it was too late to flee. Its crystal-blue eyes landed on them.

Dakon stood in front of Eve, readying himself for certain death.

The large beast huffed, sending a breath of icy wind their way.

Dakon willed all his magic to the surface, feeling it move inside him, heating his skin.

The creature lifted its head and roared to the gray sky. The trees trembled and shook against its power.

Eve stepped next to Dakon, her eyes turning that familiar red hue as she faced him. He reached out his hand, and she took it. Through the bitter cold, their touch was a welcome flare.

He closed his eyes, letting his magic take over.

Because when they opened, he knew he would not have long to live.

He would be true to his promise—he would protect her; he would die for her. Just as she would for him.

It roared again, sending shards of ice that melted as it hit their skin. He braced for the worst. Eve tightened her grip on his. They would face this threat together.

For this was not just any creature.

It was the dragon who lost its fire.

And they were the flame in the silver storm.

APPENDIX

HOUSE FARRIN

House Farrin has manned Pleasant Peak for nearly a century and is under Lord Dario's charge. It is sworn to House Ivari of Larrea and fought in its uprising against the crown under Fidel IV. After eight years of war and hardship on his people, Lord Dario brokered a deal with the crown for clemency in exchange for allowing Givensmir forces to pass through the Canys River, a stronghold of the Pleasant Peak army. Many accounts differ on the reasons for Lord Dario's decision to fold for the crown between threats of violence against his wife and children or coins being passed to assuage his guilt. The circumstances remain unknown and are spoken only in secret confidences.

Following, the fall of Fidel IV, House Farrin claimed fealty to Larrea's newest ruler, Lord Moryn of House Ivari. Yet, his loyalties to the crown remain under scrutiny as one of his sons has been rumored to commiserate with rebellious houses.

Lord Dario is the head of House Ivari.

SIGIL
River Elk

COLORS
Red and Silver

HOUSE RUBIANES

The Rubianes have stood the test of time in Serit. Their house forged from centuries far beyond that of written record. In the fertile lands of their namesake, the lineage has amassed a large fortune from their wines and other crops sent throughout the kingdom. Generations ago, Andren I of House Rubianes swore fealty to King Nikolas Ebron I after losing the Battle of the Vines. King Nikolas granted Lord Andren continued ownership of Rubianes and the surrounding lands after he successfully aided in a negotiated surrender of Larrea to the crown.

Centuries later, Lord Marcelo I was ordered to marry the first Royal Enchantress, Lady Lucia of the Blackthorn. Deemed a scandal for the known nature of witches and mortal couplings to bear no children, House Rubianes was in uproar. However, the wedding proceeded and yielded two daughters, Clarisa and Eve. The former with the magic of her mother and the latter with pure mortality.

Following the death of the treasonous Enchantress and the loss of Lady Clarisa, Lord Marcelo remarried Natalia of House Grana, a minor house in Rubianes. They have a son, Isidro who is expected to take his father's lordship.

Lord Marcelo is the current head of House Rubianes.

Lady Eve is a fugitive of the crown for the murder of King Marc I.

Her whereabouts are unknown.

SIGIL
Cross swords between olive branches

BANNER COLORS
Burgundy and Gold

HOUSE EBRON

House Ebron originated from the Mistral Islands where they saw much success in naval trade as they were positioned between the Blackthorn and mortal kingdoms. After the fall of the Blackthorn witches, Gale Ebron I took advantage of the vulnerability of the mortal lands, securing an alliance with Teros and creating the kingdom of Givensmir. Following the creation of its capital north of what is now known as Catalina's Port, Gale secured his title as Givensmir's king, a lineage that has lasted for centuries.

King Marc I is the head of House Ebron and ruler of the Givensmir kingdom.

SIGIL
A Merlion

COLORS
Gold and Black

HOUSE TEROS

Following the alliance with House Ebron, the Teros' have remained a stronghold of the north. Occupying the dense forests, silver mines, and warhorses that make up a sizeable force of Givensmir's battle trade, the Teros have long been suited for battle. Their lands are separated from the Unclaimed Wastes by the icy river of Gods' Protection with no suitable plans to occupy further. They have the highest regard for loyalty to family, duty, and honor.

Lady Tyrina is the head of House Teros.

SIGIL
A War Horse

COLORS
Forest-Green & Silver

HOUSE IVARI

Rife with internal conflict and continuous wars throughout the centuries, House Ivari has felt its share of struggle and hardships. While Larrea has miraculously remained in the hands of the Ivari lineage, it has transferred between cousins, daughters, uncles, and legitimized bastards alike. Forced into the expansion of Givensmir's kingdom, House Ivari and its lands remained faithful for a few years. Following the rise in taxes and underwhelming support of King Eryck following his ascension to the throne, Fidel III of House Ivari began an uprising against the crown, declaring themselves a separate kingdom once more. Civil war waged for eight years and three different false kings before Prince Eryce was ordered to execute Lord Fidel IV, ending the war. The immediate family was exiled to Bastard's Haven, after their acts of submission. A new noble, after swearing fealty to King Eryck and accepting terms of surrender, was appointed as the Lord of Larrea.

Lord Moryn, distant cousin of Fidel IV, is the head of House Ivari.

SIGIL
Sea Serpent

COLORS
Blue and Black

HOUSE MYTAR

The Mytars have developed a complex mining system in the mountains where they have forged precious resources and established effective trade with Givensmir. However, they remained resistant to joining the kingdom over the centuries until the year 798 when Lord Joseph I of House Mytar met with the Royal Enchantress. After a single meeting, he is rumored to have declared that he would have 'sold his left arm if only to spend another moment listening to her speak'. Lord Joseph and King Byron III of Givensmir remained steadfast companions until the king's untimely death years later.

Lord Joseph I is the head of House Mytar.

SIGIL
Cloud pierced by a Pickax

COLOR
Bronze and White

BLACKTHORN COVENS

The Blackthorn covens were created following the fall of Isila and the Original Witches. Bound to remain in the Blackthorn isles where their magic was strongest, the remaining witches formed covens which remained in relative harmony across the Dallise Sea from the mortals who sought revenge. Despite all attempts at invasion, the Blackthorn and its covens have yet to be conquered. Under the same lineage of rulers, the isles are led by its Capital coven.

One of the covens, Strix, known for their disastrous methods of witchcraft were exiled in the year 613.

Queen Saryn is the head of the Capital Coven and ruler of the Blackthorn kingdom.

SIGIL
Owl beneath Three Stars

COLORS
Silver and Black

ACTIVE COVENS
Capital

Alvyna

Luna

Veneno

Petris

Arric

EXILED COVEN
Strix

PRIALIS

The island of Prialis is a territory of Givensmir's kingdom. The people of Prialis are known for their peacemaking and tend to stray from violence. Despite much opposition, the land was claimed by King Byron III to be used as a port for supply lines running to the east during his conquering of the Larrea kingdom. At the urging of the Enchantress and the successful invasion of Larrea, King Byron largely ignored the island, deeming it a waste of resources. Prialis and its people live in villages and worship the land and sea nearly as much as the five gods.

A council of four, the eldest of the island's leaders, rules the people as is their sacred tradition.

SIGIL
A Jasmine Flower above Four Sea Waves

COLOR
White and Blue

AUTHOR'S NOTE

The first chapter I wrote for this book was Callum's.

The scene came to me as I was battling an intense bout of writer's block. I sat in front of my library computer, staring at the blank screen and the cursor blinking mockingly at me. I wrote various passages from the POVs of different characters and would delete them nearly as quickly. Nothing seemed quite right.

How do I start this story?

Where do I even begin?

What do I want to say?

I sat in my thoughts for a few moments, but they were filled with the endless, disturbing news cycles. I've always wanted to write stories that brought the parallels of real life into a fictional fantasy setting where conflicts were met from the safety of ink on paper. But this time the idea seemed daunting and, quite frankly, intimidating.

I walked around my library, by the rows and rows of books that filled its rooms and at all the people who lingered. They held books in their hands, typed fastidiously on laptops, and immersed themselves in worlds of their own away from the pressures outside the library's four walls.

One day, I thought, I want to be in this space, with all the people who are trying to escape, and I want my books to be something that someone will pick up on a bookshelf and think, *this is exactly what I need to get through today.*

Callum's chapter was a much-needed release. He was a hero that found himself in the castle dungeons where his life seemed at its end. There, in the pits of his despair, we find a different Callum than the one we had grown to love. He is now resigned, quiet, and grieving.

Enter Emilio.

He is not the answer to quell Callum's sorrow completely, but one that eases his isolation through humor and patience.

Because sometimes in a world where things are overwhelming, a touch of humor or the company of a friend can make all the difference.

I hope Flame in the Silver Storm made you feel seen, heard, and gave you an escape in a world that can feel harsh and bleak.

Remember, books have magic.

Take it and lose yourself for just a moment.

Because a moment in joy is our way of fighting back.

With Love,

Rocio

ACKNOWLEDGMENTS

Writing a novel can be daunting, but with the right people in your corner it can also be fun.

To the amazing authors, creatives, cosplayers, and other bookish people I have met along the way while writing Flame in the Silver Storm, I am eternally grateful.

To my editor, Heather, who always challenges me to be a better writer, this book is a testament to your faith in me. Your humor is just the cherry on top (and my favorite part of our chats). Thank you for being a beacon of light in this crazy, exciting, publishing world.

To the readers, who have loved, shared, and cheered me on before reading a word of this novel, my heart is yours. Thank you for sticking with me on this journey and all my quirkiness in between.

To Lesley Nolasco, who sat me down and in so many words told me to act like the author I wanted to be, here I am finally doing it. Thank you can never be enough for your wisdom and insight when I needed it most.

To Allen, Dallas, Adriana, Pedro, David, Gio, Alonso, Thalia, and Tia Terry, you all are the village that makes it possible to have my dreams come true. There are not enough thank yous in the world to show you how truly grateful I am for each of you, but hopefully these books are a start.

AUTHOR BIO

ROCIO CARRANZA is the author of this and several other works, including *Blood of the Blackthorn*, *Lana Lang*, and *Miss Reliable*. Forever a dreamer and creative, Rocio spends her free time building worlds on paper and film that may never see the light of day, but spark joy in her soul. She lives with the ever-jovial Allen and their two sons in Austin, TX. *Flame in the Silver Storm* is her sophomore novel.

VISIT THE AUTHOR ONLINE:
www.rociocarranza.com

INSTAGRAM & THREADS:
@rociocarranzawrites

TIKTOK
@rociocarranzawrites

www.ingramcontent.com/pod-product-compliance
Lightning Source LLC
Chambersburg PA
CBHW020011120726
47903CB00004B/1241